dark curls ... othes from ... d into his ... pecimen of femininity ...

His breath froze in his lungs. He experienced the same sensation he'd felt when he'd first set eyes on the blond woman at the queen's reception: a ripple of recognition, like a tiny electric current passing through his brain.

When he found himself reaching for her, he snatched his hand away. Things he hadn't seen before were clicking into place.

"There is no other woman," he said. "Is there? There is no boy who conducted her to a safe place. You're one and the same person . . . You're the woman at the reception. You're the blond who tried to kill me. I want you to start at the beginning and tell me all you know, or I swear I will have you locked in a dungeon and I will walk away without a backward glance."

Praise for

The Runaway McBride

"A charming romance . . . Thornton displays her usual deft touch, effortlessly combining delightful characters with an intriguing mystery!"

—*New York Times* bestselling author Shirlee Busbee

And for Elizabeth Thornton and her novels

"A writer of ... *omantic Times*

"An Elizabe... a powerful, entertaining, ...

... *Book Review*

"An unforgetta... —*Booklist*

"As multilayered as a wedding cake and just as delectable."
—*Publishers Weekly*

"Exhilarating Regency romantic suspense."   —*The Best Reviews*

Berkley Sensation Titles by Elizabeth Thornton

THE RUNAWAY McBRIDE
THE SCOT AND I

The
Scot
and I

Elizabeth Thornton

BERKLEY SENSATION, NEW YORK

THE BERKLEY PUBLISHING GROUP
Published by the Penguin Group
Penguin Group (USA) Inc.
375 Hudson Street, New York, New York 10014, USA
Penguin Group (Canada), 90 Eglinton Avenue East, Suite 700, Toronto, Ontario M4P 2Y3, Canada
(a division of Pearson Penguin Canada Inc.)
Penguin Books Ltd., 80 Strand, London WC2R 0RL, England
Penguin Group Ireland, 25 St. Stephen's Green, Dublin 2, Ireland (a division of Penguin Books Ltd.)
Penguin Group (Australia), 250 Camberwell Road, Camberwell, Victoria 3124, Australia
(a division of Pearson Australia Group Pty. Ltd.)
Penguin Books India Pvt. Ltd., 11 Community Centre, Panchsheel Park, New Delhi—110 017, India
Penguin Group (NZ), 67 Apollo Drive, Rosedale, North Shore 0632, New Zealand
(a division of Pearson New Zealand Ltd.)
Penguin Books (South Africa) (Pty.) Ltd., 24 Sturdee Avenue, Rosebank, Johannesburg 2196,
South Africa

Penguin Books Ltd., Registered Offices: 80 Strand, London WC2R 0RL, England

This is a work of fiction. Names, characters, places, and incidents either are the product of the author's imagination or are used fictitiously, and any resemblance to actual persons, living or dead, business establishments, events, or locales is entirely coincidental. The publisher does not have any control over and does not assume any responsibility for author or third-party websites or their content.

THE SCOT AND I

A Berkley Sensation Book / published by arrangement with the author

PRINTING HISTORY
Berkley Sensation mass-market edition / June 2009

Copyright © 2009 by Mary George.
Map by F. R. George.
Cover art by Aleta Rafton.
Cover design by George Long.
Cover hand lettering by Ron Zinn.
Interior text design by Kristin del Rosario.

ISBN: 978-0-425-22832-6

BERKLEY® SENSATION
Berkley Sensation Books are published by The Berkley Publishing Group,
a division of Penguin Group (USA) Inc.,
375 Hudson Street, New York, New York 10014.
BERKLEY® SENSATION and the "B" design are trademarks of Penguin Group (USA) Inc.

PRINTED IN THE UNITED STATES OF AMERICA

10 9 8 7 6 5 4 3 2 1

For my relatives and friends
in Aberdeen and on Deeside.
"For auld acquaintance."

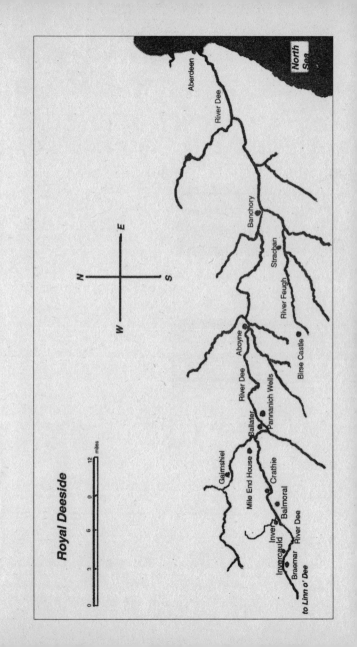

Royal Deeside

North Sea

Aberdeen

River Dee

Banchory

Strachan

River Feugh

Birse Castle

Aboyne

River Dee

Pannanich Wells

Ballater

Gairnshiel

Mile End House

Crathie

Balmoral

Inver

Invercauld

Braemar

River Dee

to Linn o' Dee

N
W — E
S

0   3   6   9   12
miles

One

⮿

Balmoral Castle, July 1885

The moment he set eyes on her, Alex knew that this woman was going to be trouble. Though she was pretty enough and trim enough to catch the eye of any red-blooded male, that was not the kind of trouble he had in mind. He was thinking about the case he was working on, wondering if she could be the one.

It was the blond hair that made her stand out. In this corner of the Highlands of Deeside, the natives were mostly dark-haired Celts like himself. This young woman had the look of an English rose. He was sure that her eyes would be blue.

She turned her head quickly, as though she realized that someone was studying her, and their eyes brushed and held. In the split second before she tore her gaze from his, he felt it: a ripple of recognition, like a tiny electric current passing through his brain. Strange, when he knew that he had never met the woman.

Watch her, Hepburn, he told himself.

After watching her wander among the assembled guests

as though she were looking for a friend, Alex dismissed her from his mind. She seemed harmless enough. Besides, it wasn't a woman he was looking for but a man. *Ca bheil sibh, Mac an diaboil?* Where are you, son of the devil?

A voice at his elbow said softly, "Her Majesty is about to make her entrance. What happens now?" The speaker was Alex's brother, Gavin. Though the resemblance between them was striking, Gavin's manner and expression possessed a charm that was entirely lacking in Alex.

"Now we wait," Alex responded.

His gaze traveled the crush of guests in the castle's ballroom, noting that the cream of Scotland's Highland society had come to pay its respects to Her Majesty, Queen Victoria. There would be no dancing at this reception. Since her husband's death, the queen had retired into semi-obscurity. Frivolity was now frowned upon.

A silence fell as the doors to the queen's gallery opened and Her Majesty entered, flanked by her kilted guard of honor. Alex had positioned himself to watch the guests. He was scanning faces, seeking out anything and everything that struck him as odd. He hoped that his counterpart on the other side was not as vigilant, because he'd soon deduce that this trumped-up drama was a lie, a carefully choreographed trap to ensnare a traitor.

The "queen" was not the queen but only someone who resembled her; the "footmen" in their dark green coats and tartan sashes were not footmen but police officers. He was not part of the official operation but worked alone and reported only to his section chief, Commander Durward, and in his absence, as now, to Dickens, the local man in charge of security.

Gavin had no part in the operation. He was one of the guests, but he'd known that something was up when his elder brother had arrived at the family's fishing and hunting lodge the week before. They expected trouble at the queen's reception, Alex had told him. He'd also told Gavin to keep his mouth shut and his eyes open, and that was the only part Alex would allow him to play. At the moment, Gavin was weaving in and out of the guests, doing much the same as Alex was.

As the queen and her escort began to process slowly down the aisle that her aides had cleared for her, every head was lowered. The ladies' skirts rustled as they made their curtsies. Alex's bow was perfunctory. When he looked up, he saw the blond-haired woman moving quickly toward him. The thought had hardly registered when she raised a revolver that had been concealed in the folds of her skirts and pulled the trigger. He heard the deafening report of the gun going off, felt the whiz of the bullet as it missed him by a hair, heard the groan of someone behind him who had been hit; then he braced himself as the crush of screaming guests surged and ebbed like waves on an angry sea. It was a relief to see that the queen's guard had closed ranks around "Her Majesty" and were hustling the look-alike up the gallery stairs and out of the reception area. When a second shot rang out, however, and hit the chandelier overhead, making it teeter alarmingly, the panicked crowd rushed for the set of French doors giving onto the gardens. The "footmen" could do nothing to hold them back.

Alex scanned the pulsating wave of people forcing their way out. There was nary a sign of the woman with blond hair.

"Gavin," he shouted above the din, "look for a woman with blond hair. Don't let her get away." He gestured to the exit he thought she would have made for.

Gavin nodded and pushed his way through the crowd.

Muttering a furious curse, Alex went down on bended knee to tend to the wounded man. He was younger than Gavin by a year or two, and his face was vivid with color. "Did you see that?" the young man demanded. "Someone tried to murder me!"

The bullet had lodged in his arm, just below the elbow, and though the wound was bleeding profusely, he did not appear to be in any danger. After fishing in his pocket for his handkerchief, Alex folded it into a pad and told the young man to use it to stem the flow of blood.

He was beside himself with fury. He'd misjudged the scheming bitch. He'd been confident that, even if she were the assassin—and it didn't seem likely that a woman would be up to the job—she wasn't in a position to get off a clear shot at the queen. It had never occurred to him that he would be her target. And he had no doubt that her object was he and not the man whom she'd accidentally shot. With him out of the way, she'd have a clear shot at her real target. That bullet had missed him by a hair. It was a miracle he was still breathing.

A moment or two later, breathless from his exertions, Gavin returned. In his hand, he held a blond wig. "I found this on the terrace," he said. "It's possible that she's one of the guests the footmen are rounding up for questioning, or she may be panicked and making for the river."

"She won't be." She was too cool and too clever not to have a well-thought-out escape route in place. He got up, helped the wounded man to rise, and taking the wig from Gavin, stuffed it into his pocket. "Get this gentleman— what is your name, by the way?"

"Ramsey." The young man grimaced in pain. "Ronald Ramsey."

"Get Mr. Ramsey medical attention, then meet me in the courtyard."

"Lean on my arm, Mr. Ramsey," said Gavin soothingly. "I don't believe we've met. I'm Gavin Hepburn, and the gentleman you just met—he of few words, and all of them orders—is my brother, Alex. We are the Hepburns of Feughside. Are you visiting in the area? I ask because I don't recognize your face."

As Gavin led Ramsey away, Alex strode for the exit. He admired his brother's tactics. Gavin might appear to be engaged in a casual conversation, but he was, in effect, getting the man's statement. There would be many state-

ments taken tonight and many frayed tempers before these
exalted guests could get to their beds.

On the terrace, he cleared his mind and took a moment
to study the lie of the land. In the Highlands, the sun set
early. Off to his left, he could see the sun's rosy rim as it
disappeared behind the peaks of the Cairngorms. In front
of him was the path to the river. A forest of trees obscured
the view as did the forest of guests who were now being
herded back into the castle.

He closed his eyes and shut off the active part of his
brain.

All his senses were humming, but the one sense that
might be of use to him, his sixth sense, had obviously
dozed off.

His sixth sense. It wasn't a joke. It was a legacy from
his granny, the celebrated Witch of Drumore, as the superstitious country folk called her. Much good it had done
him. He couldn't read minds or hear voices. The best he
could say about it was that it sometimes pointed him in the
right direction. But when he needed it most, such as now, it
would desert him like a fickle woman.

Where was the wench? How did she know that he was
the one to take down before trying for the queen? He was
supposed to be a secret service agent, for God's sake. He
was supposed to blend in with the crowd. But more important than any of that was, where was the woman now?

He dug in his coat pocket, produced the blond wig, and
crushed it between his fingers. He felt it again, a ripple of
recognition, like a tiny electric current, passing through
his brain. He rubbed it against his cheek, and the current
became stronger, more compelling.

His dark brows snapped together as he tried to recall
every small detail of the woman who had bested him at his
own game.

Average height. Delicately sculpted features. A slender
figure set off by a gown that wasn't showy but was suitable

for the occasion, a gray blue silk, as he remembered. Her eyes were blue . . . no, not blue, but gray, as gray and clear as the waters of the river Dee on a fine day. She baffled him and intrigued him. Why had he singled her out? Was it his training as an agent? Was it his sixth sense? Or was it something else? And why hadn't he acted on his first impression that this woman was going to be trouble?

He put the wig to his face and inhaled.

A picture formed in his mind. He saw a young man, a boy really, in tartan trews and bonnet, kneeling beside a spring of crystal-clear water. The boy scooped some water into his cupped hands and drank greedily. Behind him rose the peaks of the Cairngorms.

That was better. His sixth sense was working just as it should. He couldn't read minds or get premonitions from his dreams as others with his gift were able to do. His gift was most potent when he touched objects that belonged to his quarry. And that was what the blond woman was now: his quarry. The boy in his vision was surely her accomplice.

"So there you are." Gavin's voice came to him as though from a great distance. "Didn't you hear me calling you?"

The picture in Alex's mind instantly dissolved. He thrust the wig into his pocket. "I was lost in thought. Did you find anything out from Mr. Ramsey?"

"Damn little. He says that he didn't see anything. He's quite shaken up. Well, he would be, wouldn't he? All he wants is to go home and forget the whole thing."

"He must have seen the woman with the gun."

"He insists that he didn't see anything. One moment he was looking at the queen, and the next, a bullet slammed into his arm." Gavin propped one elbow on the parapet and peered up at Alex. "Are you sure it was a woman?" When Alex turned his head and gave his brother a straight look, Gavin shrugged. "Sorry I asked. Of course you're sure. It's just that it seems criminal to me to involve a woman in this kind of dirty work."

"Gavin," Alex's voice was pleasantly modulated, "they *are* criminals, traitors, in fact, and the woman must be one of their prime operators. She is bold, brave, and resourceful. I'll tell you something else. She meant to kill me, not Mr. Ramsey. With me out of the way, she'd have a clear shot at the queen."

Gavin stood stock-still. Finally, he said irritably, "What's going on, Alex? You've told me very little. I'm picking things up in dribs and drabs."

"I've told you as much as you need to know and only because you're my brother and I trust you implicitly."

"You're not acting as though you trust me."

Their eyes met, one seer of Grampian to another. Gavin's gift was to put ideas into his subjects' minds. Alex knew that if he wasn't careful, he would be blabbing like a baby, telling Gavin all his secrets.

Smiling a little, Alex replied, "I'm up to all your tricks, Brother, so don't even think of meddling with my mind. I trust you more than I trust anyone. Let that suffice."

"Don't you trust your colleagues?"

"Up to a point." He was becoming irritable, and when Gavin opened his mouth to say more, Alex cut him off. "Look, I shouldn't be telling you anything. You're not in the game. All I'll say is that someone took a potshot at me tonight, and I mean to find her."

These somber words were followed by a long, reflective silence. At length, Gavin said, "I don't suppose that erratic muse of yours can show us which way she went?"

"That depends." Alex looked toward the peaks. "Tell me, Gavin, where are we most likely to find a spring of ice-cold water?"

"In the mountains." Gavin took one look at Alex's expression and said slowly, "Where did that idea come from? Your muse?"

"Where else would I get a damn fool idea like that? We'd best get a move on."

"Are you joking? It will soon be as black as pitch out

there, and it gets damn cold in these mountains. Why can't we wait till morning?"

"And give her a head start? Not on your life."

A slow grin creased Gavin's face.

"What?" Alex demanded.

"In spite of your words, Brother, I think I've just been invited into the game."

Alex grunted.

A little later, Gavin observed, "The castle is locked up like a prison. They're not likely to give us horses. We're supposed to be guests, remember? They'll want to question us."

"They'll give us horses," said Alex, "or Her Majesty will want to know the reason why." He held up his hand. "Watch me, little brother, and see how it's done."

"The last time you said that to me," replied Gavin moodily, "I broke my arm when I fell out of our tree house."

Alex's only response was a grin, but it soon faded. As they struck out toward the stable, he was thinking of the woman, remembering another time and place, when another pretty woman, a blond, no less, had led him and three of his agents into a deadly trap.

Two

Mahri hitched up her skirts and ran like a hare, weaving in and out of the trees as though the hounds were snapping at her heels. Though she'd chosen the route that gave her the best chance of escaping detection, she did not count on it. There was always one agent sharper than the others, one who would put two and two together and realize that she'd outwitted them. While agents had followed the guests who swarmed onto the lawn, she had stayed close to the castle walls and disappeared round the corner and into the shadows.

She'd lost her wig and reticule in the panicked stampede, but that didn't worry her. They couldn't be traced back to her. She was sure that many ladies had lost more costly items.

It was the thought of the dark-haired man who worried her most. A flicker of recognition had crossed his face. She hoped he wasn't an agent. An agent with a good memory for faces was more trouble than she could handle right now.

The odd thing was, she had no memory of him, and

he was the kind of man a woman would remember, not because he was tall, dark, and handsome, but because he seemed . . . remote . . . untouchable. A challenge, in fact. But not for her. She'd had enough challenges in the last little while to last her a lifetime.

If she didn't get a move on, her lifetime would be numbered in hours. She couldn't turn back the clock, nor did she want to. She had foiled the plot to assassinate the queen. Now she'd have two sets of killers after her: Her Majesty's Secret Service and the members of her own cell.

Up, up she went until she reached the dry stone dike that marked the boundary of the old estate. Here she paused to drag air into her lungs and look back the way she had come. It was darker in the valley than it was on the slopes, and lights were winking in and out of the trees that surrounded the castle. She assumed that groundsmen were beating the bushes to flush her out. If her ruse worked, they would find the blond wig and think she was making for the river. If . . . if . . . if . . .

She lifted her head as she listened for sounds of pursuit. There was nothing, only the sound of the wind playing a restless game with the leaves of nearby trees.

Her revolver was still clutched in her hand. She set it on top of the dike and pulled on one of the stones until it fell with a soft thud to the ground. In the gap left by the stone, she found a satchel that she'd hidden there the night before. It took her only a few minutes to strip out of her own things and dress in the boy's clothes she'd packed in the satchel. Having replaced the satchel and stone, she took a step back and examined her handiwork. Perfect.

"I'll be back for you," she promised her satchel. She was almost tempted to take the dress with her, but caution prevailed. If she were captured, it would give her away.

She picked up her pistol and was off and running again.

There were great cairns of stones dotted around the estate, monuments to the queen's joys and sorrows during her long reign. One of those cairns was close to the tree line.

She hauled herself up to the top of the incline and slumped against the hard granite face. Her arms and legs ached, and her lungs burned. She could hear her breath whistling painfully between her parted lips. She was once a crack courier and was used to pushing herself to the limit, but those days were over. She could no longer race up and down hills like a fleet-footed athlete. Nor could she sustain the role of a boy except in exceptional circumstances and only when the lights were dim. Nature had done its work, softening her hard edges, adding curves. But when her life was in the balance, it was amazing how she slipped into her old skin.

Having ascertained that she was in the clear, she put two fingers to her mouth and emitted a shrill whistle. A moment later, a rider emerged from the trees leading a pony. Dugald was a deerstalker in the hunting season and a man of all trades in the summer. He was also her staunchest ally, and she had sore need of an ally after tonight's work. He'd known her since she was a babe in swaddling clothes, when he was gamekeeper on her grandfather's estate near Gairnshiel on the other side of the river. Their relationship was not that of master and mistress. Dugald was not only her mentor but also her closest friend.

"Did ye stop the bastard?" he asked. His voice was as gravelly as the rest of him. Craggy features and grizzled hair completed the picture.

"I didna kill him if that's what ye mean." Though Mahri spoke the cultured English of the educated Scot, she was just as comfortable in broad Scots or Gaelic. "I'm no a murderer."

Dugald held the reins till she mounted up. "Lassie," he said, "ye dinna have to tell me that. Did ye save the queen is a' I meant."

"Aye. She was well guarded, but I wasna taking any chances. Ramsey is a fanatic. He doesn't care if he lives or dies. He thinks God is on his side." She gave a brilliant smile. "I put a hole in his arm. It will be a long time before he uses that murderous hand to hold a gun."

"Possibly." Dugald's tone was dry. "But I'm thinking it would have been better if ye had gone to the authorities and told them all that ye know—"

"No!" She'd had that debate with herself for a long time now, and there was no easy solution. Fearing that she'd hurt Dugald's feelings, she said gently, "I can't betray my comrades. This was the best I could do."

"But if it's you or them?"

"I don't know. I just don't know."

"Whisht! What was that?"

Mahri's hands tightened on the reins, and her head came up as she listened.

Dugald held up two fingers.

She nodded. There were two riders coming their way. Dugald made another signal. He wanted them to split up. She felt a shiver of alarm, not for herself, but for Dugald. He didn't know what he was getting into. He wouldn't know friend from foe. She knew what he hoped to do. He was going to draw off their pursuers and give her a chance to get away.

Perhaps it was for the best, because if they found Dugald with her, they might well shoot him on sight. As for herself, she did not expect either side to treat her with kid gloves. They'd want to know how much she knew, and when she refused to tell them, they would turn nasty.

Dugald was gesturing to her to get going. She dug in her heels, and her pony tensed every muscle, then sprang forward.

She kept to the plan. There was a room under the name of Thomas Gordon waiting for her at the Inver Arms in Braemar. She'd arrived a few days before and told the proprietor that she had come from Aberdeen for a little visit in hopes that the mountain air would help her breathe more easily. It was a credible tale, for it was common knowledge, at least among Highlanders, that the air in the mountains was superior to all others.

The plan had gone awry, but it wasn't lost altogether. She had shaken off the rider who was following her. Dugald, she hoped, would do the same, and when he turned up, all would be well. He was going to guide her over the hills to Perth, and once she reached Perth, she would take the train south, and Miss Mahri Scot would sink into obscurity.

There was a train at Ballater going to Aberdeen, but Ballater was too close to the castle for comfort. That was how they would expect her to make her escape, on the train from Ballater. Dugald was her best bet.

Meantime, she had a part to play.

In the privacy of her small room under the eaves, she pulled her leather hand grip from beneath the bed. The first thing she did after she stripped was to bind her breasts with a linen towel, then she wriggled into a set of clean clothes. The sight of herself in tight tartan trews made her grimace. This would never do. She'd flattened her breasts, but her hips and posterior were too curvaceous to fool anyone. When she unbuttoned her deerskin jacket, she was better pleased with the result. At least her rounded bottom was less noticeable. Her dark hair was too long for a boy's, so she stuffed it under her tartan tam. The final touch was to slip her dirk into her right boot. She dithered about her gun but decided to leave it behind. It was too obvious, too hard to conceal in her boy's getup. At the reception, she'd kept it in her reticule until the last moment.

After taking a step back, she made an elegant bow to the reflection in the mirror. "Thomas Gordon," she said, "at your service."

As she continued to stare at her reflection, her expression turned wistful. She was looking at the cairngorm brooch pinned to her tam. It brought back memories of happier days when they had all been together, her mother and father and brother, Bruce. Now those happy days had turned into a nightmare.

She turned from her reflection, muttering a Gaelic curse. More irritation. She must remember that she was passing herself off as a Lowlander, and Lowlanders had allowed the ancient tongue to die out centuries before. Only Highlanders kept to the old ways.

That last thought was reinforced when she entered the taproom. Oil lamps gave out the only light. It would be a long time before electricity came to the Highlands. No electricity, no telephones, and damn few trains—so much the better for Thomas Gordon.

She found a place for herself at a table in the darkest corner, ordered a wee dram of whiskey, and took a moment to study the other patrons. They were a far cry from the guests at the queen's reception. They were all males, of course, except for the two women who waited on tables. She made a thorough inventory: estate workers, local businessmen, and perhaps the odd doctor or solicitor. In spite of it being an older crowd, they were a lively lot. But the one thing that impressed her was that word of the attack at Balmoral had not yet reached them.

The woman who waited on her was Mrs. Cluny, the proprietor's wife. "Been out walking the hills, Tam?" she asked conversationally.

"Riding," replied Mahri. "I don't know when I was last on a horse." That was a lie. Her father kept a fine stable in his house in Edinburgh.

Mrs. Cluny clicked her tongue. "I dinna know how folks can abide living in towns. Now get that down ye, shepherd's pie, made to my ain secret recipe. Ye could do with a little more padding on ye, laddie."

There was no menu in these isolated inns and no restaurants to be had. Visitors accepted what was offered at the place where they were staying, or they went hungry. Mahri tucked into the shepherd's pie, savoring each bite. She thought that Mr. and Mrs. Cluny were the most fortunate of people. The whole family was involved in some aspect of running the inn. They were not rich, but they had what money could not buy. They were a close-knit family; they were warmhearted and content with their lot. She envied them.

She toyed with the glass of whiskey and occasionally put it to her lips. She'd asked for it because she thought it made her look more manly. It also made her hoarse so that she frequently had to clear her throat, which was all to the good for someone who was supposed to be prone to lung infections.

No one gave her a second look. All the patrons accepted her as one of them, a stripling who was growing to manhood. She wondered what they would do if she shouted, *Look at me, I'm a female!* They'd probably laugh and go back to eating and drinking.

It was depressing.

She kept her eye on the door while she ate her dinner. People came and went, but there was no sign of Dugald. Her anxiety increased tenfold, however, when a gentleman, a cut above the other patrons, pushed into the taproom and paused just inside the door.

The light wasn't bright enough to see his face clearly, and he had yet to move away from the door. He had that quiet air of assurance that marked him as someone who was used to taking charge. She hoped he was a butler from one of the grand houses in the area, but she couldn't quite see him in that role. Too grand for an ordinary policeman. Ramsey's partner? Someone to take over if the plot misfired? She'd never met a member of Her Majesty's Secret Service, but she thought that he might fit that bill, too.

When he stepped up to the bar counter, she had a clear view of his face. She didn't suck in a breath; she simply stopped breathing altogether. This was the man who, she thought, had recognized her when they waited at Balmoral for the queen to make her entrance. Tall, dark, and handsome and dangerous, the man who had a good memory for faces.

She had no doubts now. It made no difference whether he was Ramsey's partner or a secret service agent. He was no friend to her.

It was time to get out of there.

She took a healthy swig of whiskey with the desired result. She started to cough, not harshly but controlled so as not to draw undue attention to herself. The fit of coughing gave her an excuse to produce her white linen handkerchief and cover the lower half of her face. Perfect camouflage, she hoped.

The stranger had ordered a tankard of ale or beer. As he turned to survey the inn's customers, she averted her eyes. She felt exposed, sitting by herself with nothing to do. She'd eaten her dinner, she'd finished her whiskey, but she couldn't smoke, not only because she didn't know how, but because it would arouse suspicion. A lad with weak lungs would be loath to put a foul-smelling pipe in his mouth. Whiskey was different. Every Scot knew that *uisque beatha* was medicinal.

She chanced a quick look at the stranger. He was propped against the bar counter, looking very much at ease as he surveyed the taproom and its patrons. She understood only too well what he was doing. He was making a mental note of all the exits and summing up each person as she had done when she'd entered the taproom. Agents were trained to notice anything that was out of place.

Her heart jumped when he exchanged a few words with the landlord, then she quickly averted her gaze when she felt their eyes on her. What had Mr. Cluny told the stranger?

She raised her head and allowed her eyes to wander, then she casually steered her gaze in the stranger's direction.

He was coming her way!

She'd been in worse fixes, she reminded herself. She'd crossed swords with the best of them. She had to forget that she was Mahri Scot and think herself into the part of Thomas Gordon.

He stopped at her table and smiled down at her. It softened his features but did not warm his eyes. "I'm Hepburn," he said, "Alex Hepburn. May I join you?" He was already seating himself before she opened her mouth.

"Thomas Gordon," she replied and stifled a yawn. "I was just leaving."

She made to rise, but Hepburn pushed on the table with both hands, pinning her in place. "Make it easy on yourself, Thomas," he said. "I don't want you. I want your mistress. Take me to her, and I'll let you go."

Mahri's mind was frozen. "My mistress?"

Hepburn slapped a blond wig on the table between them. "She left her calling card at the queen's reception earlier this evening. I don't think you're involved in that, but you're her guide, aren't you? Tonight, you led her over the hills to wherever she wanted to go. Take me to her hideout, and I'll let you go."

Mahri's mind was now buzzing. "It wasna me. I'm here for my health." She rubbed her chest. "Ask the Clunies."

"Yes, so Mr. Cluny told me. He also told me that you went out riding after breakfast and did not return until late." His smile would have done credit to a shark. "You're small-fry, Thomas. It's the woman I want."

The thought of sharks and small-fry made her shudder. "I go riding in the hills," she said, "because it's good for my lungs." When he raised a skeptical brow, she added, "What makes you so sure that I'm the lad you want?"

"Your horse is still warm. And—" He took a swig of beer, made a smacking sound with his lips, then smiled a slow smile to himself. "And you were seen, quenching your thirst from a mountain spring."

She was appalled that she'd been observed unawares as she drank from the spring. She remembered the moment well. But that was yesterday, when she'd been spying out the lie of the land and planning the route she'd take once she'd taken care of Ramsey.

A fine courier she was turning out to be!

She was, however, a quick thinker and parried his thrust with one of her own. "And where was the woman you say I was guiding over the hills?"

He shrugged. "At that point, she wasn't with you. However, only one horse in the stable is warm. That leads me to believe that you delivered her safely then came on here." He leaned forward, making her strain away from him. "Let me put this in plain language, Thomas. Either you take me to the woman or I take you back to the castle and let British Intelligence decide whether your are innocent or guilty."

Torture. The thought seared her brain. This man wasn't tall, dark, and handsome. He was infinitely dangerous. Coldhearted. Unscrupulous. And she must never forget it.

"What is it to be, then, Thomas? Do I hand you over to British Intelligence or do you take me to the woman?"

Only an agent would hand her over to British Intelligence. Ramsey and his cohorts would want a secure cellar or dungeon where they could terrorize her in private. However, they were hardly likely to tell her that.

He had the upper hand for the moment, but that could change.

"If I take you to the woman," she said, as meek as she could make herself, "do you promise not to hurt her?"

"Ah. Now we're getting somewhere. Give me her name."

She watched him warily as he pocketed the blond wig she had worn earlier. "Martha McGregor," she said, giving him one of her own aliases. "She seemed like a nice lady."

Something moved in his eyes, something hard and unforgiving.

Without thinking, Mahri edged closer to him. "Why do you hate her? What has she done?"

He scraped back his chair and got up. "First things first. When I have the woman, we'll sit down and have a long chat, you and I. There's a lot you haven't told me, but that can wait."

She thought a show of defiance might be in order, just enough to convince him that she really was small fry. "We're not going out right now, in the dark?"

"Move," he ordered. "I know she can't be far from here. You've only been back an hour or so. And don't try any foolish tricks. It will be the worse for you if you do."

Mahri believed him. The trouble was, it would be even worse for her if she didn't try to trick him. The thought stayed with her as she shuffled out of the taproom.

Three

～✦～

When she stepped out of the warm inn, the blast of cool mountain air seemed to clear her mind, and the panic that urged her to make a dash for freedom became easier to manage. There was no doubt that she would make a dash for it, but it would be at the right time, when she had a chance of escape. This hard-eyed jailer who was directing her to the stable with a hand on her elbow would not be easy to shake off. She needed all her wits about her.

A little help from the dirk in her boot wouldn't come amiss.

She chanced a quick look up at him. That granite-hard expression promised a swift and severe retaliation if she failed to disable him. Her choices were deplorable: disable a crack agent who outweighed her by four or five stone or be handed over to the tender mercies of men who were experts at prizing secrets out of people. And the law was on their side.

She wasn't panicked. She was numb with fear. Where

would Thomas Gordon have taken the woman in this isolated corner of the Highlands? Her brain was frozen.

She gave a start when Hepburn spoke to her.

"You needn't fear me." He sounded annoyed. "I'm not going to hurt you."

"Fear you?" She remembered in time that she was Thomas Gordon, and she set her chin. "I'm not afraid of you!"

"Then why are you trembling?"

"I'm not trembling. I'm shivering. I'm not used to this cold mountain air."

She didn't hear his response. Something had caught her eye. There was a peat cart in the courtyard, at the side door to the cellar, and three brawny Highlanders were unloading peat for the inn's fires while two others leaned nonchalantly against the wall, conversing in Gaelic. Hepburn had noticed them, too.

"Smugglers?" he intoned, and shook his head.

She shrugged. She wasn't going to betray Dugald's friends to an officer of the law.

"You needn't glower, Thomas. I'm not interested in smugglers. I'm not an excise man."

Smugglers. Excise men. Her brain began to thaw. She knew now where she would have taken the woman. It might work. No. It would work, if her nerve held. "We take the bridge," she said, "to the north road."

There was something different about the boy. Alex knew the smell of fear, and the boy's fear had trickled away as they jogged along this old drovers' road. They were on their way to the White Stag, a former change house that was now, with the coming of the railroad, off the beaten track. Change houses and stagecoaches were going out of style.

Darkness pressed in on them from every side, but it wasn't completely unrelieved. Moonlight glazed the dense stands of trees that flanked the road and filtered down to show them the way. They weren't alone. Smugglers were abroad, plying their trade in contraband whiskey. He heard snatches of Gaelic coming from the underbrush, and occasionally they encountered the odd traveler. Not that he understood a word of what was said.

The boy spoke Gaelic. When they were hailed by riders, he returned their greetings. About the only Gaelic Alex remembered was *uisque beatha*, and a few odd phrases. His grandmother, the Witch of Drumore, would be sadly disappointed.

Something stirred at the back of his mind, something about the boy. What was it? He was from Aberdeen, yet he spoke Gaelic. A small point. He himself was Highland bred, and his Gaelic had died away from lack of use.

Lights winked at them through the trees as they approached their destination. This was where the boy said that he had delivered the woman, to the White Stag. Had there been time, Alex would have plied him with questions. He wanted to know how the boy had met the woman and how much she had told him. He wanted to know what he had received for services rendered.

He and Gavin had counted two riders who had split up and gone their separate ways, so they had split up, too. All going well, they were to meet at the family's hunting lodge and possibly turn their captives over to Dickens at the castle. Alex liked and trusted Dickens. He would deal fairly with the boy. He couldn't say the same for Colonel Foster, who had temporarily taken charge when Durward had been called away. The colonel was all spit and polish and liked to throw his weight around. But he wasn't in charge of Dickens or Alex.

He hoped the boy was on the periphery of this conspiracy, that his only involvement had been to wait for the woman and escort her to the change house. He didn't want to make war on boys, and this beardless boy seemed too young to be let off his leading strings. Where were his parents? Who was looking after him? If they only knew the reputation of the man whose hands their stripling had fallen into, they would be shivering in their boots.

Reputation was not reality. The boy would come to no harm with him. As for the woman, that was a different matter. He knew her kind. He'd met her like once before and still smarted from the mauling he'd taken.

As he tied the horses' reins to the tethering rings in the White Stag's courtyard, Alex took a moment to get his bearings. There was no sign of contraband whiskey, but the burly Highlanders in their tartan trews and plaids looked a little too happy, as though they'd been making inroads into their private stock. Alex didn't doubt that they were smugglers. Caution had been thrown to the winds, and he thought he knew why. Every policeman and servant of the crown had been drafted into service for the queen's soiree. There couldn't be a more perfect night for smugglers to go about their business. Who was there to stop them?

They didn't know about the shooting in Balmoral. By morning, Deeside would be swarming with agents, and the smugglers would be home snug in their beds. He wasn't going anywhere, not until he'd found out who had put the woman in the blond wig up to murdering him.

As they pushed into the inn, someone struck up a tune on a fiddle. The public room was crowded. Smoke from clay pipes hung in the air. Toes began to tap, then voices broke into song. He recognized the air: "Mahri's Wedding."

The boy seemed to falter. "Steady, Thomas." Alex put a hand on the boy's shoulder. He felt a tremor but wasn't sure whether it came from the boy or was an involuntary twitch of his own fingers. He dismissed the idle thought and spoke to Thomas again. "Let's . . ." He had to raise his voice above the singing. "Let's have a word with the land-lord and find out what room Martha McGregor is in."

As it turned out, there was no Martha McGregor at the inn, though there was a Morag McGregor. Alex was watch-ing the stairs as the landlord asked whether she could be the lady the gentleman wanted. "Possibly," Alex replied, his attention drawn to a succession of men either ascending the stairs or descending them. It was becoming clear to him that there was more to the good times at the White Stag than *uisque beatha* and fiddle playing.

He looked at Thomas.

The boy answered with a nonchalant shrug. "I may have misheard the name," he said.

Alex grasped Thomas's shoulder and propelled him toward the stairs. "You young whelp," he gritted, "I know how Mistress McGregor paid you for services rendered, and you deserve a whipping. How old are you? Fourteen? Fifteen? You should be in the schoolroom learning your alphabet, not amusing yourself in the fleshpots of Deeside. You could hang as a traitor. Don't you know that?"

"For amusing myself with the lassies?" It was a glib retort, but the boy looked frightened.

Alex shook his head. He didn't know why he was angry at the boy, except that for some obscure reason, he had taken a liking to him. Still, his anger was out of place. He'd got up to a lot more mischief than amusing himself with the lassies when he was the boy's age. A reluctant smile had to be severely repressed.

"Which door?" Alex asked when they reached the upstairs corridor. There were five doors.

Thomas pointed and gulped. "Ye're no going to shame me?"

Was there anything more fragile than a young lad's confidence in his power to attract the lassies? Alex remembered his own blushes when some lass had held him up to ridicule. Gavin, of course, had never suffered such indignities. The lassies had loved him only too well.

He looked into Thomas's troubled eyes, half-fearful, half-hopeful, and he gave a resigned sigh. He was only a lad after all.

"No. I won't shame you," he said. He released his hold on the boy. "Wait here, but leave the door open. Don't move from that spot. Don't even blink."

He knocked on the door and entered on command. The woman, who was lounging in a chair, was as bonnie as they came, but she was not the woman who had attacked him in the castle ballroom. Even if she were a consummate actress, nothing could conceal her overripe curves, and this woman was so scantily clad that nothing was left to his imagination.

Uttering an apology, he made a hasty retreat.

The woman came after him. "Dinna run away," she cooed. "Ye've come to the right door. I'm the only lass that's free for the next little while, and that won't last long."

Because he wasn't a boor, he pressed a kiss to the hand that she offered him. "Alas, ma'am," he said, "I'm looking for my brother, and dare not tarry. Some other time, perhaps?"

She was cooing like a dove when he stepped into the corridor and shut the door. "Thomas?" He looked down the length of the corridor. There was no sign of Thomas. He let out a bellow. "Thomas?"

Mahri pelted down the back stairs, flung herself through the door to the cellar, and exited by a side door. She was no stranger to the White Stag, though her memories of the inn went back a few years, when her brother and she would escape the servants' vigilance and go exploring on their own.

She was in the courtyard at the front of the inn where Hepburn had tethered their horses. Hepburn would know that she'd taken to her heels, but he would want to make sure that the woman he sought was not in the other rooms. Four more doors to try, then he'd realize he'd been tricked. It would give her time to untether her pony and melt into the night.

It didn't occur to her to appeal for help to the patrons who had taken their drinks outside to escape the noise of the public room. They would believe Hepburn before they would believe her. She had to get away before he thought to look for her outside.

Her fingers had never worked faster as she tried to untether her pony. There was a knot she couldn't undo. Fear pulsed hard and fast in her blood. How had the knot got there?

"Going somewhere, Thomas?"

The quietly spoken words had all the force of a thunderclap to her panicked ears. When her heart resumed beating, she lifted her head to look at him. The light was behind him, and his silhouette showed a tall man with broad shoulders and—this might have been a trick of her imagination—long, muscular legs. At any rate, no one could doubt that he was a formidable adversary.

A few heads turned as patrons looked at them curiously.

She was struck by a blinding flash of inspiration. Pointing a shaking finger at Hepburn, she cried, "He's an excise man!"

There was a stunned silence, then everyone was on the move.

"An excise man!" a broad-chested Highlander chanted, and the cry was taken up.

No one was intent on harming the excise man. They all seemed to have the same idea: to get away before he arrested any of them. To defraud the government of the tax on whiskey carried a severe penalty. To maim or kill an officer of the law was to court the hangman's noose.

People were streaming out of all the exits. Hepburn was jostled and lost his footing. That's when Mahri made her dash for freedom. She regretted having to leave her pony, but she didn't have a choice. The wily Hepburn had knotted the reins so that, in all likelihood, he was the only one who could untie them.

She hared into the cover of the trees, crouched down, and scanned the inn's courtyard for a sign of her enemy. Carts and horses with riders were taking off in every direction. Her pony was still tethered, but there was no sign of Hepburn or his horse. Swallowing her fear, she rose to her feet and began to run.

Though it went against every instinct, she made for the ford that crossed the Dee at Invercauld. Once she crossed the Dee, she would be back in what she considered to be enemy territory, the hills bordering the Balmoral estate, the way she'd come earlier that night after she'd shot Ramsey. She didn't have much of a choice. She wanted to stay close to Braemar, where she was supposed to meet up with Dugald. The south bank of the Dee was a land of uncultivated forests, barren moors, and few people except the residents of Braemar and, perhaps, gamekeepers and shepherds. Militia, policemen, and anyone in a hurry would take the north road, and Mahri wanted to avoid them.

As her fear ebbed, her pace slowed. This felt like the longest night of her life. She'd been fatigued beyond bearing when she'd arrived at the Inver Arms, but when Hepburn had stepped into the taproom, she'd found her wind again. Now she was completely spent. She couldn't get her legs to obey the commands of her brain. She had to stop frequently to catch her breath. And if that were not enough, it had begun to rain.

Brambles snared her clothes and face. She cursed them fluently in Gaelic and pressed on. There was nothing to see now, no moonlight to show her the way. Her only guide was the sound of the river as it tumbled over its rocky bed. There were many fords over the Dee, some with stepping-stones, but this wasn't one of them. When was her luck going to turn?

Though the river was shallow at this point, it could still be treacherous. If she slipped and hit her head on a rock, she could quite easily drown. She tested the water gingerly. It did not reach the top of her boot.

She had taken only two careful steps into the water

when she heard it, the soft neighing of a horse. Her feet slipped on the stones, and she came down heavily on her rear end. All her inert instincts returned in full force. He, Hepburn, was there, stalking her.

From that point on, stealth was forgotten. Half-crouched over, arms stretched in front of her for balance, she plunged into the river.

"For God's sake, Thomas!"

She had slithered and slid to the halfway point when something caught her collar, choking her, and the next thing she knew, she was dragged and swept along the riverbed on her toes. Once they reached the other side, he dumped her, none too gently, on the muddy bank. She scrambled to her knees but that was as far as she got. He was on her in the blink of eye, hauling her up like a sack of potatoes and throwing her facedown across the saddle. Then he mounted up and urged his horse forward. She put up a feeble struggle and for her pains received several swats on her backside.

She wasn't beaten yet, she promised herself.

It was an empty promise. She'd been taught how to defend herself, but she had never been caught before, never had to come to blows with a trained killer. She was a courier, not a warrior.

It didn't matter. They'd hang her anyway.

He had hoped to clear up the business of the "blond" imposter quickly and let the boy go before his colleagues caught up with them. He had no intention of handing the woman over for questioning, not until he'd made up his mind about how deeply she was involved. Suspected traitors and conspirators, male and female, frequently met with tragic accidents before they could go to trial. The less evidence there was to stand up in a court of law, the more likely they were to come to a bad end. Once, a long time ago, he'd made a serious error in judgment. He had no wish to repeat the experience.

As for the boy, he had intended to let him off with a severe warning, but that was before the wretch had duped him, before he'd had a rude awakening at the White Stag. Thomas Gordon was no innocent bystander. He'd set a trap that could quite easily have had him, an elite member of Her Majesty's Secret Service, beaten to within an inch of his life. An excise man! Excise men were the most despised breed in all of Scotland. He himself despised them.

Master Gordon was no innocent. His subsequent flight from the inn showed forethought and cunning. He was in the conspiracy up to his neck. One way or another, Alex would pry the truth out of him, and only then would he decide what to do with him.

The pelting rain was fast becoming a deluge. Alex had hoped to return to the Inver Arms in Braemar, but the rain and the dark made it a tricky proposition. All the same, they had to get out of the rain. The nearest refuge that he was aware of was the one they'd just left.

Grunting, spewing a stream of curses, he turned his horse's head and made for the White Stag.

They were all terrified of him: the landlord, his wife, the few patrons who had not dashed from the inn in a panicked stampede. They took one look at the revolver in his hand, another at the inert form of the boy he'd hoisted over one shoulder, and they froze like icicles hanging from the eaves.

He raised his revolver as he stomped to the bar counter, pointing it at the ceiling. He was in a foul humor. If anyone looked at him the wrong way, he'd part his hair with a shot from his gun.

No one looked at him the wrong way. No one so much as blinked.

He heaved a sigh. "I am not an excise man," he said. "I don't give a tinker's cuss about your contraband whiskey. This runaway"—he slapped Thomas's rear end to make a point—"is my brother, and I aim to take him home to our father, whose heart he broke when he ran away."

He paused a moment to let the words sink in. "I don't want trouble. I want a room where we can spend the night and someone to care for our horses. I'd like a change of clothes for my brother until the clothes he is wearing have dried out." He fished in his coat pocket and produced two sovereigns, which he slapped down on the polished wood counter. "This should cover our expenses."

The gleaming coins brought an answering gleam to the landlord's eyes. It also broke the spell of silence. Men shrugged and turned to each other to resume their conversations. In no time at all, Alex and his prisoner were ushered into a snug little room at the back of the inn next to the kitchen. The heat from the kitchen ovens made their own small chamber pleasantly warm. Alex noted the bars on the only window and counted them a bonus. There would be no escape for Master Gordon now. There was one narrow bed, an antiquated washstand with a folded towel on a shelf, a small table with an oil lamp that the landlord hastened to light, and one upright chair.

"My son's room," the landlord said, "when he comes for a visit. I'll tell the wife to look out some of his clothes for the lad." He bowed himself out.

They were both wet, but the boy had taken a dunking in the river and was in far worse shape than Alex. His teeth were chattering, and shivers racked his slight frame.

Alex lowered him to the bed. He couldn't allow himself to show pity, because this boy would use it to his advantage. Keeping his voice neutral, he said, "Strip out of those wet clothes, and I'll have the landlord's wife take them away to dry."

The boy's complexion was gray; his eyes were wary. His bottom lip trembled.

Alex's lips quirked. "Don't be shy. You haven't got anything I haven't seen before. Come on, lad. Act the man."

The boy continued to sit there, staring wide-eyed at Alex.

"Look," said Alex," it's easy, see?" He put his pistol down on the table and dragged off his coat. "Now you," he told the boy.

The boy's response was unexpected. He dived into his boot and came up with a dagger. "Stay away from me, or I'll cut your heart out."

Alex might have been angry had the boy's hand not shaken like the Shakin' Briggie at Cults. When he felt himself softening, he hardened his resolve. Give this boy an inch, and he would take a mile.

"Stay away from you? You ungrateful whelp. I'm trying to save you from falling into the hands of—"

He moved like lightning. His fist lashed out, catching the boy on the wrist, and the dagger spun out of his hand. He swooped it up, tossed it on the table, then pounced on the boy, flattening him into the mattress. The boy beat at him with his fists, but there wasn't much force behind the blows. If he'd wanted to, Alex could have hurt him badly. He didn't want to hurt the boy. What he wanted was the boy's submission, and it seemed that at long last he had it.

He reached for the boy's tam, and a mane of dark curls tumbled out. Baffled, he began to strip the boy's clothes from him one article at a time. The boy protested weakly, but Alex was in no mood to listen. When soft flesh spilled into his hands, he was stunned. It took him a moment to realize that, once again, he had completely misjudged the situation. He had uncovered a perfect specimen of femininity: plump little breasts with dark crests, a long, slender waist, softly flaring hips, and skin as smooth as satin. Between her thighs, a dark thatch of swansdown protected her femininity.

His breath froze in his lungs. He experienced the same sensation he'd felt when he'd first set eyes on the blond woman at the queen's reception: a ripple of recognition,

like a tiny electric current passing through his brain. All
his senses opened to her.

When he found himself reaching for her, he snatched
his hand away. Fear-bright eyes stared up at him.

This was madness. The woman meant nothing to him.
Nothing. She'd as soon kill him as look at him.

Gritting his teeth, he got off the bed and snatched a
blanket that was folded over the chair. "Cover yourself," he
said harshly.

As she quickly did as she was bid, he reached for the
towel and mopped the rain from his face. Things he hadn't
seen before were clicking into place.

"There is no other woman," he said. "Is there? There is
no boy who conducted her to a safe place. You're one and
the same person."

When she shook her head miserably, he made an impatient, slashing gesture with one hand. "You're the woman at
the reception. You're the blond who tried to kill me. I want
you to begin at the beginning and tell me all you know, or
I swear I will have you locked in a dungeon and I will walk
away without a backward glance."

And to show her how defenseless she was, he picked up
her dirk and thrust it into the strap inside his own boot.

Four

❦

She was drawing herself into the blanket as though it were a tent when his words arrested her. "Kill *you*?" she said. "I don't even know you." She tucked the edges of the blanket under her chin.

He spoke in a voice that was all the more menacing for being soft. "Your shot missed me by a hair."

Her brain was working on several levels. She didn't know how to read this man, didn't know whether it would serve her best to appear to be browbeaten or a force to be reckoned with. Another part of her brain was sifting through his words. He thought she had tried to kill him. Was this a trick to get her to talk? And who was he? Who was he working for? She still wasn't sure.

When he slammed his hand against the wall, she blurted, "If I'd wanted to kill you, I wouldn't have missed."

"That's an odd boast for a lady to make."

It wasn't odd. It was insane. Where had her wits gone? "I wasn't boasting." She despised the wobble in her voice, and in an effort to appear more in control of the situation and of herself, she tipped up her chin. "Anyone can learn to shoot a gun. My grandfather thought it was a skill everyone should master."

When he sat down on the edge of the bed, she scuttled backward to the headboard. She did not mistake his smile for an attempt at friendliness. It reminded her of her first impression, that he was a shark on the hunt for small fry.

"Let's not play games," he said. "If you didn't try to kill me, then you were part of the plot to kill the queen."

At last she had a clue to his identity. He must be working for the authorities. Or was it a trick to lull her suspicions?

"I'm not part of any plot," she asserted with as much indignation as she could muster. "And before you say another word, I want to know who I'm talking to. You told me your name but not why you followed me. Why didn't you report me to the authorities?"

His reply was laced with irony. "I *am* the authorities. It's my job to follow runaways. You did better than run away. You vanished. Now it's your turn. Who are you, vanishing lady?"

Anyone listening to them would think that they were flirting. She shrugged off the disturbing thought and gave him another alias. "I am Margaret Blayne of Struan House by Cults." To her knowledge, there was no such person and no such house.

"You're not one of the White Stag's barques of frailty?"

"What?"

"You know, Morag McGregor, who plies her trade upstairs?"

This was going from bad to worse. When she'd set out on her mission, she'd known that she might be caught. It didn't matter whose hands she fell into; she didn't expect to be treated gently. She was coming to see that she might have underestimated the kind of torture they would use against her. This man wasn't a gentleman. She didn't like the way he was looking at her. It was too masculine, too predatory.

When he quite deliberately touched his hand to her bare foot, she jumped and quickly withdrew her toes under the blanket.

"No. I can see you are not Morag McGregor," he said. "Pity." When he sat back on the bed, she let out a shivery sigh.

"So you're Margaret Blayne of Struan House?"

"I am. Yes."

"Do you live with your parents, a husband, relatives?"

She tried not to look away from his probing stare. "I live with an aunt."

"Mmm. Well, that can be easily verified."

True, but by that time, she hoped she had given him the slip. "Mrs. Lindsay, my aunt, will vouch for me."

"What did you do with your revolver?" he suddenly asked.

She was glad to change the subject. "I left it in my room at the Inver Arms." She gave a helpless shrug. "I didn't expect to run into trouble."

"You thought you were free and clear?"

"No," she said quietly, her mind wandering, "I'll never be free and clear."

"What does that mean?"

She blinked up at him as her mind focused. "It doesn't mean anything profound. I'm tired; that's all."

His voice sounded gentler to her ears. "Shall we start over? At the reception tonight, you aimed your revolver at me and fired. If I wasn't your target, who was?"

She had rehearsed a little speech for this eventuality, but it was one thing to say it to herself and another to say it to this hard-eyed man. Something else was bothering her. Balmoral wasn't so far away. Why were they holed up here, when they could just as easily have borrowed some dry clothes and made it back to the castle where she could be questioned by other agents, too? She'd feel safer in the castle with the queen in residence. And this place was, more or less, a bawdy house. What was the significance of that?

If he thought he could cow her with these tactics, he would soon learn his mistake. She was Mahri Scot and could trace her line back to King Robert the Bruce. The blood of warriors ran in her veins. Traitors' blood, too, and the odd sprinkling of rogues' and charlatans'. But as far as she knew, none of them had been cowards.

If only she could stop her inner trembling and show her mettle.

"I'm waiting for an answer," he said.

"Ronald Ramsey," she stated baldly, "the man I hit. He was my target."

Baffled, he sat back. "Why him? What did that poor lad ever do to you? You might have killed him."

"I told you. I never miss. I didn't want to kill him, only to disable him." She paused to marshal her thoughts. There was enough truth in what she was about to tell him to persuade him to let her go. A darting look at her grim-faced jailor convinced her that she was way off the mark. This man was relentless. He would not let her go until he had verified every last detail of her story. The best she could hope for was that it would buy her a little time till she could figure a way of escape.

"Ronald is mad," she said, and that was the truth. Now the lies began. "When I refused to marry him, he warned me that he would do something spectacular to make me regret my decision. He sent me a note to say that he was going to kill the queen at her reception. I wasn't sure if he meant it, but I decided, just in case, to foil him in the act. And I did."

He grimaced in disbelief. "You expect me to believe that? The man was standing right behind me. He made no attempt on the queen's life."

"No, he wouldn't," she said crossly, "because I shot the gun out of his hand."

He took a moment to consider this. "There was no gun."

"How can you be so sure?"

"Because I'm a secret service agent. I'm trained to notice such things."

She stared at his set face, then gave a hoot of laughter. "Well, Mr. Secret Service Agent, Ramsey had a gun, a revolver to be precise. I know, because I shot it out of his hand."

Alex's lips flattened. His eyes narrowed on her. "Then where is the gun now, Miss Know-it-all?"

She gave an elegant shrug. "How should I know? I'm not the secret service agent."

His next words wiped the smile from her face. "Why didn't you warn the authorities about Ramsey? Why didn't you appeal to them to help you?"

She had warned the authorities, in a roundabout way. Much good it had done. They hadn't taken her seriously.

It wasn't supposed to be like this. She should have escaped in the panic, and Ramsey and his fellow conspirators should have run for cover, knowing that their plot had failed.

It was all such a muddle. How much should she tell him? How much did he know?

Half in earnest, half playing a part, she said, "What could the authorities do? Arrest Ramsey before he committed a crime? They were more likely to arrest me. Now you tell me there was no gun. In that case, I misjudged him, and it was nothing more serious than a lovers' tiff gone wrong."

His tone was dry. "Have done with the lies. You planned your escape with meticulous detail. A sign of a guilty conscience?"

"A sign of knowing my enemy!" she retorted. "You're all the same, you men in high places. When things go wrong, you look for a scapegoat. I'd hoped to vanish into thin air before you found one—me."

She stopped suddenly. She was talking too much, giving too much away. The trouble was, she could hardly keep her eyes open. She was losing her fear of him—she didn't know why—and the soft bed was lulling her senses to sleep.

His next question put paid to any idea of sleep.

"What happened to your companion?"

"There was no companion." He meant Dugald, of course. "I was the only one involved."

"There were two riders," he said. "You split up. I followed your trail and a colleague followed your companion."

"He might have been a smuggler. I don't know. He was no friend to me."

She wasn't unduly alarmed. Dugald was on home ground. He was a stalker. It would be different if he were found with her. Then he'd come under suspicion, too.

Something occurred to her and she said, "Why didn't you follow the other rider? Why choose me?"

"The other rider was making his way back to the castle. I knew . . . sensed . . . that it was the last place you'd want to go."

"You . . . sensed?" Her nose wrinkled. "I thought that secret service agents relied on their powers of deduction to solve cases. Too bad you didn't sense that Ramsey had a gun."

"And it's too bad for you," he snapped, "that I was on duty tonight, or you might have got away with your crime."

She'd made him lose his temper and that pleased her enormously.

After an interval of silence, he said, "How did you get past the footmen who were on the doors? I take it that you didn't have an invitation to the queen's reception?"

"I entered as though I belonged there. When one footman asked for my card of invitation, I told him that I'd given it to another. They were very polite, very helpful. Do you know, Mr. Hepburn, I think that security at the castle could do with some improvement?"

His chin jutted. Hers lifted.

There was a discreet knock on the door. He got off the bed and reached for his gun. "Who is there?"

"Mrs. Leslie, your landlady."

He thrust his gun into his coat pocket and took a quick

look around. "Do something with your hair," he growled. "You look like a girl."

He waited until she had gathered her mane of hair at her nape and covered it with the blanket before he opened the door. Their landlady, all smiles and good humor, bustled in with an armful of clothes.

"If this disna suit, let me know," she said, "and I'll fetch something else. Now give me your wet things, lad, and I'll dry them in front of the kitchen fire."

The change in Hepburn was dramatic to say the least. Mahri couldn't help staring. The landlady was an old crone who kept a bawdy house, yet he treated her with the deference due the queen. He smiled, he nodded, he blathered on about Highland hospitality and how there was nothing like it, and he secured the promise of a pot of tea and scones before the landlady left.

As soon as the door closed, Mahri said, "You can take that smile off your face, Hepburn. It's not you our landlady likes; it's the sovereigns in your pocket."

His smile vanished, and he gave her one of his glowering looks.

She smiled. "Don't tell me I've hurt your feelings? I'm sure she likes you as well as any of her customers."

Was that a smile he was trying to suppress? Evidently not, because he barked out, "Choose what you need and get dressed, unless you prefer to be naked. It's all the same to me. And do something with your hair, or I'll be tempted to cut it off."

She wasn't frightened now. She was offended. He'd treated Mrs. Leslie with deference while he had manhandled her, Mahri Scot, who was on his side and had done her best to foil the plot against the queen. For her trouble, she'd had her backside swatted and been terrorized by a string of threats. Well, he'd uttered one threat too many.

"I bet you loved your granny."

His head jerked up. "What?"

"It's obvious. You like old women, but you distrust any

female under the age of thirty. What happened, Hepburn? Did your granny spoil you? Did some young woman break your heart? Mmm?"

He had the oddest look on his face, as though someone had just walked over his grave, then his expression cleared, and in the same cutting tone, he said, "I don't have a heart, and you had better remember that. Now move your arse."

Keeping a wary eye on him, she began to pick through the clothes. When she had what she wanted, she looked a question at him.

"What?" he asked.

"I have to use the facilities."

"The facilities? Oh, I see what you mean. I'm sure there's a chamber pot under the bed."

"A chamber pot!" she gasped.

He grinned.

He seemed to be enjoying her embarrassment, and that made pride stiffen her spine. She dropped the clothes on the floor, kept the blanket wrapped tightly around her, and without a word, lay down on the bed and closed her eyes against the loathsome sight of him.

A minute went by, then another. Finally, he sighed. "Dress yourself," he said irritably, "and I'll take you to the privy. But no tricks, mind, or it will be the worse for you."

Tricks were the farthest thing from her mind. She really had to go.

She was too modest to throw off the blanket and reveal her nakedness, so she made do by using the blanket as a tent as she wiggled into a shirt and a pair of trews. When she'd done that, she threw off the blanket and pulled on her boots.

The words to thank him were on the tip of her tongue when his next words crushed the impulse.

"If you think," he said, glowering at her, "that all that writhing under the blanket will make me susceptible to your wiles, you can think again. Frankly, Thomas, I prefer my women to be a little more buxom."

She stomped out of the room when he held the door for her.

She'd fallen asleep before she'd taken more than a few nibbles of scone. He'd bundled her, fully clothed, into bed, but it soon became apparent that her borrowed garments were too tight for her comfort, too tight and too hot. He'd had to waken her to get some of them off. Naturally, she'd fought him. He'd left her with a voluminous shirt that came down to her knees, then he'd covered her with the blanket.

He had positioned the only chair in the room against the door and was sitting with his booted feet resting against the bottom of the bed. He figured that if she tried to leave the room when he was asleep, she would have to move his chair, and he would be on her before she took her next breath.

He swallowed a mouthful of cold tea as he studied her. She looked so slight and defenseless that it seemed inconceivable to him that she could be part of a plot to assassinate the queen. On the other hand, she'd led him a merry chase tonight and had damn near been the death of him. He was exaggerating, but not by much. This young woman was resourceful. She was a master of deceit. In the normal course of events, he wouldn't have allowed her to catch her breath, much less sleep. He should be firing off questions, coming at her from every direction, trying to trick her into telling him more than she wanted to. After his disastrous blunder with Ariel, he'd vowed never again to be taken in by a pretty-faced, scheming bitch.

The girl's careless words had hit the mark. *"You like old women, but you distrust any female under the age of thirty."*

He couldn't argue with that. One Ariel in a man's lifetime was more than enough—beautiful, deceitful, heartless Ariel.

She was the only woman he had ever loved. He could

think of her now without drowning in a cauldron of emotion—fury, hate, grief, and despair. It had taken a long, long time to regain his balance.

He took another swallow of tea as memories filtered into his mind. He had recruited Ariel into the service, not as an agent on active duty but as someone who could spy on the comings and goings of high-ranking government ministers and their aides. These were the circles Ariel moved in. Little did he know that Ariel's loyalties lay elsewhere, with a group of misfits belonging to a group called Demos. Their aim was to end the monarchy in Scotland and turn it into a republic. They were all talk and no action and hardly registered in intelligence reports. No one took them seriously. And they paid for their mistake. The direct result of his personal negligence was that three of his closest associates were blown up by a bomb. He was the only one to survive the blast.

He had survived, but Ariel had not. She'd fallen down a flight of stairs and broken her neck. Whether she died at the hands of British Intelligence or was murdered by a member of Demos was never satisfactorily answered in Alex's view. But Demos paid dearly, not for Ariel's death, but for killing three agents, and British Intelligence had hunted her comrades into oblivion.

After that experience, he had asked for a transfer. The glamour and excitement of the spying game had lost its gloss. He'd retreated to his desk in Whitehall and become one of the ministry's crack code breakers. There was no pain in breaking codes, no treachery and no guilt.

Life became easier to manage. Code breaking kept his mind from straying to the past. He lived comfortably in his rooms on Piccadilly, met acquaintances and associates at his club, and occasionally posted up to Scotland to reacquaint himself with his family and old friends. He wasn't happy, but he wasn't miserable either.

What had brought him back into the game was that Demos had recently burst upon the scene in a stunning revival. Attempted assassinations and bombs going off in government buildings had become the order of the day. He was a Scot, and with his experience, so his superiors told him, he was uniquely placed to smash Demos and bring its leaders to justice.

They'd had forewarning of an attempt by Demos on the queen's life. An anonymous letter had arrived that might well have been a prank but that British Intelligence took very seriously. There was a plot to assassinate the queen at her reception, the letter said. Hence the elaborate ruse of the stand-in. They'd hoped to lure the assassin into a trap.

All he'd trapped was a young woman who had attempted to kill him or the man behind him. If she had written the letter, why didn't she own up to it?

He had more than his identity as a Scot working for him now. He was a seer of Grampian with gifts neither his superiors nor Demos could possibly imagine.

That thought prompted him to dig in his pocket and pull out the blond wig. He crushed it between his hands. It still sang for him, but its energy was fading. He needed something more recent, something the girl had handled when her emotions were running high.

He reached in his boot and retrieved her little dagger. When he held it loosely in his hands, he felt nothing at all, not even a hint of emotion. He remembered how her hand shook when she waved the dirk under his nose. He hadn't felt the least bit threatened. It wasn't that he trusted her, but he didn't believe she was a killer. She lied convincingly, but any ordinary person with a modicum of intuition would have sensed that her story had glaring holes in it. Any agent worth his salt would have been pressing her for answers. All the same, he could not bring himself to hand her over to less squeamish agents than himself. He had no desire to have another death on his conscience.

He was boxing himself into a corner. If he wasn't going to take her back to Balmoral, what was he going to do with her?

He was thinking too much.

He grasped the dirk firmly in his right hand and opened his senses. This was more like it. A mist formed behind his eyes. When the mist cleared, he saw two figures, a man and a woman. Though the figures were indistinct, he knew that the woman in the bed, sleeping like a babe, was the woman in his vision.

Gradually, the scene came into focus. They were by a waterfall beside a bubbling stream. The man held the dirk in his hand, offering it to the woman. She touched it—reverently? reluctantly?—and sank to her knees. "Demos," she whispered.

Alex didn't know what broke his connection to his vision, his own shock at hearing that hateful word, or the emotion that emanated from the woman. Demos. So he was right. She was in this up to her neck!

He was incensed, now, that he'd allowed himself to soften toward her. History was repeating itself. It wasn't the woman's death he should be worried about but the death of the men who worked with him.

It seemed that nothing had changed. He could still be duped by a pretty face and a woman's winning ways. He'd even given her the bed and made do with a cramped chair to allay her virginal fears.

What a chump he was!

Well, Master Thomas Gordon—he refused to call her "Margaret," knowing that she had lied about that, too—was in for a rude awakening. He'd have her up at the crack of dawn and back in Balmoral before the birds were up.

Meanwhile—

He stripped out of his clothes till he was down to his trousers, dropped her little dagger into one of his boots, and climbed into bed. Asleep or waking, there was nothing this treacherous little bitch could do to seduce him from his purpose. And if she didn't want to share the bed, he'd tie her to the chair, but he'd be damned if she slept in comfort while he ached with cramped muscles from head to toe.

She didn't waken. She rolled into him, and her warm breath tickled his armpit. He wasn't going to turn his back on her, just in case she tried to brain him, so he anchored her with one arm around her waist. She nestled closer, all warm woman brushing against his bare skin. His breathing became labored. Lust and anger churned inside him, battling for supremacy. He shoved himself out of the bed and stood there quivering, ready to take her or ready to beat her, he couldn't tell which.

What he needed was a breath of cleansing, mountain air. After donning his shirt, coat, and boots, he left the room and locked the door from the outside. A few steps took him to the kitchen. He froze when he felt a cold draft of air. He wasn't alone. Someone had entered the kitchen through a window. He could hear quick, shallow breaths and smell the unmistakable reek of tobacco.

A smuggler wouldn't be sneaking around the house at this time of night.

Alex tensed himself to spring. Suddenly, his head seemed to shatter into a thousand shards, and he sank to the floor in a heap.

Five

❦

The professor spoke slowly and without inflection, a sure sign that he was adding things up in that razor-sharp mind of his, calculating, making connections. "I'm missing something," he said, "something important. Take me through it again, Ramsey, from the moment you were shot to the point where you stabbed the queen's chief of security and made your escape."

He turned from the window that overlooked the approach to the house and took the chair facing Ramsey's. He was a tall man, loose-limbed, with fair hair turning to silver and intelligent gray eyes in a remarkably handsome face. He'd had a varied career, first as a soldier in the Crimean War, then as a professor at Edinburgh University. He looked like a typical professor—relaxed, thoughtful, prone to long silences—but as Ramsey knew well, he was a soldier for all that.

The professor smiled. "Relax. Murray wouldn't go to bed if he were worried. Besides, if you'd been followed, the soldiers would be here already."

Ramsey made a visible effort to relax. Murray was the third member of their team, not a member of Demos but an associate whose services came at a price. It was Murray who had put him on a horse and seen him safely home.

"Go on," the professor said. "Tell me what happened tonight."

Ramsey nodded and huddled into the comfortable wing chair, careful not to jog the arm that was in a sling. He wasn't deceived by the professor's easygoing manner. He knew that he was reporting to his commanding officer. Their headquarters was this large Jacobean mansion on the north side of the river, near Gairnshiel. It had been a long ride home from the castle, or so it seemed to him in his weakened condition.

That was many hours ago. He was ready for his bed but knew that there would be no rest for him until the professor was satisfied that he'd been told every small, inconsequential detail of the debacle at Balmoral.

It weighed heavily on him. He'd made a muck of things and deserved a dressing-down, but that was not the professor's way. A word, a look, a change of inflection in his voice was enough to make a man squirm. He'd used the same tactics at the University of Edinburgh. That was where their paths had first crossed. Ramsey was a student then, and out of sheer curiosity, he'd taken a class with the charismatic professor who stood history on its head and questioned every cherished myth that the Establishment held dear. Military history was his subject. Every commander, every general, every battle had to be dissected until the truth was laid bare. His students used to joke among themselves that after one of the professor's lectures, they felt as though he'd taken their brains out, rearranged them in their proper order, and shoved them back into their heads.

The professor added gently, "Things may occur to me that may not occur to you. That's why we're going through this again."

Ramsey nodded and started over. "I had a clear shot at the queen and was bringing up my revolver when out of the blue, a woman shot me. I wasn't expecting it, wasn't prepared for it."

"What did the woman look like?"

Ramsey shook his head. "I told you, I didn't see her. My eyes were on the queen, but one of the men who helped me said that she was a blond. There's something else I should mention. There were more guards than you said there would be. I was beginning to suspect even then . . ."

"Yes?"

"That they were expecting trouble."

"You see? You've told me something new. It may mean something, or it may mean nothing at all. Then what happened?"

"Right after that, another shot went off, and everyone panicked." Ramsey shifted his position and grimaced in pain. "Two very helpful gentlemen came to my assistance. One went after the woman with blond hair, and the other stayed by my side."

"You said before that these men were brothers?"

"Hepburn was their name. Gavin Hepburn was the younger of the two, and he took me to see the doctor. There was nothing I could do. Streams of people were running in every direction, and guards were going after them."

There was a silence as the professor digested this. "Could the woman have been one of the agents assigned to guard the queen?"

"I don't think so. If she had been one of them, she wouldn't have run away."

"What about the Hepburn brothers?"

Ramsey thought for a moment. "Yes. That's more likely. They didn't panic, and they didn't run."

"You're beginning to tire. Let's move on. Tell me again about your revolver."

Ramsey hesitated. Finally, he said, "In the confusion, I

managed to retrieve it and slip it into my pocket. I thought I might have to use it to shoot my way out. I didn't expect to be searched."

"You didn't expect to be searched?" There was a trace of amusement in the professor's voice. "A gun went off at the queen's reception. You were shot, and you didn't think you'd come under suspicion?"

Faint color ran under Ramsey's skin. "No, sir. I was the victim. It never occurred to me that I would be searched. It was a stupid blunder on my part."

"You're too hard on yourself. It's too bad you fell into Dickens's hands, though. He is . . . was . . . as thorough as they come. You won't have been the only one they searched tonight. So, he searched you and found the gun. Then what?"

"I told him that the person who shot me dropped it and, in the panic, I picked it up to defend myself."

"And when Dickens examined the gun, he found you out in a lie."

"Yes, sir. It hadn't been fired, so the person who shot me could not have dropped it. Dickens knew it must be my gun."

"Don't look so stricken. It can happen to the best of us. And you redeemed yourself at the end."

The professor got up and paced to the sideboard against the wall. After a moment or two, he returned with a glass of whiskey. "You've earned this," he said, handing the glass to Ramsey. "Drink it slowly."

Ramsey appreciated the gesture. It reminded him of the good old days, when the professor would invite a few select students to his rooms, and they would argue politics well into the night. He'd been a boy then. His father had already had a career mapped out for him, so when he graduated, against the professor's persuasions, he'd accepted a commission in the British Army.

And he had eventually found himself fighting the Zulus in Southern Africa. That was when he learned that the professor knew what he was talking about. The army was commanded by a pack of blue-blooded buffoons who owed their seniority to family connections or friends in high places.

He learned something else. The professor's only son had served there, too, but had lost his life in his first engagement. The professor never talked about his loss, but there was a hard edge to him that had been absent before his son died. Now he was in deadly earnest. By fair means or foul, Scottish patriots would break free of the shackles that bound them to England.

To be a part of such an enterprise made his own heart swell with pride.

"So," said the professor, "you were found out in a lie. What happened then?"

"Dickens suddenly got up and told me that he didn't believe a word I'd said, that he believed I was part of the plot to assassinate the queen. He went to the door. I could see what he meant to do. He'd call for soldiers, and I'd be arrested."

He stopped to take a sip of whiskey, then another. "I didn't panic. It was his reference to a plot to assassinate the queen that shocked me. How could he have known about the plot, unless someone had betrayed us?"

"He may have been fishing, you know, trying to trick you."

Ramsey edged forward in his chair. "He knew something, sir. I'm sure of it. If someone had betrayed us, it would explain why there were so many men guarding the queen."

"You may have something there. Tell me what happened next."

"I couldn't allow him to leave that room alive. I'd told him a pack of lies that he could easily disprove."

The professor cut in, "Who else did you talk to before Dickens questioned you?"

"The doctor and Gavin Hepburn, but I told them nothing of any use."

"Did you lie to them?"

"No. For the most part, I pretended to be in too much pain to answer their questions."

"Well-done. Go on."

Ramsey continued, "I didn't have time to debate the point, so I picked up a letter opener that was on the desk and drove it into his neck. Then I slipped through the window and made for the rendezvous. Murray was waiting for me."

"What happened to the letter opener?"

"I left it where it had fallen on the floor. But I took my revolver with me."

After a long, reflective silence, the professor got up and began to pace. "This is what we are going to do," he said. "Tomorrow, we're going to return to the castle." He held up his hand when Ramsey tried to interrupt him. "We'll ask to speak to Dickens. We'll be shocked when we hear that he has been murdered. You'll say that he let you go last night because you were in shock and unable to answer his questions coherently but promised to return the next day. Someone will ask you the same questions Dickens asked, and you'll tell them the truth, that you're a former student of mine and we're making up a party to explore the historic sites in the area."

"But won't they know that I was the last person to be with Dickens?"

"Who would suspect a veteran of the Zulu campaign? It's not as though you were an interloper. You had a gilt-edged invitation card."

"A forgery," replied Ramsey dryly.

"An excellent forgery," the professor asserted. He got up. "I think that's enough for one night. You look all in. Up with you and off to bed."

At the door, he put his hand on Ramsey's shoulder. "I need hardly tell you that you've acquitted yourself well. We always knew that getting to the queen would be a hazardous business. Need I add that I'm very proud of you, very proud, indeed?"

At these words, Ramsey straightened and squared his shoulders. "Thank you, sir," he said.

After Ramsey left, the professor returned to his chair and considered, point by point, what Ramsey had told him. He was particularly disturbed by the presence of the woman. He didn't like killing women, but if it became necessary, he would do it. Demos was too important for squeamishness in its leader.

The newspapers called them fanatics, but that was not how they saw themselves. They were patriots, soldiers who were passionate about their cause. They wanted an end to senseless wars waged in far-flung places by power-hungry men. These were English wars, and Scotland paid for them with the lives of thousands of her young men. It was time England learned to fend for itself.

He stared into space as he considered his own experience. At twenty-five, he'd been inspired by the rhetoric of British generals to give his all for queen and country. The Crimea was where they had sent him. If these generals had only known what they were doing, it wouldn't have been so bad, but they did not know how to conduct a battle, much less a war. They were more suited to riding to hounds than to organizing an army. To them, ordinary soldiers were expendable, like pawns in a game of chess.

He had survived, but he'd come home a changed man. He married and went back to the university to teach history. And that was where he joined a group of like-minded individuals who formed a secret society. Demos talked a lot about Scotland's shame and distributed seditious pamphlets, but that was about all they did. It helped, but it was his son that gave his life purpose. Six years had passed since his son died, but the anger and anguish were as fresh as if he'd died yesterday.

His hands fisted and opened as he thought of his son. He had done everything in his power to dissuade Bruce from making the same mistake that he had made. But Bruce wouldn't listen. War was in the air, and he was caught up in the glamour and glory of a soldier's life. It was like a fever. It had to run its course.

This fever ended in tragedy. To die in battle was one thing, but to die for following an order from a commanding officer whom every soldier knew was incompetent was worse than a tragedy. It was a crime punishable by death, or it should be.

He wasn't, by nature, a bloodthirsty man. However, he could say that nothing had brought him as much satisfaction as killing the man who had killed his boy.

As he climbed the stairs to his own bed, his thoughts shifted to his daughter, Mahri. She was their courier. She should have been on the train from Aberdeen two days ago. There were important documents she was supposed to pass on to him. There was another train tomorrow. If she was not on it, he'd send someone to find out what was causing the delay.

Something moved at the back of his mind. What was it Ramsey said? Dickens had known about the plot to assassinate the queen? And how did the woman with blond hair fit in? The thought turned in his mind as he got ready for bed.

Six

His head was locked in a vise. His stomach was heaving. His chest was so tight, he could hardly draw in a breath. He was in a dark place, a cold, foul-smelling dungeon, perhaps, or a windowless cell. Water. He could feel it running in rivulets down the back of his neck, under his collar and down his spine. The floor beneath him was swaying, rattling, disintegrating.

He had to get out of here before it was too late.

A man's voice carried to him. "Listen! Did ye hear that? Riders! They'll be out lookin' for the Hepburn. I knew it was a mistake to bring him with us."

A woman's voice responded. "We could not leave him there to die. That must have been a mighty blow you gave him, Dugald. He needs medical attention."

Dugald made a rude sound. "His head is rock hard. It would take more than a dint from my fist to put a dent in it. And if he needs medical attention, why did we no leave him at the White Stag?"

"I don't trust those people. Well, you know what kind of

place the White Stag is. All that interests them is money. They would have robbed him and mayhap finished him off, yes, and I would be blamed for it."

Dugald clicked his tongue. "Lassie, ye have more imagination than is good for ye."

Alex ground his teeth. He knew exactly where he was now and what had happened to him. He wasn't in a foul-smelling dungeon. He was in one of the smugglers' carts, lying facedown on a bed of hay, and the reason it was so dark was because something—a tarpaulin?—was stretched out above him, no doubt to conceal him if they should be stopped by a policeman. His head wasn't in a vise but ached from the blow that had felled him. He assumed that the girl's companion was the rider Gavin had followed. Dugald and the girl were in the box guiding this one-horse contraption on a rickety road to God alone knew where.

When he tried to move, he discovered that he was spread-eagled on the hard floor, and his wrists were loosely bound to opposite sides of the cart. His legs, however, were free. By rolling a little, he could tell that they'd taken away his gun but not the coins that jingled in his pocket. Knowing that he was in no condition to fight his way free yet, he merely used the heel of his boot to lift an edge of the tarpaulin that was stretched out like a canopy above him. Daylight filtered through the opening he'd made. Something else came through—a pool of rainwater that doused his trousers. He bit back a furious oath and let the tarpaulin fall into place. At this rate, he'd die of pneumonia before they reached their destination.

The girl said, "Pull up under those trees, and I'll check on him."

"Check on him? Ye did that not ten minutes ago."

"He has been out for hours. I think he may have suffered a concussion."

"All the better for us when we unload him in Inver. Ye know what will happen when he comes to himself? He'll

start singing like a boiling kettle. I may have to thump him
again."

Alex was beginning to take a thorough dislike to this
Dugald fellow.

"This is not a joking matter, Dugald."

No response from Dugald this time.

Alex could tell that the cart had changed direction. A
minute or two later, it stopped. Evidently, they were going
to check on him. He wasn't going to put up a fight, not if
they were taking him to Inver. It was a hamlet just off the
main road and only a few miles upstream from Balmoral.
There would be people there to help him round up these
miscreants and march them to the nearest tollbooth.

When the tarpaulin was pulled back, Alex kept his eyes
closed and his muscles relaxed. Cool, competent fingers
felt for his pulse. "His pulse is strong," she said.

"What did I tell ye?"

"But he has a lump on his head the size of an apple, and
he has taken a soaking from the rain."

"What are ye doing?" Dugald asked, not alarmed but
not pleased either.

"What does it look like I'm doing? I'm covering him
with my cloak to keep him warm."

"But that's *my* cloak! I gave it to ye to keep *you* warm
and dry."

"I'll get you another." Her voice was light and teasing. "Dugald," she softly remonstrated, "you know you
wouldn't leave a dog out in this weather." She touched the
back of her hand to Alex's cheek. "He's not feverish, but
the sooner we get help for him, the easier I'll feel."

The tarpaulin was pulled over him, and Alex was left to
reflect on the conversation he had overheard. The woman
seemed genuinely anxious about him. They were going out
of their way to make sure that he had medical attention.
What was he supposed to make of that?

His thoughts strayed. The warmth of her body clung to
her cloak. He inhaled its scent, and every breath he took

seemed to burn his lungs. It wasn't an unpleasant sensation, far from it. When he moved, the cloak moved with him, wrapping around him like a silken web.

And he was caught.

The vision that emerged behind his eyes was of the woman as he'd seen her in the White Stag after he'd forcibly stripped her: skin like pearls; small, plump breasts; and long shapely legs.

His head still ached, his muscles were cramped, but that did not prevent the sudden wave of lust that stormed through him. He fought it off, and another vision emerged: Master Thomas, her alter ego.

Thomas wasn't fearless, far from it, but he was as brave as any man he knew. Brave, vulnerable, and in his own way, formidable. He liked the boy immensely.

Bloody hell! What was he thinking? The blow to his head must have addled his brains. The girl and the boy were one and the same person. If one was treacherous, so was the other. She was an enigma, and he was a code breaker. He was going to break her down until she revealed all her secrets.

He mustn't soften toward her. She didn't care what happened to him. It was her own neck she wanted to save. If she left him to die, she would be blamed for it. That was what she had told her henchman, Dugald.

Gavin? Where was he? Dugald must have given him the slip, but Gavin would know, when he had not turned up at their rendezvous, that he, Alex, must be in trouble. Gavin would come looking for him.

And where was his muse? It should be showing him a way out, not tempting him with lewd thoughts. Hell and damnation, how much longer before they reached Inver?

The cart had stopped moving. He raised his head and listened. Horses stamping and neighing, the jangle of harness, men's voices. The tarpaulin was removed, and someone

untied the knots on his bonds. Alex feigned unconscious-
ness, fearing that he would get another thump on the head
if he tried anything. When nothing happened, he flexed
his stiff fingers, fisted them, then rolled onto his back and
cleared the cart with an almighty heave. His eyes weren't
accustomed to the light, and he swayed on his feet.

"Here, Kenneth," said a voice Alex didn't recognize,
"gie me a hand with the poor man."

A friendly hand steadied him, Alex blinked to clear
his vision and took a moment to get his bearings. He was
in the stable yard of a small inn surrounded by a group
of stable hands. He didn't take time to answer any of the
questions that flew at him. He was scanning the stable yard
and its environs for a sign of the boy or Dugald. There was
nothing.

"I'm Jock Ogg," the man holding his elbow said, "the
proprietor of this alehouse. Och, but you'll soon come to
yourself. Come away in and get warm. A fall from a horse
is no laughing matter."

Alex had already come to himself and was impatient to
go after the girl. "Where are they?" he demanded. "The
man and the boy? Which way did they go?"

Mr. Ogg frowned and shook his head. "There was
no man, only a boy, and he rode off to fetch the doctor.
You were lucky you didna break your neck in the fall. No
one who knows the moors would dream of jumping blind
over a stone dike. You never can tell what is on the other
side."

So that was the story she'd told them, that he'd taken a
tumble from his horse. But how had she managed to disap-
pear so quickly?

Mr. Ogg was still talking, but Alex had stopped listening. His mind was working like lightning. She'd said that
she would get medical attention for him, but he doubted that
she'd gone for the doctor. Dropping him off at this small
country alehouse among friendly yokels was the only medical attention he was likely to receive. She was mounted.

He'd bet his last farthing that Dugald was mounted, too, Where had they got the horses?

"The lad was mounted, you say?"

"Not when he arrived. He brought you in on the cart, but a Highland pony was tied to the back. He was that upset that he told us very little before he went haring off. The nearest doctor is in Ballater, so it will be some time before the lad returns. Now come along in and have a bite to eat while ye wait. It wouldna hurt to brush off your clothes and tidy yourself." Mr. Ogg chuckled. "I think the cart you borrowed must have carried a load of peat at one time or another. So—"

"I need a horse," Alex said, breaking into Ogg's monologue. "You hire out horses, don't you?"

"Aye, but are ye sure you're well enough to ride?"

"I'm well enough."

The man called Kenneth cut in, "Have ye no heard about the trouble up at Balmoral?"

"I've heard."

"Well, ye won't get far. They've set up roadblocks on all the roads from Braemar to Aboyne and are questioning everybody who tries to pass. We've all been warned to stay off the roads unless we have a very good reason to be on them."

"Roadblocks?" Things were beginning to look up. The girl was too canny to be caught in a roadblock, but it would suit his purposes. She couldn't move freely. She and her cohort shouldn't be too difficult to track. "I'll take my chances. I'm known up at the castle. That's where I want to go."

He was swaying on his feet, not so much from the punch from Dugald's hefty fist, but because he'd had so little to eat in the last twenty-four hours. He stayed only long enough to satisfy his hunger and thirst, then he was up doing again. In short order, he was mounted and making his way east toward the castle. He hoped he *would* come to a roadblock. The men there would be on his side, and he'd soon form a posse to hunt the girl down. He had a good idea where she would make for. She'd make for the inn at Braemar where he'd first come across young Thomas. This was surely the route she'd planned to escape her pursuers. Beyond Braemar there was nothing but moors and mountains except for one track going south to Pitlochry, then on to Perth.

She'd be easy to catch on the barren moors, but he hoped to catch her long before that.

There was a barrier up ahead, a farmer's wagon blocking the road. He'd come to a roadblock. Alex touched his heels to his mount's sides, and the horse bounded forward.

There were only four men at the barricade, and though they weren't a cheerful lot, they were pleasant enough until he told them his name. In the next instant, their expressions went from shock to belligerence, and four pistols were raised and pointed straight at him.

"You're to come with me, sir," said the policeman in charge. He couldn't have been more than twenty. "Colonel Foster would like a word with you."

Alex didn't like Foster any more than Dickens did. The colonel had responsibility for the soldiers, and he was highly conscious of the chain of command. But he wasn't in command of Alex or Dickens. Their section chief was Commander Durward, and in his absence they reported to one another.

"What's this about?" Alex asked.

"I couldn't say, sir. All I know is that Colonel Foster would like a word with you."

Alex looked at each man in turn. *Boys,* he thought, *and still wet behind the ears.* The guns that were pointed at him, however, were just as lethal whether they were in the hands of striplings or veterans.

He tried again. "I don't report to Colonel Foster but to Mr. Dickens."

The officer in charge shrugged. "I'm just following orders, sir."

Something was seriously wrong. He could feel it in the fine hairs on the back of his neck. They were practically standing on end.

"Fine," he said, "then take me to the colonel."

The officer in charge seemed relieved at Alex's response and designated two of his companions to escort him to the castle. They fell in on either side of him, and the barrier was moved to allow them to pass.

As they jogged along, thoughts of Foster and the girl quietly slipped away, yet his mind was crystal clear. At first, he hardly knew what was happening. All he felt was a presence: Gavin. He did not possess his brother's gift. He could not put thoughts into people's minds as Gavin could. So what was Gavin trying to tell him? Listen . . .

There were no words. All he knew was that he was riding into danger and that Gavin was there.

The young policemen who delivered Alex to Foster's office lost no time in making their escape. And who could blame them? The colonel radiated all the warmth of an iceberg, not to mention that two stern-faced soldiers in Highland battle dress were stationed on either side of the door.

As soon as the policemen left, one of the soldiers ordered Alex to raise his arms, then proceeded to search him for concealed weapons.

"He's unarmed, sir," the soldier told Foster.

Foster gestured to the chair on the other side of his desk. "Take a seat, Hepburn."

Alex complied, his gaze never faltering from the man on the other side of the desk. Foster was in his early fifties, red-haired, red-faced, and with great beefy hands. He was also as thick as a plank, and in common with other stupid people who had risen to a position of authority on the strength of their years of service, he tended to be a bit of a bully.

"Shouldn't Dickens be here?" Alex asked mildly. "I'm under instructions to report only to him."

The colonel beamed at him. "Oh, that's very good, Hepburn, but not good enough. We have a witness, you see."

"A witness to what?" Alex kept his tone polite.

"To the murder of Chief Inspector Dickens," replied the colonel.

"*What?*"

Foster repeated what he'd said.

Alex stared at the other man without really seeing him. His mind was numb with horror. He was remembering how much he liked and trusted Dickens. He had risen through the ranks of the police on merit alone. In another year, he was going to retire with his wife and live the life of a country gentleman.

As his mind began to clear, he looked at Foster and wanted to choke him. He was in charge for now, and he was relishing his newfound powers.

"Tell me how it happened," he said, breaking into Foster's harangue.

"Don't play games, Hepburn. You know how it happened. You and your brother are in this together. He stabbed Dickens in the back with a letter opener that he found on Dickens's desk, then you helped your brother escape. But we caught him, and now we've caught you."

"*My brother?*" Alex demanded angrily. "My brother doesn't even know Dickens. Why would he want to kill him?"

The colonel slapped his beefy hands on the flat of the desk. His eyes were bulging, and he was breathing hard. "Because he was part of the plot to kill the queen. I presume Dickens became suspicious, whatever, and your brother killed him. We have witnesses, so don't think you can argue your way out of this. He murdered Dickens, then you procured horses to spirit him away. That makes you an accomplice, Hepburn."

Alex gave a mirthless laugh and shook his head. "You've got it all wrong. My brother was assisting me. Where is he? What have you done with him?"

The colonel linked his fingers and squeezed them tightly together, a very telling sign, in Alex's opinion. Rage was turning Foster's face purple. "Your brother," he said, "is in solitary confinement. Why don't you make things easy for him and easier for yourself? Tell us what we want to know, and we'll leave him alone. Until we hang him, of course."

Alex resisted the urge to spring at the other man and break his neck. He steepled his fingers and forced a superior smile. "You're getting ahead of yourself, Foster," he said. "I don't report to you. Commander Durward is my chief. I'll report to him and to no one else. I presume you have sent a telegram to Whitehall informing them of our situation?"

"I'm in charge here!" roared Foster. He was sucking air through his teeth. "You got away with insubordination with Durward, but you damn well won't get away with it with me."

He squeezed his linked fingers till they showed white. "This is what I think happened," he said. "Your brother was part of a plot to murder the queen. He didn't know about our decoy queen. His shot went wild and hit one of the guests, a Mr. Ramsey, to be exact. Maybe you knew what your brother was going to do and maybe you didn't, but from the moment he fired that shot, you chose him over us. You made up a story about a blond-haired woman. However, when I talked to Mr. Ramsey this morning, he said that he did not see her. I don't believe she exists. Dickens became suspicious. Your brother stabbed him to death, then you made your escape."

Alex's voice was terse with anger. "You're out of your mind!"

Foster suddenly thumped the flat of the desk with his

clenched hand. "So tell me, Agent Hepburn, where in hell have you been? And don't waste my time with fairy tales. There was no blond woman taking potshots at the queen. You didn't pursue her, as your brother wants us to believe. You were running away."

Alex kept his mouth shut.

He didn't want the girl to fall into the hands of this unscrupulous opportunist who didn't care whom he crushed to get to the top. Foster wouldn't make allowances for Thomas's youth either.

Thomas? Who in blazes was Thomas? Alex had to keep reminding himself that Thomas and the girl were one and the same person, and the girl was an enigma.

"You had better tell me what you know," said Foster, "or I'll make things very unpleasant for you."

"I'll tell you for the last time," replied Alex in a bored voice, "I have special clearance. When Durward returns, I'll report to him."

His words acted on the colonel as he hoped they would. "Teach him a lesson in manners," Foster told his guards.

They were big-fisted, heavyset men, but for all that, Alex knew that he could disable them in a fight. They hadn't been taught the tricks of an assassin's trade as he had. He didn't want to disable them. He wanted them to take him to his brother so that he could devise a way to get Gavin out of the castle. The only way that was going to happen was if he took a beating and convinced the colonel that he was in no condition to escape.

He came at the soldiers as though he were a gentleman boxer trained to follow the Marquess of Queensbury rules. The soldiers laughed at him, as well they might, but he got in a few punches before he allowed them to do much damage. The fist in his solar plexus drove the air from his lungs, and he keeled over and lay writhing and groaning on the floor.

Only then did Foster get up from his desk and come to stand over him. "You see here, gentlemen," he said, "the best that Her Majesty's Secret Service has to offer, God help us," and he kicked Alex in the back, hard. "A stint in the army is what these glamour boys need. Put him in the nursery with his brother."

The kick in the back had Alex writhing in earnest this time. He felt dizzy, disoriented, and horribly nauseated.

They hauled him up and supported him by linking their arms under his, then they dragged him away.

Mahri wanted to put as many miles between herself and the Hepburn as fast as she possibly could. They were hampered by the roadblocks that forced them to keep to the trees—the great forests of Scots pines that marched like an army over the slopes. It gave them excellent cover but slowed their progress. They'd gone only four miles, and it was another four to go before they reached Braemar. She was tired, she was hungry, and her spirits flagged. She was still thinking of the Hepburn, wondering whether he had recovered from his concussion or whether, contrary to Dugald's opinion, he was sinking into a coma.

According to Dugald, the Hepburn . . .

He shouldn't be called "the Hepburn" because he wasn't the chief of his clan. Mr. Hepburn was all that he was entitled to. Dugald had elevated him to a chieftain as a mark of respect. A warrior, Dugald called him, basing his judgment on what she had told him of her encounter with the man. He'd even laughed when she'd told him about the spanking he had administered. And she'd thought Dugald would be on her side!

She didn't think of the Hepburn as a warrior so much as a worthy opponent. A gentle warrior, perhaps. An honorable warrior, certainly. She could vouch for that. When he'd stripped her of her boy's clothes and discovered that she was a female, he hadn't tried to seduce her.

But he'd wanted to.

Just thinking about his expression when he'd seen

her naked made her toes curl. At the time, she'd known real fear. Would she ever forget the way his eyes had darkened when he'd captured her in his stare? She'd thought *rape*, *violence*, *a forced seduction*. Then he'd turned into a bad-tempered slave master and started finding fault with her.

A smile flickered at the corners of her mouth.

Her smile gradually faded. She would never see him again, not unless fate took a hand in things, and the fates had not been kind to her in the last little while. But if they should meet again in the not too distant future, would he remember her?

A blast of wind made the tall pines sway alarmingly, jerking Mahri from her thoughts.

"Whisht!" whispered Dugald, holding up his hand.

Mahri reined in her mount and looked down the slope to the road. "I don't see anything," she said.

"They've taken the barriers away. There's no a policeman in sight."

"That's good for us, isn't it?"

"Let's find out."

They came to a row of houses just off the main thoroughfare. It was too small to be a village but, naturally, it boasted an alehouse. To Mahri's surprise, the taproom was doing a brisk business, and she wondered where all these well-dressed men had come from.

"Policemen," Dugald observed under his breath. "I'd venture that they were manning the roadblocks, and now they're off duty. Ah, there's someone I know. Stay close by me, and not a word out of ye, mind."

He ordered two dinners and one tankard of ale to go with them, then he directed Mahri to a small table and told her to wait. She watched as he approached the bar counter and tapped one of the customers on the shoulder. The stranger was all smiles and thumped Dugald on the back.

Mahri's dinner arrived, the ubiquitous Scotch broth and a slice of meat pie. She was so hungry that even if a fire had broken out, she would not have left the table until she had consumed every bite.

Snatches of conversation reached her. Balmoral was mentioned, but the talk was mostly of the weather. It had been a scorching month except for the last few days, and now some of the patrons were worried. The older men talked of the great flood and how it had washed away their homes and livelihood. The younger men listened respectfully, but Mahri could tell that they weren't really interested.

A few moments after Dugald returned, his piping-hot dinner was brought to their table. "Here's how things stand," he said. "There are no roadblocks because the Hepburn has been taken into custody. It was him they was after. Seems like the policeman in charge at Balmoral got himself stabbed in the back, and there's a witness says the Hepburn brothers did it. They're both locked up at the castle."

Mahri's mind was reeling.

"Did ye hear me? I think we may be in the clear."

She put down her knife and fork. "When did this happen? When was the man killed?"

"Not long after the guests were rounded up for questioning."

"It's impossible. We know it can't be true. They were following us. They couldn't have murdered anyone."

Dugald's big hand covered hers, and he squeezed hard. "Get a grip on yerself, lass. Pick up your knife and fork and eat your dinner. Dinna draw attention to yerself." When she obeyed him, he went on, "They could have murdered the man before they came after us."

"You don't believe that!"

"I don't know the man, only what you've told me about him. And charming rogues have been known to turn out to be murderers."

"Well, I know him." Though her voice was low, it quivered with indignation. "He would never stab anyone in the back. Who says he did?"

Dugald took a long draught of his ale before he answered her. "No one knows, or if they do, they're not saying."

"Ronald Ramsey," she said, snorting derisively.

"We don't know that."

"Well, it wasn't Hepburn who stabbed that man. I'd stake my life on it."

There was a protracted silence. Finally, Dugald sighed. "So that's the way of it, is it." It was a statement, not a question.

Mahri huffed. "It's not what you think. Dugald, he would not have come to Ramsey's notice if it hadn't been for me. I don't know why Ramsey would kill that policeman, but if he thinks I'll stand aside and let Hepburn take the blame for it, he's very much mistaken."

"Lass, you're jumping to conclusions. No one has accused Ramsey of killing the policeman."

Mahri's chin jutted. "I'm saying it."

Dugald's bushy brows rose. "Even if were true, what can you do?"

"I'll go to the castle and tell them some story or other that will convince them to let Hepburn go. I'll tell them we had a lovers' tryst, and he was with me when the other man was killed." She shook her head. "I'll think of something."

"It's not as easy as you think." His eyes flicked to the policeman he'd spoken to earlier. "From what I heard, Hepburn has made a powerful enemy at the castle, someone in command who has been waiting for his chance to discredit him."

She added glumly, "And Ramsey has powerful friends in the area. Oh, Dugald, what are we going to do?"

"We're going to eat our dinner, then we'll talk."

Mahri looked down at her plate. The succulent meat pie did not begin to tempt her, but to please Dugald, she speared a morsel and popped it into her mouth.

Seven

❦

There were dungeons in the original castle but none in the brand-new edifice that Prince Albert had built for his queen only thirty years before. Alex came to himself in a cellar that had been converted to a cell. There was a barred window high in the wall. The light was fading, and he wondered how long he had been drifting in and out of consciousness.

"Alex?"

The hoarse voice came from a cot on the other side of the cell, Gavin's voice, weak and wavering. The sound of it had Alex dragging himself off the floor and stumbling toward the noise. There was only one cot in the cell.

He could barely make out his brother's face. "What happened to you, Gavin?"

Gavin let out a shaky laugh. "I didn't know your job was so dangerous," he said. "There was I at our hunting lodge, waiting for you to turn up, when some red-faced villain tried to arrest me for murder. I resisted, and he took a shot at me."

"He shot you?"

"Don't worry. He didn't hit me, but he ruined my coat and trousers. The bullet, luckily for me, went right through my pocket. An inch to two to the right, and he would have unmanned me."

Relief flooded through Alex, not because Gavin was still the same playful gallant but because no one who was seriously injured could have strung so many sentences together.

"The thing is," Gavin went on, "your colonel didn't like the answers I gave when they brought me in for questioning. I tried to tell him about the woman we were pursuing, and he wouldn't listen. He accused me of trying to kill the queen." His voice changed color, gentled, and he said, "You know that Dickens was stabbed in the back?"

"I know," Alex replied.

"I'm sorry. I know how much you liked and trusted him." He shifted his position and groaned. "Nothing to worry about," he said. "The colonel had his soldiers beat me, rather badly. I think they may have cracked one of my ribs."

"Let me take a look."

Gavin sucked in a breath when Alex gingerly pressed a hand to his side. "You're bleeding," Alex said.

"The bullet may have nicked me in passing, but no harm done. One of the orderlies tended to the wound, a very nice fellow by the name of Wilson. I don't think Foster is very popular in the castle."

Alex's tone was savage. "What you need is a doctor!"

Gavin chuckled. "I'm a prisoner, Alex, not a guest. I was lucky to have an orderly take a look at me. I'm fine, really."

Alex could hardly control his anger or his frustration. One way or another, they were going to get out of here, even if he had to carry his brother on his back. Then he'd take care of the colonel.

Gavin said, "What are you thinking?"

Alex shook his head. "None of it makes sense. Dickens wasn't attached to Special Branch or the Secret Service. He was in charge of security at the castle. He was a policeman. Why would anyone want to kill him?"

"I have no idea."

"How did it happen? Do you know?"

"All they've told me is that Dickens was in his office when he was stabbed."

"But we weren't anywhere near there."

Alex tried to visualize how the drama had played out. They'd gone to the stable for horses so that they could go after the woman who had shot Ramsey. They hadn't heard a scuffle or anyone call out. He turned the problem over in his mind. Finally, he said, "Who was the last person to see Dickens alive?"

"I have no idea." Gavin shrugged. "I took that fellow who was shot to get medical attention, left him with the doctor, and made straight for the terrace to meet you. I don't know what happened after that."

Alex tried to put himself in Dickens's shoes. What had he seen or heard that made someone want to kill him? Where was Ramsey at the crucial time? Was someone else involved? A member of Demos? Was the girl a distraction?

She'd given him Dugald's cloak to keep him warm. She'd stopped that stinking cart to check on him on that bumpy ride to Inver. Whatever else she was, she was no coldhearted killer.

But she was a member of Demos, if he could trust his vision.

Gavin said, "Did you catch up with the woman we were tracking?"

"Mmm? Oh, yes, and I was wondering whether she was telling the truth. She said that Ramsey had a revolver, but I didn't see it."

"You're thinking Ramsey may have murdered Dickens?"

"It's possible."

"Then why not shoot Dickens—oh, I see. The shot would be heard, and everyone would come running. But Ramsey was a victim, too, wasn't he? And why would he kill Dickens?"

"If I knew the answer to that question, I'd be a seer."

Gavin chuckled. "What if the girl lied?"

Alex's answer was clipped. "Well, we know that she didn't kill Dickens. We were hot on her trail, remember?"

"Ouch," said Gavin. "You like this woman, I can tell. What are you doing?"

Alex had abruptly risen and was exploring the four corners of the cell. "I'm looking for a way out."

"What about your section chief? Why isn't he here to take our statements?"

"He had to go to Whitehall on the queen's business," Alex replied, "but I'm sure when he returns, he'll soon sort Colonel Foster out."

"Maybe we should wait for him to arrive and be good little boys?"

"Foster doesn't play nice, Gavin. I'm not sure that you can take another beating. And if Durward is delayed, who knows what Foster will do to get us to confess? If he sets his soldiers on us again, I swear I'll kill him. Durward won't be able to help us, then."

Gavin had no reply to this.

After a few minutes, Alex came back to Gavin and sat at the foot of the pallet with his back to the wall. "They have to feed us, bring us water. That's when we will make our bid for freedom."

"Fine. Whatever you say."

This carefree response startled a laugh out of Alex. "I'm baffled," he said. "You were nicked by a bullet and took a sadistic beating, yet you sound quite chipper. How do you do it?"

"Ah, well," responded Gavin, "you could say I'm putting my muse to the test."

"What?"

"The gift I got from Granny. I can put thoughts into people's minds. So I thought, why not put them into my own mind? And it worked. The pain became manageable. I can move more easily. The trouble is, I haven't had enough practice and become distracted."

"If that's the case, why didn't you stop the soldiers from beating you?"

"I'm a seer, not a magician, and my gift doesn't work with everyone."

"What about me? Can you put thoughts into my mind?"

"No, more's the pity."

Alex was pleased to hear it. He didn't want anyone meddling with his mind. Hardly had the thought occurred to him than he remembered his vague uneasiness as he approached the castle: he was riding into danger and Gavin was there.

"Of course," Gavin went on, "I may improve with practice."

"Just remember, two can play at that game."

Each heard the smile in the other's voice. After a moment's thought, Gavin said, "So what do we do now?"

"We rest."

"Fine. Then you can tell me what you've been keeping to yourself."

"I don't know what you mean."

"Come on, Alex. I'm not a simpleton. Durward just happens to be in Whitehall on the queen's business? Durward and the queen are inseparable. So I'll ask you again: What's really going on? Where is Durward? Where is the queen? And where is the woman we were after?"

Alex debated for a moment as though he'd come to a fork in the road and he was deciding which way to go. At length, he said, "I never wanted to involve you in this, for your own protection, but it's gone way beyond that. But you're right. You *are* involved whether I like it or not." He shifted slightly to ease the pain in his back.

"You may remember that some years ago a group called Demos caused quite a stir. They detonated a few bombs in Edinburgh and London to draw attention to their aims."

"Yes, I remember. They wanted Scotland to become a republic, didn't they?"

"They did. But they weren't vicious with it, not to begin with. They bombed empty buildings, that sort of thing. No one got hurt and no one took them seriously until . . ."

"Until . . ." Gavin gently prompted.

"Until one of my handpicked agents infiltrated the group. As it turns out, she wasn't my agent but was working for Demos. She set things up so that three of my agents were ambushed, blown up, in fact. I was supposed to be with them, but I was searching another part of the building." He shook his head. "Suffice it to say that we began to take Demos seriously after that. In fact, we hounded them out of existence. We thought that was the end of it."

There was a short silence, then Gavin said, "What happened to your handpicked agent?"

"She died in mysterious circumstances."

"I see," Gavin said softly.

Alex shifted again. "In the last year or so, Demos has returned with a vengeance."

"Were they responsible for those bombs going off in London last year?"

"The Irish took the credit for that so we may never know. What we do know is that Demos decided to do something spectacular to make us all sit up. They decided to assassinate the queen."

"And you know this because—?"

"One of Demos's agents turned coat and informed us anonymously by letter. This time, we took the threat seriously. We didn't want loose tongues to scare Demos off, so we set things up with a decoy queen."

"A decoy? You mean that wasn't the queen at the reception?"

"No, it was someone who acted the part of the queen. We set a trap hoping to ensnare an assassin." Alex went on at some length, answering the many questions that occurred to Gavin. Finally, Gavin shook his head.

"What?" asked Alex.

"What I can't understand is why you became involved. I thought you were happy breaking codes in Whitehall." On the next breath, Gavin answered his own question. "It's a personal vendetta, then? They murdered your agents, and you want them to pay for it?"

"Wouldn't you if you were in my shoes?"

"I'm amazed," said Gavin, sounding irritated in spite of his words. "You're still playing the part of the elder brother, even in the Secret Service. You can't blame yourself for everything that goes wrong. I'm sure your agents understood the risks they were running."

Alex had nothing to say to this.

Gavin heaved a sigh. "How does the woman who shot Ramsey fit into this?"

"I haven't made up my mind." Alex shrugged. "She may be the turncoat. I don't know."

Gavin waited, and when his brother did not elaborate, he said with a hint of annoyance, "You can't stop there. I'm entitled to know whether she is on our side or not."

"She's not on our side."

"Then she's the enemy."

"She's not the enemy." Alex sighed. "I don't know, all right? I haven't made up my mind about her."

Mystified, Gavin said, "Begin at the beginning, and tell me what happened after we split up. Where did she lead you? Did you lose her? Tell me, Alex."

Alex took his time to put his thoughts in order, and the account he gave his brother was highly expurgated. The sequence of events he related was as accurate as he could make it, but those undercurrents of awareness between himself and the girl, that spark of energy that seemed to ignite between them when he let his guard down, were too personal, too annoying to share.

When he stopped speaking, Gavin suppressed a chortle.

"What?" demanded Alex, the same glower in his voice that was etched on his brow.

"Nothing. Nothing at all. What's her real name?"

"I have no idea."

"Something to do with fire, I'll wager."

"Why do you say that?"

"I was thinking of Granny, just before she died. You must remember what she foretold for each of her grandsons— you, James, and me."

Alex's voice softened to a murmur. "Yes, I remember."

They were in Drumore Castle, the seat of their cousin James's family, an imposing edifice that jutted into the North Sea. Granny McEcheran, the "Witch of Drumore" as the locals called her, had summoned her grandsons to her bedside to pass on her psychic legacy.

Her grandsons were men of the world, but because they loved their granny, they had humored her. On her death, she told them, they would become members of an honorable company with a long tradition: the seers of Grampian. They had been highly skeptical but, as it turned out, Granny was right.

Each had received a different gift: James had premonitions of the future that came to him in his dreams; Gavin had the power to put thoughts into people's minds; and he, Alex, had the gift of sensory perception. When he handled certain objects, pictures formed in his mind. He still had to interpret those pictures, and therein lay a problem. Sometimes he was right, and sometimes he was *almost* right, and that wasn't good enough.

Gavin broke into his thoughts. "Granny left each of us with a puzzle to solve, a prediction for the future. Don't you remember?"

"I remember," Alex replied. He could hear his granny's voice as if she were whispering in his ear.

"You will pass through fire, but it will not consume you if you trust your intuition. Hold fast to what you feel, Alex."

Gavin intoned, "You will pass through fire—"

"I know what Granny said," retorted Alex. "I don't need

you to remind me. But I fail to see what that has to do with the woman who shot Ramsey."

"Maybe nothing at all, but if I were you, I'd want to know her name."

Alex opened his mouth to blast his brother, but the words died on his tongue. A different kind of blast struck the barred window, shattering the glass, and a shower of fragments borne on a ferocious gust of wind hurtled inside.

After a moment of stunned silence, Gavin said, "Good God, what the devil was that?"

"I think it's the gale all the locals have been predicting in the last week."

Both brothers listened as a wild dervish raged outside their window. They could hear horses neighing and men shouting and what sounded like trees toppling to the ground.

Gavin said, "No one is going to feed us and water us with that racket going on. They'll be too busy tying everything down."

"Well, we're not tied down," said Alex. "Trust me, little brother. One way or another, I'm going to get us out of here. Now get out of that cot, and let's see if we can make a weapon out of it."

In short order, he had demolished the cot and fashioned a club from one of its supports.

Mahri, in her boy's get-up, cowered in the shelter of the rowing boat that she and Dugald had just beached under an outcrop of rock. There was no lightning or thunder, but there was enough rain to float Noah's ark. That wasn't the worst of it, though. The gale was strong enough to uproot trees. Pines and poplars were toppling over like skittles, making movement dangerous if not impossible.

Up ahead was Balmoral Castle. She could imagine the chaos inside the castle walls as everyone ran to light oil lamps and candles.

Above the roar of the wind, she shouted, "What do we do now?"

"We wait," Dugald responded, and just in case she had not heard him, he tethered her with a hand on her arm.

This was not how they had planned things when they'd set off from Braemar. She'd paid her shot at the Inver Arms and retrieved all her belongings, including her revolver, and they'd walked the distance to Invercauld, where Dugald had arranged to have a boat waiting. They had set off in the gloaming, not dusk exactly, but not far from it. They'd hoped to row downstream to Balmoral while it was still light, but the dark rain clouds that were spreading out over Deeside had turned the Dee into the river Styx.

Their plan was simple. They were going to pass themselves off as servants of one of the many Gordon lairds in the area, with a couple of crocks of whiskey for Colonel Foster, with the Gordon's compliments for services rendered. A man like Foster would be flattered by the gesture, even though he might not remember what service he had rendered. Then they'd take the colonel hostage and force him to release his prisoners.

And after that, they'd go their separate ways.

It didn't look now as though that plan would work.

Dugald said, "I don't know, lass. This doesn't look good. Maybe we should give up and try another day."

"Give up? And give Foster the chance to finish what he started? I will not! Don't you see, Dugald, the gale has made things easier for us? We don't need Colonel Foster. It will be as black as pitch in the cellars. All we need do is open the door and spirit the Hepburns away."

"Ye forgot something."

"What?"

"The key to the door."

Mahri let out a half breath. "If you won't come with me, I'll go alone." When she felt him stiffen beside her, she bit down on her lip. "I didn't mean it, Dugald. You know I wouldn't do this without your say so. You know the castle's layout, and I don't."

He snorted, but the stiffness went out of him. "There will be a lull," he said in her ear. "It will only last for a few minutes. Then we run like hell for the castle walls. Have ye got that?"

"Aye."

A minute went by then another. She heard it now, the silence as the storm abated, heavy, breathless, ominous.

"Now!" shouted Dugald.

She scrambled over the outcrop of granite that they'd sheltered under and bolted for the castle. Her feet had never moved faster as she darted into the cover of the trees; her breath—quick, shallow, and sobbing—seemed loud in her own ears. She stumbled a time or two, but Dugald was right behind her with a guiding hand. When she reached the wall, she clung to it as though it were her long-lost lover. She didn't want to let go, but Dugald gave her no respite.

He dragged on her arm and pulled her along the wall till they turned the corner to the entrance facing the stables.

And as suddenly as the silence had fallen, the storm erupted again in a roar of rage. There was no one about, everyone was taking cover, but the horses in the stable were stamping and neighing in terror, and dogs were howling like banshees.

Dugald knew his way around the nether regions of the castle, though he'd never set foot abovestairs. He was a deerstalker, and when he had business here, he entered by the tradesmen's entrance.

He hustled her through the doorway and down a flight of stairs. If it was dark outside, here it was pitch-black.

There was someone in the corridor with them, someone up ahead. "Bugger you, Willie," a masculine voice said. "I told you to shut the outside door before you opened the door to the cellars. Now see what you've done. The lamp has gone out."

They heard a match strike, saw it falter and go out. A shadow moved, then began to close the distance between them.

"Willie?" This time the voice held a thread of suspicion. Mahri felt Dugald tense to spring. Fearing the other man might have a gun, she put a restraining hand on Dugald's arm and pushed past him.

"Please, sir?" She used the most girlish voice she could muster. "Dinna be angry. I'm lost, you see. Can ye tell me what door leads to the kitchen?"

There was a silence, then the man chuckled. As he walked slowly toward her, she heard the clink of metal on metal, like a key on a ring.

"I'll show you the way," he said, "if ye gie me a kiss." He stopped suddenly when he felt the press of her revolver against his ribs.

"One word out of you," Dugald said, "and I'll have my wee friend here pull the trigger. Now, take me to the Hepburn."

A heartbeat of silence went by as the jailer seemed to weigh his options. When he let out a resigned sigh, Mahri began to breathe again, but she was still on edge.

The jailer led them to the end of the corridor. "Here we are."

It seemed eerily quiet to Mahri. She'd expected the Hepburn to call out, something.

"Unlock the door," Dugald said. He waited until the jailer complied. "Now, you first."

Mahri was truly alarmed at the silence. She had visions of the Hepburn's broken body lying in a heap on the floor. Why was it so quiet in that cell?

A voice from inside whispered, "Water . . . please . . . water."

Dugald pushed the jailer into the cell, and energy exploded around them. She heard the crack of something hitting the jailer, the whoosh of air from his lungs, then the thud of his body as it hit the floor.

"Hold off!" Dugald roared. "We've come to rescue ye both."

"Dugald?" said Hepburn incredulously.

"Aye, Dugald and Master Thomas."

Eight

~~~

It was an odd group of allies that made their escape from the castle; Alex didn't trust them any more than they trusted him. There had been no time for explanations. Those would come later. Dugald and the girl had everything planned, and for the moment, he was willing to let them have their way, but only for the moment. His purpose hadn't changed. She was his only lead to Demos, if he could believe his vision, and he had her in the palm of his hand. He had only one regret—that he had not captured her fair and square. He dismissed the thought almost as soon as it occurred to him. He was no knight in shining armor, and she was no damsel in distress.

All the same, she puzzled him. Why had she come back to rescue him?

He did not waste time debating the question. He was more concerned by the change in his brother. Now that they were on the move, Gavin was no longer so chipper, and his reserves of energy seemed to have run out. Alex and Dugald were supporting him between them, but every step forced a weak moan from Gavin's lips.

The girl was out in front, lighting their steps with an old-fashioned lantern they'd found in the cellar. Even so, it was slow going. They had to climb over fallen trees and make their way around other obstacles to get to the boat that Dugald said was waiting for them. Every so often, they ducked as a sudden gust of wind tore the slates from the castle roof and sent them flying like missiles.

To add to their misery, it was pelting rain. Their garments were plastered to their bodies, and their boots were filling with water. The girl kept looking over her shoulder as though she expected trouble, but he did not think anyone would be mad enough to venture outside until the wind became less fierce.

He had to admire her stamina. And her pluck. She might be young and inexperienced, but she did not panic easily.

What was he thinking? He knew damn well that this girl was a formidable, well-schooled opponent. She'd proved that when she'd shot Ramsey at the queen's reception then slipped through their fingers. He could admire her, as one soldier to another, but he'd be mad to trust her.

Why had she risked herself to save him?

They heard the river long before they reached it. It seemed to be in a hurry to reach Aberdeen and empty itself into the North Sea. The thought that this was going to be a turbulent boat ride made Alex balk.

"It's the only way," Dugald shouted. "Horses are useless in a storm."

"What's the plan?" Alex shouted back, but the wind carried his words away.

When they reached the river, the girl turned to the right, and they stumbled along till they came to an outcrop of rock. Here, at last, was a shelter of sorts. He left Gavin slumped against the rock face with the girl hovering over him while he went with Dugald to take a look at the boat.

"There's a wee tot of whiskey here for all of us," said

Dugald, and reaching into the boat, he produced a crock that he hoisted onto one shoulder. "It will chase the cold away afore we brave the perils o' the Dee."

"Did someone mention *uisque beatha*?" queried Gavin, his voice quavering.

That small attempt at humor from Gavin had them all smiling.

When Alex offered the crock to the girl, she shook her head. She was intent on examining the blood on Gavin's trousers. "I'm surprised he could walk this far," she said without emphasis. "He should see a doctor."

"The nearest doctor is back at the castle," said Dugald.

"Not the castle," said Gavin. "They don't like me there."

"What happened to him?" asked the girl.

Worry laced with anger roughened Alex's voice. "Foster beat him."

In the same unemphatic voice, the girl said, "There's bound to be a doctor in Ballater, but that's about eight miles downstream." She was looking at Alex, trying to convey her anxiety without letting Gavin know.

Alex inclined his head to indicate that her message was received and understood, then he crouched down with his back to the rock face and took a healthy swig from the crock before passing it to Gavin. His brother couldn't get far on foot, and even if they could find horses, they would be impossible to control in a gale. He didn't see what choice they had. They had to go by boat.

He watched as the girl climbed to the top of the rock they were sheltering under. So she was the lookout. Did she never tire? Did she never rest? What drove her like this?

She must be very afraid, not of him and not of Foster, or she would never have returned to Balmoral to save him. Was it her erstwhile suitor she feared most? Or was it Demos?

Was his vision of Demos a hoax? A figment of his imagination?

To Dugald, he said, "So, what's the plan?"

"Plan?" Dugald shook his head. "There is no plan except tae get ye out of the castle. After that, ye're free tae go where ye want, as are we. There was no storm when we set out."

"Yes, the storm changes things, doesn't it? And there's only one boat." Alex dropped his voice so that Gavin wouldn't hear him. "My brother can't walk out of here, and he needs to see a doctor. We have to go to Ballater. We have friends there who will take us in."

"What friends?" Gavin piped up, showing that he was wise to his brother's ways. "Do you mean the Cardnos?"

"Who else will take us in with no questions asked?"

"I suppose," said Gavin, sounding resigned.

Alex added, "Your cub will be safe there, too, Dugald."

Dugald turned his head and gave Alex a straight look. "Fine. Then Ballater it is. But if you harm one hair of her head, I'll break your neck, and that's a promise."

The girl came sliding down the rock, startling them all.

"What's wrong?" Dugald cried.

"Men with lanterns! They're coming this way."

That settled the matter.

They scrambled to their feet and made for the boat. Alex helped Gavin into the stern of the boat while Dugald took up the oars. The girl hung back.

"What is it, lass?" Dugald yelled.

"My cairngorm!" Her hand was on her tam. "I've lost it. I had it a moment ago. It must be under the rock. Hold on."

A sudden surge in the river propelled the boat away from the bank.

"Mahri!" yelled Dugald. "Get back here!"

Either she did not hear, or she did not want to hear.

Mouthing a furious oath, Alex leaped over the side and went after her. He caught her by the waist, dragged her to the boat, and threw her in. He had just clambered on board when the current lifted them up and swept them away.

Alex thought that things could not get worse, but he was

wrong. Someone nearby shouted, "There they are, on the river."

"What do we do?" cried the girl.

"We hold on for dear life."

Mahri's relief at evading capture did not last long. She felt as though she had stepped from one nightmare into another. Though the ferocious winds had died down, and the rain had dwindled to showers, the river was in full spate and propelled their little craft through the waves like a shot from a sling. To add to her terror, the thunderstorm they thought the gale had diffused now burst above them, lighting up the valley with streams of fire.

Dugald and Hepburn were hard-pressed to keep the boat steady. Her task was to use her oar like a barge pole to ward off objects that had been swept away in the flood: uprooted trees, kegs of whiskey, household furniture, and saddest of all, farm animals that had failed to reach higher ground. The fear that their pursuers might be close behind them was the least of her worries now.

She didn't know how long they had been on the river when Gavin pointed up ahead.

"Look!" he shouted. In spite of his wound, he was crouched beside her, bailing water as fast as it came in.

At the next crack of lightning, she saw it: the Ballater Bridge over the Dee. The bridge at Ballater had had a sad history. When the Dee was in flood, trees and other debris from upstream would slam into it with such force that supports would buckle and give way. Even now, it was under construction. It seemed to Mahri that this bridge was always under construction. At the next crack of lightning, she caught her breath. There was a logjam under one of the arches, and their little boat was going to smash into it.

Dugald was shouting orders, telling them to row like mad for the bank. Even Gavin had taken up an oar and was expending the last of his energies to do his bit. Her arms ached, her hands were stinging from splinters, she was soaked to the skin, but the will to survive drove everything from her mind except bringing their boat safely to shore.

She was jarred from her purpose by the sound of men shouting from the bridge.

"Rest your oars!" Dugald's voice. "Listen!"

When they did as they were bid, their little craft went into a spin. Mahri clung to Gavin, supporting him as the boat began to rock. Everything was moving too fast for her mind to grasp. She couldn't make out what the men on the bridge were shouting, but the Hepburn and Dugald seemed to understand. They picked up their oars and started rowing like madmen.

"Get down and hold on!" Hepburn's voice.

She dragged Gavin to the floor and held on for dear life. It felt as though they were going over a waterfall and their little boat had taken flight. She braced for the crash, but their craft skimmed the surface of the water, barely touching it as its momentum carried it forward. When the crash came, it was like hurtling into a wall of straw.

When she finally raised her head, she saw men from the bridge racing down an incline and into the lake they had landed in. Dugald and Hepburn were thumping each other on the back.

"What happened?" she asked faintly.

Gavin struggled up. "It looks," he said, "as though the good people of Ballater have come to rescue those caught in the flood."

Hepburn loomed over her, plucked her from the boat, and carried her to shore. Gavin was right. All around, there were lanterns lit, and people, both men and women, with smiling faces, were handing out blankets to the victims of the flood.

The lake, she now saw, was a flooded farmer's field, and the wall of straw was a haystack, several haystacks, in fact. The waterfall was a channel workmen had carved out to divert part of the river as they built foundations for the new bridge. If the bridge had not been under construction, she had no doubt that they would never have made it.

"We were lucky." She spoke past the huge lump in her throat. Now that the danger was over, she was beginning to feel all the discomforts she'd suffered in their mad dash to freedom.

Hepburn set her down and steadied her by cupping his hands on her shoulders. A smile curled his lips. "If you weren't dressed as a boy," he said, "I would—" He stopped suddenly.

Her heart lurched. "Yes?"

Their eyes locked. Mahri had the oddest feeling that they were in the eye of the storm. All around them, sounds became muted, and people melted into the background. A shiver passed over her, then another, but it wasn't unpleasant. Why was he looking at her as though he'd never seen her before? Why did she want this moment to go on forever?

"What were you going to say?" she asked tremulously.

His brows snapped together. "Nothing. I'd best see to Gavin."

Mahri was hardly aware that one of the rescuers had wrapped a blanket around her shoulders. Her eyes followed Hepburn as he waded through the water to their boat, and she wanted to stamp her foot. When she watched him with Gavin and Dugald, her pique gradually melted away. In spite of their differences, they were all good, honorable people. They could have been friends if the circumstances had been different. Even so, they were comrades. At least for a little while, she hoped that they could be comrades.

The glow inside her did not last long. Theirs was not the only boat to find a safe harbor. Several had been pulled out of the water and were lined up beside the haystacks. She began to scan faces, hoping that she wouldn't see one she recognized.

She jumped when someone touched her arm.

"Who are you looking for?" asked Hepburn. He and

Dugald were supporting Gavin between them, and Gavin was protesting that he didn't want or need any help.

"Whom do you think? We are fugitives from the law, are we not? Policemen? Soldiers?" She gave a helpless shrug. "There's no lack of people to choose from."

His hard scrutiny reminded her of the first time she'd encountered him at the queen's reception. His eyes saw too much.

"We'll talk later," he said, "but first things first. Let's get Gavin to a nice soft bed."

"I'd rather," said Gavin testily, "that you got me to a nice big glass of *uisque beatha*. There's nothing wrong with me that that won't cure."

Dugald settled the argument. "Laddie, ye took the words right out of my mouth. After we are warm and dry, you can have as much *uisque beatha* as you like. Thomas, make yerself useful. Pick up our knapsacks and stay close behind us."

Ballater was on the other side of the river and only accessible by the bridge, but their route took them in the opposite direction. Though Hepburn had told them that the house was close to the village, in their state of exhaustion, the going was slow and made all the more miserable by the steep hills they had to climb. The one mitigating factor was that Hepburn appeared to have eyes that could see in the dark. He kept them all from straying off the road or taking a wrong turn.

By the time they reached the house, Mahri was practically sleeping on her feet. Impressions came and went. She heard a woman's laughter and Gavin's gruff response. Someone tried to take the knapsacks from her, and she tried to fight him off. She heard the Hepburn shouting, and she cried out in panic but quieted when he said something soothing in her ear. The last thing she remembered was falling into a soft feather bed, then she slipped into a welcome oblivion.

* * *

Colonel Foster couldn't stop pacing. The bastards had got away. He was surrounded by a cast of incompetents! Somebody was going to pay for this, and it wasn't going to be him.

In sheer frustration, he threw the glass he had been drinking from into the fireplace, where it smashed gratifyingly into smithereens.

He hoped they drowned like rats. Maybe they'd done him a favor. Hepburn had always been Commander Durward's blue-eyed boy. If there were a way of rescuing his favorite from the hangman's noose, Durward would find it.

Perhaps the storm had been a godsend. Durward had been due to arrive on the morrow, but there was no likelihood of that happening now. The flood would keep Balmoral and the upper reaches of the Dee isolated for some time to come.

He was still in charge here, and so he should be. He came from a military family. He was born to command. And by the time Durward got here, he'd have taken care of Alex Hepburn and his no-account brother.

There were two others who had helped them escape. Though the guard hadn't seen them clearly, he'd heard the voices of a man and a woman. He'd find them, too, and he'd make them sorry they'd ever crossed swords with Bertie Foster.

The thought of the woman gave him pause. Not for one moment did he believe that the Hepburns had gone chasing after her to bring her to justice. If she helped them escape, she was one of them. Let Durward try to save his favorite now.

The thought of Durward and his crew made him sneer, and he stopped pacing. British Intelligence! Secret service agents! Spies! A pox on the lot of them! Some of them had never seen military service. They'd been recruited from universities and gentlemen's clubs. They were a network of chums!

Well, he'd show Durward and his chums how a soldier handled things.

He went to the door, opened it, and shouted a name. A moment later, a captain in the uniform of the Queen's Royal Guard entered.

"Sir," said the captain, saluting Foster.

Foster came right to the point. "I want these woods swarming with soldiers. I want Hepburn and his brother dead or alive. If they have drowned in the river, I want to hear about it."

"Yes, sir." The captain hesitated.

"What?" asked Foster roughly. "Spit it out, man."

"Are you giving me a 'kill on sight' order, sir?"

"That's exactly what I'm giving you."

Still the captain hesitated.

"This is war, Captain," roared Foster. "These men killed Dickens. They tried to kill the queen. I take full responsibility for the orders I issue, so go to it before I have you arrested for insubordination."

The captain saluted smartly and left the room.

Foster got up and started to pace again. Strictly speaking, Hepburn hadn't tried to kill the queen. He'd known about the stand-in. And they were still keeping up the pretense that Her Majesty was secluded in the castle. These were Durward's orders, but he doubted that Durward would be sending any more telegrams telling him what to do. The lines were bound to be down.

At last he could run things the way he wanted.

Nine

~~~

Mahri awakened to the sound of drapes being drawn back and the feel of light making patterns on her eyelids. The wind wasn't howling; there were no claps of thunder to make her start. She was warm and dry in a soft feather bed, at peace with herself and the world.

The thought made her brow furrow. She must be dreaming.

She slowly opened her eyes. A young woman with a halo of gold hair was standing beside the bed. She had a kind smile and hazel eyes that were alight with humor.

"Good morning, Mahri," she said. "My name is Juliet Cardno. Don't be alarmed. My mother and I undressed you last night and put you to bed."

Mahri lurched to a sitting position and promptly groaned. Every muscle in her body felt as though she'd been tortured on the rack. Worse by far were the blisters and splinters on her hands, blisters and splinters she had got from using her oar as a barge pole.

"Where is everyone?" she asked abruptly.

"Alex and your man, Dugald, are outside, clearing up after the storm. I'm sorry to say that our servants have quite deserted us, on account of the flood, you know. They have their own homes to go to, and their own families to see to. So, we're quite alone. But I'm sure we'll manage. As for Gavin"—Juliet shrugged—"we had to practically tie him to his bed. He wants to do his part, I suppose, but he's still a little shaky on his feet."

Mahri blinked slowly as she gazed up at the other girl. "I'm sorry," she said. "I wasn't quite awake. Could you repeat what you said?"

The other girl smiled and sat on the edge of the bed. "You're with friends, Mahri; that's the main thing. No one has come looking for you, because everyone has enough to do in their own backyard. Yes"—she nodded when Mahri's eyes flared—"Alex has told us that you're all in trouble with the law. Something to do with the rumpus up at Balmoral, isn't it? Well, of course, my mother and I know that Gavin and Alex had nothing to do with the attempt on the queen's life. You need a place to hide out until Alex clears up this terrible misunderstanding, and my mother and I are confident that he'll do that as soon as the telegraph lines are up and the trains are running again. Then he'll get a message to Whitehall and ask his section head to sort out this debacle."

Mahri took a moment to digest this. Finally, she said, "Were you at the queen's reception?"

"Ah, no. Gavin offered to escort me, but there is a gentleman I want to avoid whom I knew would be there. You know how it is." Her eyes were very wide, very clear. "We were engaged to be married once, but he threw me over for another woman. *C'est la vie.*"

This was frankness on a scale that Mahri had never imagined, and she didn't know how to respond, so she started over. "I wish I had missed it, too."

Juliet's eyes twinkled. "I'm sure you do."

Mahri cleared her throat. "What did the doctor say about Gavin?"

"Oh, he hasn't seen the doctor. Old Mac, as we call him, is too busy treating people who are much worse off than Gavin. You probably don't realize how much damage the storm caused, not only in Ballater, but in all Deeside. The roads are impassable. No one is getting in or going out. Alex bound Gavin's ribs and stayed with him through most of the night. Gavin is doing fine, Mahri, so there's no need to worry."

No need to worry? Juliet Cardno didn't know the half of it.

Mahri shook her head. "I don't understand. When we left the castle, Gavin could hardly walk. He'd lost a lot of blood. Now you tell me he is fine?"

Juliet lifted one shoulder. "He says that it's a case of mind over matter. He tells himself that he isn't in pain, and the pain goes away. Don't ask me how he does it, but it seems to work." She cocked her head to the side. "Alex tells me that you and Dugald got them out of prison last night. That was a very brave thing you did, Mahri."

"It was Dugald who did most of it." She shifted uneasily, wondering what she'd told the other girl before she'd found a bed. Juliet knew her name. What else had she told her?

Juliet saw the movement. "I hope I didn't hurt you too much last night when my mother and I undressed you?"

"Hurt me?"

"Last night. You put up quite a fight when we tried to strip your wet clothes from you. Poor Alex. You were calling out for him to help you and wouldn't let him go. The whole house was in an uproar."

A ripple of shock went through Mahri. She could see that the other girl was enjoying herself immensely. "Is this a joke?"

Juliet laughed. "What a pair you and Alex make! He is as straight-faced as you this morning. You're both too proud to admit you have feelings for each other, at least to outsiders."

"I don't feel anything for Alex. I mean, Mr. Hepburn."

"Yet you went back to Balmoral and got him out of that dungeon." Juliet threw up her hands. "Don't mind me. Everyone will tell you that I'm a terrible tease. Shall we change the subject?"

Mahri was only too happy to oblige. There was a silence while she racked her brain for something to say. Juliet, evidently, wasn't going to help. "Alex." The name slipped out before she could prevent it, but she went on seamlessly. "Alex has told me very little about you and your mother. I don't know why you should be so kind to me, but please believe that I am deeply grateful."

"You could say," replied Juliet, "that any friend of Alex is a friend of ours. No, don't frown. I'm not teasing. Our families have known each other forever. We come up here every summer. The Hepburns have a place east of here. We hardly ever saw Alex, though, after he went back to work at the Home Office. That, of course, was after that terrible tragedy with Ariel and he became . . . well . . . withdrawn. Not the same man at all, and who can blame him?"

"Ariel?"

"The girl he was going to marry. She died in an accident, oh, it must be four or five years ago." Juliet stopped. "He hasn't mentioned her?"

"No."

"Then I shouldn't either. Alex is a very private person."

There was an interval of silence, then Juliet gave an infectious laugh. "Stuff and nonsense! You should know what you're up against. Ariel, in my opinion, was a real beauty, the kind of female a man loses his head over. She had impeccable taste and the figure to show off the expensive garments she wore. She was wealthy, wellborn, and not afraid to express her opinions. Not to put too fine a point on it, neither I nor any other female of my acquaintance could stand the woman."

She suddenly stopped. "Oh dear, I brought you a cup of chocolate and put it down somewhere." She looked around, spotted it on the table by the window, and went to get it.

"I suppose that sounds cruel," she said, handing the cup to Mahri, "what with the girl in her grave, but I never felt that we should speak only good of the dead. Yes, I have good cause. I had a beau that Ariel stole from me, not the one I mentioned earlier, but that was before she met Alex. What I'm trying to say is that we're all very glad that Alex seems to have come to terms with his loss and has picked up the threads of his life again."

She wished Juliet hadn't mentioned Alex's lost love. Now she was avidly curious, and if she started asking questions, Juliet would get the wrong idea.

"What about you, Mahri? Did you grow up on Deeside?"

"No." She didn't want to say too much, because this girl's mind was as sharp as a needle, and she had plenty to hide. She chose her words carefully. "My mother was born here, and after she married, she'd come here in the summer months. My father couldn't always get away. We loved it here, my brother and I, but that was before my mother died. Afterward, it was too painful for my father to return to a place that held so many memories of my mother." It was the truth, but it wasn't the whole truth.

"Where are your father and brother now?"

To give herself time to think, Mahri took a mouthful of chocolate, and almost gagged on the lumps floating in it. Swallowing valiantly, she got out, "My father died not long after my mother, and Bruce and I went to live with my grandparents. But Bruce is gone, too. He died in Africa in the Zulu War."

She regretted having to lie to a girl who had been kind to her, but she didn't know what else she could do. Anything she told Juliet was bound to get back to Alex Hepburn.

When she allowed her shoulders to droop, as though these memories were making her sad, Juliet took the hint. "I've looked out a change of clothes that I think will fit you. We're about the same size, I believe. You must be hungry—" She suddenly broke off and exclaimed, "Good grief! What happened to your hands?"

Mahri made an involuntary movement to hide her hands, but Juliet was too quick for her. She removed the cup of chocolate, lifted one hand, then the other, and examined each closely.

"Well," she said, "Alex told us you were brave, but if I'd known you'd been to the wars, I would have tended to your poor hands last night." She pointed to a door. "The bathroom is right through there. Do what you have to do, and I'll be back with the tweezers and a salve to fix those blisters and splinters."

At the door, she turned back. "A word to the wise," she said, "or maybe I should say a word to the innocent. Watch out for Gavin. He's an inveterate flirt. No good scolding him. Just pretend that you're taking him seriously and start making plans for the wedding. It works for me. I promise you, he'll run a mile."

Mahri heard Juliet laughing to herself on the other side of the door, and her own lips turned up. There was something about that young woman that made her worries seem easier to manage.

She pushed back the covers and swung her legs over the edge of the bed. Her legs felt like noodles; her hands felt as though she'd thrust them into a hornets' nest. As she took a moment to come to herself, she studied her surroundings.

The room was uncluttered, comfortable, restful. A happy room, she decided. Could this be Juliet's room? Juliet was outspoken, outrageous, and by her own admission, a terrible tease. It would be nice to have a friend like Juliet.

She made a face. What a maudlin thought! She didn't want or need friends. Her life was too complicated to allow anyone to get close to her. What would they talk about? Fashions? Who was getting married to whom or not? Beaux?

Juliet had certainly got the wrong idea about Alex

Hepburn and her. Maybe it was as Juliet said. She vaguely remembered resisting someone who was trying to take the knapsacks away from her. If she had shouted out Hepburn's name, it was to get him to stop, not to beg for his help.

Juliet had also got the wrong idea about her going back to rescue Hepburn from prison. He had only been doing his job when he'd tried to capture her after she'd shot Ramsey, and she'd practically delivered him into the hands of his enemies! It was all such a muddle, but in her own mind, she'd paid off a debt, and that was the end of it.

It was time she stopped thinking about Alex Hepburn and started thinking about her own problems. Inhaling a long breath, she wiggled out of bed and tottered to the bathroom. On the way, she stopped in front of a long cheval mirror. The woman who stared back at her was as different from Master Thomas as day from night. She was wearing a fine, lawn nightdress with rows of pretty pink bows scattered across the bodice. Juliet had done her proud.

She turned and looked back at the bed. There was no sign of Thomas's clothes, but on the back of an upholstered chair, a brown taffeta day dress was spread out, and neatly folded on the dresser beside the chair was what she assumed were fine linen petticoats and pantalets. As long as she was the Cardnos' guest, she didn't mind dressing as a lady in borrowed finery.

Though she knew how to conduct herself in polite society, she'd never been comfortable in it. She'd missed her mother's guiding hand. It was her brother and grandfather who had raised her to be proficient in the manly arts. Her father had been too busy to pay them much heed.

As she grew up, her brother and Dugald were the only people she had been close to. She supposed, in some ways, she'd been a lonely child, especially after Bruce went away to school, but she'd never thought that she was unhappy. There were always the summer holidays to look forward to when Bruce came home from school.

It was Juliet's questions that had brought everything

back to her. Her grandparents' house was on Deeside, and when her father was too busy to take care of a young girl, she'd stayed with her mother's people. It was Dugald who had consoled her when her mother died. She was sure her grandparents loved her but, like most Scots, they were ill at ease with displays of raw emotion. Then they were gone, and Bruce was gone, and there was only Dugald.

As time went by, her father became more like a stranger to her.

She suppressed a shiver. Her grandparents' house now belonged to her. She wondered if she would ever see it again. When she felt her eyes begin to tear, she gave herself a mental shake. She didn't have time to be sorry for herself. She should be thinking of escape.

The first chance she got, she would take to the hills. But first, she had to talk to Dugald and come up with a new plan. She needed her boy's clothes back. A boy traveling through the Highlands wouldn't attract notice. A well-dressed lady would stand out like a beached whale. Aside from that, she wanted her brooch. It was all she had left of her mother, and she wasn't going to leave without it. She'd stuffed it into her coat pocket the moment before Hepburn had lifted her bodily into the boat on their wild ride to Ballater.

According to Juliet, the telegraph lines were down, and the trains were not running. That could work in her favor. Dugald knew the area far better than her father did. It wouldn't take her father long to work out that she was the one who had aborted their plan to assassinate the queen. In her father's eyes, *she* would be the traitor, and he would try to track her down. He might succeed, but he wouldn't harm her, not because he loved her but because she had something that could bring them all to ruin.

She swallowed hard. No, her father would not harm her. He wasn't a bad man but someone who had been led astray. And in his turn, he'd led others astray. Her own brother for one. Others were students whom he'd come into contact with at the university. She had never really believed that he would go through with the plot to assassinate the queen. Where would it all end?

She closed her eyes as frustration began to build in her. Life was nothing but a game of chance. If her mother had not died, her father would not have filled his empty hours by becoming involved with a group of fanatics. Her brother might still be alive, and her family could well be spending those lyrical summer months on Deeside.

She couldn't go back. She had to go forward. On that grim thought, she pushed into the bathroom. She didn't waste time in bathing, except to splash cold water on her hands and face. The soaking she had taken the night before was more water than her sensitive skin could cope with right now. She heard her bedroom door open. Juliet had come to fix her hands.

Ten

~≥

When she entered her bedroom, she came to a sudden halt.
The Hepburn was there, sitting on a chair he had pulled
close to the bed. There was a bowl of steaming water on a
tray and other objects she glimpsed in passing.

"Don't you ever knock, Mr. Hepburn?"

His brows rose. "Did someone put a burr under your
saddle? Or are you always this bad tempered when you
wake up?"

She didn't glare, but she wanted to.

"My name is Alex," he said. "If you keep calling me
Mr. Hepburn, the Cardnos are going to wonder what is
going on."

"Where is Juliet? She said that she would doctor my
hands."

"Her mother burned the porridge we were to have for
breakfast, so Juliet is making a fresh pot. She asked me to
look at your hands, and that's what I shall do."

She hid her hands in the folds of her robe, and to distract
him, she raised a point that had been bothering her. "What

exactly did you tell Juliet to explain my presence here? She was very vague, and I didn't want to encourage her until I'd spoken to you."

His eyes turned several shades lighter, and his lips twitched. "I told her, in the strictest confidence, that you were one of my own handpicked agents and that I was forced to take you with me for your own protection. Dugald is our guide."

Laughter bubbled up, slowly at first, then helplessly, until her shoulders shook with the force of it. Shaking her head, she said, "I'm surprised you could keep a straight face when you told her that whisker."

Smiling, he replied, "It wasn't easy, but it will serve. She knows that your work is secret, and she is not to bombard you with questions."

"If you think that, you don't know Juliet. Curiosity is her middle name."

"I was thinking of you. Every time she asks a question, all you need say is that you're sworn to secrecy. All that aside, we need another cover to explain our presence to the locals. The story we are putting about is that you and Gavin are cousins, come for a visit, and were caught in the storm. To be on the safe side, I've changed your surname to Robson. I'm not expecting trouble. I doubt if anyone in Ballater will remember me, but they'll know Gavin. He comes here to fish every year. Try to remember you are now Mary Robson, and if anyone comes calling, make yourself scarce." He paused then went on, "You wouldn't care to tell me your real name, would you? I mean your last name. Last night, Dugald let slip that your Christian name is Mahri."

She gave him a direct and steady stare but remained silent.

He sighed. "I thought not."

"What about you?" she asked. "Are you one of the cousins?"

"No, Dugald and I are going to be the hired hands, and

hired hands don't have names. Now get into that bed and show me your hands."

She got into bed and grudgingly allowed him to examine her hands. He stared at them for so long, she began to feel horribly self-conscious. She knew that they looked like a laborer's hands. Her nails were ragged, and some of the blisters had begun to crack. She couldn't help thinking of the divine Ariel. She imagined Ariel had beautiful long-fingered hands with delicately colored nails.

She wanted to hide her hands under the covers and was ashamed of the impulse. Let him think what he wanted.

He spoke in a gentle voice. "You weren't wearing gloves last night?"

"I took them off when I discovered I'd lost my cairngorm." At his look of puzzlement, she elaborated, "Before we got in the boat. I discovered I'd lost my brooch and took off my gloves to feel for it on the ground."

"That was why you almost got us all drowned?" His voice was rising with each word. "Because you lost your brooch?"

She made a derisory sound. "We didn't drown, did we? And that brooch means a great deal to me. It was my mother's."

He was staring at her hands, so she couldn't see what he was thinking or feeling. "Where is the brooch now?"

"It must be in my coat pocket. I mean, Thomas's coat pocket. I suppose Dugald took my clothes away to dry them."

Before she knew what he was about, he had emptied a tot glass of a pungent liquid over one of her hands. She didn't cry out, but tears welled in her eyes.

"Antiseptic," he said shortly. Almost on the same breath, he said, "What about the dirk I took away from you? Does it mean a great deal to you, too?"

"Dirk?"

"The blade you kept in your boot."

"No. It means nothing at all."

He looked up with an arrested expression then quickly looked away. She didn't know what to make of that look.

He started on the other hand. "Juliet tells me that when you were a child, you and your family used to spend the summers on Deeside?"

She knew it! He might be on the run, but that could change in the blink of an eye, then they would no longer be allies. He was still a secret service agent, still trying to pry her secrets out of her.

"That was a long time ago," she answered shortly.

She was prepared for the next dousing of antiseptic on her hand and did no more than grit her teeth. He used the tweezers to pull out the splinters one by one. It hurt, but she was too proud to show it.

Without looking up, he said, "And your mother died when you were how old?"

"I was seven."

"And your brother?"

She tugged her hands free. "I'm disappointed in Juliet. I thought she would be more discreet than run to you with my life story."

He answered mildly, "Let's not get carried away. You told her very little."

"And I'll tell her less in future."

"I'd be happy to answer any questions you put to me."

Ariel's name flashed into her mind, and she quickly crushed it. "Fine," she snapped. "Where is Dugald?"

He sighed. "He's backtracking to Balmoral, doing a little reconnoitering for me. He should be back tomorrow."

She wasn't disappointed; she was appalled. She wanted to be up and doing. She wanted to slip away before her father picked up her trail. She couldn't go without Dugald. He was her guide.

"Reconnoitering? What does that mean?"

Her thoughts scattered when he doused first one hand in the basin of warm water, then the other, and finally dried them off with a white fluffy towel.

"The worst is over," he said.

Holding one hand steady in his, he dipped his fingers into a jar of ointment and massaged the salve into her palm. She was mesmerized by the way his thumb caressed the pain away. When he started on the other hand, her eyes began to close. Suddenly coming to herself, she jerked away. He looked as shocked as she felt.

It was all an act. She must never forget who and what he was. A secret service agent didn't care what methods he used to get the information he wanted.

He recovered more quickly than she. "Did I hurt you? I'm sorry."

Scowling, she said, "You were telling me what you've done with Dugald."

"He volunteered. We have to know where we stand, and he can move about more freely than I can. Until we know what Foster is up to, we are staying right here, so don't get any ideas about slipping away on your own."

"And if Dugald tells us it's safe to leave, what then?"

He got up and set the tray on a small table beside the window. "Then we leave," he said.

"We go our separate ways?"

He turned to look at her. "I didn't say that. Listen, Mahri. We're not enemies. You proved that by coming back for me when I was incarcerated in that dungeon." He came to stand over her. "Why did you come back for me?"

She gave a careless shrug. "I knew you could not possibly have murdered Mr. Dickens. You're simply not that kind of man. And you wouldn't have been captured if I hadn't left you at the alehouse." She shrugged again. "I felt responsible."

He sat on the edge of the bed and stroked her cheek with the pads of his fingers. She should have pulled away, but she had never felt more like laying her head on his broad chest and pouring out all her woes.

He said softly, "I wish you'd tell me what trouble you're in. Perhaps I can help you. I won't always be running from the law. You helped me. I'd like to return the favor."

The moment of insanity passed. She had to remind herself that they were still on opposite sides. "I've already told you. I'm not going to repeat myself."

"Ah. You mean that you broke your engagement to Ramsey, and he threatened to do something heinous to make you sorry?"

"I told you, he's mad. He's not going to give me up."

He gazed at her thoughtfully. "There's no need to be afraid. I won't let anything happen to you. Trust me."

He was confusing her with so much kindness. She was deathly afraid, not only for herself but also for what she'd set in motion. But he was the last man she could confide in. He was too good at his job. She shouldn't have worried about him, shouldn't have rescued him. It wasn't necessary. He would have rescued himself.

She was bracing herself for the moment when he would ask her about the letter she'd sent to Mr. Dickens, the letter that warned him that Demos was planning to kill the queen. What a fool she'd been to think that they would cancel the reception! She'd improvised with her story of Ramsey making her sorry that she had jilted him. But Alex Hepburn was no fool. If he hadn't already done so, he would soon put two and two together. He'd realize that she had written the letter and that only a member of Demos could know so much, then he'd never let her go.

It was imperative that she keep a cool head and nerves like steel.

"I'm hungry," she said, "so if you don't mind, I'd like to get dressed and go downstairs."

His lips flattened. "You mean you want to do your own reconnoitering? Don't get any ideas, Mahri. I promised Dugald that you would be here when he got back, and I'm a man of my word." He stood up. "Juliet said you should wear white cotton gloves to protect your hands. You'll find them in the top drawer of her dresser."

With that, he left the room.

She had made him angry. If she had not known that he

was made of iron, she would have said that she had hurt his feelings. At any rate, he'd certainly taken *her* measure. She *had* wanted to go downstairs to get the lie of the land in case she had to beat a hasty retreat. It was what she was trained to do.

She got out of bed and began to dress. It was when she was tying the strings of her petticoats that she realized her hands no longer hurt her. Turning them over, she examined her palms. He must have used a magic salve, because the angry red had faded to pink.

It must be a trick of the light, she thought and reached for the taffeta dress.

I knew you could not have murdered Mr. Dickens. You're simply not that kind of man."

Her careless words had rocked him back on his heels. They'd carried more punch than the concussion he'd suffered when he'd fallen out of his tree house and landed on his head as a boy. In his business, that kind of trust was rare.

So why would she risk her life to rescue him one minute, then treat him as though he were her worst enemy the next? This was the thought that possessed Alex as he stomped up the stairs to the stable loft where Dugald had chosen to quarter himself.

He knew that she was brave and resourceful, but she was also stubborn. Couldn't she see that things had changed between them? He knew that she was in trouble up to her neck. He could sense her fear. There was far more to her story than she had told Juliet or him. He was beginning to fit the pieces together, but he wanted Mahri to tell him not because he'd tricked her but because she wanted to.

Why? The thought turned in his mind. Was it because this woman had captured his imagination from the moment he'd set eyes on her? And only moments ago, he'd felt that shock of recognition again? Did she know how desirable she looked in her transparent muslin nightgown that revealed far more than it concealed? How had she managed to erase those soft, feminine contours beneath her boy's clothes?

The picture that formed in his mind had his groin tighten painfully against the fabric of his trousers.

He cursed fluently. He'd wanted Ariel, but not like this. Ariel was all fire and passion. She'd enjoyed provoking him to jealousy, delighted in flirting with other men. He doubted that Mahri knew how to flirt. Her appeal was subtle, a blend of innocence and worldliness. A man would never lose his head over her, as he'd done with Ariel, but he might easily lose his heart to her. The thought made him scowl.

He'd never told anyone the truth about Ariel or the "accident" that had claimed her life. Everyone believed what they wanted to believe, that on her death, his life had shattered, and he had withdrawn into himself. And everyone was right but for the wrong reasons. He'd learned that emotions caused too much grief. Feelings could lie. He was too astute, too wary, to fall into the same trap again, or so he'd told himself. But that was before he'd met Mahri.

He stopped right there. He'd known her for forty-eight hours. He wasn't going to allow the softer feelings she evoked to rule his head. He needed a clear mind to get them out of the coil they were in.

What he should be thinking about was how to use his powerful gifts to bring a traitor and murderer to justice. And he would do it, but he'd keep Mahri out of it.

Dugald's room was spartan, but it made an excellent lookout and, of course, there were horses at hand if he had to make a quick exit. How was a deerstalker connected to a woman like Mahri? His devotion, his loyalty, yes, and his sharp tongue when his mistress took needless risks raised all sorts of questions in Alex's mind. Of one thing he was certain. Dugald trusted him, or he would never have left his cub in his care.

Thomas's garments were hung on the backs of chairs to dry. Alex lost no time in delving into the pockets of the deerskin jacket. In a matter of moments, he held it in his palm, a cairngorm brooch set in an intricate gold setting, the brooch she usually wore on her tam.

He had no qualms about unlocking its secrets. Mahri refused to confide in him. He still didn't know who she was. He couldn't help her unless he knew what he was dealing with.

He covered the brooch with both hands and centered his thoughts on its sharp edges, its cool surface, and brought to mind how she kept fingering it, as though it was her secret talisman.

Behind his eyes, pictures were beginning to form. He could feel the heat of the sun beating on his face. His head was spinning, and a kaleidoscope of color surged in waves around him, then gradually receded.

Blurred shapes became more distinct. He saw a girl on a horse; a boy—her brother?—a year or two older, riding beside her. They were in a pasture, and a man and woman were standing beside a gate, watching them, waiting for the girl to take a fence.

"Go on, Mahri," the man called out. "You can do it!"

The girl jerked round. "Papa! The fence is too high."

"Nonsense! Go on! Make me proud of you."

The woman—Mahri's mother?—touched the man on the sleeve. "William," she said, "Mahri is right. She is only a child."

The man replied, "We'll let her decide, shall we?"

Alex was appalled. Mahri's fear was coming at him in waves. She didn't want to jump the fence. He wanted to shout out to tell her not to do it, but he was frozen in place. He could feel Mahri tense. The next moment, she went thundering over the pasture. When she cleared the fence, she let out a whoop of laughter.

"I told you she could do it," said the man. "We Scots thrive on a challenge."

The scene disintegrated, and the shadows rushed in. Alex was shaking. He wanted to throttle the man, Mahri's father, if he was her father.

All the same, he was baffled. There was nothing in that scene to throw light on the puzzle that was Mahri. She'd been afraid to take the fence but, at the end, when she'd cleared it, she'd been exultant.

What was he to make of that?

There must be something here that he was missing, else why did he have the vision?

This brought to mind his vision of Mahri accepting the dirk. He'd sensed her reverence. Now the dirk meant nothing to her. If she had turned on Demos, why wouldn't she answer his questions?

He was still dwelling on that thought when he returned to the house.

Eleven

❦

Mahri straightened and stretched her aching spine. She was in the kitchen, preparing what would pass for the evening meal. It wasn't an onerous task, because there weren't many mouths to feed. Everyone was still clearing up after the flood. None of the servants had returned, and the Cardnos had gone off to Ballater, supposing the bridge was open, to gather as much information as they could on what was happening up at the castle. It also gave them the opportunity to call on Mrs. Dickens and her family to offer their condolences.

Mrs. Dickens and her family. The chance thought made her wince. She was still pondering what had happened there. It seemed beyond belief that anyone else had been involved in Dickens's murder except a member of Demos. What was becoming patently clear was that everyone connected to her was in danger. She'd dragged them all into her web of deceit, even Alex and Gavin. Colonel Foster was still trying to track them down. According to Dugald, the colonel was convinced they must have gone into hiding close by, and he was determined to find them and arrest anyone who gave them shelter.

They couldn't stay here, not for long. Yet Gavin was in no condition to travel. She and Dugald could slip away, but it seemed a cowardly thing to do.

The thought depressed her, and she absently stirred the batter in the bowl on the table. She couldn't slip away, because Alex Hepburn wouldn't allow it. Sometimes she felt that they were comrades, but when she really thought about it, as now, she felt more like his prisoner.

She beat her batter with enough force to send droplets flying to her face. She gasped, then reached for a damp cloth to clean up the mess. She shouldn't take her anger out on her pancake batter, but that man really tried her patience. By his own admission, he was well-known to Foster and his men, yet for the last three days, he'd been working outside, brazenly showing his face as he helped Dugald repair the damage the storm had caused. He had a three days' growth of beard, and he thought that would fool any unwelcome visitors into believing that he was a common laborer out to earn a few extra shillings.

And it worked. That very morning, two soldiers had appeared, nosing around and asking questions. They'd taken her for the maid of all work. She'd fussed over them and poured them a tankard of ale, all to allay their suspicions. She'd had the shock of her life when Alex sauntered in.

He'd come for a drink of water, he said, bold as brass, and after exchanging a few words with the soldiers in broad Scots, he sauntered out.

That man had the luck of the devil.

Her luck, on the other hand, was running out. How long before her father caught up to her?

Her mind was numb from so much speculation. It was her job to produce something edible from the few staples that were left in the larder, so she had better get on with it. If she hadn't taken on the job, they would have all gone hungry. No one knew how to cook except Dugald and herself, and Dugald was busy. She didn't mind. She liked cooking. Her fondest memories as a child were of helping her mother bake bread on Cook's day off. Mama believed that every female should know how to cook.

She didn't want to go down that road, so she concentrated on the matter at hand. She'd prepared a vegetable pie and was now in the process of making pancakes with a hot strawberry sauce to go with them.

The batter was too thick. She had to thin it with milk. Clutching her bowl to her middle, she walked to the pantry and pushed through the door. It took her only a moment or two to add the milk, carefully stirring the batter with her wooden spoon to test its consistency. That done, she retraced her steps and came to a sudden halt.

Gavin was there, in her kitchen, sampling the staples she had set out on the table. At her entrance, he looked up with a lopsided grin. Mahri knew all about lopsided grins and masculine guile. In her role as Thomas Gordon, she'd mixed with notorious rakes and philanderers. Not only had she learned from observing them, but she'd tried a few tricks of her own just to pass muster.

He was only a year or two younger than his brother, though he seemed much younger, a smidgen handsomer, and far more easygoing. And definitely more charming. He had the kind of smile that was calculated to soften any female's heart. She listened to her heart. It was as slow and steady as the clock on the mantel.

"Mahri," he said, almost blinding her with his grin, "or should I call you Miss Robson?"

"Cousin Gavin," she responded, raising her brows a little, "I think you are supposed to call me Mary."

"Ah yes, I'd forgotten." He pulled up a kitchen chair and eased slowly into it. "We have not had the opportunity to exchange more than a few words since you rescued me from"—he gave a faint shudder—"that vile hellhole in Balmoral. May I say, ma'am, that I shall be forever in your debt?"

Well, maybe her heart was speeding up a little. He did have a charming smile. "You should thank Dugald," she said. "I just followed his orders." When he shifted in his chair and groaned, she said quickly, "Are you all right? Can I get you something? You really should be resting in bed, you know."

He palmed his side. "Perhaps I'll have a wee tot of whiskey to dull the pain. To tell the truth, I'm bored with my own company."

Mahri fetched the tot of whiskey he'd asked for.

He downed it in one gulp, smiled, and handed the glass back to her. "If only," he said, "someone would read to me or play a game of cards with me to pass the time."

"I'm sure Mrs. Cardno would be happy to read to you."

"Yes, but she's not here, is she? And she has this peculiar idea about Juliet and me. She keeps asking when we're going to be married."

Mrs. Cardno, in Mahri's opinion, had been well primed by Juliet. She liked the lady immensely. She seemed young and spry and up for anything. Mother and daughter were well matched and a formidable obstacle to the lures of a well-practiced rake. The trouble with Gavin was, rake or no, everybody liked him, and that made him a menace.

"You're bored, and you don't have enough to do?" said Mahri, oozing sympathy.

"That's it in a nutshell, ma'am." He flashed another beguiling smile.

"Well, you've come to the right place, Cousin."

With that, Mahri deposited her bowl of batter in his lap and told him to keep stirring. The look on his face had her pealing with laughter. A moment later, Gavin joined in.

The slam of the kitchen door had both their heads whipping round. Alex stood on the threshold with a scowl on his face.

"Uh-oh," said Gavin for Mahri's ears only, "I think I've outstayed my welcome." In a carrying voice, he said, "Glad to be of service, Mahri, but I'm not so hale and hearty as I thought I was. I think I'll toddle off to bed."

He handed her the bowl of batter, said something in passing to Alex, and pushed out of the room. Alex, silent as a tomb and stripped to the waist, stalked to the sink and began to pump water over his bent head. He stopped pumping, shook the glistening drops of water from his dark hair, and reached for a towel.

Beads of water glistened on his tanned shoulders and broad chest. His waist was rock hard, as were his hips and long, muscular legs. Mahri had to admit that he was a magnificent animal. Her gaze moved to his face. Even the dark stubble on his chin added to his virility.

It was the scowl on his face that brought her out of her reverie.

His eyes narrowed on her. "What do you think you're doing?"

What *had* she been doing? He'd caught her staring, measuring him like a Thoroughbred she wanted to acquire for her stable. He would get a good laugh out of that.

She tried for a lighthearted air, lighthearted and sophisticated. It was either that or die from embarrassment. "A cat may look at a queen," she cooed.

"What?" He looked baffled.

She set her bowl on the kitchen table and stirred vigorously. "It's all right, Hepburn," she said in the same amused tone. "You're safe from me. In my role as Thomas Gordon, I've seen my share of naked men." She gave a tiny shrug. "I promise not to run screaming from the room."

His dark eyes locked on hers. With the grace and stealth of a jungle cat, he crossed to the table. "Are you daring me to do my worst?"

"What?" Now she was baffled.

"Run, Mahri, run!"

He was threatening her, and that got her temper going. The man was a boor! He was also moody. She never knew where she was with him. He'd bathed her hands and found her cairngorm brooch for her. He'd acted as though he wanted to be her friend. Today was a different story. She couldn't do a thing right. Well, he'd better watch his step, or she'd crown him with her bowl of batter.

She gave what she hoped was a ladylike snort. "Don't try my patience, Hepburn. You should know by now that I'm not afraid of you."

"I can change that."

The menace in his voice mystified her. What had she done now? "What's your point?" she demanded crossly.

He slapped his palms on the flat of the table and leaned toward her. Through his teeth, he bit out, "Didn't your mother ever teach you that flirting with men could get you into trouble?"

"Flirting?" She felt the angry color rise in her cheeks even as she admitted to herself that he might have mistaken her slow appraisal for something she had never intended. To cover her confusion and give herself a moment to regain her balance, she moved away from him and set her bowl on the sideboard. Now she felt not only foolish but cowardly as well.

She marched back to the table but was careful to keep to her own side. "You conceited ass," she said. "I never flirt. Men are not that important to me."

"You were making eyes at Gavin, and don't think I didn't see how you were playing up to those soldiers this morning. Have a care, Mahri. You were playing with fire there. And while we're at it, leave my brother alone."

"Gavin? What a filthy mind you have! I was talking to him to pass the time of day. He's an invalid. I wanted to help him; that's all."

"You were making eyes at him. Try that on the wrong man, and you could end up on your back with your skirts around your waist."

For a moment, she was speechless, taken aback by his crudity, then she crouched as though she would spring at him. "Where did you learn your manners? In the bawdy houses in the docks of London, I don't doubt."

He showed his teeth. "I think you must be confusing me with Thomas Gordon." His smile vanished, and his voice rose a notch. "Mind what I say. No more flirting, or suffer the consequences."

She made a scoffing sound. "I know how to take care of myself, as you should know."

He moved so fast, she was taken off guard. One moment, he was on the other side of the table, and the next, he was on her side and had grabbed her by the upper arms. She braced for a shaking. Instead, he yanked her against him and covered her lips in a bruising kiss. It was so bruising, it hurt. It was so bruising, she forgot she was holding the wooden spoon, and it dropped from her fingers to clatter on the stone floor. It was so bruising, she forgot to breathe.

He pulled back a little, muttered something harsh under his breath, then he kissed her again and again, whisper-soft kisses this time that confused her even more. She stopped struggling. As those kisses lingered, all her frustrations and anger quietly slipped away. Hardly aware of what she was doing, she went on tiptoe and twined her arms around his neck.

When his tongue entered her mouth, she thought she would faint with the pleasure of it. Heat spread from her lips to her loins and all the way to her toes, then licked along her spine, melting her as though she were a little wax doll.

As suddenly as he had grabbed her, he wrenched himself away. With his back to her, shoulders hunched, he tried to even his breathing. "I apologize," he said finally. "The fault is mine, not yours." He did not turn to look at her. "It won't happen again."

It took her a moment to realize that she had been rejected, that what had been a wondrous experience for her was to him nothing but an error in judgment. Her lips were still burning, her breathing was uneven, and her legs were refusing to obey the commands of her brain. She had to lean against the table for support.

What a fool she had made of herself. But if she was a fool, he was a rogue.

"Ah, Dugald," said the rogue, "I thought I heard your step."

Her gaze jerked to the door. Dugald was there, looking suspiciously from one to the other. How long had he been watching them? To cover her confusion, she picked up the wooden spoon and wiped it off with a dishcloth.

The rogue was not in the least embarrassed by Dugald's presence. In fact, he seemed relieved to see him. With a man-to-man grin, he said, "Keep your cub on a leash, Dugald, or the next time she provokes me, I may be tempted to put her over my knee and wallop her backside."

The suspicion in Dugald's expression instantly vanished. Smiling ruefully, he walked to the sink and poured himself a cup of water. By the time he had finishing drinking it, Alex had gone back to work.

Shaking his head, with a wry twinkle in his eye, Dugald said, "Lass, lass, what tricks have you been up to now?"

"None! I didn't do anything. It was a misunderstanding; that's all. Why are you taking his part?"

Dugald had wrung out a cloth and was wiping the sweat from his brow. "I'm no taking anyone's part," he said. "I've more sense than to come between a man and his maid."

Mahri had no patience with this kind of talk and no wish to prolong the conversation. "Dugald," she said, appealing to him, "we have to get away from here. There's nothing to stop us from leaving, is there?"

Dugald's brows beetled. He said slowly, "The Hepburn would stop us." When she started to protest, he clicked his tongue. "Mahri, Mahri, have we no enough enemies without bringing the Hepburn's wrath down upon our heads? Be patient. He means you well. And things have changed since we first set out. The woods and hills are crawling with soldiers. There are only two of us. The Hepburn would be a good man in a fight."

"Fight?" She said the word as though it were a profanity. "I don't want to fight. I want to run. I want to escape. We're prisoners here, don't you see that? Who knows what the Hepburn has in store for us?"

He regarded her thoughtfully for a long moment. "I'll talk to the Hepburn," he allowed, and that was all he would say.

With no servants to wait on them, they ate at the kitchen table, with the exception of Dugald, who always took the first watch. Mahri need not have worried about the awkwardness between herself and Alex or what she would say to him. There were enough people there to take up any slack in the conversation, and Alex wasted no time on small talk but began to question Juliet and her mother about their visit to Mrs. Dickens before they'd taken more than a few bites of her vegetable pie.

At one point, in answer to a question from Gavin, Juliet said, "The locals know you too well, Gavin, to believe you murdered Mr. Dickens." She flashed a smile at Alex. "Alas, they don't know you, so no one rushed to your defense. However, Mr. Stevenson from the bank whispered in my ear that everyone in Ballater thinks that it's another of Colonel Foster's cock-ups, and it will all be sorted out in due course."

Gavin stirred himself and replied with a smile, "It's more than a cock-up; it's a conspiracy. Foster has witnesses. Who are they? That's what I'd like to know."

Mahri was struck by how tired he looked, yet he'd been resting for most of the day. She couldn't see him riding a horse or tramping over the moors to safety. No wonder his brother was in no hurry to leave. Gavin needed time to heal, but time was something they did not have. She was certain of one thing: Alex wouldn't leave without Gavin. That was one thing she'd learned about the Hepburn. He was loyal to his friends. Gavin was both brother and friend. Lucky, lucky Gavin.

The conversation had moved on to Colonel Foster, who, it seemed, had also come calling on Mrs. Dickens to offer his condolences.

Juliet said, "I asked Colonel Foster about the witnesses, but he just smiled knowingly and said that all would be revealed in good time."

Mrs. Cardno interjected, "He's not an easy man to like. He's so full of himself."

"Mother, you're too kind. The man is a horse's arse, and I got that from Dugald."

When the laughter died away, Alex said, "What else did Colonel Foster say?"

Juliet replied, "He told Mrs. Dickens that he had arranged for a guard of honor to be present at her husband's funeral, and that he would be at their head. It was embarrassing. He looked as though he expected us all to applaud."

"A guard of honor?" said Gavin. "What about the castle? Won't that leave the queen open to an attack? It's a big castle to guard."

He and Alex exchanged a veiled look. Though everyone was under the impression that there had been an attack on the queen, not one word of the decoy had got out, and that was how Alex wanted to keep it. It was what had been decided by Whitehall even before the attack took place. As long as Demos thought that the queen was still in Balmoral, the safer the real queen would be.

"True," replied Juliet, "but since the colonel believes that you two are the villains, and you're on the run, he may think that he has nothing to fear."

At this point, Mahri interjected, "Was anything said about Dugald or me? Is the colonel hunting for us, too?"

"Not specifically." Juliet thought for a moment. "They

know that a girl and a man helped Gavin and Alex escape from the castle, but that's all they know."

"A girl?" She remembered, then, that she had tricked the jailer by pretending to be one of the maids. She might fool the authorities for a little while, but not the one she feared most.

Juliet's gaze rested on Gavin. "You look all in." Her voice held a trace of annoyance. "You should be in your bed." To Alex, she said, "He really should see a doctor."

Gavin gave a snort of derision. "Stop fussing, woman. I don't need mothering. What I need is a tot of whiskey to ease the pain."

Juliet's brows rose. "Whatever happened to mind over matter? You said that—"

"I know what I said." His chin jutted. "I get distracted; that's all."

Juliet said something under her breath, but everyone heard it. "Horse's arse."

Gavin's straight lips gradually turned up. Finally, he laughed. "Your point, this time, Ju, but I'll have my revenge."

Mrs. Cardno entered the conversation with a sly smile. "Henry Steele was there, too. Such a gentlemanly man, and so considerate of an old woman's foibles. He is still single, you know. Some lucky girl is bound to snap him up before long."

Mahri said, "Who is Mr. Steele?"

"Oh," replied Mrs. Cardno with a sideways glance at her daughter's bent head, "he is the proprietor of the estate on the other side of the river. I'm sure Dugald must have worked for him at one time. He has turned his grand house into a hotel."

"Mother," said Juliet. There was a distinct edge in her voice. "Mr. Steele may not be a horse's arse, but he lacks something essential in his character."

"Yes," replied her mother placidly, "I believe you're right. He is human, isn't he, and has failings just like the rest of us."

Mahri took a quick inventory of everyone's expression. No one was embarrassed or offended. Everyone seemed to find this banter between Mrs. Cardno and Juliet amusing. She wasn't sure that she was amused. For a moment there, she thought she'd detected a flash of pain in Juliet's eyes.

Smiles faded, and now it was back to business.

"Anything else you can think of?" asked Alex. "Anything at all?"

"Tell him about the trains," said Mrs. Cardno.

"They're running again," Juliet said. "They cleared the tracks of all the trees and debris that the flood caused, so we're not completely cut off from the outside world."

Alex rested his hands on the table. "You're sure about the trains?"

"Oh, yes. We saw the train from Aberdeen. When we left Mrs. Dickens's house, we heard the whistle blowing. There was great excitement in the village. People came out of their houses and made for the Station Square. Mother and I did, too. When the passengers alighted, a cheer went up."

"Were there any strangers among the passengers?"

"Not that I noticed. Why do you ask?"

Alex shrugged. "I was hoping that someone from Aberdeen might take over my chief's job, at least as a temporary measure, but I don't suppose that word of the attack on the queen has reached them yet."

Mahri didn't hear the next exchange. She was thinking that her father would have expected her to be on that train, yes, and on the last train before the flood.

She was scared, but another emotion was at work in her. A slow-burning anger bubbled and simmered. Her father had duped her, used her, and abused her trust. He was in the wrong, but he would never admit it.

Alex scraped back his chair and got up. "I'll go and relieve Dugald so that he can have his share of this delectable dinner before my brother scoffs the lot."

Everyone laughed and complimented Mahri on her skill

as a cook. By the time Dugald entered the kitchen, his dinner was cold, and Mahri wondered what he and Alex had talked about for so long.

John Murray propped one shoulder against the window frame and looked over at his employer. The professor was sitting at his desk, as still as a statue, his eyes closed. Only his clasped hands, squeezing till the knuckles turned white, betrayed his state of mind. The professor was in the grip of some strong emotion. Anger? Fear?

The professor removed his spectacles and pinched the bridge of his nose. "She wasn't on the train," he said softly, then viciously, "She should have been here four days ago, before the flood."

Murray didn't reply. He was thinking that in another era, as the messenger of bad news, he might have been killed on the spot.

The professor gestured to the sideboard. "Help yourself to a glass of whiskey and bring one for me. A large one."

Murray obliged. He was about forty years old, was neither tall nor handsome, but like many in Demos, he'd seen military service, though he'd worked mostly in intelligence.

He wasn't one of the university crowd. He didn't have money behind him or believe in causes. He hired himself out to the highest bidder, one contract at a time. That made him an outsider in the professor's circle. Murray didn't mind. Money was money.

"She's the informer," the professor said. "My own daughter."

Murray sipped his whiskey and said nothing.

"It's all falling into place. There was a woman involved in the debacle at the castle. She shot the gun out of Ramsey's hand. Dickens told him that they knew of the plot to assassinate the queen. The Hepburn brothers were arrested, but they escaped with the help of a man and a woman." The

professor smiled faintly. "If that was not Mahri, then she's
either seriously disabled, or she's dead."

Murray knew the value of silence, and he kept his mouth
shut. When the silence became prolonged, however, and it
looked as if the older man had forgotten his presence, Murray said, "What do you want me to do?"

The professor tapped his fingers on the flat of his desk.
"Find her and bring her to me. There's a man called Dugald, a deerstalker. If Mahri is in the area, she'll be with
him."

"What about the brothers she helped get out of prison?"

The professor nodded. "If we find them, we'll find
her." He leaned back in his chair. "You have contacts. Use
them."

"I'll need more money."

"I'll see to it. But remember, I don't want her hurt. I
don't care what happens to the others."

When he was alone, the professor got up and took a turn
around the room. He always tried to appear calm and collected. The absentminded professor role had served him
well. But this betrayal not only cut him to the quick, it also
filled him with dread. She knew too much. She could put
the whole mission in jeopardy, and it wasn't over yet.

How much did she know, and who had she told? What
had she done with the documents she should have delivered
to him?

And if worse came to worst, what was he going to do
about his own daughter?

Twelve

Looks like half the garrison is off to Mr. Dickens's funeral," said Dugald.

"So much the better for us," replied Alex.

They were crouched down in a stand of firs, on a hill behind the castle, with a fine view of the private bridge that linked the queen's summer residence and the road to Ballater. They made an impressive picture, these mounted soldiers with their green and gold tunics and plumed bonnets. At their head, naturally, rode Colonel Foster in full regimental dress.

Dugald said, "I dinna like it, coming here in broad daylight."

"Trust me, Dugald, with Foster and half the garrison gone, our job will be easier. We didn't meet any soldiers on the way here, did we?" When Dugald made a harrumphing sound, Alex went on, "I know I have you to thank for that. You know this valley and woods like the back of your hand."

"I care nothing for that. It's this scheme of yours. It's daft."

Alex was losing patience. "It's risky, but I don't have a choice. Gavin isn't getting better; he's getting worse."

What troubled Alex was not his brother's ribs but the unlucky shot that had pierced Gavin's thigh close to the joint of his leg. Every night and morning, Alex changed the dressing, and every night and morning, the wound seemed to be worse. He wondered if a piece of the bullet had broken off and was festering inside. Gavin had to see a doctor.

There were, however, few doctors on Deeside, and Alex had no doubt that they wouldn't lift a finger to help a man accused of trying to kill the queen. After weighing his options, he'd decided that his best bet was to get Gavin to Aberdeen, where they had friends. It wasn't safe to travel by road, and Gavin wasn't fit to outrun pursuers, so Alex had made up his mind to get him away by train.

It wasn't impossible. He had a friend at the castle who could arrange it, if he could be persuaded.

Dugald said, "This friend of yours, Miller, how long have ye known him?"

"We met at university. Mungo was obsessed with the theater club. He directed all our plays. No one was surprised when he took up acting as a career."

"And he took the queen's place the night of the reception." It was a statement, not a question.

"And fooled everyone into the bargain."

When Dugald mumbled something under his breath, Alex said crisply, "I'm holding you to your promise. You're not to tell anyone, not even Mahri."

"Then why did ye tell me?"

"In case anything happens to *me*." Alex clasped Dugald's shoulder. "You've got to take my place. You've got to look after the others. There is no one else to do it. You know that, don't you?"

They plodded on. After a while, Dugald said, "I would do it anyway, but if it's a promise ye want, I'll give it tae ye."

"Thank you."

"I just pray that no one recognizes ye."

"What, in this getup? Don't I look like a forester?"

Dugald's gaze wandered over Alex, from his tartan trews to his torn leather satchel and cracked, scruffy boots. When Alex raised the ax he held in his hand, Dugald grinned. "With that fur on your face, your own mother wouldna recognize you."

"That's the general idea. Now let's move."

They stayed in the shelter of the trees as they made their way down toward the river. Alex meant what he'd said to Dugald. If anything went wrong, one of them had to take charge and see the thing through, and there was no one else he could rely on but Dugald. Mahri might not like the way the scales had shifted, but she wouldn't take off without Dugald. Meantime, she had her hands full as head cook and nurse. At least Gavin was in no condition to work his rakish charm on her.

He felt himself cringe inside. He was a fine one to criticize his brother. Gavin was honest. He loved all women, whereas Alex had pounced on Mahri and used her as though she were the veriest strumpet—he, Alex Hepburn, who had been raised to treat all women with chivalry. And the awful thing was, he couldn't wait to do it again.

Bloody hell! He could feel his groin tightening. Forget her! Focus on his reason for coming here!

"This will do," said Dugald.

They were in full view of the castle and the soldiers on guard. "We'd best get started, then," said Alex, and he raised his ax and brought it down hard against the trunk of an ailing poplar.

They had felled two trees before one of the soldiers wandered over to investigate. They paid no attention to him but carried on with their work.

After a moment or two, the soldier said, "No one told me that these trees were going to be cut down today."

"I don't know about that," Alex replied. He mopped his brow with the back of his sleeve but barely spared the soldier a glance. "One of the groundsmen hired us, but I forget his name."

The soldier squinted down at Dugald. "Don't I know you from somewhere? Aren't you a deerstalker?"

"That I am, but this isna the hunting season, and a man has to earn a few shillings where he can."

The soldier grunted. "What's wrong with the trees?"

"Poplar beetles. If we dinna cut them down, the beetles will spread and eat up all the poplars on the estate. The queen loves her poplars."

The soldier looked at the tree, then at Dugald. "Well, don't waste time. Get on with it," and he walked back to his post.

"Poplar beetles?" asked Alex.

They both chuckled.

They were making their way to a small stone rotunda at the edge of the formal gardens that were off to the side of the ballroom. At this point, they withdrew into the shrubbery, but not stealthily. To anyone watching, they wanted to give the impression that they had nothing to hide. The rotunda had only one entrance facing the castle, but the walls came no higher than a man's waist. They left their axes outside but kept their satchels and swung themselves over the back wall.

Alex rummaged through his satchel and produced his watch. "Not long to wait," he said, "five minutes, maybe ten. Mungo is a man of habit. He can't do without his cigarettes for more than an hour at a time. We may as well make ourselves comfortable while we wait."

Dugald dug into his satchel and came up with a cheese and pickle sandwich. He munched on it without really tasting it. He was thinking of the preposterous story the Hepburn had told him when he'd taken the first watch the other night. The queen was not the queen but a decoy. The gentleman who played her part was Mr. Miller, whom the Hepburn had known from his university days and who had subsequently become an agent. The real queen had never left Windsor Castle, and that was where she was now, or she should be, if British Intelligence was doing its job.

Though they didn't know it, the soldiers were guarding nobody. Mr. Miller played another role—Her Majesty's private secretary—and no one was allowed into the queen's presence without his say-so, except for others in the know such as Colonel Foster.

He swallowed a mouthful of sandwich and said darkly, "What's the point of this elaborate tomfoolery? Why not let everyone know that the queen is safe and sound in Windsor?"

"Think of what would happen next. The vultures might descend on Windsor and try again."

Dugald gave one of his noncommittal grunts. He was thinking of Mahri and how she'd tried to save the queen. She'd be crushed when she found out that it had been all for nothing. He couldn't tell her. He'd given the Hepburn his word.

The tread of footsteps approaching the rotunda alerted them to another presence.

The man who entered blew out a stream of smoke. He seemed surprised but not put out to see two laborers sharing his little sanctuary. In Dugald's opinion, the only thing Mungo Miller had in common with the queen was that he was small in stature with the delicate bones to go with it.

Miller said, "You're trespassing, but I don't mind, not if you don't mind if I smoke. The queen detests the weed, and anyone caught smoking inside the castle would face instant dismissal."

Alex got to his feet. In a cultured voice that was at odds

with the clothes he wore, he said, "So you're still going on with the charade, pretending the queen is in residence?"

Miller stared and gaped. "Alex? Is it you?"

"Himself."

The other man looked fleetingly over his shoulder toward the castle. "You're mad to come here. Don't you know that Foster is out for your blood?"

"So I believe. Sit down and enjoy your cigarette."

"You were always a cool customer."

Miller sat on the stone bench and took several quick pulls on his cigarette. Dugald could see that he was on edge. Bloody hell, so was he, and he was wishing that he'd brought his pipe if only to chew on it. The Hepburn, on the other hand, seemed relaxed.

Alex said, "This is my guide, and he has my complete confidence."

Miller looked at Dugald. "So that's the way of it. How do you do, Mr. No Name." He breathed deeply. "To answer your question, I can't leave, even if I wanted to. You know that. Only the bigwigs in Whitehall can close down this operation, and last I heard, they wanted us to wait until they had consulted with the minister. That, of course, was before all the lines went down."

He inhaled and let out another puff of smoke. "All right, Alex. What is it you want? I know you didn't come here to ask after my health."

Alex smiled. "That's what I like about you," he said. "No questions about my guilt or innocence. You've always taken my word on faith alone."

Miller laughed softly. "I may not know your brother, but I can't believe that he was part of a conspiracy to kill the queen or that he murdered Dickens. No, and I can't see you aiding and abetting him if he did."

"Foster had witnesses to prove that I'm in it up to my neck."

"Stable hands," retorted Miller, "and all they can say is that you and your brother commandeered a couple of horses not long after all hell broke loose in the ballroom. Of course you didn't come back right away. Even so, Foster jumped the gun. He should have waited until he had all the facts." He squinted up at Alex. "Why didn't you come back right away?"

"Long story, and we haven't got time to go into it right now. To get back to your point. I want your help."

"That goes without saying, or you wouldn't be here."

"First off, I need a letter opener, but not any letter opener. You'll have to break into the evidence box to get it."

There was a long silence. "You said 'first off.' What else do you want?"

"A couple of uniforms of the queen's guard, and a letter with the official heading to give us a safe pass."

"You have nerve, I'll say that for you!"

"Will you do it?"

Miller laughed. "Why not? I'm bored out of my mind, twiddling my thumbs with nothing to do. Now start over. Tell me what this is about."

The moment he touched the letter opener, he felt the familiar sensation. But it was Miller's impression that came to mind: Miller, as gleeful as a schoolboy up to mischief as he unlocked the evidence box. Alex couldn't help smiling. Miller had always been ready for mischief, even at university. He thought he understood. Miller was the last person to touch the letter opener.

He shooed him away and focused on the person he wanted: Dickens's murderer. The world receded, and a picture formed in his mind, indistinct, but gradually coming into focus. He saw Dickens at the door, and the flash of the blade as Ramsey rammed it into Dickens's back. He knew it was Ramsey because he was in the killer's mind.

Heart racing. Breathing labored. Panic. Where was Murray? What would the professor say? What would the professor—?

"What's come over ye, lad?"

The vision disintegrated, and Alex blinked rapidly. Dugald's expression was an odd mixture of perplexity and alarm. They were in a leafy glade, on their way home, and he hadn't been able to resist palming the blade that had killed Dickens.

"Who is the professor?" Alex asked.

Dugald's expression instantly became guarded. "The professor? Professor who?"

"That's what I'm asking you."

"Well, ye're asking the wrong person. What would a deerstalker know about professors?" On the same breath, he went on, "Why are ye loitering when we should be making tracks for home?"

Dugald didn't wait to see if Alex was following him but strode into the queen's forest as though he knew every inch of it, which he probably did. Alex glanced back. They'd left everything as though they were experienced woodsmen: three trees down and neatly stacked along with their branches for carting away. The head groundsman might scratch his head, wondering who had ordered the job, but he wouldn't lose any sleep over it.

He soon caught up to Dugald. "You're not helping Mahri by keeping secrets from me. You must know that I want to help her. You know who the professor is, don't you?"

Dugald didn't stop walking. "I willna betray the lass, and that's all I'm going to say on the subject."

Alex recognized a brick wall when he walked into it.

Later that evening found John Murray in the Black Sheep, an alehouse that was a mile or two west of Ballater. Since the night before, he'd stopped off at every change house in the district in his hunt for information on the professor's daughter, and he was beginning to develop a hearty dislike for the local ale that he felt obliged to drink, but a man without a drink in his hand in an alehouse would have stood out like a hawk among pigeons, and Murray wanted to blend in.

When asked, he explained his presence by saying that he'd come into the area hoping to find work with the railway and was forced to stay on because of the flood. He didn't mention the girl, because he knew that if he found Dugald or the Hepburns, he was sure to find her, too. Besides, the last thing the professor wanted was to draw attention to her. If and when she was found, she would be dealt with in private.

He'd given a lot of thought to the girl's connection to the Hepburns. Like the professor, he was convinced that she was the woman who had helped them escape. How did she know them? She was a turncoat. Only one of the Hepburns was involved in security at the castle, the elder brother. Was that how she'd come to know him? Was he her contact at Balmoral? It seemed more than likely.

For the moment, he'd given up trying to pin down the deerstalker. No one knew where he lived, supposing he had a permanent home to go to, nor could they remember when they'd last seen him. In the summer months, he occasionally took odd jobs, but when the hunting season began, he was much in demand as a deerstalker and made more than enough money to tide him over to the next season.

He was nursing a tankard of ale at the bar counter, reflecting that the crowd was more subdued than usual, the result, he supposed, of the funeral that had taken place earlier in the day. It seemed that most of the customers had attended the service for Dickens and were still lamenting not only the death of a man they respected but also the brutal way his life had been cut short.

"It's a sad business," Murray observed to the man standing beside him. He'd discovered that noncommittal remarks served him better than direct questions when he was trying to gather information from unsuspecting subjects.

"Sad, did you say?" said the man beside him. "It is tragic. Dickens was due to retire before Christmas. We've never seen anything like this in Deeside. Mark my words, the English are behind it."

The man on the other side of Murray made a rude sound. He looked remarkably like the first man: red-faced and beefy. They might have been brothers.

The first man took offense. "So what's your theory, Tam o' Shanter?"

"Tam Shackleton is the name as you know very well! It's obvious what happened, isn't it? Dickens was stabbed in the back. He was a careful man. He'd never let an Englishman get close to him unless he were a friend."

If you only knew, thought Murray. That's all it took, one careless mistake, and it was game over, and it could happen to the best of them. When Dickens turned his back on Ramsey, he hadn't understood that he was dealing with a fanatic. A fanatic wouldn't think about consequences. He'd come at you anyway.

The first man said, "That Hepburn fellow is more English than Scot, isn't he? He was Dickens's friend. Leastways, he pretended to be. They came in here from time to time. I never could like him."

"Me neither," said the other. "He just wasn't sociable, not like the other fellow who occasionally came in with them."

"You mean the one who smoked like a chimney? The queen's secretary?"

"Aye. Mungo Miller he calls himself, but I still say he is more English than Scot. You have only to hear him speak."

Holy Jesus! These yokels sounded as mad as the professor and his equally demented disciples. No wonder Scotland was a hotbed of hotheads. He wasn't complaining, not when his services were in demand.

There was a spell of silence as both gentlemen slurped down a healthy swig of ale. *Maiden's water,* Murray thought, but he managed to swallow another mouthful, just to appear sociable. But he wasn't a sociable animal. Emotion played no part in how he lived his life. It wasn't a choice. He was born cold-blooded. He never hated or disliked his targets. He never took sides. Whoever paid him was his master, for a little while.

The temperature of the conversation had cooled, and Shackleton said in a confiding tone, "It wouldn't surprise me if yon queen's secretary was hiding the Hepburn brothers out in the woods."

"What makes you say that, Tam?"

Shackleton's voice dropped to a whisper. "Who else would hide Hepburn? Miller is the only friend he has."

"I think he's long gone."

The temperature was rising again. "Oh, you do, do you? Then tell me this. Why does the queen's secretary creep out of the castle at all hours of the day and night? Mmm? My Jack works at the castle, and he has seen it with his own eyes. Rain or shine, there goes Mr. Queen's Secretary, skulking among the bushes."

The other man gave a scoffing laugh. "He goes out to smoke! I thought everybody knew it! And you're exaggerating. He doesn't skulk among the bushes. There's a little stone shelter hard by the castle wall. That's where he goes. And he's not the only one either."

He emptied his tankard and slapped it down on the counter. Shackleton did the same. They glared at one another. Murray was acutely aware that he was on to something. He didn't want the conversation to end or develop into a quarrel, but he didn't want to appear too eager or too inquisitive. Curious strangers were often regarded with suspicion in small villages.

"Here," he said, "let me buy you both a drink."

Shackleton regarded Murray with a trace of calculation in his expression. "That is very kind of you, sir," he said. "I'll have a whiskey."

The other man nodded affably. "I'll have the same."

Whiskey cost a lot more than a tankard of ale. *Trust these Highlanders to nail an unsuspecting Lowlander,* thought Murray. He dug in his pocket, found some change, and slapped it on the counter.

"Landlord, I'll have a whiskey," he said, "and the same for my friends here."

Thirteen

～

They were late home for supper, but there was no supper waiting for them, no aroma of freshly baked salmon from the catch Dugald had made the day before.

Juliet met them at the back door. Her complexion was like parchment. "She has gone," she said. "Mahri has gone."

"Gone? Gone where?" Alex pushed into the house and made straight for the kitchen as though he expected to find Mahri there. It was spanking clean with everything tidied away. Nothing was on the table to show that anyone had made a start on getting supper ready.

The others crowded in behind him. Dugald said, "She wouldna leave without me." He didn't sound as though he believed his own words.

"Tell me what happened," Alex said, looking at Juliet.

"We don't know. Mother and I came home from the funeral to find the house just as you see it."

"Gavin?"

"Mother is with him now. We think Mahri gave him

something to make him sleep. When we ask him questions, he rambles, but none of it makes sense."

A wave of emotion tightened Alex's throat. That she would have left his brother alone at a time like this! He wouldn't have believed it of her. Her conscience wouldn't have allowed her to desert someone who needed her. That was what he'd thought when he'd set out with Dugald that morning. He'd trusted her, and she'd let him down.

All that aside, she was taking appalling risks, a young woman alone, roaming the hills.

Juliet seemed as upset as he felt. "I blame myself," she said. "I told Mahri that Mother and I would be back in an hour, but it was closer to two hours before we arrived home."

Alex nodded. He was still thinking of a young woman on her own.

He abruptly turned and made for the stairs. In Mahri's room, he started opening drawers. Most of them were empty. There were only two dresses in the wardrobe, the brown taffeta she'd worn the night they arrived and the gray dress she wore during the day.

"Thomas Gordon," he said savagely. She had reverted to her role as a boy.

From there, he went to Gavin's room. Mrs. Cardno was at the bedside, bathing Gavin's brow with a cloth wrung out in cold water.

"He's burning up," she said, "and his mind is wavering."

"Nothing of the sort," Gavin retorted.

Alex smiled. "He seems lucid enough to me."

"Mind over matter," Gavin muttered. "She's a witch, Mahri told me."

When it looked as though his brother was falling asleep, Alex squeezed his shoulder. "Gavin, what did she give you?"

No response.

Alex straightened and looked down at his brother. When he'd left that morning, Gavin had been pale and hollow-eyed, but not like this. The sudden turn in his condition left him shaken. He was the elder of the two. He'd always looked out for Gavin.

That wasn't precisely true. After Ariel, he'd withdrawn into himself. Numbers and codes demanded less attention than people. They could be trusted. He'd become emotionally detached, a lone wolf. What a fool he'd been to think he could maintain the shell he'd built around himself.

That shell had shattered into a thousand shards. He'd never known such helplessness. He was facing a terrible dilemma. He had to choose between Mahri and Gavin. His brother needed a doctor, not tomorrow or the next day, but right now. Mahri had to be rescued from her own rashness. She could become lost in the hills and die of exposure.

He went downstairs. "Dugald," he said, "it's not the soldiers Mahri has to worry about. They're not really interested in her. It's the professor she is running from. Am I right?"

"Aye," Dugald replied, drawing the word out as though he was reluctant to say it.

"Can you track her?"

"I can try."

Juliet said, "Where are you going, Alex?"

"I'm going to Ballater to kidnap a doctor for Gavin. Don't worry. I know what I'm doing. And Dugald"—he paused at the door—"say good-bye to Mahri for me. Tell her I wish her well."

Juliet was wringing her hands. "What are you talking about? Surely Dugald will bring Mahri back here?"

Dugald responded as though Juliet had not spoken. "I'll tell her, lad."

"Take good care of her, Dugald."

"Ye can count on it."

The back door creaked open, and a gust of chill mountain air blew in. There was the sound of voices in the back hall. Alex waved everyone to the side of the room. With his revolver in one hand, he edged behind the kitchen door.

Two people entered, a tall muscular woman in her midforties and a boy with a tartan tam.

"Mahri!" said Alex, then more fiercely, "Mahri!"

Dugald's grin was slow and wide. "Mistress Napier," he said, "the Witch of Pannanich Wells." He turned to Alex. "Mahri has brought us home a healer."

She had changed from her boy's getup into her day dress, and Alex could hardly take his eyes off her. Though Miss Napier had taken charge and cleaned the festering wound, Mahri was right beside her, next to the bed, using a clean linen rag to mop up the trickle of blood. Cool, calm, and competent under duress—that was Mahri. Not for the first time, he acknowledged that there was more to her than that. She was like one of the complex codes that came across his desk. Bit by bit, he invariably unlocked its secrets, and he was bound and determined to do the same with her.

He wondered how much she'd told Miss Napier. The woman was the least curious female he had met. No questions asked. No explanations necessary. He wasn't uneasy or anxious about her motives. *Trust your instincts,* his grandmother had told him often enough, and his instincts were telling him that the witch wished them all well.

His gaze shifted to Gavin. He was resting quietly now, but his cheeks were pale, and there were bruises under his eyes. Mahri had told him that she'd given him a mild dose of laudanum before she left to fetch the witch. She hadn't broken faith with him. She hadn't deserted Gavin and left him to fend for himself. She'd gone for help. She did what had to be done, she'd said, that was all.

"More," said Mahri, practically glaring at him.

"Right."

It was his job to spoon the witch's herbal tea past Gavin's lips in order to bring down his fever. She'd brought the herbs with her as well as water from the famous wells of Pannanich. And it seemed to be working. He thought that there might also be a mild sedative in the tea. Certainly, Gavin was out of it. It was just as well. Alex did not think his brother would take kindly to having two females doctor him when the only thing between their eyes and his nakedness was a decorously draped sheet.

She'd told him that she'd seen her share of naked men. Maybe it wasn't a joke. Frankly, he didn't care. The kiss they'd shared was like one piece of the code he'd broken. Mahri was innocent of a man's passions, but she was ripe for the plucking.

And he'd break the arm of the first man who stretched out his hand to take her, even if he had to break his own arm.

Miss Napier said, "Mahri, fetch me the salve."

Mahri obediently felt around in a jute satchel and produced a jar, which she opened and handed to Miss Napier.

"The wound," said Miss Napier, "never had a chance to heal. See how the dressing has rubbed it raw? Your brother must have overexerted himself. Either that or a speck of dirt or something was left inside it. Keep it clean, apply the salve as often as you change the dressing, and keep your brother off his feet."

"Mind over matter," said Mahri. To Miss Napier's questioning look, she answered, "Gavin thought he could make the wound heal by sheer force of will. He fooled us all."

"There's something in what he says," said Miss Napier. "A positive attitude can help in healing, but it would be foolish not to employ all the accumulated knowledge of doctors and herbalists over the centuries."

Alex had never heard of the Witch of Pannanich, but Miss Napier put him in mind of his own grandmother, the Witch of Drumore: educated, well-spoken, and gifted in ways that ordinary mortals could barely imagine.

To Miss Napier he said, "You have a gifted touch. Is that why the locals call you a witch?"

She was winding a strip of linen around the fresh dressing. "They're confusing me with my aunt." She looked up with a smile. "She believes in the old magic. I put my faith in my herbs."

"If I'd known you lived close by, I would have sent for you sooner. Mahri, you should have told me. Pannanich is only two miles along the road, isn't it?"

Mahri regarded him from beneath her brows. "If I'd told you that I'd gone to consult a witch, you would have laughed yourself silly. You wanted a doctor, a real doctor."

His lips twitched. "You don't know me half as well as you think you do."

Miss Napier began to tidy up. "Make sure he rests for the next day or two, and I'll leave the salve and bag of herbs in case he becomes feverish again. Mahri, you know what to do?"

Mahri nodded.

"Good girl."

Miss Napier couldn't be induced to stay and have supper or to take money for her labor, though she happily accepted one of the fat salmons Dugald had caught. Dugald was to escort her home, but she lingered on the back porch to have a private word with Alex.

"My aunt gave me a message for you before I left," she said.

"Your aunt?"

"The Witch of Pannanich Wells."

She seemed reluctant to say more, so he said seriously, "What's the message, Miss Napier?"

She said with a laugh, "I'm not sure that I believe in this hocus-pocus."

"Please," he said simply.

She heaved a sigh. "'Break your journey in Aboyne,' that's what she said. 'Break your journey in Aboyne.'"

"A remarkable woman, Miss Napier," said Alex. "How did you come to know her?"

He looked at the cards in his hand and arranged them

in order. He and Mahri were in Gavin's room, keeping an eye on their patient. The Cardno ladies were downstairs, clearing up after they'd enjoyed Dugald's mouthwatering salmon, and Dugald was, as usual, prowling around outside.

Mahri threw down her cards. "I can't concentrate. What time is it?"

"A few minutes after ten. You haven't answered my question."

Her mind did a quick inventory. She couldn't see any potholes, so she replied naturally, "My parents rented a cottage one summer near Pannanich Wells so that my mother could take the waters. They're famous for their curative powers. That was when I met Miss Napier. She'd come to look after her aunt. The old lady was ailing, you see, and had taken to her bed."

"The Witch of Pannanich Wells?"

"Yes. There have been witches there for generations, if you can believe what the locals say."

"Oh, I believe them. Go on."

She gave him a sharp look. He was careful to keep his lips straight.

"I was just a child, but it seemed to me that the witch must be a hundred." Dimples flashed in her cheeks. "In fact, she was in her sixties. There was something seriously wrong with her; I can't remember what. At any rate, Miss Napier was an herbalist. No one can say what cured the witch, whether it was the waters or Miss Napier's skill, but the old lady is still going strong."

"Strange."

"What is?"

He shrugged. "Miss Napier is obviously well educated and gifted. Why would she want to bury herself in the middle of nowhere?"

"Because," she said sharply, "she was needed. She is her aunt's only living relative. Who else would look after the old lady if not her niece?"

"And when her aunt's health improved?"

"She'd fallen in love with Deeside and couldn't bear to leave it."

He looked at her over the cards splayed in his hand. "It sounds as though you knew her well."

She shrugged. "Not really. I met her through my mother. I'd practically forgotten about her until Gavin took a turn for the worse. I was at my wits' end. Then I remembered Miss Napier and her aunt. I wasn't even sure that they were still there."

He looked over at the bed. "Thank God they were."

"Yes."

"What about your mother? Was she cured?"

She shook her head. "My father was never happy with folk remedies. He said that the witch and her niece were charlatans. He put my mother under the care of what he called a real doctor, but the doctor said that he'd left it too late."

"That must have been hard on you. I know when my mother died, I was inconsolable."

Struck by his words, she gazed at him, then nodded slowly. "That's how I felt, too."

"You see, we're not so very different."

"In some things, perhaps."

"Family is important, wouldn't you agree?"

This was leading somewhere; she knew it was leading somewhere, and that put her on her guard. She picked up her cards and pretended to study them. "I suppose."

He sat back in his chair. "You suppose? It sounds to me as though your family meant a great deal to you."

Treading carefully between truth and fiction, she replied, "Well, they did, but they're all gone now." It was how she felt. "I won't even have a niece to keep me company in my old age."

Laughter gleamed briefly in his eyes. "I think I can say, without a doubt, that you're talking nonsense. You'll have your own husband and children. I guarantee it. I've kissed you, remember?"

Her eyes smoldered. "You can stop right there! Don't think I don't know what you're doing. You're a secret service agent, and this is an interrogation. You're trying to throw me off stride so that I'll tell you whatever you want to know."

"Now why would you think that? I paid you a compliment. I'm sorry it started off badly, but I can't remember when I enjoyed a kiss more."

Color bloomed in her cheeks. The memory of that kiss made her skin tingle. Then he had gone and spoiled it. Through her teeth, she said, "If this isn't an interrogation, what is it?"

"I'm merely trying to understand your character."

"I've told you all you need to know!"

"That piffle about a thwarted suitor attacking the queen to make you sorry for jilting him?"

"So, it *is* an interrogation! I knew it!"

There was no pretense at playing cards now. Though they kept their voices down, their glances clashed and held. He relented first.

"Listen to me," he said. "I know that you were a member of Demos." He was remembering his vision of Mahri accepting the dagger at the waterfall. "I don't think you knew what they were really up to, and when you found out, you were devastated. I understand your loyalty to them. They're the family you loved and lost."

He gave a half smile. "I've seen the kind of person you are. You don't desert your friends, no, not even when you don't owe them anything. I'm thinking of myself and Gavin. But misplaced loyalty is dangerous. Demos has tried to assassinate the queen. There will be other targets. Can you stand idly by and see innocent people die?"

As though she had not suffered torments deciding what to do for the best! She'd started off with good intentions, but now the whole enterprise was turning into a nightmare.

Her silence tried his patience. "How can you be loyal to that scum? Do you have any idea what they do? No? Let me tell you. Your precious Demos killed three good agents who happened to be my friends. They were blown up by a bomb. I barely escaped with my life and only because I was checking out another part of the building. Do you know what carnage a bomb can cause? It was worse than a slaughterhouse."

"Stop it!" She paused till she felt in control of her voice. "If you're trying to play on my sympathies, it won't work, because I can't tell you what I don't know. So stop badgering me. I—"

He broke in roughly, "I'm telling you because I want to help you. We're not enemies, Mahri; we're allies."

"Then let me go."

He shook his head. "I can't agree to that."

She got up, spine straight, chin tipped up. "So now we know where we stand. Good night, Mr. Hepburn."

He watched her as she walked to the door. "Who is the professor?" He called out and winced when she slammed the door shut behind her,

He'd made a bullocks of it. He didn't know what had come over him. He never spoke of the day his friends died. What the hell did he think he was doing?

It was her devotion to Demos that riled him, a group of lunatic subversives who cared nothing for justice or law, except as it served their own ends. Demos. Assassins. Murderers. Misfits. How had someone like Mahri come to be mixed up with that fraternity of traitors?

Mahri was too loyal and too honorable for her own good. She was also strong-willed, compassionate, selfless, and an accomplished liar.

He frowned. She would leave him the first chance she got. He wasn't going to allow that to happen. He wanted to keep her safe. He wanted to keep her . . .

That was the rub. He wanted to keep her.

Restless now, he got up and began to prowl. There was a movement at the bed. He crossed to it and felt his brother's brow. The fever was down a little, and Gavin's eyes fluttered open, then closed again against the light from the lamps.

"Thirsty," he whispered.

Alex reached for the cup of Miss Napier's tea and carefully dribbled a few drops past Gavin's dry lips.

"More," said Gavin, and Alex obliged.

Alex said, "As soon as you feel up to it, we're going to make a little trip. We're getting out of here, Gavin, just as soon as you . . ."

Gavin had slipped into sleep again.

Alex put down the cup. He felt overwhelmed and unequal to the task of keeping everyone safe. The witch had said that they should break their journey at Aboyne, but he didn't want to stop at Aboyne; he wanted to go to Aberdeen. Gavin had to see a doctor. He had colleagues in Aberdeen who could help them. They could telegraph Durward at Whitehall. The plan he had devised to get them away was risky but not impossible. The only fly in the ointment was Mahri. She would bolt the first chance she got.

He returned to the chair he had vacated and closed his eyes. He was a seer. That should give him some advantage. His mind emptied, and he kept it blank for a full minute, then slowly opened it to whatever occurred to him.

Apart from Mahri's dirk, the only connection he had to Demos was the letter opener that Ramsey had used to kill Dickens. The last time he'd seen the blond wig was at the White Stag just before Dugald clobbered him.

He got up and opened the wardrobe where he'd stowed his satchel. It took him only a moment to retrieve the letter opener. Miller's impression came to him, as it had the first time he'd palmed the letter opener, and he tried to shoo it away. It was Ramsey he wanted. But Miller wouldn't be shooed away. He burst into Alex's mind like a fireball. There was no picture this time, only a torrent of emotions and a jumble of words.

Alex opened his hand. His fingers were trembling. He didn't question how this vision had come to him or why it was different from the others. His gift was new to him, only a few months old. He had a lot to learn about seers and what they could and could not do. All he knew was that his friend Miller was in trouble.

The words. What were the words that came to him from Miller's mind? What were the words? There were no words now, only an awful silence.

Everything inside him, all his instincts, all his senses, were suddenly honed to a razor-sharp edge. It was now or never.

Fourteen

Alex had them all up at the crack of dawn. When Mahri came to herself, her first thought was that something had happened to Gavin during the night. Reaching for her wrap, she threw it over her shoulders and went tearing along the corridor to his room. When she saw that the bed was empty and unmade, her heart lurched.

She met Juliet and her mother at the top of the stairs. Like her, they had thrown a shawl over their nightclothes. They weren't sure what had wakened them, and they hovered, undecided, until a door opened downstairs and a masculine voice bellowed that they were to come, just as they were, and have breakfast.

Alex met them at the door. He looked very serious. "Come in, ladies," he said. "Breakfast is waiting. I'm sorry if I alarmed you, but time is of the essence. The sooner we leave this house, the easier I'll feel."

Mahri was struck by several things. Alex was clean-shaven, and he'd cut his hair. The same went for Dugald.

But it was the sight of Gavin that startled her. Though he was dressed in a crumpled suit, and his face was still very pale, he had obviously recovered some of his strength and all of his wits.

Miss Napier's credit could not have stood higher in Mahri's eyes.

"Alex tells me," he said, managing a painfully faint smile, "that we're taking the train out, and we're to leave almost at once."

"To where?" asked Juliet, clearly confused.

"To Aberdeen, of course," Gavin replied. "Where else does the train go? No need to look so glum, Ju. I'm going to travel in style."

Mahri sank into the nearest chair. Her eyes were steady on Alex's. She sensed the urgency in him vibrating beneath that calm exterior, and her heart began to race.

"What has happened?" she asked. "Who is leaving?"

"All of us."

He took his own place at the table and passed around a jug of milk. "Porridge," he said, as though they might not recognize what was in the bowl in front of them. "It's the only thing I know how to cook."

No one cared about breakfast. They were all looking expectantly at Alex.

He put down his spoon. "It's like this," he said. "Up till now our luck has held, but that could change. The flood helped us, but now that everything is almost back to normal, soldiers will be free to return to their duties. You see what this means? The search for Gavin and me—and you, too, Mahri—will begin in earnest. For my part, I'd rather fall into the hands of my colleagues in Aberdeen than be taken by Colonel Foster. Look what he has done to Gavin already."

Gavin cut in, "You're not thinking of giving yourself up, are you?"

Alex shook his head. "Not unless I'm ordered to by my section chief. Durward is a good man, a fair man. When we get to Aberdeen, I'll telegraph him and tell him all I know."

Juliet looked more confused than ever. "But Gavin isn't fit to travel. You heard Miss Napier. He is supposed to rest and—"

Gavin cut her off gently but firmly. "Alex knows what he is doing. I trust his instincts."

Mahri glanced at Alex then looked down at her bowl. She trusted Alex's instincts, too, but there was something he wasn't telling them, something critical. She glanced at Gavin. He was the exception. He looked as calm and determined as Alex. Yes, she thought, Alex had taken Gavin into his confidence. She didn't feel offended or left out. Alex Hepburn was a good, decent man. Everyone in the room knew that they could count on him.

Where did that leave her? Could she count on him, too?

What did it matter whether or not she could count on him? She trusted her own instincts. So what were her instincts telling her? The answer invaded her mind like a Highland mist creeping into a fortress. She couldn't keep it out. *Oh, no!* she told herself sternly. *You're not so stupid as to let one careless kiss addle your brains.*

She wasn't falling in love with him. When this hair-raising adventure was over and she had begun her new life, Alex Hepburn would fade from her memory.

Alex said, "You're very quiet, Mahri. What are you thinking?"

What was she thinking? She swallowed a mouthful of lumpy porridge as she tried to gather her thoughts. Finally, she said, "I was wondering why you did not bring this up last night. Why wait till now to tell us that we're all moving out this morning?"

A shadow seemed to pass over his eyes, but it quickly cleared. "I had to see whether Gavin was well enough to make the journey."

That did not satisfy Mahri, but before she had formed the words to question him, he said, "Now here's the plan."

* * *

They left the house in two groups. First went the Cardno ladies with Mahri posing as Juliet's cousin, not as a female, but dressed as a young gentleman in the garments of Juliet's late father. In Alex's opinion, it was an improvement on Thomas Gordon. Mahri was too well-rounded to sustain a boy's role. He could hardly believe how well she had fooled him—but not for long.

The second group was made up of Dugald and himself, dressed in the green tunics of the Queen's Royal Guard, and Gavin, in his rumpled suit, looking deliberately the worse for wear, who was posing as their prisoner.

The first test came as they made to cross the bridge into Ballater. There were two guards at each end, but there were also workmen there, repairing the damage of the flood to the bridge. Juliet played her part well—the consummate flirt. She was dressed for the part, too, in a fitted brown linen gown with a flared skirt and a hint of a bustle. Her mother was dressed in black and leaned heavily on Mahri's arm. When Mrs. Cardno stumbled and fell on her knees, the guards rushed to help Juliet and her cousin raise the old lady to her feet.

It was quite a performance.

"Now," said Alex softly.

They stepped onto the bridge, with Gavin giving the impression that he'd been soundly beaten. His chin hung on his chest. His feet dragged. One of the guards came to meet them, but half his attention was still on Juliet, who was blathering on about going to Aberdeen for the day to do a little shopping. In one hand, Mahri clutched a leather traveling bag. If asked, her story was that her holiday with her cousins was over, and she was going home to Aberdeen. Her other hand was in her pocket where her fingers were curled around the butt of her little revolver.

Dugald whispered from the side of his mouth, "Here comes trouble."

"Nonsense," replied Gavin. To Alex, he said, "Remember who our grandmother was. I've been practicing. There's nothing to it."

They stopped when the guard came up to them. Alex said, "We're taking this man by train to Aberdeen for questioning. Here are my orders signed by Colonel Foster."

The paper he presented was the official notepaper of the queen that Miller had filched for him. The orders and Foster's signature were a forgery, Alex's handiwork. It helped that Alex had an aiguillette denoting his rank as captain pinned to his left shoulder.

The guard scanned the document. When he looked up at Alex, there wasn't a hint of suspicion in his eyes. "You'll want someone to clear the way for you, Captain," he said.

"Thank you."

"Come this way. I'll take you to the station."

Gavin smirked. Alex frowned. This was too easy.

They crossed the bridge without a challenge and were soon trudging up Bridge Street toward the Station Square. It seemed to Alex that Gavin was leaning more heavily on him, and he was beginning to wonder whether he'd done the right thing by attempting to make for Aberdeen. It was the vision from Mungo that had galvanized him into action. *Now or never.* That was the message, but what had disturbed him more was the awful silence that followed.

He couldn't think about Mungo right now. He needed all his wits about him to pull this off.

Mahri and the Cardnos went to the ticket office to buy their tickets. After that, they were to wait in the station house to make sure things were running to plan before they boarded the train. The train was already getting up a head of steam. There were few passengers on the platform, but that would change when they stopped at every small village on the way. There were only five or six miles between stations, and by the time they reached Aberdeen, the train would be crowded with people.

The stationmaster came forward and looked askance at the soldiers and their prisoner. Alex gave him the forged orders, and once again they were allowed to pass. They chose the last carriage, for first-class passengers only, and would have barred anyone else from entering it, not that anyone tried. A carriage with armed soldiers guarding a possibly dangerous criminal was something everyone seemed determined to avoid.

They waited till they were alone, then Dugald removed Gavin's manacles while Alex did a quick inspection of the other two compartments that made up their carriage. His brain clicked automatically, noting doors, windows, and exits. As long as the train was moving, they could fend off an attack. If trouble came, it would be at one of the many stations between Ballater and Aberdeen.

He looked out the window to see Mahri and her companions boarding the carriage next to his own. There was no way to join them. Every carriage was a closed unit, completely isolated from its neighbors. Until the train reached Aboyne, there would be no communication between them.

"Break your journey in Aboyne."

Not if he could help it. They would be no better off than if they stayed in Ballater. He had to reach Aberdeen. Besides, many old women in Scotland claimed to be witches. Who was to say whether the Witch of Pannanich Wells was a genuine witch or just a superstitious old woman?

He should talk. Who was to say that he was a genuine seer?

The train jolted into motion. Shaking his head, smiling a little, he dropped into the nearest banquette and focused his thoughts on what might lie ahead.

Mahri appeared to be calm, but beneath that cool exterior, her nerves were stretched taut. She was thinking that this was too easy. The guard on the bridge was too compliant, and the same could be said of the stationmaster. They should have asked more questions, shown some reluctance to let them pass. It made her wonder whether they had walked into a trap.

She couldn't dwell on her worries for long, because Juliet and her mother kept drawing her into their conversation. They talked of the dress shops in Aberdeen, the beautiful scenery they were passing through, and shook their heads over the flooded fields and the hardships that that would bring to the farmers and their families when winter set in. At every station, however, as more passengers got on the train, the tension in their small compartment was almost palpable.

After the last stop before Aboyne, the idle chatter died away. Mahri was rehearsing in her mind the next part of Alex's plan. He didn't want to arrive in Aberdeen in uniform. He wanted to melt into the crowd as quickly as possible, just in case something went wrong. That made a change of clothes necessary, and she had them right there in her leather traveling bag, as well as supplies Miss Napier had left to treat Gavin.

Aboyne came too soon for her liking, when she was still rehearsing what everyone was supposed to do. Metal screeched on metal, the engine belched a cloud of steam, and doors were flung open even before the train had come to a stop.

"Ready, Mother?" said Juliet.

The old lady's eyes held a feverish sparkle. "The last time I felt this ready was the day I married your father."

Juliet winked at Mahri. "I don't think I want to hear any more in that vein."

Mahri smiled, but her eyes were trained on the platform outside their window. She saw Alex stepping down from the carriage. Hawkers were coming alongside the train, selling newspapers from Aberdeen and hot buns and pies from local bakeries. Alex bought a newspaper and appeared to scan the front page. This was their cue to get going.

Mahri passed the traveling bag to Juliet and opened the carriage door. Once on the platform, in true gentlemanly fashion, she helped each lady to descend. They were taking a little walk to stretch their legs, or so they hoped it would appear to anyone who was watching.

When they came level with Alex, Juliet bent down to remove a piece of grit from her shoe. When she straightened, she was no longer carrying the bag. Mrs. Cardno had spread her voluminous skirts to conceal the transfer. It was Mahri's job to act as lookout.

"It's done," said Juliet in Mahri's ear. "Alex has the bag."

Mahri nodded absently. Her mind worked the same way as Alex's, and she was busily sorting and assessing the people milling around on the platform. They all seemed innocent enough. All the same, as she hoisted herself into the carriage, she surreptitiously looked over her shoulder.

And she froze. Some tardy passengers, well-dressed gentlemen, one in a long brown coat, were converging upon the last carriage on the train, Alex's carriage. She recognized one of them, though he wouldn't have recognized her. It was Murray, her father's henchman.

It took her only a split second to decide what to do. She jumped onto the platform and slammed the carriage door behind her.

John Murray, the man in the long brown coat, had been the first passenger to alight from his carriage. Close behind him were three companions, crack shots all, who fanned out as he began to walk slowly to the end of the train. He thought he had everything figured out. Alex Hepburn was posing as a soldier. The young man whom he'd half dragged, half carried into the station at Ballater must be the girl, and the other man, also posing as a soldier, had to be Hepburn's companion, whom Miller had referred to as "No Name." They should have been actors, they were so convincing.

Murray hadn't expected Hepburn to make his move so soon. Miller had told him, under torture, about the uniforms and the letter giving Hepburn the authority to commandeer a carriage on the train, but he had sworn that he did not know where Hepburn was or when he intended to leave. It was as well for him, John Murray, that he never relaxed his vigilance, or he might have missed Hepburn altogether.

It wasn't Hepburn he wanted, of course; it was the girl. She was worth a lot of money to him alive. But he didn't underestimate Hepburn. He would try to protect her. The girl was his passport to clearing his name. Whether she was a willing or an unwilling hostage made no difference. She knew too much. Hepburn had to be stopped before he handed her over to the authorities. Once the girl was back with her father, Murray's job would be over, and he would walk away a much richer man.

He was a cautious man. Though he'd had a clear shot at Hepburn in Ballater, he had decided that soldiers from the barracks would be swarming all over the place if they heard the shot. He'd have a much better chance of bringing down his quarry in this quiet country town.

The train was ready to move. He nodded to his best marksman, the signal to enter the carriage and deal with Hepburn and Mr. No Name. He would follow closely and deal with the girl.

"Stand where you are, or I'll pull the trigger."

Murray turned swiftly to see a young man with a revolver in his hand, pointing it straight at him. Everything clicked into place in an inkling of a moment. "Get her," he shouted. "That's the girl."

The gun wobbled as he knew it would. "There are four of us," he said pleasantly, "and only one of you. Who will you shoot first?"

"Why you, of course," she said, and she pulled the trigger.

The whistle blew, and steam belched from the engine, covering the report of the gunshot. The only fatality was Murray's hat. It went flying from his head onto the track. Guns drawn, the men approached her slowly. She was completely cut off.

* * *

Alex dug into the traveling bag and produced dressings and salve for Gavin's wound as well as a bottle of Pannanich water.

"I'm not drinking that slop," Gavin protested when Alex thrust the bottle into his hand. "Who knows what's in it?"

"I think the lad is getting better," said Dugald with a grin. He was rummaging in the bag, laying out each article of clothing as he unpacked it.

When the train jolted into motion, Alex folded himself into the well-upholstered banquette. Gavin was stretched out on the other side, using the banquette as a bed.

"Well," said Alex, "I think that went off rather—"

He sat bolt upright. Outside the window, he saw the figure of Mahri in her man's clothes, making for the exit. She wasn't alone. Accompanying her were three well-dressed youngish gentlemen.

A red mist swam before his eyes. She'd never had any intention of going with him. She'd lulled him into thinking that she was docile, when all the time she was plotting how she could escape. She had betrayed him. Somehow, she'd got word to her friends that they'd be on the train.

He jumped to his feet at the precise moment that a shot plowed into the banquette he'd been reclining against. A man was framed in the doorway. Before the thug could fire again, Alex slammed his forearm down on the man's wrist, and the gun went slithering into the corridor.

Time receded. Alex was no longer the Alex Hepburn who sat behind a desk in Whitehall, breaking codes no one else could break. He was a covert field agent in Her Majesty's Secret Service with authority to kill.

They came at each other again. There was nothing Dugald or Gavin could do to help, because Alex and his assailant were in the small corridor that joined the three compartments that made up the carriage, and Alex had his back to them. He brought up his knee like a battering ram, aiming for the man's stomach. The man grunted, retreated, then lunged toward Alex, swiping at his throat with the back of his hand. Alex caught the outstretched arm by the elbow and wrenched it as high as it would go. There was a sickening crunch, and the man roared in anger and pain.

Alex relaxed his guard and paid for it dearly. A knife appeared in the man's other hand and grazed the fleshy part of Alex's shoulder. Alex lashed out his right foot, catching his assailant on the knee. They both went down, grappling for the knife. A fist crashed into Alex's jaw, stunning him. Remembering his training, he rolled from that flashing blade, but he couldn't roll far in the confines of that narrow corridor.

He was pulling himself into an empty compartment when his attacker loomed over him, ready to plunge the knife into his chest. A triumphant smile was etched on his face. That smile brought Alex to his senses. He wasn't ready to die yet. As the knife plunged down, he bent his knees and smashed his booted feet into his attacker's chest. The man reeled back against the carriage door. Alex was on him in an instant. He shoved the door wide and shouldered the man out onto the track.

When he turned back, both Gavin and Dugald were standing there gaping. He was breathing hard. When he had caught his breath, he said, "The fall won't kill him. I can run faster than this train is moving." He took another breath. "I have to go back."

"Go back for what?" Dugald demanded, angry and baffled at the same time.

There wasn't time to explain, and Alex didn't want Dugald to know that Mahri had left the train. He would insist on going with him.

"There was trouble at the station," he said. "Stick to our plan, and if we don't meet up in Aberdeen, look for me in Feughside."

He opened the carriage door, waited until the train was passing a bank of broom, and jumped. His teeth jarred, the wind was knocked out of him, but there were no bones broken. When he got to his feet, he dusted himself off. He was still wearing the uniform of the Queen's Guard.

"Break your journey in Aboyne."

The old witch must be laughing her head off.

Fifteen

She'd taken a brutal knock on the head, and she wakened, disoriented and nauseated, to find that she was slung over the back of a horse with her hands and legs tied to the saddle. Logical thought came back slowly. She remembered the train, the platform at Aboyne, her shock of recognition when she caught sight of Murray. She'd taken a lightning impression of his accomplices and knew at once that these men were not members of the Demos she knew. Like Murray, they were hard-faced, sharp-edged mercenaries. Dear God, how far had her father sunk?

She thought of Alex, and panic swelled in her chest till she could hardly breathe. She remembered the shot she'd heard coming from his carriage. The thought that they might have killed him was too horrible to be borne. She wouldn't believe it. She refused to believe it. It would take more than these hard-faced louts to get the better of him. *Alex is alive.* She repeated the words over and over like a litany. Alex was alive, and he would come for her.

In the meantime, all she could do was take the measure

of the men who had abducted her so that she could even the odds when the time came. No sooner had the thought occurred to her than she began to question her sanity. Who did she think she was fooling? She was defenseless, a sitting duck, making grandiose plans she hadn't a hope of carrying out. At the station, she'd made a muck of things. She could have shot one of them, maybe two, but people got in her way—passengers, vendors, and newspaper boys—and she wouldn't risk hitting innocent people, so she'd taken to her heels with some wild idea of drawing them off to save her friends.

She'd chanced one look back and had seen one of the thugs enter Alex's carriage. When she'd heard the shot, she'd turned back. That was when Murray had felled her with a mighty blow to the side of the head.

She blinked rapidly to clear the haze from her eyes. When the haze did not clear, it came to her that it was, in fact, one of those capricious Highland mists that was rising from the ground and draping everything in its way in a translucent shroud.

No wonder their progress was slow. The horses were being kept to a walk. How many horses? How many riders? She strained to hear every sound and counted three mounted men. At the station, she'd counted four men. One was missing. Her spirits soared. One down, three to go. This was Alex's doing. She held on to that thought. Alex was alive. He was coming for her.

Over the next hour, she learned a lot more. They were traveling west, going back toward Ballater. She knew what that meant. Murray was taking her back to her father. It gave her a small advantage. Murray might hurt her, but he would not kill her. If he did, he wouldn't earn his bounty.

Every so often, they would stop and take cover in the trees. She heard other riders pass by, soldiers or smugglers who swore copiously as they came to grief when they inadvertently strayed from the road. At this point, Murray gagged her, fearing, she supposed, that she would cry out and alert soldiers to their presence. She wouldn't have, of course. She feared the soldiers almost as much as she feared Murray and his cutthroats, not for herself, but for Alex.

One of her abductors mentioned the name Mungo Miller, and the others sniggered, as though it were a private joke. For the most part, however, they were silent, silent and watchful.

They veered off the road and followed a dirt track that led down to the river. A hovel appeared out of the mist. On closer inspection, she saw that it was an abandoned cottage that the storm had battered so badly that half the roof had caved in and doors and windows had blown out. Here they halted. Her bonds were untied, and rough hands dragged her off the horse. Her legs were so stiff that they buckled under her, and she fell on her knees. Her muffled cry of pain was greeted with raucous laughter and lewd threats from one of her captors about what they would do to her if she gave them trouble.

"Shut your mouths," Murray hissed to his men. "Do you want the soldiers to hear us?" He hauled Mahri to her feet. "Leave the gag," he warned when she made to tear it off.

A shove sent her stumbling to the hole where the door should have been. Though it was dim inside that hovel, the mist had been kept at bay by the cross breeze that whistled through the windows, so that she could see her captors more clearly. She wished the breeze could have done something about the water that lapped at her feet.

Only two of the men had entered the cottage with her, Murray and a younger, dark-skinned, dark-haired man who could have passed for a gypsy. She thought of Murray as a stern-faced, thin-lipped schoolmaster, and the third man, whom she assumed was taking care of the horses or keeping watch, made her think of a ticking bomb. He didn't say much, but his eyes spoke volumes.

"Sit," said Murray, pointing to a rickety chair.

When she obeyed, the gypsy got behind her and tied

her to the chair with a length of rope. He could have made
it tighter, more unpleasant, and she flashed him a grateful look. When he leered suggestively, she quickly looked
away.

The reason they had stopped soon became clear. They
hadn't chosen this hovel at random. They'd stowed a box
with fresh clothes to change their appearance. She could
hear Murray and the gypsy talking in an alcove that served
as a bedroom. They were worried about a man called
Frenchie. If he didn't catch up to them soon, Murray said,
one of them would have to go back to find out what had
happened at the station. But whether Frenchie turned up or
not, as soon as it was dark, the rest of them would press on
to Ballater with the girl.

It took a moment before the full import of his words
registered. So she was right. One of Murray's men was
missing. He had to be the man who entered Alex's carriage.
If she hadn't been gagged, her smile would have split her
face.

She looked up to find the gypsy hovering over her. Her
throat went dry. One by one, he began to undo the buttons
on her shirt. She looked frantically for Murray, but he was
still in the other room.

The gypsy's hand slipped inside her shirt. The binder
that she'd used to flatten her breasts had slipped to her waist
so that his hand touched bare skin. He caressed the fullness
of one breast, then the other. Fear raced along her spine and
edged her toward panic. She didn't think about what she was
doing, didn't care about being tied to a chair. She jumped
to her feet. Crouched over, with head down, she charged,
and they both went down in a jumble of arms and legs. The
chair suffered the most. It fell to pieces, leaving Mahri free
to make a dash for it. She tore off her gag and ran.

Murray caught her before she had taken more than a few
steps along the track. He grabbed her by the hair, dragged
her head back, and his hand lashed across her face, sending
her to her knees. He hauled her to her feet again.

Teeth gritted, he said, "Little girls who misbehave must be taught a lesson."

He thought she was at fault. She tried to explain, but he wouldn't listen. He hauled her to the side of the cottage, to where there was a trapdoor. He removed the bar and kicked the door open.

"Get in," he ordered in the same hard voice. "I'm warning you, if I hear one cheep out of you, I'll turn you over to Archie. He likes playing with little girls."

The gypsy—Archie?—had come out of the cottage, and he strolled toward them. "If we have time to waste," he said, "why don't we have a little fun—"

Murray felled him with one blow. "Didn't I warn you not to handle the merchandise? You never could keep your hands to yourself. One more trick like that, and you'll be in the root cellar and not the girl. We're being paid to bring her to her father intact. Have you got that?"

The gypsy said something coarse under his breath, but he pulled himself to his feet and stumbled back to the cottage.

"Move!" Murray ordered.

Mahri looked down into what seemed like a bottomless pit. The cellar was in complete darkness. What was worse was the stench. She thought she might be sick. She glanced at Murray. There was no relenting in that hard face.

She stepped onto the first stone step and hesitated. One shove from Murray made her lose her balance. She sat down with a thud, and her feet went sliding into an unspeakable midden of garbage and rotting vegetables. She heard the door slam and the bar thud into place.

Heaving, straining away from that veritable cesspool, she hoisted her bottom up to the next step. Sludge still lapped at her feet. She dug in her heels and managed, by sheer force of will, to lever herself higher. She stopped on the fourth step up. There was nowhere else to go. There was no room to stand unless the trapdoor was opened.

She crouched there, shivering, hugging herself with her

arms, devising all kinds of deaths for Murray and his thugs, each one more gory than the last.

He'd been right about the man he'd thrown from the train. The fall hadn't killed him, but he was hurt. He was lumbering through the underbrush like a wounded bear. Alex didn't have to see him to know where he was. All he had to do was follow the sound of his progress.

Alex dropped down behind an uprooted fir tree when his quarry stopped, either to get his bearings or because he was cautious, making sure that no one was following him. The mist was a godsend, obscuring him from the man he stalked as well as concealing them both from any patrol they were likely to encounter. There were none, as far as Alex could tell. Only smugglers.

Why wouldn't the man move? He'd considered breaking his fingers one by one until he told him where his friends had taken Mahri, but if Demos had sent him, he wouldn't frighten easily. Besides, his quarry knew where he was going. They were both on foot, and by his reckoning, they'd come about three miles. Mahri had to be close by.

He was trying to give her the benefit of the doubt, trying to convince himself that she hadn't left him of her own free will, but at the back of his mind he was remembering that she had never concealed her intention of escaping him the first chance she got.

There was more to it than that. She'd had her revolver with her. She could have got off a shot if only to warn him. Maybe she hadn't known about the thug he was following, the thug who had tried to kill him, but she'd known something was afoot. With his own eyes, he'd watched her leave the station with her comrades-in-arms.

Had she been part of the plot to assassinate the queen? Was that why Demos was after her, not to punish her but to rescue her? Had he allowed himself, once again, to be taken in by a pretty face? When all was said and done, his record with women was hardly stellar.

He ground his teeth together. When he caught up with her, there would be no more deferring to his code of honor. He would get to the truth, even if he had to beat it out of her.

When he heard the soft whinny of horses, he melted into the shadows, thinking that it might be a patrol. The man from the train must have heard it, too, but it didn't seem to alarm him. They'd come to a small clearing. Ahead of them, Alex could just make out a derelict building. On his left, tied to a fence pole, and the only part of a fence left standing after the flood, were three horses, maybe four.

The man stepped into the clearing. Revolver in hand, Alex tensed to rush the building. Suddenly, all hell broke loose. A volley of shots came from behind him. They whistled through the air, and the man crossing the clearing dropped like a stone. Alex dived for the nearest hedge and flattened himself on the ground.

"We got one of them, sir," a voice shouted.

More shots followed and were returned by those inside the house, then everything went quiet.

Soldiers were taking cover behind trees and anything else they could find as they advanced on the ruin. Alex slipped in beside them. He was in uniform and hoped that in the half-light, they would take him for one of their own.

Two soldiers burst into the cottage. Alex was hard on their heels. There was no one there. He looked at the broken chair, the length of rope, a discarded cravat, and a man's coat flung carelessly over a sideboard. A brown coat, he noted.

One of the soldiers ran to the door. "Sir, they're not here. They must have gone out the back."

"After them! They can't go far."

Alex melted into the gloom of a small alcove bedroom. Mahri's essence seemed to fill his nostrils, his mouth, his head. He sensed her presence, but he couldn't deny what his eyes told him. There was no one there.

Horses' hooves pounded outside as the patrol went in pursuit. He waited a moment then slipped soundlessly outside. There wasn't a uniform in sight, not even a sentinel to guard the horses that were tied to the fence rail. It was no bloody wonder that the British Army lurched from one disaster to another.

But where was Mahri? Fear began to steal into his mind. He'd sensed her presence, could still sense it, but was she alive or— He couldn't complete the thought. Frantic now, he made a circuit of the house and came upon the root cellar. He was afraid to lift the trapdoor, afraid of what he would find. She must have heard the shots going off. Why hadn't she called out?

His fingers shook as he threw back the door. In the next instant, he was bowled over by a hissing, biting, scratching wildcat.

He rolled with her on the ground. "You little spitfire!" he bit out. "You didn't think I'd catch up with you, did you?"

Her fist landed on his chin and brought tears to his eyes. Heaving, kicking, she strained away from him. He rolled on top of her and caught her wrist just before she could rake his face with her nails.

"If you don't behave yourself," he said tersely, "I'll be forced to tie you up and gag you."

She stopped struggling. "Alex, is it you?"

"Who else would it be?" He was still angry, still unsure of her.

"Then get off me, you big lump. I can hardly breathe!"

He helped her to her feet. The stench clinging to her clothes made him want to gag. "Why in blazes did you hide in the root cellar?" he demanded.

"I didn't hide. They put me there." She removed the coat. "I can't wear this."

Her coat was drenched in the stench of rotting vegetables and only God knew what else. He took it from her and threw it away. "They put you there? Don't lie, Mahri. You're adept at landing on your feet when everyone around you is toppling like pawns. What were you going to do, creep away after the soldiers were gone? Did you think even once of the people you'd left in the train? I suppose you'll tell me that you would have found a way to catch up with us?"

She didn't seem to understand the trouble she was in. "Well, of course I would. Is everyone all right?"

"As happy as harpies!" he replied savagely. Grasping her wrist, he dragged her into the cottage.

"We haven't got time for this," she protested. "Murray might come back at any moment. So might the soldiers."

"Who is Murray?"

"He was the leader." She added quickly, "I heard someone say his name."

Alex picked up the brown coat. The left pocket was bulging. He removed a fat purse, transferred it to his own pocket, then wrapped Mahri in the coat. "Now we can leave," he said. But there were still a lot of questions he wanted answers to.

When they passed the body of the man who had been shot, he turned her face into his shoulder. There was something odd going on here. Those soldiers had known about the hovel. They hadn't been lying in wait, exactly, but they'd been close enough to take Mahri's abductors by surprise. They hadn't told the man he was following to halt or surrender. They'd opened fire and shot anything that moved.

What was he missing?

The noise of gunfire had frightened the horses. They were pulling on their tethers, rearing and stamping in an effort to get away. He untied two of them and whacked them on the rear end to hasten their flight.

When he and Mahri were mounted on the other two, he kept the horses to a walk and his eyes peeled. The short hairs on this neck began to rise, and he whipped his head round to look back at the cottage. A shadow moved within shadows. He heard the creak of the door to the cellar as it was opened.

"Murray!" Mahri breathed out.

Alex answered softly, "Let's move."

He touched his heels to his mount's sides and broke into a canter. Mahri followed him.

Sixteen

❧

All she had to do was follow him.

Mahri screwed her eyes closed then opened them wide in an effort to stay awake. She didn't know how long they'd been traveling, but she thought it must be for hours. Though the light was fading, there was no mist here to obscure her vision. Not that there was much to see—no mountains, no castles—only rolling hills and various cottages they passed on the way. Evidently, they'd moved well out of the river's reach, because there was little sign of flood damage here.

When she felt herself slip from the saddle, she quickly righted herself. She wasn't going to let Mr. Secret Service Agent know that she was just about all in. He'd hardly said two words to her since they'd set out. *Keep up* seemed to be the only words in his vocabulary. He wouldn't believe a word she told him, and that made her spitting mad. After all she'd done to keep them all safe, a few words of praise wouldn't have come amiss.

There was another reason for her bout of misery. She still stank of the filth in the root cellar. The smell clung to her clothes, her skin, her hair. Why couldn't he see her, just once, all prettied up and at her best? She sniffed back a snort. It wouldn't make a bit of difference, except to her vanity. According to Juliet, though Alex Hepburn could have his pick of the beautiful and accomplished women he met in the salons of London, his heart still belonged to Ariel.

He had a heart? No one would have believed it if they could see how he maltreated her.

She was falling asleep again. *Stay awake. Don't complain. He'll only tell you to keep up in that obnoxiously superior voice of his.*

𝔄lex looked back to assess how she was coping. She was doing just fine. He didn't know another female who could have lasted this long. He'd set a grueling pace. He didn't expect to meet many patrols so far from Balmoral, but Demos's agents were another matter. They wanted Mahri, either to rescue her or to punish her for breaking ranks. Which was it? The question gnawed at his mind, making him by turns suspicious of her and impatient with himself.

He heard her muttering to herself.

"What is it now?" he asked.

"What is it now?" she mimicked. She sounded tearful. "I'll tell you what it is. My last meal was a bowl of lumpy porridge. I've been set upon by thugs, chased by soldiers, and captured and carried off by an agent of Her Majesty's Secret Service. And he asks, 'What is it now?'"

She reined in and started to dismount, all the while muttering to herself.

"What do you think you're doing?"

She bawled the words. "I have to use the facilities!"

"The what?" His brow cleared. "Oh, I see."

They'd stopped at a wooden bridge with a stream rushing over rocks beneath it.

He took the reins of her horse. "Don't try any tricks," he

warned. "We're in my neck of the woods now, and I know every inch of it."

He could hear her muttering to herself as she climbed down the incline to the underside of the bridge. A moment later, she gave a startled shriek.

His heart lurched. Quickly tethering the horses to a rail on the bridge, he leaped down the bank. Mahri was doing a little dance, hopping from foot to foot, her hands fluttering as she swiped at her shirt and trousers. Her coat was draped over a bush. She wasn't in danger as far as he could tell.

Because she had frightened him, his voice was harsh. "What in Hades is the matter with you?"

"Maggots!" she cried. "My clothes are teeming with them. Ugh!"

"Maggots?" Hands on hips, he frowned down at her. "Is that all?"

His words had no effect on the horror that seemed to grip her, an irrational horror, in his opinion. After all she'd come through, how could a few harmless maggots bring on this fit of feminine vapors?

With quick, impatient movements, she pulled off her shoes, then her stockings, and went tearing into the water. He watched as she submerged herself time after time, as though her clothes were on fire.

"Mahri!" he said sternly, hoping that the tone of his voice would bring her to her senses. "You're a grown woman. Act like one."

She gasped, spluttered, and emerged from the water, then advanced toward him. He couldn't help noticing that her white shirt was open to the waist, revealing the creamy swell of her breasts. He was fascinated by the way her hard, plump nipples thrust against her shirt. Her waist was no bigger than a man's hand span, and her dripping-wet trousers sheathed her hips and legs.

His mouth went dry, and the inevitable happened. His groin tightened painfully against the fabric of his trousers.

He was exhausted; every muscle in his body ached; he'd

had a hellish day. How could he possibly have these carnal fantasies about a woman who showed her disdain for him in every possible way? He must be insane. He was a rational man, he told himself, but the hardness in his groin was telling him how primitive he really was.

A word penetrated the fog in his brain. "What did you say?"

Eyes spitting fire, she stared doggedly into his face. "We can't all be like Ariel," she flung at him, "with never a hair out of place. I don't suppose she ever saw a maggot in her life."

"Ariel?" he replied, as though he'd never heard the name before. Those creamy breasts were jiggling with every angry breath she took. He fisted his hands to make sure that he didn't reach for her. "What has Ariel to do with anything?"

She took a step away from him, then swung back to face him. "You expect every woman to be like her. Oh, Juliet told me all about her, how she was picture-book perfect and always immaculately dressed. Well, some of us are not so lucky. We get abducted and locked up in maggot-infested cellars, then some boor makes fun of us." The spate of words dried up. Then, squinting up at him: "Are you laughing at me?"

"No. I swear it." His nose wrinkled. "You smell as though you'd bathed in a sewer."

Her sense of injury boiled over, and she gave him a mighty shove. He teetered on the edge of a rock but could not find his balance and fell heavily on his rear end. Mahri took off like a rocket.

"Mahri! Get back here!" he bellowed.

She ran like a frightened deer, jumping over small obstacles in her way. She was too angry to think clearly about where she was going or what she would do if she managed to outrun him. She hated him so much in that moment that she never wanted to see his arrogant face again.

She leaped onto a spur of rock, and something cold and squiggly moved beneath her bare foot. She leaped off that rock as fast as she'd leaped onto it. An adder raised its head and uncoiled its sinuous, twitching body. It was ready to strike. Slowly, carefully, she eased away from it, then made a sudden feint to the left. When the adder struck, she pounced and seized it by the neck. Alex caught up to her just in time to see her throw the creature into a clump of heather well off the track.

"Good God," he said, awed. "Who taught you that trick?"

"My brother," she said simply.

"Did it bite you?"

"I don't think so. It wasn't expecting to be stepped on."

"Let me see." Adder bites could be fatal. He pushed the fearful thought from him and went down on one knee. He lifted one foot and gently probed with his fingers. "Tell me if it hurts," he said.

It didn't hurt. It made her ache. It made her dizzy. It made her want to weep. She felt herself melting and put a hand on his shoulder to steady herself. He was the most perverse man she had ever encountered, and she did not know why his good opinion should matter to her, but it did.

"It doesn't hurt," she said, injecting some starch into her voice. As her sense of ill-usage receded, she began to take stock of her position. She didn't know where she was or where to turn for help. A woman on her own with no money, no clothes except for the stinking weeds she was wearing was bound to attract attention. She had to stay with him. She had no choice.

"Give me your other foot."

His voice sounded strange to her ears, hoarse, as though he were coming down with a cold.

"No," she said, "that wasn't the foot that stepped on the adder."

She yelped when he gave a hoot of laughter and suddenly scooped her into his arms. "You're fearless with poisonous snakes," he said, "but turn into jelly over a few paltry maggots. Explain it to me."

"There's no explaining it," she said crossly. "Some people are afraid of spiders. I'm afraid of maggots. They make my skin crawl. Aren't you afraid of anything?"

His answer was instantaneous. "I'm afraid of innocent young women who think they can take me in with their winsome ways. They never do, you know."

She thought, for a moment, that he was paying her a compliment. Realizing her mistake, she said caustically, "You have a high opinion of yourself. No female in her right mind would try to win you over. You're as winsome as a block of marble. Well? What do we do now? I'm soaked to the skin, and you're not much better off than I am. We need to find shelter. We need to dry off our clothes. I'm hungry, but more than that, I'm tired, so tired that I'd be happy to present myself at the first tollbooth we come to and beg them to lock me up. At least they would give me a bed."

"What we're going to do," he said, "is stop at the first inn we come to, rest, clean up, eat, and go on from there."

"And who is going to pay the shot?"

"Why, I am, Mahri, with the fat purse I found in the pocket of your coat. You know, the coat that one of Murray's people left in that hovel?"

Her emotions had worn themselves out, and she felt resigned, or as resigned as anyone could be under the circumstances. She was in dire straits, but she wasn't alone. The man who held her so confidently as he struck out along the track made her feel safe and protected. The warmth of his body took the chill from her own frozen limbs. Maybe she was clinging a little too desperately, but she needed that warmth. She needed his strength.

She restrained a sigh. If only he weren't so stubborn and pigheaded, she wouldn't have run from him and wouldn't need to be carried.

"Thank you," she said when he helped her into the brown coat once more. "It was good of you to carry me. I don't think I could have walked barefoot along a track where adders lie in wait."

He hoisted her into the saddle. Looking up, he said, "If you weren't so stubborn and pigheaded, there would be no need to carry you. Don't you know that adder bites can be fatal?"

There was a moment of silence, then Mahri chuckled. The chuckle swelled and she gurgled with laughter. "Stubborn and pigheaded," she got out. "Oh, that's rich."

Alex was struck with the thought that she didn't laugh nearly enough to suit him. He experienced an odd softening in his midsection. Disregarding it, he said with a frown, "If you're over that bout of insanity, I suggest we get moving."

Seems like déjà vu," Alex said.

They were in an upstairs bedchamber that overlooked the stables in the Feughside Hotel. Mahri had bathed and washed her hair, and the fragrance that perfumed her skin had wafted to every corner in the room.

Alex was well aware of why she'd doused herself in the bottle of lavender water she'd found on the washstand. Now she smelled as fresh as a spring morning.

He set down the tray he was carrying, a late-night supper of cold meats, plenty of fresh bread and butter, and a rhubarb pie.

"Déjà vu?" Mahri shook her head.

She was kneeling in front of the fire, fluffing out her hair to dry it. Alex couldn't tear his eyes away. Tiny curls of glossy dark hair framed a face that had the purity and delicacy of a cameo brooch. She looked fragile, but he knew how misleading her looks were. Though she could not match him in strength, she was as slippery and agile as the adder she had stepped on.

And he, and only he, was going to tame her to his hand.

Where had that insane thought come from?

Frowning, he tore his eyes away and concentrated on dividing their meal onto two plates. He gave one to her with only a fork to go with it.

"It's not the same at all," she said. "This is luxury beyond imagining."

And it was. Though the room was small, it was furnished with good pieces, a fire had been lit to take the chill off the air, fresh clothes had been found for them and their ruined garments taken away to be burned, and finally, the landlady had provided this handsome supper to fill their empty stomachs.

Mahri reached for a chicken drumstick and daintily bit into it. She didn't know what story Alex had fabricated to explain their situation, but she heartily approved. She was now clothed in a woman's fine lawn nightgown and a warm wrap to go over it. Laid out on the chair was a set of woman's clothes to tide her over till they reached the next stop on their journey, all courtesy of their landlady, who said that the garments were left behind by careless guests who had never returned to claim them.

Alex was rigged out in a new set of clothes, too. While she had languished in luxury, he'd been out and about, taking care of the horses, conferring with the landlord, giving her time to have her bath in private. His plum-colored coat and skintight trousers were more suited to a dandy than a secret service agent. She swallowed a giggle.

He'd forced her to drink a small glass of whiskey when they first arrived, to stave off the interminable bouts of shivering that had taken hold of her. Maybe that was why she wanted to giggle.

"This is an out-of-the-way place," she said, "yet it's crowded with guests. Why is that?"

"They've come for the local games, you know, athletes competing for a place in the Braemar Gathering."

"What if someone recognizes you?"

He flashed her a smile. "I don't have the kind of face that people remember. Besides, I haven't been in Feughside in years. I left to go to school and rarely came back."

She wasn't going to tell him that he had the kind of face a *woman* would remember—not handsome exactly, but with straight dark brows, intelligent blue eyes that missed nothing, and a strong mouth and chin. He would think she was using her so-called winsome ways to take him in. As though she would! As though she could! This man was impervious to females.

"Stop frowning," he said, "and eat your dinner."

She picked up a drumstick and made a show of eating it.

Seventeen

❧

A rap on the door announced the maid with a pot of tea. She was very young, with very pink cheeks, and could hardly raise her eyes to acknowledge their presence until Alex pressed a coin into her hand. Then she wished them a happy life together, bobbed a curtsy, and bolted from the room.

Mahri didn't want to giggle now. "What," she said ominously, "have you told the landlord and his wife about us?"

He answered casually, "That we're newlyweds. It was the only way I could be sure of getting a room. You saw their expressions when they first saw us. We looked like a couple of tramps."

"You could have told them that we are brother and sister."

"That wouldn't do. They would have turned us away. On the other hand, everyone wants newlyweds to have a bed on their first night of marriage, especially after they've been set upon by brigands and robbed of all their worldly goods. That's what I told them, by the way."

"What about your fat purse?"

"Now that was a stroke of genius on my part. I told them that the brigands missed it because it was hidden in an intimate item of my wife's clothing. Newlyweds and a fat purse—what could be more appealing to a hardheaded, romantic Scot?"

The more she frowned, the more he grinned.

She bit ferociously into a crust of bread and chewed on it as she thought things through. Finally, she said, "I prefer to have a room of my own."

"Don't we all? But that wouldn't suit in our case. If there is trouble—and I'm not expecting any—I want you close by. I don't want to risk life and limb chasing you down again."

She took that to mean that he was afraid she might try to run away. She wouldn't, of course. For one thing, she didn't know the area, and she didn't know what might be waiting for her around the next corner. For another, she wanted to find out what had happened to Dugald and the others. Alex seemed confident that they'd got safely away, and they'd meet up at his place. She couldn't leave till she knew every-one was all right.

So they had to share this small room, because he didn't trust her. "There is only one bed," she pointed out.

He cut into a piece of ham and chewed on it before answering her. "True, but it's large enough for two people."

Her nostrils quivered. "Never, in my whole life, have I shared my bed with a man."

One corner of his mouth curled up. "As I am well aware."

It seemed to her that he was referring to the punitive kiss he'd forced on her in the Cardnos' kitchen. She searched her mind for a suitable retort. Nothing came to her, so she said truculently, "Pass me my knife. I want to cut up this slice of ham."

"Mahri," he said shaking his head, "in your hands, a dinner knife is a lethal weapon. I'll cut your meat for you."

That was the final insult. She surged to her knees. "You stupid, muddle-headed imbecile!" she railed. "You're clever with codes and numbers, so I've heard, but I can't see it. Secret service agent?" she scoffed. "A plank of wood could work things out better than you. As I tried to tell you, I didn't leave willingly with Murray. I hoped to draw him off so that the rest of you could get away. I couldn't empty my revolver because I might have hit innocent bystanders. I got off one shot, then I was hit on the head and abducted. The reason they locked me in the cellar was because I attacked the gypsy."

"I might believe you," he said, "except that there was no bar across the trapdoor. You could have left anytime you wanted."

She drew in a broken little breath. "When the shooting started, someone came to get me, Murray or one of his minions; I don't know who. Then he ran off. He must have unbarred the door."

She stopped. What did it matter what he thought? Picking up her fork, she speared a chunk of ham and bit into it.

Her anger, no, her outrage, and the incipient tears she was too proud to give in to acted on him powerfully. His suspicions began to seem absurd. She wouldn't have put them all in danger. She might run from him, but betray Dugald? Betray Gavin? And Juliet and her mother? Mahri was loyal to a fault. She had yet to learn that sometimes a person was forced to choose sides.

He had his own weaknesses to contend with. He didn't give his trust easily. He'd been so filled with rage at her apparent betrayal that he hadn't been thinking straight. What had she called him—a stupid, muddle-headed imbecile? She had a point.

He had the strongest urge to take her in his arms and tell her that he was sorry for misjudging her. But they weren't done yet. One thing, one insurmountable problem, made him steel himself against her. She was still shielding a gang of terrorists whom he was sworn to bring to justice or wipe off the face of the earth. Once Durward arrived on the scene and took charge of the investigation, he, Alex, might not be in a position to protect her. He was thinking of Ariel. He had always suspected that his own people had had a hand in her death. Traitors were rarely tried for their crimes. They simply met an untimely end.

He wasn't going to let that happen to Mahri.

"We walked into a trap today," he said quietly. "You know that, don't you?"

Her head came up, and her gaze collided with his. "Of course I know it! Murray and his minions were on the train with us from Ballater. I hope you're not accusing me. You didn't tell us your plan until this morning, so no one at the Cardnos' house could have set things up."

"One other person knew my plan, the person who supplied me with uniforms and the safe pass for the train. He is the queen's private secretary, and his name is Mungo Miller."

She repeated the name softly. "I've heard that name recently." She thought for a moment. "When they were taking me to that awful cottage, one of my abductors mentioned his name, and the others sniggered. What does it mean?" When she saw his expression, she caught her bottom lip between her teeth. A moment went by. "You think he betrayed you?"

"I hope to God I'm wrong, but I think he may be dead."

He was sorry that he'd been so blunt. Her eyes were wide and disbelieving. He wanted to put her on her guard, not scare the life out of her. "I may be wrong," he went on, trying to allay her fears. "You know your abductors better than I do. Are they killers?"

"I don't know, but it wouldn't surprise me. Murray especially." She shivered. "They were all afraid of him."

Since the hand holding her fork had developed a tremor, he steered the conversation into a less harrowing channel. "You mentioned a gypsy," he said. "Who was he?"

She spoke to her plate. "Archie. I didn't know his name, but he reminded me of a gypsy, so that was what I called him. Then I heard Murray call him Archie."

"You'd recognize him again?"

"I never forget a face."

He was impressed. Neither did he, but he'd been trained to remember faces. "Why did you attack him?"

She lifted her chin and looked at him with what he took to be a challenge in her eyes. "I didn't like the game he wanted to play with me, so I went for him. I didn't hurt him, because I was tied to a chair. I will say this for Murray: he didn't like it either. I think he may have broken the gypsy's nose. Then Murray locked me in the root cellar."

Alex remembered the broken chair and the rope he'd seen at their hideout, and he wanted to kick himself.

She had stopped eating and was staring vacantly at her plate. He didn't like to see her beaten like this, but there would never be a better time to wring the truth out of her.

The thought of wringing the truth out of her made him grit his teeth. Only the desire to keep this brave, tenacious, and strangely vulnerable young woman out of harm's way gave him the determination to persevere.

He reached for her shoulders and drew her toward him so that she was kneeling at his feet. The fact that she didn't struggle was a sure indication of her fatigue. It was like reeling in a spent fish.

He kept his voice gentle but firm. "I believe everything you've told me, but you've left a great deal out. Some things I know, but some I'm guessing at, and you won't enlighten me. How can I help you when you continue to mislead me?"

She blinked up at him, trying to concentrate on his words, when all she wanted was a nice, soft bed.

When she didn't answer, he went on, "Here is what I know. Contradict me if I'm wrong. You're a member of Demos." There was no response. "You wrote the letter that warned us of the assassination attempt on the queen."

"Much good it did me," she responded bitterly. "I thought the reception would be canceled, but the powers that be let it go forward."

He was speechless. At long last, she was giving him answers. Of her own free will, she was cooperating with him. It didn't matter that he already knew the answers to his questions. This was a milestone. She was learning to trust him.

"So," he went on finally, "you broke ranks. You betrayed your comrades." He cursed himself. Wrong choice of words.

Her fatigue began to ebb. "I betrayed their plot to assassinate the queen. I didn't betray them."

"Is Ronald Ramsey a member of Demos?"

Now she was fully alert. "I suppose so, but I'd never seen him before the night of the queen's reception."

He knew that she was lying. Her eyes gave her away. "I think he murdered Dickens," he said.

All the color washed out of her face.

He twisted the truth a little. "It must be either Gavin or Ramsey. They were the only ones near Dickens's office at the crucial time. I know it wasn't Gavin. He's not a member of Demos. Ramsey is. Do you see the kind of people you're protecting?"

She wrenched free of him and rubbed her arms where his fingers had grasped her. "You want me to go to the police, is that it? Why would anyone believe me? I am—was, a member of Demos. The police are just as likely to believe that I killed Dickens."

"Or I did. You're my alibi, and I'm yours. We're both in this up to our necks. We're both on the run. The difference is that you know what you're running from. If I'm to help you, and myself, and Gavin, I need to know what I'm up against."

He took a quick breath. "You have something Demos wants. What is it?"

Her eyes were wide and unblinking. "I don't know where you got that idea."

"Don't you? Then think about this. You weren't rescued tonight by your comrades. They didn't greet you with open arms. They captured you, terrorized you—if what you've told me is true. Help me, Mahri. Tell what's going on."

Her throat worked, but no sound came; then she raised herself on one knee, then to her feet, and walked to the window. Arms folded across her breasts, she stared blindly out on the stable block. She was silent for so long that he thought she wasn't going to answer him. When she spoke, her voice sounded a long way off, as if she'd put a great distance between them.

"My brother recruited me to Demos. I never met any of the other members of our cell, not to begin with. I was a courier, carrying messages from one dropping-off point to another. Bruce was my only contact with other members of my group. I was young, sixteen to his eighteen. I thought I was doing something patriotic. Bruce fired my imagination." She turned her head to look at him. "And we Scots had good cause to be dissatisfied with our lot."

She seemed to expect a response, so he said neutrally, "What made you change your mind?"

"I got older. Bruce got older. We approved of Demos's aims but not the methods it used."

His tone was dry. "You mean planting bombs? Recruiting mercenaries? Assassination?"

"No. We were small fry. We knew nothing of that. I meant burning postboxes, cutting telephone lines, that sort of thing." She gave a short, mirthless laugh. "Unfortunately, no one is allowed to resign from Demos. Bruce, however, found a way to escape. He joined the British Army and died in the Zulu War. He was only twenty years old."

She left the window and took the chair opposite his. "Ironic, isn't it? Bruce joined the British Army. In his letters home he told me that he didn't like the army's methods any more than he liked Demos's methods."

"I'm sorry," he said, and felt the inadequacy of those sterile words. How many times had he said them? How many times had he meant them? He wanted to comfort her, but if he tried, she was more likely to spit on him than thank him. He made do by simply shaking his head.

"Tell me about Murray," he said. "You recognized him at the station, didn't you?"

She nodded.

"Is he a member of Demos?"

"Until today, I'd only seen him from a distance, but I know that Demos employs him for special jobs."

"Like what, for instance?"

"I don't know. I was only a courier. But I'll tell you one thing: the men who abducted me from the train are not like any of the members of Demos I've ever met. They don't believe in causes. They are mercenaries."

Alex was still thinking about Murray and his mercenaries when she stirred. Adjusting her wrap, she said, "Is the interrogation over?"

His jaw tensed. She always found a way to put him in the wrong! He said shortly, "How did you find out about the plot to assassinate the queen?"

She shrugged. "Since I was disillusioned with Demos, my conscience wasn't troubled when I read the messages I was carrying. I'd done it before, but I'd never come across anything like that. I knew I had to stop it or make the attempt. I also knew that once I showed my hand, Demos would be on my trail like a pack of hounds. I had my escape route mapped out until"—she pinned him with a look—"until you stumbled across my path."

A thought occurred to him, something he didn't want to share with her in her overwrought state. If she knew too much, why hadn't Murray killed her to silence her? Why abduct her? He stored the thought in his mind for further reflection.

"Who are they, Mahri? What are their names?"

Her laugh was brittle. "I don't know. That's the thing about secret societies, they're so terribly secretive. We have

code names. It's safer that way. Ronald Ramsey doesn't
exist. Murray doesn't exist. I don't know their real names."

"The leader of your cell must know who the members
are. What do you call him, 'the professor'? He is the leader,
isn't he?"

When he heard her quick intake of breath, he pressed
his advantage. "Do you really want to fall into his hands?
Give me his name, or tell me where I can find him, and
you'll never have to worry about him again."

She got slowly to her feet and took a step toward him.
Whether or not it was deliberately done, she had the advantage of looking down on him. "I'll never have to worry
about him again?" she queried. "Then why are we on the
run? Why do we have two sets of villains after us, Demos
and your incompetent secret service and its cohorts? Don't
you know by now, Demos has influence? Its members are
everywhere. There are many cells."

"That may be true, but if we kill the root, its branches
will die."

She gave a weary sigh. "I've said all I'm going to say.
Now, if you'll excuse me, I'm going to bed."

She dropped her wrap and crawled into bed with all the
indifference of a child in the presence of her father. And
just as though he were her father, he tucked her in and drew
the covers up to her chin.

Her dinner plate was on the floor beside the fire. He
picked it up and shook his head. She'd hardly touched the
food he'd brought for her. He should have waited until she'd
eaten before he bombarded her with questions.

Sighing, he picked up her discarded wrap and sank into
an upholstered chair, a lady's chair, if his cramped legs
were anything to go by. There was no question of sharing
the bed with her. She might not know it, but he was well
aware that they were like dry tinder. One spark could start
a fire that he might not be able to put out.

The whiskey bottle was close at hand. He poured a

healthy measure into a teacup and sipped absently. He was reflecting that he was pinning all his hopes on Durward to sort this mess out. He was a good man, a thorough man, but he would not make allowances for Mahri's reluctance to disclose the names of her former comrades. Alex's standing with his chief wouldn't count for much then. He had no rights, no court he could turn to, to plead her cause.

He thought of Ariel again and shuddered.

It would never come to that. He'd keep Mahri out of harm's way until everyone in that damn secret society was behind bars or scattered to the far corners of the earth. He would take care of it personally. And when he had finished with Demos, she'd no longer be of interest to British Intelligence.

He couldn't keep her out of harm's way, because she wouldn't listen to reason. The moment his back was turned, she'd slip away. Where would she go? Who would look after her? And this woman badly needing looking after. If it were up to him, he would keep her under lock and key.

His legs were cramping. He got up and took a turn around the room.

Eighteen

~❦~

He returned to the chair and spread his coat over himself to keep warm. In the Highlands, the temperature could plunge drastically when the sun set. He'd left the lamp burning in case Mahri wakened in the night and couldn't get her bearings. The fire had burned low. He looked over at the bed. She was restless. He wished he could get inside that convoluted mind of hers and discover what she was thinking, plotting, feeling.

Sadly, that wasn't how his gift worked. He couldn't read minds, but he was sensitive to strong emotions. He had to be close to his subject or touch an object that belonged to them to get an impression. Impressions and visions, that was all he had to go on. And impressions and visions could be misleading.

Since meeting Mahri, his muse had become erratic. Or maybe he'd become erratic. He'd lost his focus. The trouble was, he had never quite managed to see her as a subject. She was a free spirit, a hummingbird that was tantalizingly out of reach.

He focused his thoughts on Mahri. His eyelids grew heavy; his breathing slowed. Images came fleetingly and faded away. The room gradually receded. The lamp flickered and went out. He was in a cold, desolate place. Mahri. He was reaching for her, reaching, straining every muscle. Suddenly, she was in his arms, and he went spiraling down into a nightmare.

She had lost something precious, and no one and nothing could console her. Alex could feel her terror, her disbelief, her denial. Her emotions buffeted him as though he were one of the principal actors in the drama. Panic wrapped around his throat, almost choking him.

"No," she moaned, "no." Then, deerlike, she bounded away on an invisible path that only she could see. Alex felt the constriction in his own chest as he fought to keep up with her. Why wouldn't she slow down?

It came to him that they were going downhill, that Mahri was no longer running in circles but had a destination in mind. He could hear water cascading over rocks. They'd come to one of those small waterfalls that was common in the foothills of the Highlands.

And he recognized the spot. He'd seen it in his vision of Mahri when he'd palmed the dirk he'd taken from her the night he captured her. She was on her knees, and a young man was presenting her with a dagger. She kissed its hilt. She was now a fully fledged member of Demos.

That was where Alex's vision had ended, but Mahri's dream wasn't over yet. The young man disintegrated, leaving her alone. She got up and, with a cry of mingled rage and despair, flung the dirk into the river.

The scene suddenly changed. He saw blazing-hot skies and scorched scrubland that seemed to go on forever. He felt Mahri's anguish. She was looking for someone, but there was nothing to see. The landscape was empty. There was no one there.

A thin, high wailing sound jerked him out of her dream. Mahri was trying to fight herself free of the covers. He bounded from the chair and reached the bed in two strides.

When he laid his hands on her, she came awake on a panicked cry. Frozen with fear, her face chalk white, she stared unseeingly into his face.

"Mahri!" he said. "Mahri! It's all right. I'm here."

There was a moment when he thought she might resist him; then, with a little cry, she kicked off the covers and launched herself into his arms. He could never afterward remember what he said in those first few moments when he tried to comfort her. He vaguely remembered soothing words that a father might say to a child. It was a bad dream, only a bad dream, and he was there to fend off anything that might try to hurt her. Truth to tell, he was as shaken as she. Her heart was beating frantically against his ribs, and she was sucking air into her lungs in great, sobbing gulps.

The minutes passed, and he did nothing more than brush his hands over her back, calmly, ceaselessly, as the shudders that racked her slender body gradually died away.

"Feeling better now?" he asked softly.

"This isn't like me," she mumbled into his shoulder. "I'm sorry I woke you."

"I wasn't asleep."

He tried to adjust his position and smiled when her arms tightened around his neck, keeping him close. When she came to herself, he thought wryly, she'd be sorry that she'd let down her guard even for a moment. She liked to think that she was self-sufficient and didn't need anyone. He amended his opinion almost at once. Dugald was the exception. She was close to Dugald. Alex wondered how much she had confided in her stalwart deerstalker and was glad that she'd had him there to take care of her.

"Tell me about your dream," he said.

He expected an evasive answer and was staggered when she nestled her head in the crook of his shoulder. It seemed natural to do what he'd wanted to do for a long, long time. He feathered her hair with his fingers, absorbing its silky texture, savoring the faint fragrance of lavender that clung to each strand.

"I was dreaming about my brother," she said. "I suppose it was talking about him tonight that brought the dream on—the trick he taught me with snakes, the time he recruited me to Demos, and losing him in a senseless war he didn't really want to be involved in."

He made a soothing sound but kept his opinions to himself, believing that any interruption at this point might distract her from sharing something that obviously weighed heavily on her mind.

She gave a shivery sigh. "After he was killed in action, I used to dream about him all the time. I don't think I ever believed that anything bad could happen to him. He was so full of life. I'm not saying that he was perfect, but he had a sunny disposition. Everyone liked him."

"Especially his little sister," he added when she paused.

She looked up and smiled. "He teased me unmercifully, but yes, I adored him. You might say that he was my champion. He might give me a swat, but he wouldn't allow anyone else to do it." Her smile gradually faded, and she blinked back tears. "He shouldn't have enlisted," she said, then more fiercely, "I shouldn't have encouraged him. I should have tried to talk him out of it. He would have listened to me."

She looked up at him, waiting for him to respond. He felt as though his next few words would seal his fate. Treading carefully, he said, "He chose to enlist. You can't be blamed for what happened to him. Look, Mahri, I know about young men, and I can tell you categorically that when they make up their minds to do something, a little sister's persuasions count for nothing. Think of Gavin and me. Would I listen to him? Of course I wouldn't, because I'm the elder."

She shook her head. "It was so senseless! He'd only been in Southern Africa for a few weeks. We heard that it was a slaughter. The Zulus slaughtered over twelve hundred men that day, and my brother was one of them."

He was tempted to take her guilt and put it where it

belonged—on the members of Demos. It was to escape their clutches that her brother had enlisted, or so she'd told him. He let it go. He didn't want anything to disturb this newfound harmony between them.

"Do you know," she said, "this is the first time our conversation hasn't deteriorated into an interrogation?"

"If I seem hard on you sometimes," he said, "it's only because I want what's best for you."

She made a scoffing sound. "You can't help yourself, can you? You always know best. Well, you said it yourself just a moment ago, didn't you? You're the elder. You make all the decisions."

She was in a playful mood, and the change in her was captivating.

And alluring. And seductive. And, above all, dangerous.

He had to get out of that bed.

Her hand briefly touched his. "It was a joke," she said. "I wasn't serious. I didn't mean anything by it."

He smiled into her eyes. "No offense taken, and I'm sure Gavin would agree with you. Perhaps I am a little overbearing at times, a little too inclined to think I know best."

Her smile faded. "You seem very sure that the others are all right."

"As sure as I can be of anything. Just think about it, Mahri. When the train stopped at Aboyne, Murray and his thugs came for us—you and me—not for the others. That's what makes me believe that the others are safe. What we have to think about now is ourselves." He tried to edge away from her. "Get some rest. We have a long day ahead of us tomorrow."

"No," she replied quickly and grasped the sleeve of his shirt. "I'm not tired, and I don't want to fall asleep reliving the past. Talk to me, Alex, please."

He wasn't immune to the appeal in her eyes. All the same, he didn't think it wise, in their state of undress, to be lying supine on a bed. Just thinking about it was making him break out in a sweat. Short of detaching himself forcibly from her grasp, there was nothing he could do.

Resigned to acting the part of a monk, he said, "What shall we talk about?"

"Tell me about yourself. What were you like as a boy? Were you always this serious?"

"Serious!" He broke into a smile. "You abominable girl! You like to cut me down to size, don't you? If you must know, I was a tearaway, always getting into trouble, playing tricks on unsuspecting people. I've had more beatings from my father than you have had hot dinners."

"Whatever happened to that boy?" she teased.

"You said it yourself. He got older. He grew up. Things changed when my parents died. I became the head of my family."

"You mean, you felt responsible for Gavin?" She answered her own question. "Well, of course you did. It's in your nature to protect your own."

"I could say the same about you."

"And I would agree with you, but it's a trait I admire. I don't want to change you. You, on the other hand, want to change me." She seemed to realize that she'd strayed into a bog and quickly changed direction. "How did you come to work for the secret service?"

He yawned, but she didn't take the hint. Sighing, he said, "I was recruited by a friend. That's how it's usually done. We recruit people we know, people we can trust. You've heard me speak of Durward?"

She nodded. "He's the one you think will clear you when he takes charge of the investigation."

"Well, he taught me mathematics at St. Andrew's. Brilliant teacher. I was in the chess club, as was Durward. What I didn't know was that he was also a code breaker attached to Whitehall. When he became section chief of espionage, he asked me to take his place as a code breaker. And that was what I did. He is short on charm, doesn't suffer fools gladly, and is a law unto himself."

"You like him?"

"I respect him." He shrugged. "That's how I was recruited, because of my aptitude at chess and at breaking codes."

Her brow creased. "Were we at war back then?"

"We're always at war, especially in times of peace. Spies can always find work ferreting out their enemies' secrets."

She was indignant. "That sounds like a great piece of nonsense to me! No wonder we're always at war with our neighbors."

"Don't blame me. I didn't invent the system." He shook his head. "It wouldn't be necessary if we were all good people."

"Yes," she said, as to herself, "it's surprising how easily good people can be corrupted." Her reflective look vanished, and she went on, "How did you go from working with codes to active duty in the secret service?"

"By accident."

She raised her head to look at him. "By accident?"

He nodded. "Durward needed an extra man, and I was the only one available. I acquitted myself well, so I believe, and developed a taste for a more adventurous sort of life than sitting in a room all by myself, poring over numbers and letters."

She started to laugh, as she was meant to, but stopped abruptly. "But something went wrong, didn't it? You went back to your little room in Whitehall? Is that when Ariel died?"

He said savagely, "Little brothers should mind their own business."

She took offense at this. "Just be grateful that you have a brother who worries about you. I would do anything, give anything, to have my brother back. And you are mistaken. Gavin said nothing to me." She paused and lowered her voice. "I'm sorry. I shouldn't have mentioned her name."

He felt horribly chastened. After what she'd told him about her own brother, he should have had more tact. "I *am* grateful that I have a brother who worries about me,"

he said, "and I'm sure Gavin would say the same of me."
There was a brief silence. "You're right, of course. Something did go wrong, terribly wrong. It was all my fault.
Someone I trusted, someone I recruited, not as an agent
but as a source of information, deliberately lured me into
a trap, and not only me but three of my comrades. I've told
you this before."

"Yes," she whispered. "You blamed Demos."

"She worked for Demos! Oh, yes, it has branches in
England as well."

Her head came up, and her eyes searched his. "She?"

"Ariel." He kept his voice neutral and steady. "The
woman I thought I loved. She was in an ideal position to
observe and pass on information. Her father, a Scottish
peer, was in the House of Lords. She was his hostess. Ariel
heard things she wasn't supposed to hear, saw things she
wasn't supposed to see." He heard the bitterness creep
into his voice and checked it. "You might say that she was
everyone's favorite confidante, including mine. She sent
me to a house in Kennington where the leader of Demos
was supposed to be hiding out."

She took his hand and put it to her cheek. "What happened to Ariel?" she asked softly.

He gave a mirthless laugh. "She was the daughter of
a peer. She thought she was untouchable. She told me so
when she visited me in hospital. If I'd been able to move, I
would have strangled her with my bare hands. As it turned
out, she was found with her neck broken at the foot of the
stairs in her own home. I never found out who was responsible, Demos or my own people."

"It might have been an accident."

"Not in the game I'm in."

Brows drawn, he watched as she got off the bed and moved
to the table. When she returned, she offered him a cup.

"Whiskey?" he asked, his smile breaking out again.

"Why not?" She sat on the edge of the bed. "I think we
deserve it after what we've been through. Frankly, I don't

know how you can sleep at nights after what Ariel did to you."

He took a healthy swallow, then another before handing her the cup. She made a face but managed a few dainty sips before returning it to him. He bolted what was left.

"You've got it wrong," he said. "It's not Ariel's betrayal that disturbs my dreams. It's my own bloody naïveté that cost the lives of three of my friends." He broke off and looked down at the empty cup. "This was a mistake. I've never told anyone outside the service about Ariel. All that my family knows is that we were going to be married, and when she died I went a little crazy. By that I mean that I cut myself off from everyone. Mahri, what are you doing?"

She'd taken his face between her hands. With eyes wide on his, she said, "Are you or are you not still in love with Ariel?"

At first he was baffled; then, as his brain began to add things up, he grinned hugely. "Are you jealous of Ariel?"

"I suppose I must be. Everyone keeps telling me what a paragon she was and how your heart was broken and would always be hers. Only Dugald was skeptical."

"And what did Dugald say?"

"Oh, he said that if your heart was broken, you wouldn't always be following me with your eyes."

Without warning, she climbed on the bed and half sprawled over him.

He held her away with his hands on her shoulders. "You can tell Dugald," he said hoarsely, "that—"

She stopped his words with a kiss. Her lips brushed over his, and when he relaxed his grip on her shoulders, she moved in closer. But when he didn't respond, she pulled back to get a better look at him.

"What?" he asked when she laughed.

"You look like a cornered wild thing."

And that was exactly how he felt.

She shook her head. "I've already made my decision, and I won't let you stop me."

"We'll see about that."

She stopped him from rising by pushing on his chest. "You did not answer my question," she said. "Are you still in love with Ariel?"

"Of course I'm not in love with her! I only thought I was. But that does not mean that I'd take advantage of an innocent young girl."

"I'm twenty-four." She nibbled on his ear.

His hands fisted on the quilt. "And I'm . . . and I'm . . ."

"Thirty-one," she supplied. "So we're both old enough to know what we're doing."

She was tracing his lips with her fingers. "I've wanted to do that for a long, long time." She dimpled. "Well, at least for a week."

He made one final attempt to bring her to her senses. "It won't stop at a kiss."

She gurgled with laughter. "Simpleton," she murmured. "I'm not so innocent as you seem to think. As Thomas Gordon, I learned a few things about relations between the sexes that would make you blush to the roots of your hair."

He put his lips to hers. "Little liar," he breathed into her mouth.

She laughed. "Put it to the test if you don't believe me." Suddenly, she turned serious. "I'm not asking for your undying love. I'm not asking for anything. We both know that our loyalties will take us in different directions. I want you to know I will never forget you, Alex Hepburn."

Her words set his teeth on edge. She was still resolved to slip away and start a new life where neither Demos nor he would ever find her. It didn't work like that. One day, she would grow careless and give herself away; then Demos would take its revenge.

Not if he could help it.

He knew how to hold her. He knew what would bind her to him so that she wouldn't want to run away.

With infinite care, he cupped her face and brought his lips to hers.

Nineteen

As the kiss lingered, he drew her to his side and used his weight to anchor her to the mattress. She twined her arms around his neck and melted against him. She could have wept at such intimacy, but the intimacy was bittersweet. All she could be sure of was the present moment. All her tomorrows were here, right now, in the arms of the man she loved.

His mouth on hers was warm and gentle; she felt safe and sheltered. It was an illusion, of course. She had dragged him into something that was infinitely dangerous. The longer she stayed with him, the more she endangered him. How could life have dealt her such a blow?

But her sadness went deeper than that. She wasn't seeing him as a secret service agent, a latter-day centurion who faced danger without flinching. She was seeing him as that bookish young man in a small room in Whitehall, devoting his life to numbers and codes. No wonder he'd jumped at the chance to escape that sterile world. And wasn't Ariel all the colors of the rainbow?

And Ariel had betrayed him.

How long had he been alone?

They weren't so very different. If only . . .

He sensed the darkness in her and he raised his lips an inch from hers. "You're wrong," he said. "This isn't the end for us. It's just the beginning."

She smiled. "What's this? You can read minds now?"

"No. But a famous seer foretold this moment. I didn't understand her prophecy at the time. In fact, I was skeptical. Now I believe her."

When he was silent, she prompted, "And what did this famous seer foretell?"

The words were branded into his mind. He selected the part that he thought would comfort Mahri. "She said, 'Hold fast to what you feel, and all will be well'—or words to that effect. And that is what I intend to do."

Hold fast to what you feel, she noted, *and not to the one you love.* What difference did it make? She was leaving him anyway.

"I thought," she said, "you didn't believe in seers and witches and so on."

"Well, most are charlatans, but a few are genuine. I believe what my seer told me."

"You're just trying to humor me."

He felt the darkness in her turn to light, and he smiled. "Remind me, one day, to tell you the whole prophecy, but not now, not when I'm waiting with baited breath to discover what tricks you learned as Thomas Gordon."

She looped an arm around his neck. "I learned that some women are predators, and the only way to escape them is to run like blazes. I'm not exaggerating. There were times when poor Thomas was lucky to escape with his virtue intact."

His shoulders shook. "Should I run?"

"Too late. I've got you just where I want you."

All humor left her face, and she looked directly into his eyes. "Let's agree on something. Let's agree not to think of tomorrow."

He didn't tell her that tomorrow had already arrived. "I agree," he said, "and not only that. Let's pretend that there is no Demos, that we're not on the run, that we don't have a care in the world."

She tilted her head so that she could see his face, and her heart cramped. The light from the lamp brought his features into sharp relief. The abrasions on one cheek were deeper than she'd realized, and an ugly cut scored his chin. His injuries, she knew, were the result of the fight on the train. If he hadn't met her, none of this would have happened to him.

"What have I done to you, Alex?" she asked softly.

He gave a throaty chuckle. "What you have done," he said, "is waken me from my stupor. For the last few years, all my actions have been governed by a healthy dose of cynicism. Since our paths crossed, I've experienced every emotion under the sun. And, let me tell you, I'm not sure that I like it."

He rested his brow on hers. "I may regret the way we met, but I shall never regret meeting you."

His smile coaxed a smile out of her. "It's been the same for me," she said.

He could feel his heart turn over. There was no other way to describe it. This slight slip of a girl had taken on burdens that most men would have broken under. Ariel had broken him, but nothing had broken Mahri, not for long, not just because she was strong but because her passion for life was irrepressible. He swore then, as God was his witness, that he'd rather cut off his right hand than hurt her.

He drew her close on a moan and kissed her softly, carefully, when what he really wanted to do was devour her. *Slowly, easily,* he warned himself.

She pulled back with a laugh and licked her lips. "You taste of whiskey," she said.

"So do you. From this day forward, whenever I taste whiskey, I'll think of you."

"Is that a compliment?"

He raised his head and gave her one of his wickedly roguish grins. "Of course it's a compliment. Show me a Scot who doesn't like whiskey."

"You're looking at one, and I consider myself more of a Scot than you."

There was an impish gleam in her eyes. It occurred to him that there was a double meaning to her words, but before he could reflect on it, she began to undo the buttons on his shirt.

When her fingers slowed then stopped, he said, "You're having second thoughts about this?"

"No. I may have exaggerated my competence; that's all."

"You mean, you're a novice?"

She nodded. "I'm afraid so."

He couldn't help laughing. She was such a delight to him. Kissing the pout from her lips, he said, "I feel like a novice, too. It's never been like this for me, before you."

He said something else, something about his right hand that she didn't understand, then his lips were on hers, not so gentle this time, open, hot, sweetly passionate. Her bones seemed to melt, her blood heated, and there was a pleasant buzz in her head. She had no idea why she felt like crying.

His hands left her shoulders and brushed over every curve and valley, but fleetingly. He wanted to accustom her to the intimate touch of his hands, not frighten her. He should have known that Mahri didn't frighten easily. Her hands began to brush over him, touching him as intimately as he was touching her.

When they broke apart, Alex was appalled. He was trembling like a callow youth. He could hardly get his breath. His fingers fisted helplessly in the soft curls at her nape. He thanked the deity that he was still fully clothed, else he might have fallen on her like a love-struck schoolboy.

For her sake, he had to slow down. Mahri didn't understand. She was back to undoing the buttons on his shirt. If she knew how intensely his body craved hers, she wouldn't look at him with such big, trusting eyes.

When she parted the edges of his shirt and put her hands on his bare skin, a jolt of desire whipped through him. On a shaken laugh, he captured her wrists. "Mahri," he said, "I'm outpacing you. Can we prolong the pleasure? And this time, be gentle with me."

He tugged on her wrists, bringing her down to his level, and he buried his face against her hair. "You have to understand how it is with me," he said. "I've never wanted a woman more, never dreamed there could be someone like you for me."

She turned her face till their lips met. "I've used up all my competence," she said. "I really don't know how to seduce a man."

"Seduce?" He sounded angry. "Didn't you hear a word I said? You don't have to seduce me. I have never wanted a woman more."

She looked into his eyes, and what she saw there took her breath away. He wasn't trying to hide his feelings. There was desire there, and something else, something she was afraid to name.

She knew that she couldn't hold a candle to the women he mixed with in London. At her best, she was passing pretty; that was all. She couldn't imagine what he saw in her, but she knew how he made her feel. Special. Unique. Confident . . .

Her eyes were tearing again, and she blinked the tears away. Her voice was husky. "I'll try to do right by you."

Her words arrested him.

Fearing she had said too much, she rubbed her body suggestively against his. "All right, Mr. Know-it-all," she said playfully, "show me how competent *you* are."

He sucked in a breath, and the question that was forming in his mind quietly slipped away. He reached for her and rolled with her on the bed. When he ground himself into her, letting her feel his hard shaft, she went perfectly still.

He raised his head. Eyes wide with surprise, she said, "Thomas doesn't know nearly as much as he thinks he knows." Then, smiling, she stretched catlike and molded herself to the length of his body.

Alex's breath was practically strangling him. When he could breathe again, his mouth took hers in a ravenous kiss. She answered that demand with a passion that made his heart sing. A torrent of heat engulfed them both.

He tried to slow down, but she'd taken the initiative away from him. He wasn't leading her; she was leading him.

She had no fears, no inhibitions. She was a beautiful and desirable creature who had captured the man she loved.

He began to disrobe. Mahri lost no time in following his example. His hands didn't brush over her now. They took possession of every curve and valley, playing her like a highly strung violin, but the only sounds that came from her lips were soft mewls. She moved restlessly as he replaced his fingers with his lips and tongue, and she clutched at his shoulders as though she were drowning. When he laughed low in his throat, obviously relishing her distress, she reared up and pushed him into the mattress.

With slow deliberation, she explored every inch of his body as he had explored hers. She reveled in the sound of his breathing, rasping in and out of his lungs, delighted in the feel of hard, masculine flesh that tensed beneath her fingertips. She thought him the most beautiful man she had ever known.

"Alex," she cried softly, "Alex."

He seemed to know what she wanted. He knelt above her and spread her legs. Eyes on hers, he slowly entered her. And stopped.

"Mahri," he said, "I don't want to hurt you, but the first time, so I've heard, is never easy for a woman."

"I know." She could hardly catch her breath. The full-

ness inside her was almost unbearable. This was no time to
be cowardly. "Thomas told me."

With that, she scored his back with her nails. He jerked
involuntarily and thrust forward, breaking the delicate barrier. She sucked in a breath, held on to it, then let it out
slowly.

When he raised his head to look at her, he said sternly,
"I suppose Thomas taught you that trick, too?"

She nodded. "It's amazing what a lad can pick up in
inns and alehouses. You were supposed to distract me.
Since you didn't, I decided to distract you."

In the same stern voice, he said, "It's amazing to me that
you have managed to remain a virgin all these years. Don't
you know—"

She stopped his words with a kiss, a slow, openmouthed
kiss that made him forget what he was going to say. When
he could breathe again, he kissed her brows, her ears, her
chin. Then he began to move. Each thrust had her gasping for breath. Never had she been so aware of every pulse
point in her body. Never had she felt sensations that were
part pleasure, part pain. The need built slowly till she was
frantic for something she only half understood, something
just out of reach.

Her little sounds of arousal almost broke his control.
His skill and experience counted for nothing now. This was
primeval; this was dark and glorious and unlike anything
he had ever known.

As his rhythm became reckless, faster, unrestrained,
she wound herself around him and locked his body to
hers. All sense of time and place vanished. There was only
Alex. Her muscles strained; her body tightened. When
she thought that she could not bear it one moment more,
she gave a helpless little cry and shattered into a thousand
pieces. Alex was only a heartbeat behind her. As the rap-
ture hurled him over the crest, he buried his face against
her throat.

When they could catch their breath, he held her close. Mahri turned into him, gave a sigh of repletion, and promptly slipped into sleep.

He pulled the quilt over them and, while Mahri slept, he lay with fingers laced behind his neck, staring up at the ceiling. His body was exhausted, but his mind was alert. He was remembering the glint in her eye when she'd told him that she was more of a Scot than he. There was a double edge to that artless quip, a message that she hugged to herself like a child with a secret. She should have remembered that breaking codes was child's play to him.

More of a Scot than he. She spoke Gaelic. As Thomas, she wore tartan trews. She could eat lumpy porridge without batting an eyelash. But she didn't like whiskey. He had her there. A true Scot would never confess that he didn't like whiskey. He was more of a Scot than she.

He started over. Who was a true Scot and who was not? He let the thought revolve in his mind. She was a Scot, more of a Scot than he, because he was . . . he was . . . a Hepburn.

Mahri Scot? His tardy sixth sense came fully awake. An impression skirted the edge of his mind. *We Scots.* Where had he heard that recently? Not an impression but a vision. Mahri taking a fence on her horse. A male figure applauding. What was it he said? *"We Scots thrive on a challenge."*

Scot. Was that her family name? Mahri Scot. Why was she frightened of Demos? And why wouldn't she give him their names?

That brought to mind the question that had been puzzling him for some time. If Demos was afraid that she would give the authorities enough evidence to hang them all, why not simply kill her? There had been ample opportunity for Murray to do it when he'd abducted her. They'd tried to kill him, but they'd spared her. Why?

They'd want to know who she'd spoken to and how much she'd told them. They must know they were safe, or they would all have been rounded up and arrested by now. So what were they truly after? What did she have that they wanted?

It wasn't over yet, not nearly over. He'd told Mahri one part of the prophecy, but the rest was still to come. *"You shall pass through fire, but the fire will not consume you if your trust your intuition."*

He could almost hear his granny's wavering voice as she'd warned each of her grandsons what lay in store for them. Each had a different prophecy, and not one of them had taken Granny McEcheran's words to heart. But that was before the gift she had passed on had begun to manifest itself.

Trust your intuition. To his granny, that meant one thing: *Trust your psychic powers.*

She could have taught her grandsons so much more when she was alive if they had not been such confirmed skeptics. Now, with no Granny to guide them, they were like fledglings who had never learned to fly.

From the very beginning, when he'd first set eyes on Mahri, he'd been given a sign. When their eyes met, he'd felt as though an electric current had passed right through his brain. His intuition had been going full blast then. But instead of doing everything in his power to protect her as he was sure now that he was meant to do, he'd hunted her and terrorized her and accused her of plotting to kill him.

It had to be Mungo who had betrayed them. He was the only one who knew their plan. He didn't know how Demos had found out about Mungo, but he could imagine the methods they had used to get Mungo to talk. And when they got the information they wanted, Demos would have killed him.

He shoved the thought away from him. Not again! He'd lost three friends he had recruited to the service. If there were a God, he wouldn't let it happen again.

He made himself a silent promise. If Mungo were dead, he'd make them pay for this crime and everyone else who had a hand in it. He'd track them down and annihilate them, one by one.

There would be no need to track them down, because he had something they wanted: Mahri. When they came for her, as they surely would, he'd be ready for them. He thought of what had happened to Ariel, and fear tightened his chest. It wasn't going to happen to Mahri.

He had to find a way to keep her in his orbit.

Bending his head to hers, he whispered, "If you want to do right by me, you'll marry me."

A fleeting smile touched her lips. Her body was lax. She was steeped in the afterglow of pleasure. Her lashes fluttered, then her eyes flew open. There was a moment of incomprehension, then she hauled herself up. "What did you say?"

"I said that if you want to do right by me, you'll marry me."

Her jaw went slack. "You're joking, of course."

"It's hardly something I would joke about."

Her eyes searched his face. His gaze was guarded; his thoughts were veiled from her. This honorable proposal was not what she wanted to hear. "If this is an attack of conscience on your part, I absolve you. You didn't seduce me. I came to you of my own free will."

"Tell that to my granny. No. Listen to me, Mahri. I knew what I was doing when I claimed your innocence for myself. Marriage is the only way for us. You're not cut out for an affair, and neither am I. Besides, think of Dugald. He will kill me when he catches up to us."

"Dugald will never know. I won't tell him, and I'm sure you won't tell him either."

He laughed softly. "He'll know without our telling him. He'll see how I look at you and how you look at me. I won't be able to keep my hands off you." He warmed to his part. "Can you keep your hands off me? We'll be tiptoeing along dark corridors to each other's bedchambers—"

"I don't think that's funny!" She chewed her bottom lip.

"Anyway, I won't be here long enough to tiptoe along dark corridors."

His brows rose. "You're thinking of going somewhere?"

A guilty blush ran under her skin. "We're fugitives, aren't we? We can't stay in one place for long."

He was serious now. "Yes, but that's not what you meant. You're still thinking of finding a safe place to hide from Demos. I know Demos, Mahri. They won't give up until they find you. You have something they want, don't you? What is it? Why won't you tell me?"

"I told you. No one is ever allowed to resign from Demos. They want to make an example of me for foiling their attempt to kill the queen."

Her eyes never lied to him, and he could tell that she had told him a half-truth. He didn't belabor the point. An argument was the last thing he wanted. "All the more reason," he said, "for us to be married at once. I know how to take care of my own. They'll have to remove me before they can touch you."

He was winning her over. He could read it in her eyes. Then her eyes went blank, and she gave a derisive snort. "It may have escaped your notice," she said, "that you're a fugitive, too, not only from your own people but also from Demos. A fine pair we'd make, running from two packs of bloodhounds. If we separate, we'll even the odds. Demos will come after me, but they'll leave you alone."

"I don't care whether they leave me alone or not. Don't you understand anything? It's *you* I want to keep safe."

If only it could be that simple. She had no doubts that he wanted to keep her safe, but he was even more resolved to crush Demos and see all its members go to the gallows. He couldn't do both.

She swallowed the tightness in her throat. She was totally sunk in love with this man, and because she loved him, she had to send him away.

But not yet.

When she shook her head and opened her mouth to

speak, he held up a finger, silencing her. "We're going to do this my way," he said.

"Now just a minute!"

"Better get this through your head. I'm not giving you a choice. Do you think I would have a moment's peace knowing that you were in danger? I feel responsible for what happened to you. If I hadn't interfered, you would have been long gone by now. I can't change the past. I don't want to change the past, but I'll be damned if I'll wash my hands of you. We stay together, Mahri, come hell or high water."

He used his weight to carry her back against the pillows. "Trust me, Mahri," he said. "Our being together is in our stars."

She thought he was making a joke at her expense, but when she looked into his eyes, she saw that the humor was mixed with an equal part of gravity, and the hands that were pushing him away gradually relaxed. Someone to watch over her and someone to watch over. It felt so right, so good.

Against her lips, he whispered, "Will you do right by me?"

"Always," she said.

"You'll marry me?"

"That wouldn't be doing right by you."

"I'll be the judge of that. Say yes."

She managed a wobbly smile. "Oh, Alex," she said and shook her head, then added impulsively, "I need time to think about it."

His eyes narrowed on her face. "I know what you're thinking, and you couldn't be more wrong."

"What am I thinking?"

"You're thinking that this marriage may never take place, that we're on the run and don't know where we'll lay our heads from one day to the next. We won't have time to find a minister, let alone say our vows."

"It may have crossed my mind," she allowed.

"If you think that, you don't know me. I'll have my ring on your finger before you can say your own name."

She laughed. "Mahri—" she began and fumbled. Recovering quickly, she finished, "Mahri McGregor. See, you were wrong!"

He swung his legs over the edge of the bed and reached for his clothes. "Get some rest. We have an early start tomorrow."

She should have left it at that. That was the trouble with love. It made you weak when you should be strong.

To his back, she said softly, "My name is Mahri Scot. I'm sorry, Alex. I should have told you right out."

He stilled. With shoulders hunched over, he inhaled a long breath, then he turned and cupped her chin in one hand. "That wasn't so bad, was it?"

Her voice was husky. "No. I suppose not."

He came down beside her again. "You've given me a priceless gift."

"And what might that be?"

She sounded sulky, and that made him smile. "Your trust."

She swallowed hard. "There are others who trusted me. I can't hurt them. You see that, don't you?"

"I'll only hurt them if they try to hurt you. I'll never ask you to betray them."

"But—"

He stopped her words with a kiss. The sudden jump of her heart had his pulse jumping in counterpoint, but there was no frantic haste to possess her. He wanted to touch and savor. He wanted to imprint himself indelibly not only on her body but on her mind. So he told her that she was light to his darkness; he told her that she'd brought beauty into his world; he told her that he would never let her go now. And he meant every word.

Their breathing grew thicker. She became bolder, restless. With her hands on his shoulders, she urged him to cover her. When he filled her, she let out a keening cry of pleasure. At the end, she buried her head against his chest and wept.

Twenty

They didn't make an early start in the morning. They wakened at noon to the bellow of bagpipes outside their window. Mahri shot out of bed. Alex groaned and shoved his head under a pillow.

After slipping into her nightgown, she ran to the window and looked out. "Oh, what a braw sight!" she exclaimed. "Highlanders in kilts! It's a long time since I've seen so many different tartans all together. Do you think there will be dancing?"

Alex could hardly think for the racket of the pipes. "Dancing, throwing the caber, putting the stone—but above all, eating and drinking."

He reached for another pillow to block out the din, remembered the events of last night, and dragged himself up. One quick, comprehensive glance made the hard knot of tension inside him relax. Mahri looked clear-eyed and happy. He didn't know what he had expected. Tears? Blushes? Fireworks?

He loved watching her—the way she moved, the way

she looked at him, the way she laughed. He was struck
again by the contradiction in her character—the odd blend
of innocence and worldliness. He knew now where the
worldliness came from; Master Thomas Gordon had a lot
to answer for.

"Well, get up." She came to stand over him and did a
little jig on her toes. "I want to wash and, well, you know,
use the facilities, so make yourself scarce."

Alex dragged a hand through his hair. He knew what
that meant. He had to go down to the cold, cold, wash-
house, euphemistically called a bathhouse, on the main
floor, and wash himself there. The privy, naturally, was
outside, a good hike from the hotel itself.

"How did you manage to preserve your modesty when
you were Thomas Gordon?" he asked.

"Use your imagination."

"Never was my strong point. Look, I'll tell you what I'll
do. I'll cover my head with the covers, and you won't even
know that I'm here."

"Alex," she said quietly, seriously, "if you don't take
yourself off, I may disgrace myself."

He grinned. "I'll think about it."

The next thing he knew, she had stripped off the covers and was pelting him with his boots, coat, and trousers.
Then she marched to the door and held it open. A chamber-
maid stood frozen in the corridor. She took one look at the
naked man trying to dress in a hurry, squealed with fright,
and took to her heels.

"Out!" Mahri commanded and pointed as though he
needed a signpost.

When he came level with her, he said, "Don't I get a
kiss?"

He was through the door before she could do him bodily
harm. The door slammed behind him. A moment later, her
laughter rang out. He smiled, on the edge of a laugh, and
traipsed downstairs to speak to the innkeeper. A few min-

utes later, he had fresh towels and other bits and pieces he needed to complete his toilette.

The beaming proprietors, Mr. and Mrs. Crimmond, watched Alex as he sauntered down the corridor to the bathhouse.

"There goes a happy man," said Mr. Crimmond, and he sighed.

His wife punched him in the ribs. "You have nothing to complain of, Andy."

"You must be joking." There was a twinkle in his eye. "I thought the ceiling was going to come down around our ears last night, and if the slats on that bed are not broken, my name is no Andy Crimmond."

"Aye," said his wife, smiling and tucking her head to the side, "there's nothing quite like young love to warm the cockles of your heart. It brings back memories."

"Memories be damned!" said her husband. "There's life in the old dog yet. But maybe no as much life as in that young spark. At any rate, they're staying on for another night."

"Why is that?"

"He said that they didna want to travel in the dark, not after what happened to them on the road here."

"And you believe him?"

He swatted her on the backside. "What do you think? They're newlyweds. They won't be going anywhere in a hurry, except maybe to bed."

Laughing together, they entered the dining room to see to their customers.

When Alex started up the stairs a short while later, there was a spring in his step. He felt as though he had shed ten years. Everything was new to him. The sun was brighter, his senses were keener, and the sound of the bagpipes . . . No, he couldn't go that far, but at least he could say that the noise was less grating. It was enough to make a man think he was falling in love.

He entered the room he shared with Mahri and came to a sudden halt. The insane smile on his face died. There was no Mahri. Though there was nowhere for her to hide in that small chamber, he looked inside the wardrobe anyway, and called himself all kinds of a fool when he found it empty. Her nightdress was draped over a chair, but the clothes the landlady had given her were gone. She had no money. The purse was still in his coat pocket. How in hell's name did she think she would manage? Cursing fluently, he turned on his heel and thundered down the stairs and out the back door.

It was mayhem out there in the stable block, with a crush of gigs and ponies belonging to contestants and their families who had come for the day. He soon learned, however, that no one had borrowed or taken out a pony. People were arriving, not departing.

He returned to the inn and strode through the length of the corridor, barely glancing at those he passed, and pushed through the front doors. What met his eyes was a sea of people navigating booths and tents that were set up on the village green. Beyond the green the road rose steeply toward the field where the games were taking place.

He didn't know where to begin to look for her. He felt angry, helpless, and alarmed, all at the same time. Overriding these emotions, however, was a sense of wounded pride. He'd been taken in by her empty promises yet again. How could she do this to him after last night?

"Alex!"

His head whipped round.

"Over here."

Mahri was waving to him, Mahri, as pretty as a picture in her cast-off blue gown that might have been made for her. On her head, she wore a tartan tam with an eagle's feather perched on top. She looked as jaunty as a young cockerel.

He clamped his teeth together. He was ready to blister her ears when he crossed to her, but the first words out of his mouth surprised him. "You didn't run away."

She tucked her hand into the crook of his elbow and urged him to one of the booths. "I'm ravenous, and they're selling Forfar Bridies. I haven't had one of those in years. I hope you've money to pay for them."

He stopped her in her tracks and turned her to face him. Ignoring the jostling crush, he said, "I think I deserve an answer, Mahri, after what happened between us last night. So, I repeat, you didn't run away."

She had no quick retort, no glib response to avoid giving him a direct answer. All she knew was that something fundamental had changed between them. It wasn't only that they were lovers. She'd told him more about herself than she'd told anyone. He hadn't tricked her. He deserved the same honesty from her. Anything less would cheapen what had happened between them.

"I wouldn't run from you," she said, "not now. If I decide to leave, I'll tell you. What happened in this case was that I came downstairs for breakfast, or at least for something to eat, and was lured outside by the sound of the pipe band. Then, of course, I smelled the tantalizing odor of Forfar Bridies—so, here I am, thirsty, starving, and with no money to pay for anything."

He realized that she'd made a huge concession. She wouldn't slip away secretly in the middle of the night. She'd tell him to his face that she was leaving, probably after she'd tied him naked to the bedpost and taken away all his clothes. All the same, this was progress.

"It's not as funny as all that," she said, squinting up at his crooked grin.

"I understood that you had agreed to marry me," he replied mildly.

"Did I? I don't remember that." She put her fingers to his lips to silence him. "Let's take this one day at a time. We have to meet up with the others and see how they have

fared. You have to meet your section chief and clear you
name. After that's done, we can think about the future."

"What about Demos?"

"When they come, I'll be ready."

There was enough ambiguity here to raise the hairs on
his neck. He let it go, reminding himself that he was now
one of the favored few, along with Dugald. He was one of
Mahri's inner circle. When Demos came for her, he would
be ready for them as well.

"Let's get you that Forfar Bridie," he said.

Forfar Bridies had never been one of Alex's favorites.
They were made of minced beef and onions baked in a suet
crust, and they oozed grease. Mahri wolfed hers down like
a starving dog and asked for another. Alex was amused. She
ate like a peasant but had the delicate frame of a dancer. It
was this contradiction between strength and vulnerability
that intrigued him. He wondered about her involvement
with Demos. She'd been a courier, she'd told him. Small
fry. Then why were they determined to capture her?

And why was he worrying when she appeared to be as
carefree as a child?

"Alex," she said, licking the grease from her fingers,
"are you going to get me another Bridie or not?"

He'd prefer to stay and help her lick her fingers. "Right,"
he said, "another Forfar Bridie for milady."

He returned with the Bridie and also a small basket of
fruit and cheeses that they could munch on as they wandered among the booths and tents.

Most of those who were on the green had brought their
own food and were making a picnic of it. It had the feel of a
country fair. There were no lords and ladies of the manor to
kowtow to, no well-heeled landowners watching the comings and goings of their tenants. All the bigwigs would be
taking in the games and handing out ribbons to the various

competitors. Every once in a while, they heard the roar of the crowd as a favorite took the prize.

At one point, Mahri said, "If Dugald were here, he would be in his element. I'm not joking. When he was younger, Dugald was the champion putter of the stone in the whole of Scotland. My brother and I used to follow him from one gathering to another."

"You traveled all over Scotland?" He was amazed.

"Hardly. We took in the local games, but Scotland came to us. Braemar, Alex. Eventually all champions come to pit their skill against each other at the Braemar Games."

She was halfway through her second Bridie and stopped eating. "I'm not really enjoying this," she said.

"Then why did you ask for it?"

"Because Dugald and my brother scoffed them down by the score. I suppose I wanted to share in the camaraderie, so I ate them, too. Luckily, we only got them at the games. My grandparents wouldn't allow them in the house—too much grease for Granny's delicate digestion. I suppose munching on a Forfar Bridie brings back happy memories. Unfortunately, it also brings on a stomachache. I'd forgotten about that."

"Your grandparents didn't come out to watch their gamekeeper's skill putting the stone?"

"They didn't travel much, but every year they would make the trip from Gairnshiel to Braemar, and Dugald appreciated the gesture. My grandfather said that one of his proudest moments was pinning a blue ribbon on Dugald's chest. The ribbon also came with a purse. That was a golden day."

She was staring into space as if she'd been transported back in time to that golden age. He was thinking of Gairnshiel. He knew the name but couldn't remember where it was located.

Alex disposed of the half-eaten Bridie by throwing it to one of the many stray dogs that followed the crowds. She dug in the basket, came up with an apple, and polished it on her sleeve.

"What happened to your grandparents' house?" he asked casually.

She was on the point of biting into the apple when his question arrested her. There was a moment of complete and utter stillness before she turned to look at him. "What happened to *your* grandparents' house?" she asked.

He answered easily. "It came to me on their deaths. We're going there now." He could have bitten his tongue out. He shouldn't have asked such a pointed question. Now she was wary of him.

"I could say the same. On my grandparents' death, the house came to me. My solicitors rent it out. Well, it's too big for one person, but I can't bear to sell it. Anyway, when I'm in Deeside, I'm rarely here for more than a few days at a time. I stay with Dugald."

He knew when to press for answers and when to back off. Nevertheless, her wariness irked him. They were lovers. He'd asked her to marry him. There should be no secrets between them. He should come first with her, just as she was first with him.

She interrupted his train of thought. "Listen!" she said.

"What?"

"The pipes. In the marquee? I think the dancing may have started. Don't you like Highland dancing?"

"Well enough. As long as no one expects me to dance."

"No one will. For one thing, you're not wearing a kilt, and for another, these are exhibition dances. Only the best are allowed to take part."

His resigned expression brightened considerably.

"Do we have time to take in the dancing?" she asked.

"What?"

"You said we should get off to an early start."

"That was before we slept half the day away. I've reserved our room for another night."

"In that case, what are we waiting for?"

* * *

She knew how to put on a good show, but behind her smiles and ready laughter, her mind was hard at work. He was still digging for answers, still looking for discrepancies in every careless remark. Alex would never give up. It seemed she couldn't win. Alex wanted to annihilate Demos, and she couldn't allow it.

There was only one thing to do. She had no choice. She had to face her father and tell him and his cronies that their days were numbered. She had the means to bring them down. She had to convince her father that she was desperate enough to do it.

It was her loose tongue that had brought her to this fix. She shouldn't have mentioned Gairnshiel or the house, shouldn't have forgotten even for a minute that Alex was an agent of the Crown. His agile mind would soon put two and two together.

She wasn't going to trick him. She wasn't going to lie to him. But that did not mean she had to tell him all her secrets. One day, perhaps, but not yet.

Meanwhile, she tried to appear happy and unconcerned. After taking in the Highland dancing, they wandered among the tents and booths in a desultory way, stopping to admire the work of local artisans. They were on their way back to the hotel when they came to a tent with a sign outside it. There were no words on it, only a sketch of a crystal ball.

"I've always wanted to have my fortune told," said Mahri.

"I can't think why. You've already met your Mr. Tall, Dark, and Handsome."

"True. But Dugald says he's too old for me."

"Very funny."

She grinned. "I'm not joking. I asked him to marry me when I was about six years old. That's when he told me he was too old for me. I, of course, was brokenhearted."

Alex wasn't quite sure how it happened, but he found himself inside the tent before he could dig in his heels or voice a protest.

"Mahri," he said, "you're not taken in by this flummery, are you?"

"Oh, don't be such a killjoy. It's only a bit of fun."

It was as dark as pitch in that small tent, and it smelled distressingly of incense and candle grease. Alex chuckled. "So must the blasted heath have looked when Macbeth met the witches. Come along, Mahri. This is nothing but theater."

But Mahri would not budge. "Wait," she said, "the smoke is clearing."

Alex peered into that dim interior, and gradually there emerged the figure of an old gypsy woman with a shawl around her head, sitting at a lace-covered table. In the center of the table was a crystal ball.

"I have been waiting for you," said the gypsy. Her voice was low and musical with a decided Gaelic lilt.

If Mahri had not been there, Alex would have turned on his heel and walked out. He had no patience with fortune-tellers who made a mockery of things they did not understand. He stayed because Mahri seemed set on taking part in the gypsy's games.

The gypsy said something in Gaelic. Alex understood the odd word, but that was all. Mahri pulled up a chair and sat down. After a moment, Alex followed suit.

The gypsy's eyes bored into Alex's. "I don't tell fortunes or make prophecies," she said as though she could read his mind. She pushed the crystal ball toward him. "The crystal speaks for itself."

"Well, go on," said Mahri when Alex hesitated. "Hold it."

Forgive me, Granny, Alex silently prayed, then he grasped the crystal with both hands and stared into its depths. It was just as he expected. Nothing happened. There were no pictures, no visions, no voices, not even a reflection of his own face. The crystal remained impersonal and silent. After a moment or two, he set it back in the center of the table.

"Nothing," he said, "not even a whisper. Your crystal ball isn't speaking to me."

"That," said the gypsy, "is because you have shut your mind to it. Would the lady like to try?"

Mahri darted a glowering look at Alex then smiled into the gypsy's eyes. "Of course I want to try," she said. "I have great respect"—another darting glance at Alex—"for the old ways and the old knowledge."

There was a softening in the old woman, and she smiled fleetingly. "If the crystal speaks to anyone, it will speak to you," she said.

Alex sat like a block of stone while Mahri reached for the crystal. He watched her fingers close around it. She seemed calm and collected. She was breathing normally. A minute ticked by, then she let out a long breath and released the crystal.

"Well?" said Alex. One corner of his mouth turned up. "Did the crystal speak to you?"

"Didn't you hear it?"

He straightened in his chair. "No. I heard nothing. What did it say?"

"It said—oh, it doesn't make sense."

"Tell me!"

"It said that I would pass through fire but would not be consumed by it. What a strange thing to say!"

They both turned at the same moment to look at the gypsy. Her chair was empty, but behind the chair was another tent flap that fluttered in the breeze. They looked at the table. The crystal ball had vanished as well.

"We didn't even pay her," said Mahri.

It wasn't trumpery," said Mahri. She idly arranged the cutlery on the table as she thought things through. "I heard a voice. You'll just have to take my word for it. And I could not have made up that strange message. '*You will pass through fire, but the fire will not consume you.*' I know it sounds crazy, but that's what I heard."

"You don't have to convince me. Didn't I tell you that a famous seer once laid a prophecy on me, too?"

They were in the dining room of the Feughside Hotel, waiting for their dinner to be served. Massive dark beams crisscrossed the ceiling, and a plethora of stags' heads on the walls stoically surveyed the diners. There were few tables still available, and the babble of conversation made it necessary for Alex and Mahri to keep their heads close together.

Mahri said, "Yes, but you gave me the impression that you didn't take it seriously. Well, I'm not exactly a true believer myself, but there are some things that defy explanation."

They pulled apart as a serving girl delivered their first course, fish soup with oatcakes. Mahri took a spoonful of the broth before going on. "Who was this famous seer, anyway?"

"My granny," responded Alex simply.

There was a moment of complete silence. "Your granny?" she finally said.

"My granny," he repeated.

She chuckled. "Yes, well, doesn't every old woman in Scotland think that she's a bit of a witch? I know my granny did."

"Very true, but my granny was the genuine article. It runs in the family."

He continued eating his soup, while Mahri stared at him with narrowed eyes. "Alex," she whispered, "are you . . . are you a wizard?"

He used his napkin to dab his lips. "What do you think?"

Her narrow-eyed stare suddenly dissolved in laughter. He laughed along with her.

"Seriously," she said, "what do you think the prophecy means?"

For the rest of the meal, they speculated. Neither was inclined to take the prophecy at face value. It seemed to Mahri that the fire referred to their present troubles, and they were going to come through them unscathed. It was what they both wanted to believe. Alex didn't tell her that they shared the same prophecy, thinking that it would only make her suspect his motives. Her eyes were clear, her smiles were natural, and that was what he wanted for her.

The evening passed pleasantly. By tacit consent, they avoided any subject that might lead to disharmony between them. When they entered their chamber, they undressed slowly and slid into bed. There was no frantic haste to possess or be possessed. They touched, they stroked, they kissed. Everything was mellow. Their movements were fluid and languid. Time seemed to slow. Passion hovered, but they kept it at bay.

"I want this to go on forever," she murmured. She was lost in the feel and taste of him.

He settled his lips on hers. "Don't worry. It will."

"You're very sure of yourself."

"I should be. I'm a wizard, remember?"

Her laugh turned into a moan. Magic, she thought, magic fingers, magic kisses. Maybe he was a wizard after all.

He took his mouth over the crest of one breast, then the other, and laved each distended nipple with tongue and lips. When he slipped his fingers between her thighs to find her hot and wet for him, his lips curved in a smile. The smile became a groan when her hands closed around his jutting sex and caressed him voluptuously.

Pleasure, he discovered, could not be delayed for long. It beat through his blood in an ever-quickening tempo. He swallowed the small sounds she made as the pleasure rose in her, too. Their breathing grew thicker, their movements erratic.

Even when he filled her, he would not yield to her pleas for haste. He teased and tormented and kept the pace slow, drawing out every nuance of sensation until she was shuddering beneath him.

"I thought you wanted this to go on forever," he said.

Her nails scored his back and, just like the first time, he thrust and buried himself deep inside her. The pleasure was so intense, he had to grit his teeth to hang on to his control. There was no going back now.

"Little cheat," he said on a strangled laugh.

He raised on his arms to make their joining as deep as he could. She gasped and clutched at his shoulders. She was as desperate as he and matched his fervor kiss for kiss, stroke for stroke. At the end, as he emptied himself into her, she muffled her cry of release against his throat.

When he could breathe again, he slipped from her body, raised on one elbow, and studied her face.

"What?" she asked. She was breathless.

"Are you going to leave me, Mahri? After this?" He palmed her breasts. "Well?"

"Have I said so?"

He might have pushed her. What stopped him was the look in her eyes: fragile, pleading, uncertain. She wanted his understanding. And he would give it to her, up to a point. All the same, he felt disappointment shimmer through him. They were back to playing games.

Twenty-one

❧

They'd been following the Feugh, a tributary of the Dee, and were almost at the village of Banchory, when Alex changed direction. It seemed to Mahri that they were going south, but after an hour or so, when they came to a cross-roads, she realized that he had changed direction again.

She reined in. "We're going back the way we came," she said, "only we're taking a more convoluted route."

He stopped as well, removed a gauntlet, and stroked his mount's neck. "We're not likely to meet any patrols on this road." He glanced at her. "Besides, I've left a trail that should lead anyone following us to Banchory. Now we're doubling back by a different route."

"You left a trail? What does that mean?"

"I told them at the hotel that we were going to take the train from Banchory to Aberdeen."

She made a scoffing sound. "Foster will know you're too clever to do anything of the sort."

He grinned. "Was that a compliment I heard?"

She scowled. "What name did you use?"

"Alexander. Mr. and Mrs. Alexander. Now what?"

"That's your own name! You might as well have called yourself 'Hepburn.' Anyone with a modicum of intelligence would know that you're trying to lay a false trail."

"Lucky for us, Foster is as thick as a door."

"And you think you're being clever, going back into enemy territory? I call it madness."

"You may be right, but in the heat of the moment, when someone tried to kill me on the train and you were going off with those thugs, it was the only rendezvous that came to mind. That's where the others will meet up with us."

Mahri made a harrumphing sound and touched her horse's sides with her heels. "Feughside," she said. "Is that the name of your house?"

"It is, though it's more like a hunting lodge now. When we're not using it, we rent it out to hunting parties."

"Is that where Gavin was shot when he was captured by the soldiers?"

His tone was mild, untroubled. "There won't be soldiers there now. Gavin was captured because he wasn't expecting trouble. We'll be more cautious, and at the first sign of trouble, we'll take evasive action."

There was no point arguing with him. If he'd told the others that they'd all meet up at his hunting lodge, then that was where they had to go.

She liked it even less when, some hours later, they passed the ruins of Birse Castle. Out of sight, across the river Dee, lay a back road to her grandparents' house near Gairnshiel.

They were all too close for her comfort.

Enemy territory, she thought.

Feughside House made a favorable first impression on Mahri. It had three gables facing west to catch the setting sun, and was nestled in a grove of poplars. There was no flood damage here, because the house was on a rise, but the storm had brought down plenty of trees.

A young boy came running from the stable to take their horses. His face split into a huge grin when in answer to his spate of questions, Alex was able to reassure him that Mr. Gavin was fine and would soon be joining them.

As the boy led the horses away, she said, "I thought the house would be deserted, especially after the soldiers arrested Gavin."

"No. Calley—that's Gavin's manservant—has been here for years. He has nowhere else to go, and Danny, whom you just met, is in much the same case. You'll find my brother has a soft spot for strays."

Calley opened the door to them. He was a compact, sturdy man, well turned out, with age lines on a long face but no laugh lines. There was only a hint of Scotland in his accent, indicating to Mahri that he had held a superior position in some gentleman's service at one time.

While he and Alex talked in muted tones about the debacle at the queen's reception and its aftermath, she wandered through the dark paneled hallway to what appeared to be the main reception room, and here her first impression quietly died. Someone had been using the room for target practice. The usual complement of stags' heads on the walls looked as though the person who had hung the poor beasties was highly intoxicated at the time. There were bullet holes in the ceilings and bullet holes in the walls. Though there were no signs of bottles, the very air stank of stale beer and whiskey. She looked down at the floor. The Turkish carpet had been liberally christened with only God knew what.

Alex either sensed her distaste or saw something in her expression that made him join her. "You must remember," he said, "that this is a bachelor establishment. Men like to throw off the trappings of civilization once in a while."

"If I might point out, sir," intoned Calley in his flawless accent, "most of the damage was done by the soldiers who took Mr. Gavin away. A few stayed on and, shall we say, decided to throw a party?"

Mahri was curious about Calley. He was one of Gavin's strays? Why would such a superior servant bury himself in this isolated spot? She didn't ask questions, because she knew only too well the awkwardness of trying to protect her own secrets. It could turn a person into a liar. Live and let live—that was her motto.

Alex was showing her the cellars where the stores were kept when a scuffling sound behind an ancient, broken-down boiler had her head whipping round. Her first thought was that a badger or a fox had got into the house, but a series of snuffles, barks, and whines made her brows climb.

"A dog?" she said, glancing at Alex.

In the next instant, what appeared to be a filthy, trussed-up rug came barreling out of the boiler and practically bowled Alex over.

"Down, Macduff!" he said sternly, then to Mahri, "This ugly brute is another of Gavin's strays. His name is Macduff. Gavin will be glad to see him. He thought that the soldiers who arrested him had maimed or killed him."

Mahri went down on her haunches and looked into the softest brown eyes she had ever beheld. His nose was scorched; the paw he offered her was badly lacerated, and the stench clinging to his coat would have turned the stomach of the most hardened tinker.

It was love at first sight.

She opened her arms, and Macduff fell into them as though he belonged there. "Oh, you beauty," she breathed out. "What were you doing in the boiler?"

"The old boiler," Alex said, "is the entrance to a secret underground passage that comes out at a stone cairn farther down the hill."

He opened the door wide to let Mahri get a better view. She saw a trapdoor with stone steps leading down into a stygian darkness.

"And Macduff knows how to open the trapdoor?"

He shrugged. "You'd be surprised what Macduff can do. He likes to come and go as he pleases. But he would never have left Gavin if he had not been hurt really badly."

"Yes, he looks as though he has come through the wars." She scratched Macduff's ears and was rewarded with a toothy grin. "I suppose the secret passage was an escape route for Jacobites during the rebellion?"

"What makes you think that?"

"Well, this is Deeside, isn't it? It was a Jacobite stronghold. There's hardly a house here that doesn't have a secret passage to hide Jacobites during the rebellion."

"Nothing so romantic." He was amazed at how docilely Macduff allowed Mahri to remove burrs and thorns from his matted coat. Only Gavin was ever allowed that privilege. "It was used to transport contraband whiskey from the illegal still that my great-great-grandfather set up in what is now the wine cellar." He pointed to a door behind Mahri. "I'm afraid we Hepburns were an unsavory lot."

"Don't blame yourself. We can't choose our relatives." Thinking that she might have said too much, she went on quickly, "I'd like to see it."

"I'll show it to you tomorrow. Right now, I want to wash, change, and eat, in that order."

She stopped petting Macduff and straightened. "You mean you're going to give up your dandy outfit and become Mr. Sobersides again?"

"Hardly. I'll be borrowing Gavin's things."

"And what am I going to wear?"

A memory came to mind of Mahri, sleek and loose-limbed, with not a stitch on her.

She glared at his foolish grin. "Come along, Macduff," she said. "Let's find you something to eat. Then we'll see what those soldiers did to you."

From then on, Macduff became Mahri's slave. He tolerated Alex, but if he put his hands on Mahri, the dog insinuated himself between them and growled like a bear. Alex's hopes of a romantic interlude before the others arrived dwindled to nothing.

The following morning, when he took her into the secret passage, Macduff nosed his way in, too. "If there's any trouble," Alex said, "this is the place to be. What I mean by that is, if soldiers come back, it's a good place to hide. Don't touch anything, though. It's filthy down here. It hasn't been cleaned out in years."

With lantern in hand, he led the way.

She didn't care about getting her gown dirty, because she was wearing the same gown she'd worn for the last three days. She was hoping that Juliet would arrive soon so that she could borrow some of her finery. There were bits and pieces of ladies' clothing in the wardrobe in her bedchamber, but not what she considered suitable. Evidently, Gavin liked party girls. Or, she thought churlishly, maybe they were strays Gavin had taken in from the goodness of his heart.

She checked herself. She tried not to worry about the others, but she couldn't control her fears. As Alex had pointed out, they had been separated for only four days. If they hadn't turned up by the end of the week, they would go to Aberdeen and join them.

None of this would have happened if Demos had never been born. Her own guilt weighed heavily. She could stop it. No. She would stop it. She couldn't involve Alex. He was in enough trouble as it was. This was something she had to do by herself.

"Careful," Alex said when she stumbled.

The earthen floor was littered with debris: wooden kegs, stone bottles, broken glass and pottery, and a plethora of chamber pots.

"Chamber pots?" she said, surprised into laughing.

"I'm assuming," replied Alex, "that our smugglers had to hide out for long hours when the excise men came calling. Those were the only facilities that were to hand."

Mahri wondered who had the job of emptying them

but refrained from voicing the thought, not because it was indelicate but because something else had occurred to her.

"I don't hear Macduff," she said.

They both stopped and listened. The dog had been jogging ahead of them, sniffing at various objects of interest in its path. All they heard now was silence. They turned to look back the way they had come.

"I would have known if he had brushed by me," Mahri said. "He must still be ahead of us."

Alex wasn't worried about the dog. Macduff could take care of himself.

He set the lantern on the floor and took a step toward Mahri. Chuckling, he said, "If this doesn't bring Macduff to us, nothing will." He put his hands on her shoulders. They were both smiling when their lips brushed.

Mahri lifted her head. "Macduff?" she called. "Here, boy."

No response.

Alex said, "Let's give him something to worry about. Now, kiss me as if you really mean it."

He brought his lips to hers in a long, openmouthed kiss. When he raised his head, she licked her lips. "I love the taste and scent of you," she said.

Her careless words changed a lighthearted flirtation into something quite different. "I'm *starved* for the taste and scent of you."

He unbuttoned the bodice of her dress and yanked it down to her waist. Her small, firm breasts were made for his palm, made for his mouth. He teased and laved the pebble-hard nipples with lips and teeth till the need inside him was more pain than pleasure.

His weight carried her back against the wall; his hands slid around her waist then dropped lower to cup the soft swell of her bottom. Her little trilling cries made him desperate for more. When he lifted her into his hard groin and ground himself into her, she arched her neck and bit back a moan.

The blood was thundering in her ears. Heat raced along her skin. Was this the fire the gypsy foretold? The gypsy was wrong. It was stealing her breath, burning her lungs, consuming her.

He raised his head and spoke against her lips. "You see? Everything is easy. I don't know why you have to make things difficult."

He was dragging her skirts up, positioning her for the hard thrust he was sure she was as eager to receive as he was to give, when she splayed her hands against his shoulders and shoved him away.

He was stunned.

She felt as though she'd been shaken awake by a douse of cold water. Everything wasn't as easy as he seemed to think. It was chaos, a labyrinth, and she had to find a way out for both their sakes.

She held him at bay with one hand against his chest. "Now you listen to me," she finally managed. "I won't be seduced into betraying my comrades, so don't even try—"

He lashed out with his fist, smashing the wall behind her, making her jump. He was shocked at his violence, but he couldn't seem to stop himself. "Is that what you think of me?" he demanded angrily. "That I would stoop to that level?"

"You're a secret service agent. I was a member of Demos. What else should I think?"

"That's not what you thought at the hotel." His eyes narrowed on her face. "What is going on in that devious mind of yours?"

She couldn't look him straight in the eye, so she focused on adjusting her dress. He was right about the nights they had spent in the hotel, but she was right, too. The magic couldn't last in the real world of spies and traitors. One thing she never doubted: Alex was good at his job. He picked up clues the way a magnet picked up steel pins. His brain was a filter. Once his name was cleared, he would go after Demos like a hound on the scent of the hare.

It was frightening how much she wanted to confide in him, be held by him. She cleared her throat. "You know as well as I," she said, "that the nights we spent in the hotel were an interlude, something divorced from reality. Now we're back to reality. We're on the opposite sides. We can't get around that."

She could see the violence flaring in him again.

"Opposite sides?" he said savagely. "Are you deaf and blind? I'm in love with you. I'm on your side."

Her heart stuttered then righted itself. "You say that now, but what will you say when you have Demos in the palm of your hand?"

He said wearily, "You've made your point, quite eloquently, in fact." He picked up the lantern. "The point of bringing you here was to show you another way out in case the soldiers come looking for us. So let's keep to the real point, shall we?"

He stalked ahead of her. She had to pick up her feet to keep up with him. She was, by turns, angry and teary. Doing the right thing shouldn't make her feel like this.

They came to the end of the corridor and turned a corner.

"I thought as much," said Alex.

"What is it?"

"Macduff is up to his old tricks. See?" He pointed to a hole in the dirt floor where a mound of earth lay against the stone wall. "He has dug under the wall so that he can come and go as he pleases."

She wasn't terribly interested in Macduff. She'd been in an enclosed space long enough. "Yes, Alex, but how do we get out of here?"

"We use the door, of course."

He went down on his haunches and used his shoulder to push against what turned out to be a loose section of the wall. Stone grated against stone. The rock he was pushing against gave way and fresh air rushed in.

Mahri was astonished. "It's not much of a door, is it?"

"It wasn't meant for ladies, but for smugglers. Come on. And duck your head."

She ducked her head and crawled after him. For a moment or two, she was blinded by the intense rays of the sun. When her eyes became accustomed to the light, she saw that the opening they'd come through was in the base of the stone cairn.

She got to her feet and walked slowly around the cairn. It reminded her of the towering cairns on the slopes of the Balmoral estate, only this one was smaller.

"Not much cover here," she said, looking down toward the valley of the Feugh.

"All the better to see your enemies," Alex replied.

After heaving the stone back to conceal the exit, he got up and shielded his eyes against the sun. "So that's why Macduff deserted us," he said and pointed. "Gavin has come home." The look he gave Mahri was level and steady. "Seems like you've lost your appeal, Mahri."

She was left to chew on his words as he bounded down the slope toward a buggy that, she now saw, was making for the house. Trotting beside it was Macduff.

Let me see if I've got this straight," said Alex. "You sent a telegram to Whitehall, but it didn't reach Durward till yesterday, and by then he had already arrived in Ballater?"

"That about sums it up." Gavin watched Alex as he began to pace. "They rerouted the telegram to him, and he lost no time in coming to see me."

They were in the small library on the main floor, having enjoyed a scrumptious dinner laid on by Calley, whose culinary skills had been learned in the famous gentlemen's clubs of London. Alex was nursing an after-dinner whiskey, while Gavin sipped what he called "Pannanich tea" from a pewter mug.

"Tell me again," said Alex, "what you learned from Durward."

Gavin gave a hoot. "Very little. He is so closemouthed that I found myself rambling on about trivialities just to fill the silence."

From the room upstairs came the sound of feminine laugher. Gavin gave a sheepish grin. "Juliet," he said, "is no doubt having a laugh at my expense. There was this nurse, you see . . . Well, suffice it to say that she took a shine to me. It was embarrassing. There is nothing like an amorous nurse to help a patient recover in double-quick time. I couldn't wait to get away."

Alex stopped pacing and raised an amused brow. "What in hell's name do women see in you, Gavin?"

Gavin grinned. "I have never met a woman I did not like. They know it and respond accordingly."

"Why flee from the nurse, then?"

Gavin took a sip of tea. "She got the wrong idea about me. I can't possibly marry every woman who takes my fancy. It's illegal."

Alex shook his head and sat down on the chair facing Gavin. His nose wrinkled. "Your dog is in here somewhere," he said. "I can smell him."

A white woolly head poked from under a sideboard and showed Alex his teeth.

"It's all right, Macduff," Gavin said, "Alex is joking. He knows you've had your bath."

The woolly head disappeared.

Alex said, "I wonder about that dog sometimes. It's as though he understands English."

"Yes, well, I've been teaching him a few words, you know, *sit, stay*, that sort of thing. He's a quick study."

Alex sat back in his chair and stretched out his long legs, crossing them at the ankles. As he sipped his whiskey, he took stock of his brother. He seemed fully recovered, a circumstance Gavin attributed more to the Pannanich water that Juliet had forced him to drink every day than to the pokings and proddings of the eminent doctor who had him under his care. The Pannanich water, however, was all but gone, and Gavin had insisted that they get a fresh supply, even if he had to go to the witch himself. That was where Dugald was, at Pannanich Wells, not only to get more water but to look over the lie of the land.

"To get back to Durward," Alex said. "He knows about our arrest and escape from the castle?"

"Oh, yes. Foster has done his job well. Now Durward wants to hear your side of the story."

"And how were things left?"

"I told him that you'd send a telegram saying when and where you would be willing to meet him. He's putting up at the barracks in Ballater, by the way. So this morning, before boarding the train, I sent him a telegram in your name, advising the commander that you would meet him tomorrow in the lobby of the Huntly Arms after the train from Aberdeen gets in."

"So, he thinks I'm in Aberdeen?"

"He does."

Alex took a moment to think things through. "Didn't it occur to you that if Durward didn't trust us, he could have had you clapped in irons and marched to the nearest tollbooth?"

"I thought about it, but you're a bigger catch than I am, so I was betting that he'd hold off until he had you in his sights, and I wasn't going to lead him to you if I could help it."

"That's why you left Aberdeen right after you'd sent him the telegram?"

"I thought it was a brilliant idea. This way, you get to call the shots."

"Perhaps Durward was one step ahead of you."

Gavin shook his head. "No one followed us, if that's what you mean. There were no policemen hanging around stations. We split up. Juliet and I traveled first class and Dugald went third. As I told you, Mrs. Cardno was persuaded to stay on with friends in Aberdeen. Juliet thought it best. If anything went wrong, she didn't want her mother involved."

Another burst of laughter came from upstairs. "So what's happening with the fair Mahri?" Gavin asked. "She seems happy enough."

Alex got up. "Her name is Mahri Scot, or Scott with two *t*'s. Does that name mean anything to you?"

"There are hundreds of Scots in this neck of the woods."

"Her grandparents had a house near Gairnshiel."

"Where in hell's name is Gairnshiel?"

"On the other side of Ballater, I think. Mahri said that her grandfather once traveled to Braemar to watch Dugald participate in the games."

Gavin shook his head. "I've heard of Gairnshiel, but I can't for the life of me place it. You think that that's where her friends are hiding out?"

"Are they her friends?" When Gavin cocked his head and looked up at his brother, Alex said, "I'm not sure what's going on, and that's the truth. I'm going for a walk. Care to come with me?"

"Thank you, no. I've had enough excitement for one day. I'll just choose a book and toddle off to bed."

After Alex left, Gavin drummed his fingers on the armrest and stared into space. He was pulled from his thoughts when Macduff whined and put a paw on his knee.

He scratched behind Macduff's ears. "I'm not sad," he said. "It's just that I have a lot to think about."

Macduff lowered his chin on his master's knees and stared up at him with soulful eyes.

"Mahri," said Gavin, returning Macduff's stare. "She's in trouble up to her neck, and it's up to us to keep a watchful eye on her."

Macduff thumped his tail on the floor.

He felt like a bloody idiot. This was Alex's thought as he undressed for bed. He tossed one boot over the footboard, then the other. He'd gone to her room after everyone was asleep, hoping to straighten everything out between them. He'd half expected a locked door. What he'd found barring his entrance was seventy pounds of quivering, ferocious dog. He couldn't understand it. He and Macduff had been friends at one time.

Bloody dog!

He was seething with resentment. Didn't she know that she could be hanged as a traitor? Didn't she understand that his one aim was to protect her, not only from her own people but from his as well? What really rankled was that while she'd put the members of her cell before him, she was and would always come first with him.

How had he ever allowed a woman to gain such power over him?

He settled himself in bed, staring into the darkness with his fingers linked behind his neck. He was missing something. What was it?

Piece by piece, he began to arrange the puzzle of Mahri in different formations. There was a gap, something he had overlooked, one of his visions that perhaps he had misinterpreted.

When that didn't work, he went back to the beginning and set the events of the last few weeks in chronological order: plans for the queen's reception, the arrival of Mahri's letter, setting up Mungo as the decoy, the assassination attempt, Dickens's murder, and so it went on.

He drifted into sleep, then suddenly jolted awake. All the pieces were beginning to click into place.

Foster. Why did he keep coming back to the colonel?

Twenty-two

&c%

Commander Durward was a fifteen-year veteran of Her Majesty's Secret Service. Before that, he had been an academic in some of the most prestigious schools and universities in both England and Scotland. He was still an academic, but now his keen intelligence had a narrower focus. It was his job to protect the queen. He was in his midfifties, as lean as a whippet, and had the face of a poet that was at odds with his caustic tongue and abrupt manner. The commander had no patience with incompetence in any shape or form.

"The man is an idiot," he said in his gravelly voice. He was referring to Colonel Foster. "I knew it was a mistake to leave him in charge, but the decision wasn't mine. It came from Whitehall, and my orders were to protect the queen, not her stand-in. Her Majesty was in Windsor, so that was where I had to go. Besides, we thought it might be a hoax, and Dickens was a good, capable man." Durward shook his head. "What a bloody botch of things Foster has made."

He and Alex were sitting at an alcove table in the

baronial foyer of the Huntly Arms in Aboyne. Though it was still light outside, the interior of the hotel was gloomy, and several lamps had been lit. Durward was under the impression that Alex had arrived earlier on the train from Aberdeen, and Alex had decided not to correct that impression. His natural caution inclined him to keep the commander guessing.

The waiter arrived with a whiskey for each of them and, after toasting the queen, they settled back in their comfortable upholstered chairs to continue their discussion on what had transpired on the night of the queen's reception.

"I've heard Foster's story," the commander said. "Now I want to hear yours."

Alex had to suppress a smile. He was remembering the year he had spent at St. Andrew's University as a young man and how, whether in the right or in the wrong, he had always squirmed under Durward's killing stare. He was no longer that young man, but old habits were hard to break. They'd developed an easy rapport over the years, but Alex never forgot or was allowed to forget that Durward was his superior. All the same, this was an unusual situation. He and the commander didn't usually meet for drinks in a public place. They met in the offices of Whitehall, or they contacted one another by coded messages.

"At the queen's reception," Alex said, "a woman with blond hair shot Mr. Ramsey; then she made her escape. My brother and I gave chase but split up when we came to a crossroads. My path took me to Braemar, where I spent half the night combing through taverns and alehouses trying to find her. The next day, I tried to report to Colonel Foster and was immediately arrested and incarcerated. That's when I learned that Dickens had been murdered."

"And your brother?"

Alex took a small sip of whiskey. "He would say much the same as I, except that his path took him in the opposite direction, to Ballater and Aboyne."

They went back and forth, Durward picking at every

loose thread in Alex's story, Alex taking care not to implicate Mahri. Finally, Alex said impatiently, "The woman is irrelevant. She shot Ramsey, not the queen. Ask Ramsey why the woman would try to kill him."

Durward's reply was just as impatient. "Ramsey has already been interrogated and allowed to go. He has no idea why anyone would try to kill him. As for the woman, the chief of security at Balmoral Castle is stabbed to death the same night that a woman takes a potshot at one of the guests, and you say that she is irrelevant? You sound just like Foster."

"I meant to Dickens's murder. Gavin and I went after her. She wasn't anywhere near Dickens when he was murdered, and neither was Gavin or myself."

"I believe you, Alex, but I can't simply disregard Foster's charges against you."

"Who are his witnesses?" Alex demanded. "Stable hands, so I've been told, and all they can tell the colonel is that we borrowed a couple of horses. I hope you asked Ramsey where he was at the crucial time."

The commander said, "I have yet to question him, but I've read his statement. There's nothing in it that implicates you or your brother. Your trouble was that you acted like a guilty man. According to Foster, you did not surrender. You were captured. But that's not all, is it, Alex? You broke out of prison. Foster has taken that as an admission of guilt." He held up a hand to silence Alex before he could respond. "And you had help. The guard on duty said that he was waylaid by a man and girl. Who are they?"

"They're friends. I'll give you their names just as soon as my brother and I are cleared of these charges."

The commander cocked a bushy brow. "I trained you better than that. In this game, we have no friends."

Alex replied mildly, "When one's colleagues become enemies, one finds one's allies where one can."

Durward regarded Alex steadily over the rim of his glass. After draining it, he said, "I trust you, Alex, not because I know you're a good agent—even the best can be turned—but because Foster is such an incompetent clown, and that is putting it mildly. He knows nothing of police work or checking out witnesses' statements. He is convinced you are guilty because you disappeared right after Dickens was murdered and didn't return of your own free will."

He spoke over Alex's protest. "I'm going to do what Foster has failed to do. I'm going to chase down witnesses and get their statements again. However, I'm advising you and your brother to give yourselves up. If you don't, you know what comes next. A 'kill on sight' order will go out on both you and your brother. Do I make myself clear?"

Alex's brow pleated as he gazed at the older man. "Kill on sight? That's a bit extreme, isn't it?" He thought for a moment. "Something big is coming up. What is it?"

Durward squeezed the bridge of his nose between thumb and forefinger.

Alex said, "It must be something to do with the queen."

"You'll know soon enough. It will be in the papers. Queen Victoria, against the advice of her ministers, will arrive in Ballater on Saturday. She was furious when she heard that she'd been delayed at Windsor for her own safety, and beyond rage when she learned that a decoy had taken her place at the reception. Well, you know how Her Majesty feels about her duty. She is no coward. However, it's *my* duty to keep her safe, and regardless of our long friendship, Alex, I'll do everything in my power to see that you are taken out of play before she arrives. I'd be failing in my duty to the queen if I did anything less."

"I understand," said Alex quietly. And he did. If their positions were reversed, he would say the same to Durward. "You think I'm a member of Demos?"

The commander's gravelly voice rasped with irritation. "Of course I don't think anything of the sort! But it's what Foster thinks. I repeat: I'm only doing my duty."

He reached in his pocket, produced a handkerchief,

and peeled back the edges to reveal a badge, a silver stag's head, and beneath it, the motto, *Bydand*. "Do you recognize this?" he asked.

"It belongs to Mungo," Alex said. "That's the Gordon crest. It means 'stand fast.' It came to him from his maternal grandfather. He said it was his good luck piece. Where did you find it?"

"Among his things in his room at the castle. I know how close you and Mungo were. I thought you might like to have it." He wrapped the handkerchief around the badge and placed it on the table.

A deep breath caught in Alex's chest. He shouldn't be shocked like this. He'd had a premonition that something bad had happened to his friend, but he'd hoped for the best. "You wouldn't be giving me this," he said, "if you thought Mungo was still alive. What has happened, Commander?"

Durward sighed. "We found a body washed up on the bank of the river just below Linn o' Dee. The corpse we found is about a week old and took a terrible battering from the rocks. But, yes, we think it's Mungo."

"What was he doing at the Linn of Dee?" It was a remote place beyond Braemar, where the river suddenly gushed through a narrow gorge between jutting rocks and tumbled onto more rocks below. Few who had the misfortune to lose their footing at this point in the river ever survived to tell the tale.

"We have no idea," Durward replied. "Foster had patrols out looking for him. I was hoping that he would be with you, or you could tell us where he was likely to be."

Alex shook his head. Mungo was dead. It was just sinking in, and his mind resisted the awful reality.

Durward said softly, "I'm sorry, Alex." He got up. "I'll give you till midnight to speak to your friends and give yourselves up."

"Where will you be?"

"Not at the castle. I don't think I could stomach Foster. Send word to me at the barracks, and I'll find you."

Alex watched the commander leave the hotel. It was time for him to go, too. Thoughtful now, he picked up Mungo's badge still wrapped in its handkerchief and quickly slipped it into his pocket. He wasn't ready to palm the badge and discover its secrets. He felt horribly guilty for involving Mungo in his troubles. If it hadn't been for him, Mungo might still be alive.

He waited a few minutes, then made his way to the back of the hotel. Dugald was inside the door, holding a workman's voluminous jerkin and a tartan tam. Making sure that no one was watching, Alex quickly donned his workman's disguise. The bootboy who handed them each an empty wooden crate had already been well paid for his trouble.

Dugald kept up a one-sided conversation in Gaelic as they made their way to a horse-drawn cart that was tethered to the side of the stable. In a matter of minutes, they were making their way home. There were no soldiers in sight. No one followed them.

Alex felt the fine hairs on his neck rise. It was too easy. He knew Durward. They might have a truce, but the commander would be derelict in his duty if he did not pursue every avenue of discovering his quarry's hideout. He was reminded of their escape on the train, which turned out to be no escape at all.

It was too easy.

Calley met Alex as he entered the house. "The others are in the library, sir," he said.

Alex nodded. "Were there any signs of soldiers or strangers in the area while I was away?

"No soldiers," Calley replied, "but there were three riders who passed this way, oh, about an hour ago."

"Which way did they go?"

"Up the hill, toward Birse Castle."

Alex thought for a moment then quickly and precisely told the manservant what he wanted him to do. Without hesitation or protest, Calley left the house by the back door.

The hubbub in the library died before Alex had a chance to remove his disguise. "What's all the excitement about?" he asked.

"Juliet," said Gavin, "took it into her head to go into Aboyne to pick up a few things and came back with a copy of the *Aberdeen Journal.*"

"And it says right here," said Juliet, holding the paper under Alex's nose and pointing to a column with a belligerent finger, "that the queen is arriving in Ballater on Saturday. She wasn't at the reception at all. You were expecting an attack and used a stand-in for Queen Victoria. That's what it says. That was very clever, but what, in the name of God, was the point in keeping it a secret after the attack failed?"

"It wasn't my decision," Alex replied wearily and sank into a wing chair. He spoke to Mahri, who was regarding him as though he were a horrid maggot that she had just discovered crawling across the hem of her gown, a dark green twill that he'd never seen before. Juliet's doing, he thought idly.

"Mahri," he said, "I couldn't tell you that the queen's visit was postponed. It wasn't my decision to make. And if you think about it, you'll see that she was safe as long as we could keep the fiction going that she was in residence at Balmoral Castle."

Gavin interjected soothingly, "It was a good plan. Her Majesty was well protected in Windsor Castle."

Juliet snapped, "What irks me is that Alex told *you* about it, Gavin, but he didn't tell Mahri or me. I thought we were in this together. I thought—"

Gavin abruptly interjected, "Well, now you know. Can we move on? I, for one, want to hear what happened with Durward. What did he say, Alex?"

Mahri, Alex noted, looked as animated as an ice sculpture.

He steepled his fingers. "The commander," he said, "will try to correct the blunders Foster has made, but until he has enough evidence to clear us, Gavin, you and I are still under suspicion for Dickens's murder."

As he went on, he chose his words slowly and thoughtfully, not wishing to alarm the ladies, and omitting any reference to Mungo's death or the badge that weighed so heavily in his pocket. Finally, he said, "The truce ends at midnight. After that, we're fair game for the hunters."

"What does that mean?" asked Mahri sharply.

He gave her a long, narrow-eyed look. "It means that if Gavin and I have not surrendered by midnight tonight, we'll be shot on sight."

Gavin made a scoffing sound. "And I thought Durward was your friend!"

"He's my superior!' Alex said. "And he has a superior to whom he must report as well." He was becoming restless under Mahri's stare. In her own way, she was a soldier, too. She should know that he wasn't free to make his own choices. She did know it, because the same rules applied to her.

"I don't imagine," said Mahri in a voice that breathed out arctic air, "that your commander is sitting in front of a warm fire, nursing a glass of whiskey, waiting for your truce to end. From what I've observed of the secret service, he'll soon be camped outside, waiting for us to show our faces, if he's not there already."

"Act as though he is already watching us," said Alex, "and you won't go far wrong."

He saw the flare of understanding in her eyes and her darting glance in Juliet's direction.

"We can't stay here." Gavin touched Alex lightly on the wrist, drawing his attention away from Mahri. "Now that your people know we have come back into the area, this will be the first place they will look."

"I'm aware of that."

Juliet cut in, "We could go to my house. No one will look for you there. And I'm not suspected of anything. There's no reason for anyone to break down my door."

"I think," said Mahri, "that Alex has already decided what we should do and is choosing the right moment to tell us."

"Thank you," Alex responded. "We have less than an hour to get ready before our time runs out. This is what I propose."

Dugald and the ladies were to leave the lodge by the secret passage, while Alex and Gavin stayed behind and gave them a head start. "Don't wait for us," Alex said. "It's best if we travel in two groups. If you're found with Gavin and me, you'll be incarcerated, too. There will be horses waiting for you at the cairn. Danny is taking care of that right now." He looked at Mahri. "In the event of something unforeseen happening, Dugald will decide what to do."

Juliet said quietly, "Alex, what are you expecting to happen?"

He gave a careless shrug. "I'm being cautious, Juliet, nothing less, nothing more."

"You will catch up with us?" said Mahri.

He loved the worried look that had come into her eyes. "Yes," he said, "but it will be daybreak by the time we reach Juliet's house. We'll rest up there, but when night falls, Gavin and I will set out for Balmoral."

"Balmoral?" Mahri said faintly. "Why Balmoral?"

"Unfinished business with Colonel Foster," Alex replied. And more than that, he would not say.

He was in the garden, going over things in his mind while he waited for the others to get ready to leave. This was where Calley found him.

"There are only two men out there," said Calley, "but they're not soldiers. I'd say that they are scouts. They've taken up a position in the ruined castle."

"Could they be the riders you saw earlier?"

"Indeed they could, not that I recognized them, but one of the horses is a palfrey. I recognized the horse."

Not soldiers but scouts. Who was giving the orders? Durward? They'd taken up their positions before he and Dugald had returned from Aboyne. Durward had been one step ahead of them.

"Thank you, Calley," he said. "You know what to do?"

"Aye. Make it look as though the house is bursting with people."

"Then go to it. But no heroics! If the house comes under attack, you and Danny are to hide in the tunnel."

"Aye, aye, sir," Calley replied and turned and left him.

Alex's hand brushed against his jacket, and he felt the pull of Mungo's good luck charm. It was guilt that made him delay taking it into his hand. He was afraid of what he might see or hear. How many good people had he recruited into the service, only to see their lives snuffed out?

He fingered the badge through the fabric of his jacket and still he hesitated. *Bloody coward!* he thought viciously and, thrusting his hand into his pocket, he withdrew Mungo's badge still wrapped in its white linen shroud.

Even before he'd begun to unwrap the badge, he sensed a malevolent power at work. Bracing himself for more horrors, he removed the handkerchief and stuffed it into his pocket. As his fingers closed around the Gordon crest, the garden quietly receded, and a gentle mist wrapped around him. He heard laughter, a man's and a woman's, and his lips softened in a smile. Gradually, the mist cleared, and the woman's face emerged. She had dark eyes, dark hair, and a beautiful smile. He recognized her at once. He'd seen a photograph of her. She was Mungo's wife, who had died tragically some years ago.

So this was who Mungo was thinking of just before he died.

He blinked hard.

A sudden movement behind him had him pivoting to ward off a blow. Mahri blocked the slash of his hand by throwing up her arm.

She cursed long and furiously in Gaelic. Finally, she got out, "You bleeding imbecile!" She was hopping from foot to foot, cradling her arm against her breasts. "Didn't you hear me call your name?"

"No. I'm sorry."

He was still in the throes of the vision that had filled his mind, still steeped in the guilt he felt over Mungo's death. He wanted to touch her, hold her, make sure that she was all right. He reached for her, but she danced away.

His hands fell to his sides. "You shouldn't be out here alone," he said. "You blocked my first blow, but if I'd been an enemy, you wouldn't have stood a chance."

"I'm not alone," she snapped. "Macduff is with me, and so are you."

At the sound of his name, Macduff pushed his way between them and began to lick Alex's hand.

Mahri said, "A fine guard dog you turned out to be!" She rubbed her sore arm.

Ignoring her, Macduff whined and offered Alex a paw.

Alex bent down to stroke Macduff's head and smiled a little when the dog began to purr like a cat. Straightening, he said, "Time is wasting. So what did you want to say to me?"

He seemed sad, lifeless somehow. Even Macduff sensed the change in him, and that blunted the sharp edge of her words. "Why didn't you tell me that the queen was in Windsor?"

"What difference would it have made?" When she was silent, he went on, "Oh, I see, you could have warned your friends in Demos, and they would have dispersed. But the flood put a stop to that, didn't it?"

She preferred his temper to this cool disdain. "Is this another trap? Is there another decoy queen who will be arriving on Saturday? What's going to happen, Alex?"

He gave a strained laugh. "I'm not in a position to know. Have you forgotten that Gavin and I are the prime suspects? Durward isn't a fool. He's not going to tell me anything. I'm as much in the dark as you are. Maybe it's a test. Who can say?"

She studied his face, the harsh lines of weariness; the dark, turbulent eyes; and her throat ached. "What is it, Alex?" she asked softly. "What's bothering you?"

"Nothing!" His reply was abrupt. A moment of silence went by, then he went on in a different tone, "Mungo is dead. Durward confirmed what I suspected."

"Mungo?" She knew the name. Alex had told her that he feared for his friend.

"He set up our escape by train. We'd been friends since university days." He broke off and shook his head. "I recruited him to the service, but he never would take the danger seriously. He wasn't cut out to be an agent." He inhaled a slow breath. "Do you know how many agents I've recruited who have met with untimely deaths?"

"It's not your fault. They must have known the risks. Isn't that what you told me about Bruce?"

His smile was so painful that it made her heart clench. She surprised them both by grasping his hand and bringing it to her cheek. She couldn't find words to comfort him. "I'm sorry," she said. "I'm so sorry." She was sorry that Demos had caused so much havoc. She was sorry that she'd ever played a part in its schemes. She was sorry that the world wasn't a better place. But most of all, she was sorry that she and Alex were on different sides.

He cupped her chin in one hand and, smiling a little, as though he'd heard all her unspoken words, began to dab at her wet cheeks with a handkerchief he'd pulled from his pocket. Suddenly, his smile died. He stared at the handkerchief in his hand and swayed on his feet.

"What is it, Alex?" asked Mahri.

Juliet's voice, strident, impatient, came to them from the kitchen door. "Mahri, what's keeping you? It's time to go."

Alex held Mahri at arm's length. "Don't take any foolish risks," he warned. "Stay close to Dugald, and you'll be safe."

She managed a laugh. "I'll be waiting for you, Alex."

She turned away before she could make a fool of herself.

Twenty-three

What in hell's name was he doing here, when he'd promised himself that he would never again involve his brother in the game? It was just like when they were boys. Gavin could always talk him into taking him along with him. And when they were scolded by Granny for getting into mischief, he, Alex, always bore the brunt of it because, of course, he was the elder. So here they both were, crouched behind one of the broken-down ramparts of Birse Castle, watching the movements of the two scouts who had their hunting lodge under surveillance.

"They're not in uniform," Gavin whispered in Alex's ear.

"Demos agents, I presume, or their lackeys."

Silence followed Alex's terse reply.

The scouts had lit a small fire that could not be seen from the lodge. One was sitting on the ground with his back to a wall; the other was obviously taking the first watch, but it wasn't a close watch. They obviously weren't expecting trouble. Calley had done well. Lights were shining from every window of the lodge, giving the impression that the occupants were still up and about.

Three scouts and now there were two. It didn't take a leap of the imagination to figure out that the missing scout had ridden to his master to tell him that the Hepburn brothers were taking cover in their hunting lodge. It was the logical place for them to go. If these scouts were attached to Demos, who or what had brought them here? Foster? Mahri? The professor?

His mind kept straying to the broken-down cottage and how soldiers had been lying in wait for Murray and his conspirators. The soldiers had started shooting almost at once. They'd been shooting to kill. Who had informed on Murray? Would the soldiers have killed Mahri if she'd shown herself?

Who was the enemy, Demos or Colonel Foster?

And whose handkerchief was wrapped around Mungo's badge?

The handkerchief seemed to be burning a hole in his pocket. He'd used it to dab the tears from Mahri's cheeks, and the dark energy that it had given off had practically scorched his fingers. Emotions had pumped through him, making his stomach heave. All he had was an impression of overweening arrogance. What he had to do now was test his suspicions. His psychic power was inclined to lead him astray. He wanted proof before he acted.

"Ready?" he asked Gavin.

A fraction of an inch at a time, they slid from their perch till they were on the same level as the scouts. "Stand and deliver!" Alex barked out as though he and Gavin were highwaymen.

One man brought up his gun, and Gavin blasted it out of his hand. It was all over in minutes. It wasn't only surprise that had won the day. These men were big and brawny, but they were untrained and no match for a disciplined agent of Her Majesty's Secret Service.

"What are you going to do with us?" asked one as Alex trussed the man's hands behind his back.

"We're going to hand you over to Colonel Foster for questioning," he said.

It was only a six-mile trek to Juliet's house, but it was slow going because they kept off the beaten track. Alex didn't want to take the chance of running into any Demos agents, and he was sure now that it was Demos who would hunt them down. They were expendable, but Mahri was not. He'd convinced himself that they wouldn't hurt her, not until she had given them what they wanted.

He kept thinking about her, how she rode astride like a man. How she never seemed to tire. She had plenty of pluck, and she could withstand hardships.

So why did he worry about her like a mother hen with only one chick?

"*We Scots always rise to the challenge.*" That was Mahri.

But who was in the vision with her? She'd told him that her father had died of a broken heart when she was still a child. Was that a lie, too?

Gavin's voice interrupted his train of thought. "I hope we did the right thing, letting those scouts go."

"They're not Demos agents," Alex replied, "but lackeys, locals who were hired by the third man to report our comings and goings."

He'd decided that he wasn't going to be burdened by two insignificant yokels, so when they were in the middle of nowhere, he'd turned them loose. It would take them a long, long time to reach the nearest hamlet.

"Lights up ahead," said Gavin. "We've arrived."

The sun was just beginning to appear on the horizon when they rode in. They stabled their own horses and, after rubbing them down, made for the back door.

Dugald was the only one at the kitchen table, and he was making short work of a beefsteak sandwich. "Help yourself," he said, indicating a plate of sandwiches.

"Where are the others?" Alex asked.

"Washing the dirt o' the journey from their faces. They've already eaten, so they may go straight to bed.

Alex was disappointed. Though they were all tired out after making an exhausting journey during the night, Mahri had said that she would wait for him.

Gavin grinned. " 'Woman, thy name is fickle,' " he quoted. "Ah, here comes Macduff. If you want fidelity, Alex, best get yourself a dog."

"What we'd best get," Alex replied with a glower, "is a sound sleep and something to eat before we tackle Foster."

He stomped upstairs in a filthy mood, slammed the door, and lost no time in tearing off his clothes and pouring a pitcher of ice-cold water over his head and naked torso. In the castle, there were servants falling over themselves to see to his comfort. They'd heat the water for his bath, brush and press his clothes, bring him a sandwich on a pretty plate with a tankard of ale to go with it. On Deeside, servants were as scarce as hens' teeth. They all wanted the glamour of working at Balmoral.

He was drying himself off with a scratchy linen towel when the door opened, and Mahri stepped into the room. She'd brought him a sandwich on a pretty plate and a tankard of ale to go with it. A smile lit his eyes the moment before it touched his lips.

She was staggered by his beauty: his harshly chiseled face; his broad shoulders; his long, muscular legs. When he dropped the towel, she sucked in a breath. It was the laughter in his eyes that made her put down the plate and tankard of ale, then catlike, with supreme confidence, she crossed to him. Going on tiptoe, she wound her arms around his neck.

"I've told you before, Hepburn," she crooned, "I don't shock easily. In my other life as Thomas Gordon, I've seen it all. It's not the size of a man's sex that makes a woman go weak at the knees but his capacity for caring. Don't ever lose it, Alex. That's what makes you special."

What had started off as a lighthearted play on words had become something else, something serious, something she meant with her whole heart. He was a beautiful man on the inside, and that's what counted. His mind, his heart, his scars, especially his scars, made her want to share his burdens. He blamed himself for Mungo's death and, before that, for the colleagues who had been blown up by a bomb. *"Do you know how many agents I've recruited who have met an untimely death?"*

They were more alike than he knew. She, too, dreaded the thought of sending her father and his agents to their deaths. She couldn't, dare not confide in him. Alex's avowed mission was to hunt down Demos and destroy it, root and branch.

He sensed the change in her, and he drew her close. "What is it? What put that look on your face?"

"I have a confession to make. I'm in love with you, Alex Hepburn."

Though she meant every word, she'd succeeded in deflecting him from asking questions that she wanted to avoid.

"Was it so hard to say?" he asked softly.

If they went on like this, she'd break down and start crying like a baby. She said archly, "Don't you want to know when it suddenly struck me that you're the only man for me?"

"Maybe. All right. Yes . . . I think." His eyes were crinkling at the corners.

"When I walked into this room and saw you in all your naked glory."

With a great whoop of laughter, he dragged her to the bed. It started slow and easy, as though they had all the time in the world, but danger was an ever-present companion. The knowledge that all they could count on were a few stolen hours changed the tone of their lovemaking from playful to torrid in the space of a heartbeat.

She tore out of her clothes as if she were on fire. He spread her legs, knelt between them, and wrapped them around his waist. He loved the dazed look that came into her eyes when he joined his body to hers, loved the way her body clamped around his, drawing him deeper as he moved inside her. Each and every shudder from her found an answering beat in him.

He wanted more.

His mouth found one puckered nipple. He kissed it, sucked it, then moved to the other. His mouth and hands were not gentle, but it was exactly what Mahri needed. She nipped at his shoulders with her sharp teeth. Her nails scored his back.

She couldn't breathe. He couldn't drag air into his lungs. Their movements became frantic. Their pleasure sharpened, hovered, then soared. At the end, spent, they collapsed into the mattress, just as the sun's rays streaked across the sky, heralding the beginning of a new day.

Alex didn't get up till late in the afternoon. Mahri had gone back to her own bed, and that came as no surprise. The others might have their suspicions, but Dugald, especially, would not tolerate his "wee lamb" living openly in sin. In fact, Alex wasn't going to tolerate it either. The first chance he got, he would marry Mahri and make everyone happy.

His sense of euphoria did not last long. The only person up and doing was his brother, Gavin. He was at the kitchen table, buttering a slice of toast.

"Where is everybody?" Alex asked.

"They're still abed, except for Dugald. He's scouting around outside."

"I told him to take the first watch," said Alex. "Now it's my turn."

Gavin gave a huge yawn. "I feel as though I rode sixty miles last night, not six."

Alex's response was dry. "It's about half the distance from our rooms on Piccadilly to Richmond Park, and I don't remember you complaining about that."

"Ah, but I never ride out to Richmond unless I have a beautiful girl riding beside me. You should try it sometime, Alex. There is nothing like a beautiful woman to make a man forget all his troubles."

This was an argument Alex knew he could not win, so he speared a slice of toast, bit into it, and went outside to relieve Dugald.

He found Dugald in the stable loft with stubble shadowing his chin and lines of weariness etched on his face. But he was still on duty, still scanning the road for signs of trouble. Alex felt like a sulky schoolboy. Of course Mahri was still in bed. She wasn't avoiding him. Everyone was exhausted from being up all night. And she had more than a sleepless night to exhaust her.

Over the next few hours, when she didn't come downstairs, he changed his mind.

"I think she's coming down with something," Juliet told him. "Nothing serious. But I've given her a powder for her headache."

When the hours passed and there was still no sign of Mahri, Gavin asked the question that seemed to be on everyone's mind. "What's this all about? Have you two had a falling-out? What have you done or said to upset her?"

The sun was setting, and they were in Alex's room, getting ready to move out. Alex was dressed in the slightly tattered uniform of a captain of the Royal Guard—the uniform that Dugald had worn on the train. He'd had to discard his own uniform at the Feughside Hotel. Gavin was dressed as Gavin.

He pinned the aiguillette denoting his rank to his left breast. "Concentrate on the task at hand," he replied curtly.

"You mean your tête-à-tête with Colonel Foster?"

"That's exactly what I mean." And before Gavin could continue the conversation, he left the room.

Mahri came downstairs to see them off and wish them luck. She did look pale, but she would hardly look him in the eye or leave Juliet's side, and that made Alex deeply uneasy. Was he imagining things, or was she up to something? It was too late to have it out with her. He trusted Dugald to keep her out of trouble.

He managed a few words in private with Dugald. "Don't let her out of your sight," he warned.

"Ye canna think she'll run away?"

"I'm thinking that they may come for her. This may be your last chance to tell me. What does she have that Demos wants?"

Dugald's expression betrayed his anguish. "I dinna rightly know, but it's more complicated than ye can guess."

"How is it complicated?"

"I canna go against the lass."

Seething with resentment, Alex mounted his horse and urged it into a canter. Gavin followed after him.

Dugald didn't seem to understand that she came first with him. He didn't give a damn about whose side she was on. He would always be on her side, and he expected the same from her.

He wished to God that he had never met her.

It wasn't true. But it was humiliating to admit that she thought she could run rings around him just because he loved her. She would soon see how wrong she was.

If she lived that long.

God, he hoped he knew what he was doing.

Gavin caught up to him. "What's your hurry? I can hardly keep up with you."

Alex slowed his mount. Frowning, he said, "You don't have to come with me if you're not up to it. I can manage on my own."

"Not up to it? I've never felt better. It's you that is acting like a crazy man. What's got into you, Alex?"

Fear. Doubt. Resentment. *Trust your instincts, Alex.*

"We don't have much time," he said. "That's what's wrong with me."

"You're thinking of the shoot to kill order?"

"No one is going to shoot us, Gavin, unless they take their orders from Demos."

"I was thinking along the same lines. Foster will want to take us alive. If he thinks that *we* are members of Demos, he'll try to break us into betraying our friends. Why *are* we going to see him, Alex?"

"To clear up a few points that have been bothering me."

There was a pulse of silence, then Gavin said, "I'm a big boy now, Alex. You don't have to protect me. We're in this together. So tell me!"

Alex heaved a sigh. With some reluctance, he told his brother about his suspicions, and afterward, much to his surprise, felt as though a yoke had been lifted from his shoulders.

"Then what are we waiting for?" cried Gavin. "*En avant!*"

Alex shook his head. "You were always the reckless one," he said, but he laughed and followed Gavin's lead.

Because of the dark, it took them two hours to reach the castle. As though their mission was of the highest priority, they galloped up to the side door with no attempt at concealment. While Gavin held the horses' reins, Alex ran up the steps and presented the guard on duty with a letter.

"From Commander Durward to Colonel Foster," he said, spitting out the words like an officer of the Guard. "He is to come with us."

He hoped to God that Durward had meant what he said, that he wouldn't stay at the castle because he couldn't stomach Foster. He didn't wait for a response but quickly marched to the side of the entrance, where his face was hidden in shadow.

From the side of his mouth, Gavin whispered, "Why isn't Foster out looking for us?"

"You'll have to ask him that."

Foster appeared at the steps, buttoning his tunic as he came. "Commander Durward wants to speak to me?" He quickly descended the stairs.

"Yes, sir."

"Where is he?" He was blinking up at Alex, whose back was to the lantern on the wall.

"This way, sir."

All unsuspecting, Foster followed them to the rotunda where Alex had persuaded Mungo to help them escape by train. The colonel stepped inside. "I don't see anything."

He turned to face Alex, and that was when Alex slammed his ironclad fist into the beefy part of Foster's belly. The colonel gasped, sank to his knees, and began to retch.

"Now that *that* is out of the way," said Alex pleasantly, "we can talk." He waited until Foster had control of his breathing. "You can begin by telling me where I can find Mr. Ramsey. You remember Mr. Ramsey, don't you?"

The colonel blustered, he fumed, but point by point, he answered each of Alex's questions. He wasn't a coward. He didn't mind taking a beating. What shocked him was Alex's conviction that Demos was still active in the area and was plotting to kill the queen. No one had informed him of such a thing.

As the mills of Foster's brain slowly began to grind, he looked up at Alex. "Why didn't you go to Durward with your suspicions? You're old school chums, aren't you?" He made no attempt to keep the sneer from his voice.

"Haven't you figured it out? Durward is the power behind the throne. Now here's what I want you to do."

Mahri reined in her pony and looked back the way she had come. Below her, the lights of Ballater were almost completely extinguished. She was on the other side of the river, on her way to her grandparents' house. Mile-End was her house now, she corrected herself. She thought of her father and steeled herself against him. She was past giving him any more chances to redeem himself. The stakes were too high. The queen was returning to Deeside on Saturday. She had no doubt that Demos would be waiting in the wings to do its worst.

Not if she had anything to do with it.

She stifled a panicked laugh. If she truly wanted to stop Demos, all she needed to do was give Alex the information that could send Demos and its sympathizers to the gallows or to prison for a long, long time.

No one should have to face the choices she had to make.

After tonight, she wouldn't have a friend in the world. She'd duped Dugald, knowing that Alex had set him to spy on her. She'd duped Alex. She'd duped her father. Of the three, Dugald was the only one who would forgive her.

She could not remember a time before him.

It had not been easy getting away from him. Even in sleep, he could detect any furtive sound. So she'd pretended to be delirious with a fever. And while he had gone to fetch Miss Napier, she had picked herself up and left the house, overriding Juliet's wringing hands and warnings of dire consequences.

She hadn't had everything her own way. As a precaution, either Alex or Dugald had hidden her boy's clothes so that she was forced to wear her voluminous skirts. She wore a beret on her head and pinned to her cloak was her precious cairngorm brooch.

She wasn't alone. Macduff had appeared out of nowhere and was trotting ahead of her as though he knew the way. She was glad of his company. Dogs didn't ask questions or suspect motives. They gave their love unconditionally. Now, why did that make her go all teary?

All was quiet. Nothing stirred. But that was a false impression. When one was raised in the Highlands, as she had been, one listened with a different ear. Stoats and weasels were creeping out of their burrows to hunt the hare. Foxes were slinking into farmyards for easy pickings.

Macduff knew it. She could hear the soft growl that vibrated deep in his throat.

"No," she said, and the growling stopped.

She thought of Alex, and something inside her pulsed to life. She would make a bargain with the devil if it would save him.

She'd come to the ruined foundation of what had once been a chapel of the Knights Templar. A snatch of memory flitted through her mind. She and Bruce, as very young children, pretending to be postulants of the knightly order. They'd had tests of valor to undertake and acts of charity to perform.

Their future had stretched out before them like a golden ribbon of light.

She shivered and raised the hood of her borrowed cloak to shield her from the cold, but a cloak was useless against the kind of cold that gripped her.

Not far to go now.

The house was up ahead, but even in daylight, it was hard to see for the stands of Scots pines that screened it. It was a children's paradise, no secret tunnels or passages, but with rooms running together and staircases that came out at brick walls, the result of succeeding generations of her family adding to or remodeling the interior to suit their individual tastes.

It really was an ugly house, but she loved it anyway.

"Watch out for adders," she told Macduff.

She was attuned to the sounds around her, and Macduff's lack of a response gave her pause. "Macduff?" she whispered. Her eyes searched the dark, but she saw little beyond shadows moving within shadows. "Macduff?" she prompted, a breath of a sound.

Noise erupted around her—a lion roaring, a gun going off, a man cursing. The silence that followed filled her with dread. Every muscle tensed for action. She slipped her hand into the pocket of her cloak and withdrew her revolver. Eyes peeled, ears straining, she slowly dismounted and stood there waiting, hesitating, undecided. Her finger curled around the trigger. "If you have hurt my dog," she said, "there will be hell to pay."

A shadow moved in front of her. She pulled the trigger just as someone hit her from behind.

Alex and Gavin were about a mile from Ballater when the sound of a dog barking made them rein in. Gavin knew the sound of his own dog and quickly dismounted. Alex took a moment to look around him. They hadn't run into any patrols. There were no guards on the bridges, because Foster wasn't expecting trouble. Durward had not told the colonel of his meeting with Alex in Aboyne. The commander thought that everything was going to plan. He would soon have a rude awakening. The question was—where in hell's name was he? No one seemed to know.

"Macduff, where are you?" Gavin called softly. "Where are you, pup?"

It sounded like a baby crying, but it was Macduff who crept out of the underbrush. Gavin went down on his haunches. "What is it, boy?"

He ran his hands over Macduff's coat. "There's blood on him," he said. "And there's a hole, here, on the tip of his ear, a slice really. A bullet or some predator has taken a bite out of him."

Macduff licked his face. "Where is Mahri?" To Alex, he said, "I told him to watch over her just in case."

Alex said, "Your dog understands English now?"

"No! He understands my thoughts! I'm a seer, for God's sake! Alex, this is serious. If Macduff is here, he must have followed Mahri."

"Christ Jesu! Where is Dugald? He would never have allowed her to leave the house."

"It's possible that she was abducted at gunpoint. Maybe they both were."

This did not resonate with Alex. "I'd bet my last farthing," he said, "that she has been waiting for the right moment to make her bid for freedom, and tonight I gave it to her."

"But where will she go?"

"Foster told us when he told us where to find Ramsey. He's visiting Professor Scot, who has leased Mile-End House for the summer months."

This bitter response was followed by a long silence. Finally, Gavin said, "It would explain a lot."

This time there was no response from Alex, and Gavin went on, "Do you think Foster will do as he promised?"

"I'm counting on it."

"And Durward?"

"I don't underestimate him. I think that he may be one step ahead of us."

"Sounds as though it's going to be quite a party."

"It's going to be a hell of a party," Alex said savagely.

Twenty-four

❧

Where are the lists you were supposed to deliver?"

Mahri gurgled and choked and coughed, and came to herself with the taste of whiskey in her mouth. She didn't open her eyes right away but took her bearings through her senses. The windows were closed. A fire was burning in the grate. The lamps were lit. The not unpleasant odor of old books filled her nostrils. She was in the library, and she was not alone.

"Father," she said, and opened her eyes.

Only three weeks had passed since she'd last seen him, and she thought the change in him was alarming. He seemed smaller, older, and as far removed from the pleasant, absentminded professor as night from day. She could see that he was in the grip of some strong emotion, but that came as no surprise. By his lights, she was a traitor.

He slammed the half-drunk glass of whiskey on his desk and turned back to loom over her. His breathing was audible; his eyes were bulging. "Do you have any idea what you've done? This isn't a game, Mahri. You've put our lives in danger. You never intended to bring those lists to me, did you?"

"No." She put a hand up to rub the back of her head, but it did nothing to ease the blazing pain. Her words were slow and precise. "You lost my loyalty and sympathy when you decided to murder the queen. I never thought you would go through with it, but I was wrong."

"You shot Ramsey." It was a statement, not a question.

"You left me no choice. Where is everyone?"

"Men are patrolling the area, so there is no escape. They're waiting for the commander to arrive. Someone has gone to fetch him. Now that you are here, they'll be expecting trouble. You should have stayed away. Why did you come back?"

"To stop you from making another attempt on the queen's life and to warn you. I think Hepburn is on to you. And who is the commander? You've never mentioned him before."

He took the chair behind his desk and linked his fingers. "The commander has several cells under his oversight. We are just one of them. Mahri"—he shook his head—"don't you understand anything? They'll kill you, and they'll kill me. We've failed in our mission. No, it's worse than that. They'll think we're in this together, so they'll kill us both, but not before they've tortured you into giving them the information they want. So, I'll ask you again. Where are the lists you were supposed to bring? It's the only thing that can save us."

The confidence that had fueled Mahri's actions was beginning to founder. Her father wasn't afraid. He was terrified. And who was the commander? As far as she knew, her father was the leader of this section of Demos. She hadn't come this far to give in now. If her father couldn't help her, she'd bargain with the commander.

The professor said, "We can make up a story to explain the delay. We'll say that Hepburn forced you to go with him, and when you finally made your escape, you came straight here to me. Only tell me where you've hidden the lists, and we may yet scrape through this disaster."

"Listen to me, Father." Her voice shook with emotion. "I came to make a bargain with you. Forget about the commander. Leave Deeside at once. Take your cohorts with you, and these lists will never come to light."

He sat back in his chair and looked at her as though she were mad. "Haven't you heard a word I've said? There is no going back. Even if I could do what you say, we're only one cell. There are others who will take our place. And Demos has a long memory. They'll hunt us down like vermin."

"If anything happens to me," she replied coolly, "those lists will be passed to British Intelligence. Let Demos try to make a bargain with them."

He began to laugh, but it was a mirthless laugh bordering on panic, and that threw her off balance. "My dear child," he said, "you have nothing to bargain with."

He was afraid, mortally afraid, and she'd never seen him like this, not even when Bruce went off to war. His fear made her own nerves stretch to the breaking point.

A board creaked on the other side of the library door. The professor straightened then gulped in a great draught of air. He put a finger to his lips, warning Mahri to be silent. His words were so soft, she had to strain to hear them.

"It's too late for me, but not for you. If you get out of this alive, don't go to the authorities. They can't be trusted. Find your deerstalker—"

When another floorboard creaked just outside the door, he got up. He had a gun in his hand. "Hide, Mahri," he whispered urgently. "The jib door!"

Mahri was paralyzed with indecision. The jib door was on the other side of the room and was made to look like the paneled wall. No one could tell it was there if it hadn't been pointed out to them. It wasn't a secret passage, but a door to the old servants' staircase. No one had used it in years.

She'd waited too long. The door was opening. Her father yanked her down and pushed her under the desk. All she could see from her vantage point was feet. But she could feel the tension in her father. Two men had entered the room. Her father moved in front of the desk, shielding her from view.

"Commander," he said, as calm as she had ever heard him. "Ah, you here, too, Ramsey? This is a surprise. I understood, Commander, that you wanted to cut yourself off from all contact with Demos until our mission is complete."

"We know she is here," said a voice that Mahri did not recognize.

"I suppose you got that from Murray. Yes, she was here, but I let her go."

"That wasn't very wise of you," said the stranger gently. "Ramsey?"

Ramsey was obviously looking around the room, searching for her, but it was a cursory search. There was nowhere to hide except under the desk, and Ramsey didn't think to look there.

"She's not here," he said.

"I'm sorry it has to end like this, Professor," the commander said.

A volley of shots rang out. Mahri jerked then cowered underneath the desk. Her father's body had fallen in a boneless heap in front of her. She put a hand over her mouth to stifle her whimpers.

"Torch the place," said the stranger. "Let Colonel Foster make what he likes of it. No doubt he'll blame it on the Hepburn brothers, and that will play right into our hands."

Ramsey said, "She didn't get away, sir. Murray would have known if she had. I think she is still hiding somewhere in the house."

"Find her. But don't waste too much time on the search. I want all evidence of our presence here obliterated. And the fire may drive her into the open."

"What about the lists, sir?"

"If they are found, they'll come to my desk. Let me worry about the lists."

Trembling with terror and with her skirts bunched around her, she tried to choke back tears. Her father was dead, and she was to blame. How could it have come to this?

The footsteps retreated, and she heard the click of the door as it closed. She was still numb from the horror of seeing her father executed before her eyes, and that was what it was, an execution.

Commander, her father had called the man who ordered his execution. And the commander said that if the lists were found, they would come to his desk. He had to be Commander Durward, the man whom Alex trusted implicitly. Durward's name had not been on any list.

The tread of footsteps on the other side of the library door galvanized her into action. She scooped up her father's revolver and moved swiftly to the jib door. It was so out of use that she could hardly get it open. It creaked, it groaned, but inch by slow inch it opened, and she slipped through to the narrow staircase.

When someone entered the library, she froze, and when the tread of footsteps came closer, she held her breath. She hadn't shut the door properly. The man on the other side of the door seemed to know it.

"Mahri, I know you're in there." Ramsey's voice! "Give yourself up, and I promise nothing will happen to you."

She acted instinctively. She raised her father's revolver and waited. The door was suddenly flung open, and Mahri pulled the trigger. A body fell forward, on top of her, and warm blood covered her hands. She didn't have time to be squeamish. Others had heard the shot and were converging on the library. She dragged the inert form into the staircase and shut the door with a snap.

"Ramsey?" she heard someone shout. "Ramsey, where are you?"

There was, of course, no response, because Ramsey lay dead at her feet, and she had killed him. When she'd first met him, he'd seemed like a pleasant young man with a bright future. Then he'd got in with the wrong people. It was what had happened to her father.

"Forget about Ramsey!" The voice of authority, Commander Durward. "Forget about the girl. Torch the house! Pass the word. Torch the house!"

She wished with her whole heart that it was Durward who had opened the jib door. Then she would have emptied her revolver into his black heart without a ripple of conscience.

She could smell burning carpets, and smoke was creeping into the staircase from cracks in the paneling. It was so dark that she might as well be hiding in a hole. All she had to guide her was her sense of touch. Which way should she go?

Outside, they were waiting for her. They would shoot her down like a rabid dog. Where was Macduff? What had they done with Macduff? She started to cough. She couldn't stay here. She had to choose. There was another way out, if she was willing to risk it.

She held on to the handrail and began to climb up the stairs.

Alex rode like a madman. He couldn't have kept to that frenzied pace if Macduff had not been out in front to guide him. The bitterness he'd felt when he'd realized that Mahri had slipped away to be with her father had been consumed by an alarm that was bordering on panic. She'd expected her father to greet her with open arms. It was the dog that had shot that hope to pieces. Gavin was right. Macduff wouldn't have left Mahri's side unless something dire had happened. He was taking them to her.

With him went a small troop of Guards, courtesy of Colonel Foster. He hadn't offered them amnesty, though. That would come, the colonel said, when he had tested Alex's theory, and it proved to be true. Meanwhile, they were going to Mile-End to arrest the professor and his "guests" and bring them in for questioning.

He was wrenched from his thoughts when a rider suddenly appeared in front of him. His horse reared up, almost unseating him.

"Hold yer fire! Hold yer fire!" Dugald's voice.

"Dugald?" Alex could hardly believe his ears. "Where did you come from?"

"It's a long story. The lass tricked me but not for long. I knew she would come here."

There wasn't time to go into explanations. Macduff was whining and running forward then back again as if to tell them that time was running out.

"These men are armed and dangerous," Alex said. "They won't take prisoners. Our job is to rescue the woman."

"Sir, look!" shouted one of the troopers.

A red glow appeared over a stand of Scots pines just ahead.

"The devils have set fire to the house," yelled Dugald.

"Forward!" Alex shouted, and he bounded forward with the others close behind him.

It took them only a few minutes to get to the house, but by that time flames were shooting through one part of the roof. Funnels of flames erupted through a downstairs window.

They fanned out and took cover. Bullets were flying in every direction, but no one broke through the cordon of soldiers. Murray and his henchmen were outnumbered.

"Pray God she is not in there," said Gavin.

Alex's voice was grim. "We know that she is in there. Look at your dog, Gavin."

Macduff was on his belly, creeping toward the house inch by inch, and the sounds that came from his throat resembled a baby crying.

Alex said, "Give my your cloak, Gavin."

"You're not going in there!"

"I must."

"Then I'll come with you."

Alex shook his head. "You're forgetting the prophecy

Granny McEcheran passed onto me. *My* prophecy, Gavin, not yours."

Gavin didn't argue the point. Alex draped Gavin's cloak over his shoulders and zigzagged toward the back of the house where the flames seemed less fierce.

And he came face-to-face with Murray.

Ʂhꝰ couldn't see a thing in that dark tunnel and feared that she would suffocate in the heat and smoke. What kept her going was the prophecy from the gypsy's crystal. *"You will pass through fire, but the fire will not consume you."* No. The fire wouldn't consume her. She would die from smoke inhalation.

She'd had a plan when she'd started up the staircase. What was it? All she could remember was that she had to get to the old dining room. Odd thoughts occurred to her. She should have paid the gypsy for her prophecy. She loved this ugly old house with all its oddities. It was hopeless. She couldn't go on. Where was the door to the dining room? She felt along the wainscoting with her hands. If she could only get to the old dining room . . .

I'm going to cut out your heart," Murray spat, and he darted forward with a blade in his hand, forcing Alex to retreat.

"You've used up all your bullets," said Alex. "Don't they teach you anything in traitors' school?" With that, he shot Murray in the knee.

Murray went down like a howling banshee, and Alex picked up the knife. With his free hand, he grabbed a fistful of Murray's hair and arched his throat back. "You have one chance to answer my question, and if I think you are lying, I'm going to slit your throat. Understand?"

Murray nodded.

"Where is the girl? Where is the professor's daughter?"

"I don't know."

The knife made a small incision and droplets of blood oozed out. "Last chance," said Alex.

Perhaps it was Alex's calm demeanor that terrified Murray, or perhaps it was the sudden shower of burning debris that fell on them, but he couldn't get the words out fast enough.

"We thought she was in the house somewhere, but when we searched it, we couldn't find her." He groaned and groped for his knee. "She must still be in there or she is outside hiding somewhere."

If she had been hiding outside, Macduff would have found her. So she was still in the house. "Where did you see her?" Alex asked roughly.

"In the library."

"And where is the library?"

"Above the front door."

"If you're lying to me," said Alex, "I'll come back and put a bullet between your eyes."

Murray didn't have the breath to howl. He lay on the ground, writhing and whimpering.

Alex entered the house. The paneled walls were beginning to blister. At any moment, they would burst into flame. He didn't give himself time to think of what he was doing. Instinct had taken over. He draped Gavin's cloak over his head and dashed for the stairs.

The floor was so hot, he could feel the heat through the soles of his boots. It occurred to him in passing that there was more than one fire burning in the house. Several people must have set fires in different areas.

When he pushed into the library, the fire was just getting a hold. His heart almost stopped beating when he saw the body of a man in front of the desk. He thought it must be Mahri's father. He crossed to it and saw that the man had been shot to death. Had he been trying to protect Mahri? Then where was she?

"Mahri?" he roared.

No one answered.

He went down on one knee, tore off a glove, and touched a hand to the professor's throat, not feeling for a pulse, but to determine how long he had been dead. He was still warm. As Alex's touch lingered, a tide of powerful emotions seemed to surge from the professor into himself, making him tremble. Fear. Grief. Horror. Love. Above all, love for his daughter. And when these powerful emotions began to ebb, at the end, something incongruous. A jib door.

Alex knew about jib doors. There were many such doors in the queen's summer residence. Servants disappeared into walls like wraiths. God forbid that one of Her Majesty's guests should come face-to-face with a lackey.

If the last thing the professor had thought about was a jib door, it must be significant. Alex found it in a matter of moments. There was blood smeared on the floor and on one section of paneling.

Fear gripped his throat. Whose blood? He found the recessed handle and yanked with all his strength. A panel came away in his hands, then another. Smoke belched through the opening, and Alex began to cough. All the same, his hopes soared. He'd found the concealed entrance to a servants' staircase.

And right inside the door he found another body. Ronald Ramsey. Blood soaked the dead man's coat and shirt. A trail of blood led up the stairs. When he looked down the stairs, his hopes faltered. The fire roared to life, cutting off his retreat.

"Mahri!" he yelled, and he followed the trail of blood going up the stairs. He found her one floor up, with her skirts hiked up to cover her mouth and nose. For one heart-stopping moment, he thought that he had lost her, but when he couched down and gathered her in his arms, she clung to him like the pet monkey he had once owned.

"I knew you would come for me," she said, burrowing her head against his chest.

He allowed himself one moment of weakness, only one moment to savor the feel of her in his arms, before he shut his mind to everything but how he could get them out of there.

He removed Gavin's cloak and draped it around her head and shoulders.

"What are you doing?"

"We're going to make a run for it. We have to go down those stairs before the house collapses around our ears."

"No!" she said, pushing out of his arms.

"There's still a chance." Even as he said the words, he doubted that they could make it. "Remember the prophecy. *You will pass through fire—*"

"Yes, but there's no need to do it the hard way!"

She grabbed his arm. "Follow me. I know another way."

He almost resisted. Two things made him follow her lead. The first was that the fire was spreading rapidly now and they would never make it to the bottom of the stairs. The second was the prophecy. *Trust your intuition*, his granny had told him, and his intuition was telling him not to let Mahri out of his sight. On hands and knees, he crawled after her.

They came to a landing. "Push the door in," Mahri said.

He got up and kicked it in. The draft of smoke-free air that swept over them gave them some relief. They both gulped in air and coughed to clear their lungs. The flames had yet to reach this part of the house. As soon as they were clear of the door, Alex shut it to keep out the smoke, and he helped Mahri to her feet.

"As God is my witness," he said, "I shall never smoke another cigar or cigarette."

A cursory glance at the room told him that it was used to store old furniture. There was no paneling here, but smoke was beginning to creep through the floorboards. And where the smoke went, the flames would soon follow.

"Pray as you've never prayed before," she said, "that the lift still works."

"The what?"

"The lift." She opened the door of a cupboard and sobbed with relief. "It's still here, thank God! It's a lift to bring hot food from the old kitchen to the old dining room. When the new kitchen was built, the lift became obsolete. The thing is, the old kitchen became the gardener's store. They won't be expecting us to come out there. Get in. It's our only hope."

"You first."

"Oh, no. I'm not going without you. See, there's room for two. Besides, I don't know if I can work the chain."

Pieces of plaster fell on them, and from another part of the house, they heard a muffled explosion. Alex picked Mahri up, pushed her into the lift, and crawled in beside her. "Now show me how this bloody thing works."

Later, he would reflect that what had saved them were the brick walls that encased the lift. Also, his fingers had never worked faster to pull on the rusty chain that worked their descent. Even so, he felt as though he were roasting in an oven. When the mechanism stopped working, he used both feet to kick out the door. Dragging Mahri into his arms, he ran like hell and leaped through a wall of flames into the cold night air.

She was lying on the grass, looking up at Alex. "You look like a chimney sweep," she said and sniffed.

He was lying beside her. "You should see yourself." His breathing was labored. "This house is a nightmare to navigate."

"It was a children's paradise." She managed a tortured smile. "The result of successive generations of my family indulging their whims and fancies." She touched a hand to the cut on his cheek. "Ramsey and your Commander Durward killed my father."

"And you shot Ramsey."

"You know about Durward?"

"I know."

She swallowed a sob that was stuck in her throat. "Yes, I killed Ramsey. I didn't have a choice. I'm sorry, so sorry. Nothing turned out the way I hoped it would. I wanted to make a bargain with them. I must have been out of my mind. They weren't interested in the lists I'd stolen. They weren't going to give up and go away."

"Hush!" His eyes were hot and intense. "Do you think I care about that? Where are your gloves? Look at your hands." He turned her hands over. "They're going to hurt like the devil in another hour or two. Have you no sense, woman? You should have kept your gloves on."

She would have blasted him with the sharp edge of her tongue if he hadn't raised her hands to his lips and kissed them reverently.

Men came out of the shadows, soldiers with prisoners, and Gavin and Dugald. Alex got up and moved away. "Where are you going?" she cried out.

"Unfinished business," said Alex.

"Durward?"

"Yes, Durward. We'll talk later."

She sat up and would have gone after him, but Dugald was kneeling beside her, scolding, clicking his tongue, and Macduff was licking her ear. Then they were hemmed in by soldiers and watched as the house began to collapse upon itself.

Alex found Murray propped against a tree with a soldier standing guard over him. "Where did Durward go?" he asked.

When Murray hesitated, Alex raised his revolver. Murray could see that he meant business and blurted out, "He went to his house, the Cove. We were to meet there."

To the soldier, Alex said, "Shoot out his other knee if he tries to get away."

And mounting up, he took the road to the north.

Twenty-five

⁓

Alex slowed his furious pace when he heard hoofbeats gaining on him.

"Alex," shouted Gavin, "will you wait up?" When he came abreast of his brother, he said between gasping breaths, "Mahri says that you're going after Durward."

"I won't kill him, if that's what you think."

"I was more worried about him killing you. That's why I've brought a couple of troopers with me."

"It won't happen."

"How do you know?"

"He'll want to talk. Tell me how clever he is." He was thinking of the handkerchief that had been wrapped around Mungo's badge and the sense of overweening arrogance that had engulfed him when he'd touched it. It was worse than arrogance. *Hubris*, his granny would have called it. "Find Foster and tell him I'll be at the Cove. And take the troopers with you."

"But . . . how do you know that Durward will be at the Cove? He could be anywhere—Ballater, the castle—"

"No. He didn't pass us on the way down. He has nowhere else to go but up. Besides, Murray told me."

"He's gone to ground?"

Alex gave a short, mirthless laugh. "I doubt it. Men like the commander don't go to ground. They regroup, plot how to retrieve themselves from an impossible situation. Now go! And tell Foster where to find me."

He heard Gavin curse savagely at his back, but the hoof-beats grew fainter, and soon Alex was the only rider making for the Cove. That was all that remained of the vast lands in Deeside that the great family of Durward had once held, this cottage on a few acres of land. Their trouble was, they'd never fought on the winning side. It was a story the commander often told with relish, as though, he said, ancient history mattered a jot! What mattered was what a man made of himself.

Although they were at the very least a mile apart, in this barren landscape of moor and mountain, Mile-End House and the Cove were practically neighbors. But Durward did not live in the cottage. It was a relic, all that remained of his heritage, and he could not bear to part with it. And he had laughed at his fanciful turn of mind.

Alex had laughed along with him. He wasn't laughing now. A man whom he had admired and respected, a man whom he had trusted with his own life as well as the lives of his comrades, now filled him with a murderous rage.

The rage had to be put on a tight leash. He had questions to ask, and he wanted answers. If Durward escaped retribution now, too many lives would be in jeopardy. He'd be free to silence anyone who had dared to oppose him, and Mahri most of all. It was she who had brought Durward's plans to ruin.

As he approached the house, there was no attempt on Alex's part at subterfuge. He was well aware that the commander would be expecting Murray to make a report. Alex's appearance on the scene might put him off his stride, but he'd want to know how much Alex knew and whether or not he should brazen it out or make a run for it.

The Cove was nestled in a small depression between the moor and an outcrop of rock. From that vantage point, it was impossible to see the fire that had razed Mile-End House to the ground. But the smell of smoke was in the air, and a curious neighbor would surely have climbed the rise to investigate. There was no sign of a curious neighbor, no sign of anyone, only a light shining from a downstairs window.

After tethering his horse, Alex walked boldly up to the front door and hammered on it with the knocker. The door was opened at once by Durward. He had a gun in his hand. Alex's uniform seemed to confuse him, but he kept the gun pointing right at him. "Alex, is it you?"

"Come to make my report, sir," Alex managed. He looked to be on the point of collapse, and it was more than a ruse to deflect Durward's suspicions. He'd lived through a hellish night, and it wasn't over yet.

"Come in, come in, and tell me what has happened." Though Durward's voice was solicitous, he kept the gun pointing at Alex.

They entered a small parlor with comfortable leather chairs and a small fire burning in the grate. Though it was quite unpretentious, it put Alex in mind of one of the gentlemen's clubs in and around Whitehall.

He took the chair indicated and was soon nursing a small glass of whiskey. The commander, Alex noted, did not pour a whiskey for himself but nursed his gun instead.

"How did you know where to find me?" asked Durward pleasantly.

Alex knew that he couldn't pretend that he knew nothing of the fire. He was covered in a white ash, and his clothes smelled strongly of smoke. Besides, he had decided on a different cover—the loyal agent who cannot believe that his chief is a traitor.

"You mentioned the house before," he said, "but it was Murray who told me. I don't know if he is still alive. He was in bad shape when I left." He leaned forward slightly, unthreateningly, and said hoarsely, "Commander, I don't know what is going on, but I know that you must go into hiding at once. Soldiers are combing the hills for you." He touched a hand to his uniform. "They think I'm one of them. That's why they didn't arrest me."

"Alex, you're overwrought. Remember that you are an agent. Now tell me slowly and succinctly what happened tonight."

Alex had his story ready, but it left out a lot, and he improvised where he thought it would help him. He told the commander about setting out for Mile-End, hoping to find Demos agents, but when he got there, it was already too late. The house was on fire, and he left soldiers and Demos fighting a fixed battle.

"There was a woman there, too," said Alex. "Professor Scot's daughter. I thought she was on our side, but she was just waiting her moment to get away from us."

The commander cocked one brow. "*Our* side?"

"My brother's and mine."

"Now, that makes sense."

"She escaped the fire, but she's under arrest. She's offering to make a bargain—a list of Demos agents for amnesty."

The commander melted into the back of his chair. "The lists are not important," he said. "You see, Alex, my name isn't on them."

Alex's head came up. "What?"

"And who is going to believe the word of Professor Scot's daughter? She's one of them, an agent of Demos."

"But . . . what are you saying, Commander?"

The commander laughed. "Your trouble, Alex, was that you were always too trusting. That was your greatest failing. So trusting to come here and warn me of danger. You see, I wrote those lists and sent them from Windsor to Professor Scot. They comprise the names of likely prospects for our cause as well as the names of sympathizers who support us financially. He was supposed to approach these people and enlist them as full-fledged members of Demos. His daughter, one of our couriers, was to take those lists to her father." His voice hardened. "As things turned out, she decided to use them for her own ends."

It took all of Alex's willpower not to spring at the other man and choke the life out of him, but the commander had taught him the value of discipline, and he held to his plan.

"You're not the power behind Demos," he said. "You can't be!"

"I assure you that I am. If you could only see your face! Think how well placed I am. I move freely between Windsor, Whitehall, and Balmoral. I have the ear of the home secretary. All matters of security for the queen come to my desk. Nothing can touch me, Alex, nothing."

It was all there in the commander's face, the arrogance, the hubris, his overmastering sense of superiority, and Alex felt sick to his stomach. But the game wasn't over yet. He still had a few moves to make.

He shook his head. "But how can that be? You knew that there was a stand-in for the queen at her reception. You knew there was a turncoat. Why wouldn't you warn Demos off? If you were one of them, then why let them continue with the attack and put themselves in danger?"

The commander was highly amused. He got up, kept his eye and gun trained on Alex, moved to the table with the decanters on it, and poured himself a neat whiskey. When he settled himself in his chair again, he said affably, "My dear boy, it was too risky for me to interfere. I was in Windsor, remember? And this was their show. I had to let events run their course. If Demos had succeeded in killing the decoy queen, then all credit to them, but you must see that my hands were tied."

"When did you know they had failed?"

"Oh, Professor Scot sent me a telegram the following morning, and I left for Balmoral almost at once."

"And got marooned in Aberdeen because of the flood," said Alex.

"Quite." Durward sipped his drink slowly.

Alex stretched his cramped muscles. "That poor woman. I mean the professor's daughter. She thinks those lists contain vital information that could prove lethal to all her friends in Demos."

"She's partly right, but since my name isn't on them, I have nothing to fear."

"And what about the people whose names are on those lists? Have they nothing to fear?"

The commander shrugged. "There comes a time when one has to cut one's losses. This is one of them."

Alex had to look away to conceal the disgust he knew must be reflected in his eyes. He hunched his shoulders and let his arms swing between his spread legs. When he was sure his gaze was neutral, he looked up. "I had my suspicions," he said. "I began to see that Demos had a powerful friend in Balmoral. I thought it might be Foster."

"Foster?" The commander chuckled. "That clown? I'm almost insulted."

"However, it didn't take me long to realize that it couldn't be the colonel. It had to be someone who returned to Deeside after the flood."

The commander wasn't smiling now. "And how did you work that out?"

"Mahri, the girl. Even though she shot Ramsey and foiled the attempt on the queen's life, well, Mungo's life really, Foster wasn't interested in her. He didn't know how important she was. She was just the woman who shot Ramsey." He gave a half smile, as though he regretted having to point out a few moot points to his superior. "My first inkling came when we escaped by train. The guards on duty let us pass without incident. We could have over-powered them very easily if they tried to stop us, and you wouldn't have wanted that. As you know, of course, Demos was waiting for us at Aboyne. They wanted Mahri, but not to kill her. They could have killed her at the station. Instead, they abducted her. Now here is where things get curious. A troop of soldiers was lying in wait for Murray and his thugs, and they were shooting indiscriminately. They didn't care whom they killed."

"Interesting," said the commander.

"Yes, isn't it? Here's what I make of it. At this point, Demos was taking its orders from the professor. He, of course, wanted to protect his daughter. The soldiers were taking their orders from you, and you, understandably, wanted her dead."

"Not from malice. Not because the lists were important. She'd become a liability, but naturally, I couldn't tell her father that."

"Of course you couldn't. You must have been reluctant to countermand his orders. After all, he was the leader of Demos in Deeside at that point. I doubt that the members of his cell even knew of your existence."

"Do I look like a fool? Of course they didn't."

Durward got up. Keeping Alex under close watch, he sidled to the window. A quick look through the glass seemed to reassure him and he returned to his place. "You were saying?" he prompted, just as though he were the host at a dinner party.

"After that fiasco," Alex said, "you knew you had to take the reins of Demos into your own hands. They were, by that time, mostly mercenaries anyway. You made them a better offer, and from that moment on, you had them in your pocket."

"Where is this leading?" The commander was becoming testy.

"You didn't disband them. Now, that was a serious mistake. They'd failed in their attempt to kill the queen. After the floods receded, they should have dispersed. But they stayed on. Why?"

"You tell me."

Alex spread his hands. "I'm guessing, and it's only a guess, that someone in the know told them that the first attempt had been a hoax, but the queen was returning to Deeside and they could try again."

Not a muscle moved in the commander's face, not a twitch to betray what he was thinking. "This is all conjecture on your part," he said. "Nothing can be proved. Any evidence there might have been burned to a cinder when Professor Scot's house was torched tonight." His bushy eyebrows snapped together. "How did you know about the house? How did you know I'd be there?"

"I suppose you could say that Colonel Foster told me. You see, he and I had a long conversation earlier tonight. It was an oversight on my part. My excuse is that I was a fugitive, and I had bigger things to worry about than Ramsey."

"What are you talking about?"

"Ramsey's address, you know, where he was staying when he was in Deeside. You can imagine my shock when Foster told me that he was staying with Professor Scot at Mile-End House. Mahri Scot. Professor Scot. That couldn't be a coincidence."

The commander had nothing to say to this.

Alex went on. "Your lack of diligence was another serious mistake, and so unlike you. After our meeting in Aboyne, I expected soldiers to come for us. Instead, there were only a couple of yokels. Now, that told me that something big was about to happen, something that required the services of the Royal Guard. Tonight, Colonel Foster told me what it was. The queen isn't arriving on Saturday morning as the papers reported. That was a blind to fool her enemies. She would arrive by train in the wee hours of this morning and would be whisked away by the Royal Guard to the castle, with no one the wiser. I believe it was your idea, you know, as part of your job to protect the queen. But you and Demos have other plans for the queen, don't you, Commander?"

The commander's eyes strayed to the clock.

Alex went on in the same unthreatening monotone, "I didn't expect to find you at Mile-End. It was Professor Scot I wanted to talk to. We rescued Mahri, and she told us that you'd been there and that you and Ramsey had shot her father to death. I'm afraid it's over for you, Commander."

Durward studied Alex's face. "You'll never prove anything, and the word of that little bitch will be laughed out of court if she gets that far."

Alex ignored the provocation. "There's not much time left. Tell me where you set the bomb, and I won't kill you."

A sneer curled Durward's upper lip. He got to his feet, and his finger curled around the trigger of his revolver. "The bomb? I don't remember mentioning a bomb."

"You didn't. I worked it out. You may remember that you were my chess master when I joined the university chess club. The one thing you dinned into me was to know my opponent and anticipate his moves. So I asked myself, what would I do in Durward's shoes? Once the queen steps off that train in Ballater, she'll be surrounded by soldiers. Demos no longer has the element of surprise, and they're too few in number. If you're going to assassinate the queen, it must be now or never."

"You don't know what you're talking about."

"Don't I? Tell me about Dickens."

"I had nothing to with that. Ramsey panicked and killed him."

"And Mungo? Tell me about him."

"What's to tell? He, too, had become a liability. But I had nothing to do with his death."

"Why on earth did you give me his badge?"

"Because . . . because you were friends. I thought you should have it."

Alex's head drooped, and once again, he let his arms swing between his spread legs. "Commander, I'm overcome," he said. "Beneath that tough exterior of yours beats a heart of gold." He shook his head. "I know better than that. I'd bet that when I was captured, Mungo's badge would be in my possession, and everyone would think that I had murdered him."

He looked up and caught Durward looking at the clock again. Chuckling, he said, "I think your clock must be fast. You see—"

A tremendous blast coming from the direction of Ballater shook the windows. Alex had been expecting it, and his hand slipped inside his boot to find the dirk he had once taken from Mahri. In one rapid movement, with the flick of his wrist, he embedded the blade in Durward's arm and the gun fell to the floor. Alex kicked it out of the way.

Grimacing in pain, the commander hissed through his teeth, "It's finished. She's finished, your precious Majesty."

All the rage that Alex had ruthlessly suppressed now boiled over. He pulled the dirk out of the commander's arm and pressed the point of his blade against the older man's throat. "Wrong again," he said. "Colonel Foster made a phone call. The queen left the train at Aboyne. She is nowhere near that bomb."

"You're lying!"

"You'll soon find out that I'm not, just as everyone will soon find out what a murdering devil you are."

"I'm a patriot!" the commander shouted.

"Patriot! Colonel Foster is twice the patriot you are! Oh, yes, he's a clown, but that's because you were always holding him up to ridicule. You could have made something of him. But that's not your way, is it? You're like a male lion that eats its own cubs if they get in his way."

He drew in a quick breath.

"You were responsible for the deaths of my friends. You deliberately set a bomb to blow them up, yes, and me, too."

"I should never have recruited you. You were always too clever for your own good!"

"You murdered Mungo and Ariel, didn't you?" Alex's voice had risen by several notches.

"Not Mungo! I had nothing to with that."

"But you murdered Ariel."

"She knew my identity. She couldn't keep secrets. You know she couldn't."

"And you would have murdered Mahri tonight. Burned her alive, in fact."

"What else could I do? She would have betrayed us."

The commander's sneer shattered when Alex tossed the dirk aside and slammed his fist into Durward's mouth. But the commander knew how to defend himself. Before Alex could hit him again, he brought up his knee, catching Alex in the groin, and Alex went staggering back. Durward fell on top of him and straight into an elbow to his jaw. They rolled on the floor, kicking, gouging, grappling with each other in a brutal contest for supremacy. Only one of them would come out of this alive. Neither man heard the sounds of horses' hooves or feet racing up the path.

The door burst open, and Colonel Foster strode in, followed by several troopers. It took two soldiers to pry them apart.

Durward's breathing was labored, but he spoke first. "Colonel Foster, I demand that you arrest that man. He tried to kill me." He clutched the wound in his arm, drawing everyone's attention to the blood that had seeped through to his coat.

Colonel Foster barked out, "I'm sorry he didn't succeed!" To Alex, he said, "You were right, and I was wrong. There was a bomb at the station, in the queen's waiting room. There wasn't time to find someone who knows how to defuse these little buggers, so we packed it in an old carriage on an isolated part of the track to wait for it to blow itself up. I'm assuming that's what we heard just now."

"There could be other bombs," said Alex.

Foster's voice acquired a little starch. "Mr. Hepburn, I'm not stupid. The queen will remain in Aboyne until we've done a thorough search."

"Sorry, Colonel." Alex gave a contrite half smile. "I wasn't suggesting that you weren't doing your job."

"Well, well, the queen is safe and sound. That's all that matters. There's a little lady waiting for you outside. I wouldn't like to keep her waiting. She's got quite a temper."

Alex left first. He was hardly through the door when Mahri flung herself into his arms. She allowed herself one quick hug, just to make sure that he was in one piece and lucid, then she let fly with a string of Gaelic curses.

To the troopers who were standing by, Alex said, "Those are Gaelic love words." The troopers laughed and turned to each other, conversing in fluent Gaelic.

Durward, flanked by two troopers, came out of the house. When they were level with Alex, Durward halted. "This will never go to trial, you know," he said.

Remembering how Ariel had died, Alex replied indifferently, "I wonder who will get to you first, them or us?"

When the soldiers marched off with their prisoner, Mahri took a closer look at Alex. Before Foster and his troopers had stormed the house, she had been shivering with terror. Now that she saw that Alex was standing on his own two feet, the terror evaporated, leaving her distinctly annoyed.

"You're bleeding," she scolded.

"It's only a bloody nose." He wiped his nose on his sleeve.

"It could have been so much worse."

He shrugged and put up with the scolding, because the worried look that he loved had come into her eyes. "So much worse for the commander," he said. When he stumbled, it began to dawn on him that Durward had given as good as he'd got and that it wouldn't be long before each punch and gouge would begin to make itself felt.

Mahri slipped her arm around his waist. "Lean on me," she said, "at least until we get you to a horse."

She was coddling him, and Alex was thoroughly enjoying the experience. Not slow to take advantage of her softer feelings, he made his limp more obvious and draped an arm around her shoulders.

"You can take that smile off your face, Hepburn," she said. "What you did tonight was stupid. There was no need for you to go after Durward. You should have sent the troopers."

He shook his head. "Oh, no. Durward has a silver tongue.

He lies almost as well as you do. He would soon have had those troopers eating out of his hand. And," he went on, interrupting her next scold, "who are you to speak? You went off without a word to anyone and almost got us both roasted to a crisp."

There was something important he had to tell her, something that would mean all the world to her. What was it?

He tipped up her chin. Tear-bright eyes blinked up at him. "Mahri," he said seriously, "if it's any consolation, your father did everything he could to save you. It was Durward who decided that you had become a liability. It was Durward from beginning to end."

Her face began to recede, and he felt himself swaying. He heard voices. Gavin's? Dugald's? Gentle hands helped him mount his horse. The ride to Ballater was made in a haze.

They stopped at the nearest hotel and put him to bed, but he made a fuss when they tried to send Mahri away. He slept fitfully, but whenever he wakened, she was there to give him a drink of water or mop his brow with a cool cloth. He wanted to kiss her, make love to her, but he hardly had the energy to lift his head from the pillow.

The next time he wakened, Mahri was on top of the bed, curled into him. Sunlight streamed through the window, and he could hear the sounds of people inside and outside the hotel going about their daily business.

His mind was crystal clear. "Mahri," he said, "Mahri."

Her lashes lifted, and she stared into his eyes.

"The lists?" he said. "They're not important. There's nothing in them to earn anyone more than a slap on the wrist. And," he added truthfully, after giving the matter some thought, "perhaps a large fine. But nobody is going to hang for being on those lists."

"You want me to hand them over to Colonel Foster?"

"No. I want you to give them to me. I want you to trust me, as I trusted you tonight."

He had a swollen eye, a bloody nose, and a scrape

on both cheeks. She swallowed and sniffed before she answered him. "You want me to trust you because you followed me up a flight of burning stairs and climbed into a lift that might have cooked us like two trussed chickens for Sunday dinner?"

"That's it in a nutshell."

"Why did you do it?"

"You know why. Because I love you."

She kissed him slowly and carefully on the lips. "Later," she said, "we'll talk later, after I'm all prettied up."

He admired beautiful women. What man didn't? He thought Mahri surpassed beauty, Mahri with her singed hair, sooty nose, and the stench of smoke still clinging to her skin.

Something moved deep inside him, and he smiled in spite of his aching jaw. "Yes," he said, "we'll talk later. Now go tidy yourself, woman."

Twenty-six

❧

The queen was safely ensconced in her castle. Murray wasn't saying anything except that it was all a ghastly mistake, and that he had simply been in the wrong place at the wrong time. And the commander wasn't saying anything at all.

Mahri listened to the conversation going on around her with half an ear. They'd stayed on at the hotel because it was close to the center of things, and Juliet had arrived to join her companions and learn what had happened in the interim. Also, it was the hotel that Juliet's erstwhile suitor owned, and no one wanted to snub Mr. Steele when he went out of his way to make sure that they had everything to make them comfortable. Only Juliet was reserved with him.

They'd just eaten a late breakfast and were seated in a quiet corner of the hotel's foyer. Alex had to retell his account of his meeting with Durward and answer questions as they occurred to the others. Mahri's mind was taken up with the lists she'd promised to give Alex.

She'd thought she had something to bargain with, but

Alex said that the lists were worthless. That was not what her father had thought. "*Where are the lists you were supposed to deliver?*" He'd been beside himself with fear. She hadn't realized then that he wasn't afraid for himself, but for her. In his last moments, he'd tugged her down to hide under the desk, then stepped in front to shield her from view. To her dying day, she would never forget it.

He'd known that he was finished, but he'd thought only of her. It made her feel small for ever having doubted him. At the same time, his unselfish act made her feel as precious as priceless porcelain and just as fragile. She should have loved him more.

She wouldn't make the same mistake with Alex.

A light touch on her neck drew her eyes to his. "It's time," he said.

It was time to take him to where she'd hidden the lists. The story that she'd told her father, that she'd given the lists to her advocate with instructions to give them to the authorities if Demos struck again was sheer fabrication from beginning to end. She really wasn't cut out to be a spy or a secret service agent. No one had taken her seriously.

"I'm ready," she said.

Two horses were already saddled and waiting for them. Mahri didn't have to think about it. She rode astride like a man, with her dress kilted up to allow her freedom of movement. Two of Her Majesty's guards were holding the reins. They were there because Alex had asked Colonel Foster's permission to cross the bridge into the Balmoral estate. Security in the castle and its environs was so tight that nobody could get in or out without a safe pass.

They entered by the queen's private bridge at Balmoral and jogged up the path to the ballroom. Soldiers in green tunics were very much in evidence. They jogged past the ballroom and took the path that Mahri had taken the night she'd shot Ramsey. The sun was on her face; a light breeze was blowing; the scent of pines hung heavily in the air. She looked over at Alex and met his troubled eyes.

"I've been thinking," he said. "You don't have to do this, Mahri. Foster doesn't know that the lists exist; leastways he hasn't mentioned them to me."

"Ah, but you know, and that's what matters." She laughed, as though a great burden had been lifted from her shoulders.

Her laughter made him smile, and he fell back a little as she led the way.

She was remembering her mad dash along this track after she had shot Ramsey, how her muscles had cramped and her breath had rushed in and out of her lungs. Alex had given chase even then. She wondered how it would have ended if he hadn't caught up to her.

They would have found each other. Somehow, somewhere, they would have found each other.

They came to the dry-stone dike where she'd hidden her satchel and the dress she'd worn to the reception. Alex helped her drag away the stone that concealed her hiding place. A torrent of water gushed out. Her satchel was soaked through.

"The floodwater got to it," she said faintly.

From the satchel, she drew out a sodden heap. "This was the dress that I wore that night," she said. Last of all, she found what had caused so much trouble: the lists she had failed to deliver to her father.

Alex took them from her. Taking the greatest care, he separated the two pages of names she had handed to him. The paper was so wet it shredded in his hands. The writing on the paper ran together, making the words completely illegible.

He looked at Mahri. She looked at him. They both began to laugh.

Later that night, when Mahri entered her bedchamber, Alex was right behind her. She said, "What's the matter with Juliet? She had nice Mr. Steele falling all over her. He is obviously smitten. I thought she was in love with him, yet she sulked all through dinner."

Alex allowed himself the pleasure of running his fingers through the ends of her hair. She'd snipped off the singed pieces without design or care and managed to look as though a man's fingers had possessively combed through her tresses. His fingers, he thought and smiled.

She turned to look at him, brows raised.

"Juliet," he said, trying to remember the question.

"And Mr. Steele, you know, the man who owns this hotel. I thought she was in love with him, and they had quarreled."

"No. I don't think so. It's Gavin whom Juliet wants. She has been in love with him for years."

"Are you sure?"

"Positive."

"Does Gavin know?"

"No. He looks upon Juliet as a sister or a cousin, and every other woman as fair game."

"Mmm. There's something in what you say." She was remembering the one and only time Gavin had tried to flirt with her. "But he takes a refusal gracefully. All the same, he attracts women like moths to a flame, if the ladies I've seen in this hotel are anything to go by. I don't know how he can bear it."

Straight-faced, he replied, "It isn't easy, but he manages." He captured her wrist and tugged her down to sit beside him on the bed. "Let's forget about Gavin and his women. There is something important I have to tell you, something you need to know before we marry."

He waited a heartbeat, thinking she might protest that he took too much for granted, but when she looked up at him with those big, trusting eyes, he knew everything was going to be all right.

"What is it?" she gently prompted.

"It's like this," he said. "When everyone was asking me

questions about Durward, you know, about how I was so sure that he was directing Demos, I gave them reasons that they could accept."

She nodded. "You figured out that someone at the castle might have had a foot in both camps?"

He nodded. "Yes. But what really convinced me that it was Durward was a handkerchief he gave me. I told you I was a bit of a wizard. Well, Durward's handkerchief had his character embedded in it. I knew, then, that he was a black-hearted devil."

"You're a wizard?" she said. "Just like Miss Napier's aunt is a witch? You mentioned it once before. Can you read minds?"

"No."

"Can you make prophecies?"

"No."

"But your grandmother could make prophecies, couldn't she? I remember you telling me that."

"Yes, well, she was more powerful than I'll ever be."

Her eyes were alight with laughter. "Then if you're a wizard, what can you do?"

"I . . . well . . . I sense things. I have—" He broke off. "You're not taking this seriously, are you?"

She looped her arms around his neck. "Of course I am. I'm a bit of a witch myself. I'm not saying I'm infallible, but I can make prophecies, too."

"Don't stop there. Tell me what you see."

Between kisses she said, "We'll marry the first chance we get. We'll have children, lots of them, and we'll make sure that they know we love them. I can't see where we will live because it's unimportant, just as long as we're together. And we'll have a dog, just like Macduff. He really is amazing. If I didn't know better, I'd think he was one of us, you know—"

He cupped a hand over her mouth and bore her back against the mattress with the press of his weight. "You," he said, "are one of those far-seeing witches. I, on the other hand, can't see farther than the next few minutes. No. Make that an hour."

Her eyes sparkled. "So, what do you see?"

"I'll show you," he said.

Later, her last words before she slipped into sleep were, "You really are a sorcerer. Who would have believed it?"

"Witch," he said, and kissed her.

Enter the rich world of
*historical romance
with Berkley Books.*

Lynn Kurland

Patricia Potter

Betina Krahn

Jodi Thomas

Anne Gracie

Love is timeless.
penguin.com